THE
MAYFLY

D0230417

04451755

Before turning his hand to writing, James Hazel was a lawyer in private practice specialising in corporate and commercial litigation and employment law. He was an equity partner in a regional law firm and held a number of different department headships until he quit legal practice to pursue his dream of becoming an author.

He has a keen interest in criminology and a passion for crime thrillers, indie music and all things retro.

James lives on the edge of the Lincolnshire Wolds with his wife and three children.

THE MAYFLY

JAMES HAZEL

ZAFFRE

First published in Great Britain in 2017 by
Zaffre Publishing
80-81 Wimpole St,
London W1G 9RE
www.zaffrebooks.co.uk

Copyright © James Hazel, 2017
All rights reserved.

No part of this publication may be reproduced,
stored or transmitted in any form by any means,
electronic, mechanical, photocopying or otherwise,
without the prior written permission of the publisher.

The right of James Hazel to be identified as Author of this
work has been asserted by them in accordance with
the Copyright, Designs and Patents Act, 1988

This is a work of fiction. Names, places, events and
incidents are either the products of the author's imagination or
used fictitiously. Any resemblance to actual persons,
living or dead, or actual events is purely coincidental.

A CIP catalogue record for this book is
available from the British Library.

Trade Paperback ISBN: 978-1-78576-300-7
Paperback ISBN: 978-1-78576-297-0
Ebook ISBN: 978-1-78576-296-3

1 3 5 7 9 10 8 6 4 2

Typeset by IDSUK (Data Connection) Ltd

Printed and bound by Clays Ltd, St Ives Plc

Zaffre Publishing is an imprint of Bonnier Publishing UK,
a Bonnier Publishing company
www.bonnierpublishing.co.uk

To Jo
Words are meaningless without you.

'[Men are] creatures among whose instinctual endowments is to be reckoned a powerful share of aggressiveness. As a result, their neighbour is for them not only a potential helper or sexual object, but also someone who tempts them to satisfy their aggressiveness on him, to exploit his capacity for work without compensation, to use him sexually without his consent, to seize his possessions, to humiliate him, to cause him pain, to torture and to kill him.'

Sigmund Freud, *Civilization and Its Discontents*

December. Post-festivities. The frozen earth was veiled in a thin covering of snow that crunched under Detective Chief Inspector Tiff Rowlinson's boots. In a glade, the log cabin looked as though it had come out of a fairy tale, complete with a tall stone chimney and heart-shaped etchings above the door. A local landowner had built it for his daughter as a summer house sixty years ago, but it had long since been abandoned, and was now swathed with climbing plants and moss. A sanctuary built out of love and innocence, defiled in the most grotesque manner.

Rowlinson slowly circled the little wooden structure, his hands behind his back and his coat collar turned up inside the white plastic overall. The crime scene investigators mingled uncertainly, watching where they trod. They had established a perimeter with reams of blue-and-white plastic tape around the glade. Rowlinson had been here before, too many times. He had seen too many bodies, too many weeping loved ones and too few prosecutions. He didn't feel much anymore. The endless cycle had anaesthetised him.

Except in these woods.

In these woods, Rowlinson felt again.

He approached the entrance to the cabin and ducked through the doorway. Inside, the air was stale and heavy. He fumbled for the inhaler in his coat pocket. Felt a little relief at feeling the familiar plastic tube and the tip of the metal canister. He no longer noticed the bitter cold.

The room was empty, save for the victim. And the flesh-eating flies swarming around what was left of him. The victim's head was slumped over the back of a wooden chair, mouth and eyes wide open. His skin was yellow and withered. A reaction to the poison, Rowlinson had been told, but he now understood a comment one of the SOCO team had made a short while ago – 'Poor bastard looks like someone sucked his soul clean out.'

He was naked and his arms were covered with deep lacerations, but that was nothing compared to his chest. The flesh was hanging off, exposing a crimson network of muscle and tissue. There were similar wounds on the lower half but everything was so saturated in blood, it was hard to make out which parts of him remained intact and which didn't.

'Jesus,' a voice behind Rowlinson gasped.

He turned to find Hardwick in the entrance, hand over his mouth.

'What the hell have we got here, guv?'

DS Hardwick was a foot shorter than his superior but still managed to fill the little cabin with his portly frame. He was a city boy with a swaggering gait, but a decent copper despite his lack of charm.

'The damage is self-inflicted,' Rowlinson said quietly.

'He tore his own skin off, boss?'

Rowlinson peered more closely. Ptyalism – excretion of foamy saliva, but to such an extent that the victim had been unable to control it by swallowing alone. At some point, he had introduced his fist into his mouth in order to induce vomiting but had ended up biting down so hard that he had almost taken his hand clean off.

'The alkaloid caused unimaginable pain for many hours. To combat it, the victim attempted to fillet himself.'

'Why?'

'To get at his heart, Hardwick. It was the only way to end the pain.'

∽

Three hours earlier, Sir Philip Wren had been sitting in the study of his Kent home, his belly full of port and chicken, and his mind full of gushing phrases to use during his acceptance speech for an OBE. He had received the phone call only yesterday in the strictest confidence – the Honours Committee had resolved to acknowledge the incumbent Attorney General's services to the legal profession and Her Majesty's Government in the New Year's Honours list. Finally, a lifetime's commitment to public service was to be recognised and Wren had spent the last twenty-four hours in a state of euphoria.

But his jubilation had been short-lived and he was now in south Wales, cold and anxious, and with a sharp pain in his head.

The scene was as he had expected – a glade swarming with a forensic team. Blue flashing lights. A feeling of uncertainty hanging in the air. And in the centre, a little wooden cabin with hearts carved above the door.

It's happening again.

He had been told that the detective in charge, Rowlinson, was competent. He had no doubt that this was true, but a local detective couldn't possibly keep this case. Not if Wren's fears were realised. He found Rowlinson standing with another man by the cabin door, looking at him with the same expression of uneasiness as all the detectives he had seen over the years. He didn't blame them. If he could have it any other way, he would leave them to get on with their job – but he couldn't. Not this time.

He walked across the glade, conscious of the questioning eyes following him.

'Philip Wren.' He offered his hand and received a firm grip in response.

'DCI Rowlinson. We weren't expecting the Attorney General, sir. Is there a jurisdictional issue I should be –'

'Not at all. No one wants to tread on any toes here, Chief Inspector. Your authority is not in question.'

It was a lie. There was a task force already in place to take over the investigation, a sub-division of the National Domestic Extremist Unit. A covert, specialist Met unit.

'Then I don't see –'

'May I see the body, DCI Rowlinson?'

Rowlinson shifted his weight from one foot to the other. The Attorney General had arrived in a Jaguar XJ accompanied by a small company of dark-suited men. These men had gathered the bewildered SOCO team together and were issuing them with confidentiality agreements to sign. After a further moment's hesitation, Rowlinson stood aside.

Wren inhaled the cold air greedily before stepping inside the log cabin. His stomach churned. He didn't want to see that chicken again.

Rowlinson stood in the doorway watching him curiously, hands wedged in his pockets.

He cleared his throat.

'The poison was administered through a catheter in his wrist, probably while he was unconscious. The poison takes over the whole body, arrests every single nerve. The pain is excruciating, but the brain is too overloaded to shut down. The sensation apparently lasts for hours, during which, as you can see, the victim mutilated himself.'

'Is there anything in his mouth, Chief Inspector?'

Rowlinson faltered. 'What?'

Wren felt a lump in his throat, something restricting his airway. 'His mouth, Chief Inspector. Is there anything in his mouth?'

Rowlinson looked behind him, as if he thought it might be a test, before taking two strides across the floorboards to within touching distance of the victim. The foam around the victim's gaping mouth had begun to congeal but some of the froth dripped down the side of his face like egg white. Wren watched as Rowlinson peered in.

'There's nothing there.' Rowlinson straightened up.

'Check again.'

Rowlinson bent over the body again and looked closer. Wren balled his hands into fists. Perhaps Rowlinson was right. Perhaps there was nothing there.

'Hang on,' Rowlinson said, digging a pen and a pair of blue plastic gloves out of his pocket. 'There is something . . .'

Wren felt the tension in his body snap as Rowlinson re-positioned himself, dipped the pen into the victim's mouth and gently eased it back out.

'What in God's name is that?' He held up a black object to the light.

Behind him, Philip Wren walked swiftly out of the cabin.

2

6th April, 1945
Buchenwald concentration camp, Germany

Captain Ainsworth stood outside the main gate, a cigarette clinging perilously to his bottom lip. The rain had let up in the last hour and sunlight was daring to penetrate the cloud covering.

The 89th Infantry Division had arrived two days earlier. They had been up for a fight, but instead they had found the camp under the control of its inmates. News of the arrival of the British and American armies had reached the camp a few days previously and the Germans had begun a hasty retreat. With the command structure dissolved and most of the guards having either fled or committed suicide, a group of inmates had stormed the watchtowers. The plucky inmates – most of them Communists – had been hiding weapons for years, which they were now, finally, able to put to good use. They had even had the guts to take prisoners, showing mercy to the Nazi wardens who had shown them nothing but inhumanity.

Ainsworth's men had been ill-prepared for what lay waiting for them at Buchenwald. They had heard about the camps of course, and heard rumours of mass killings with gas. A

Polish-Jewish lawyer named Lemkin had even coined a new word for it. Genocide. But words were so easily absorbed into the skin. Seeing a man so overwhelmed by the relief of his emancipation from a hell on earth that he fell to the floor dead at your feet. Nothing had prepared Ainsworth for that.

They had met the Czechs first. Thousands of them crammed into spaces designed for a few hundred at most. Stripped naked except for loin cloths. Freezing. Dying. Their bodies had shrivelled through malnourishment to such an extent that they barely resembled human beings anymore. The walking dead, with yellowy-white skin that tore as easily as paper, stretched so taut that Ainsworth could count every single rib.

With their last remaining energy, the inmates had greeted the 89th Division like heroes. So weak they could hardly walk, but somehow, they had managed to hoist up some of the infantry-men – lean and heavy lads, at that – to parade them around the camp in triumph. Embarrassed, but desperate not to offend, the soldiers had reluctantly allowed them to do it, although some of the inmates had collapsed from the effort.

They were a mixed bunch, from what Ainsworth could gather. There were the Czechs, but then there were Poles, Soviets, French, Croats. Women too, Many of them had been forced into sexual slavery in the camp brothel. Perhaps most satisfyingly for Ainsworth, there were a few of their own: American airmen who had been shot down over occupied France; British, too. The false papers they had carried that were supposed to have helped them escape from enemy territory had backfired. When they were captured the Nazis treated them as spies and shipped them to Buchenwald along with the Jews.

Jews. An entire race the Nazis branded the 'useless eaters'.

There was a polite cough. Ainsworth had been lost in his own thoughts, hadn't noticed the corporal behind him. Henderson was a good soldier and bright for an infantry lad, but, like the rest of the boys, he looked pale and sickly.

'First part of the roster, sir,' said Henderson.

He handed over some papers, which Ainsworth took but didn't read. Instead, he gazed over at the horizon, past the battered-down gates and across the yard to where he could see a sign that had been torn from the wall and stamped into the muddy earth. *Arbeit macht frei*. Work sets you free.

After a while, Henderson said, 'We don't have enough medicine for these people, sir. We can't stop them dying.'

Ainsworth nodded grimly. 'If you can't stop the bleeding, that's no reason not to try to stem the flow.' His stomach was churning – the chlorine tablets they added to the water didn't agree with him. After a brief pause, he said, 'Doesn't make any sense, does it, Henderson?'

'Sir?'

'Hitler knew the tide of war had changed months ago. The invasion of Russia was a fiasco. He needed resources, but he prioritised trains transporting Jews to death camps over his own army convoys. Tanks, soldiers, weapons, munitions. They could have made a difference. Doesn't make an ounce of sense.'

'Some say they were making sacrifices to the Norse gods, sir.'

'Is that what you think, Henderson?'

The soldier hesitated. 'Maybe, sir.'

'Did you see the Dora on the way up here?'

'We all did, sir.'

The Dora had been abandoned, but even though it was unmanned, the 89th had approached the massive railway gun with considerable apprehension. Weighing 1,350 tons, the only way for the gargantuan barrel to be moved was on double tracks. The techs had doubted it was ready for combat, but the estimated range was over twenty-eight miles.

'You think a race capable of producing a weapon as advanced as that also believes in resurrecting gods through human sacrifice?'

Henderson didn't answer. He had turned at the sound of an engine. In the distance, a car was approaching, its wheels kicking up dust and dirt along the track. Ainsworth looked at Henderson, who turned back and barked a series of orders at nearby soldiers. They spread out across the entrance, taking shelter where they could, rifles at the ready.

Ainsworth stood stock still in the open, a revolver hanging loose at his hip. He doubted very much the Nazis would return to try to salvage anything, and even if they did, they were hardly going to show up in a Rolls Royce.

The car pulled up facing Ainsworth. The chassis paintwork was splattered with dirt but the areas not covered in mud were otherwise clearly well maintained. This was not a civilian car. Ainsworth held his hand up, signalling to Henderson and the rest of the boys to back off. Weapons were lowered.

A tall man with wavy blond hair emerged from the back seat. He put on a hat and pulled a trench coat over a pinstripe suit, the coattails flapping helplessly in the breeze. He was young for someone being chauffeured across hostile territory.

'Captain Ainsworth, I presume.'

Ainsworth raised an eyebrow before taking the visitor's hand. He was English, but what the hell was he doing out here? Ainsworth registered the tight grip on his hand. *Not a reporter or a politician, then.*

'Welcome to Buchenwald,' Ainsworth grunted. 'Mr –'

'Ruck. Colonel Ruck.'

The visitor handed Ainsworth some papers and this time he read them with care. When he had finished, he looked up sceptically. 'British Secret Intelligence?'

'The very same. Military Intelligence, Section Five, actually.' Ruck smiled pleasantly, the pencil moustache above his top lip curling upwards like a second mouth. His voice was as smooth as his manners.

'And how is it that I can help you, Colonel Ruck?'

'First, may I congratulate you, Captain, on an outstanding operation.'

'Yeah. Several years earlier and perhaps we'd have actually done some good.'

'Please, Captain, don't belittle your achievement. Your very presence here had the Jerries scurrying for cover, did it not? A most satisfactory victory, I'd imagine.'

Ainsworth resisted the temptation to say 'get to the point'. This man was a bureaucrat. A pen-pusher. He wouldn't have survived a battlefield.

'Hardly a victory, I'd say. Forgive me, Colonel Ruck, but what is it that you're doing here?'

Ruck motioned for Ainsworth to re-examine the paperwork. 'You'll find a letter explaining everything at the back.'

Ainsworth found the letter and read it through carefully.

'I've never heard of these people,' he declared.

'Perhaps you would be kind enough to make some enquiries, Captain.'

Ainsworth turned to look at Henderson. His glance was met with a blank expression. The letter had been signed by Fleet

Admiral Leahy – Roosevelt's chief of staff. The seal looked genuine enough. The signature was a good one, too. Then he looked beyond Ruck for the first time, at the Rolls and the two Yankee soldiers now standing either side of the gleaming bonnet with red spearheads on their shoulders. Black Devils. Commandos. Escorting a British secret agent with a letter from the highest-ranking military officer after the President himself, ordering Ainsworth to hand over a bunch of people under his control *if* they were found alive in Buchenwald.

Ainsworth hesitated. *Time to buck my ideas up a bit.* 'We don't have a complete list of inmates yet, sir,' he explained, handing the letter back to Ruck. 'It could take days to find these people.'

Ruck smiled curtly. 'Read the letter more closely, Captain. They're Nazis I'm after – not Jews. Doctors, actually.'

'Doctors?' Ainsworth couldn't help but chuckle. 'There aren't any doctors here, Colonel Ruck. This place wasn't designed to prolong human life. This is – *was* – an extermination camp. Tens of thousands of people were behind these walls, kept in worse conditions than poultry. Those that aren't dead aren't far off. There are no doctors here.'

Ruck shrugged and lit a cigarette produced from a small packet hidden in his coat. One of the commandos by the car shuffled his feet impatiently.

'Have you found a surgery here?' Ruck asked.

'A *surgery*? There's no such thing. All we've seen are huge rooms where they crowded in hundreds of scared people and gassed them. Then they got the ones who weren't gassed to drag the bodies to giant pits and throw them in. That's what's here. If you're expecting a cosy waiting room with a fish tank and a copy of *Punch* on the coffee table, then you're a long way from home, Colonel.'

Ruck sniffed the air and for a moment Ainsworth was reminded of a predator sensing its prey. 'Aside from those rooms, then. Something smaller. Instruments, perhaps. Saws, scalpels, masks. That sort of thing.'

Ainsworth shook his head. 'Only death and –'

'Sir?' Henderson interrupted. He coughed nervously. Ruck and Ainsworth turned to look at him. 'What about the Hell Rooms?'

3

Charlie Priest was pan-frying sole.

It hadn't been a particularly successful enterprise, so far. The pan was too hot and the butter was foaming around the edges. The fish was crimping at the ends, shrivelling up before his eyes like paper curling in a flame.

'Too much heat,' he muttered.

He chucked his failed experiment in the bin with the two previous attempts and threw the pan in the sink. It hissed angrily. Even the cookware was disgusted with his efforts.

He wondered about another takeaway but was distracted by the sound of someone rapping on his door.

There was a little security monitor in the hall; all the new penthouses had one. Someone could jab a knitting needle through a spyhole too easily if they wanted. Priest glanced at the monitor. *Great. This evening's getting better by the minute.*

He unbolted and opened the door.

'Evening, Officer,' he sighed.

Priest's visitor smiled. The sort of smile where the mouth twists upwards at the corners but all the other facial muscles remain completely motionless.

'Mr Priest?'

'Yes.'

The policeman was clutching a box. Just a regular cardboard box, nothing exciting. A bit bigger than a shoe box. He was around Priest's age, maybe a few years older, with strands of greasy black hair protruding from underneath the custodian helmet. The Brunswick Star gleamed in the light cast out into the hallway from Priest's penthouse.

'Can I come in?' the uniform asked.

'Is there any food in that box? I'm starving.'

'Perhaps if I could just come in, sir.'

Priest shrugged and stood aside. *Why not?* The fake smile reappeared momentarily before Priest led him through to the kitchen. The policeman placed the box carefully on the side. His uniform was immaculate. *Must be new to the job.*

'Nice place,' he remarked, looking round, taking it all in.

It was a showroom kitchen. Black granite surfaces on soft-coloured wooden units. Streaks of lime green across the back wall over the appliances, reflected on the tall bar stools. The smell of burnt fish lingered in the air.

'The smell . . .?' the officer asked.

'Lemon sole.'

'I see. Easy thing to burn.'

'Not really. It's actually quite hard to mess up.'

A sympathetic but unconvincing smile.

'So what can I help you with, Officer?'

'Well, the Super sent me over. They're clearing out the archives and came across a load of your old stuff. Actually, I've never heard of you but the Super says you were a big deal in the Met and I should deliver this back personally.'

'I left CID ten years ago.'

'Really? You obviously left an impression.'

'Seemingly. Can't say I recall missing anything from ten years ago.'

'Well, let's see what we got here.'

The uniform reached over and flipped the lid of the box and brought out a long, metal object.

'T-baton,' Priest said. 'American truncheon. Circa nineteen nineties by the looks of it. Never owned one.'

'Really?' The uniform glanced down at the baton, apparently surprised. He studied it again, as if it might reveal some hidden secret. He tested the weight in his hand, softly shaking his head.

'You say the Super sent you?' Priest queried.

'Yeah.'

'Pritchard?'

'Yeah.'

'DSI Pritchard?'

'Yeah.'

Priest went down hard against the corner of the breakfast bar. His head took two impacts. One from the tip of the baton as it swung violently at him, catching the side of his temple – he'd anticipated the blow a fraction too late. The second was his head against the corner of the granite top. It was the second blow that turned the lights out.

❧

Priest opened his eyes and for a moment there was nothing. Just the sound of blood rushing past his ears.

Pritchard had retired three years previously. The uniform was real but the man wearing it hadn't been. Priest should have guessed earlier. He'd been wearing a helmet. The nearest police station was three miles from here. Helmets were what beat officers wore – officers who travelled in cars wore peaked caps. There was no way this guy had walked three miles in a helmet carrying a compendium of Priest's old stuff.

Bloody idiot. Burning the fish was bad enough . . .

At first Priest couldn't detect anyone else in the room but he was sure the fake copper was still there, somewhere. He had been dumped in a chair. His wrists were tied to the chair arms with cable ties, as were his legs. The plastic cut into his skin. Some involuntary movement while he was unconscious had drawn deep lacerations across his ankles. There was duct tape wound around his chest, binding him to the chair. He could move his head a little but not much else.

There was a wet tea cloth on his head, restricting his view. He could have been anywhere but the stench of burnt fish told him he was still in his own kitchen.

He tested the restraints around his wrists and pain seared up his arm in response. He wasn't going anywhere in a hurry. So far, the upper hand was with the man in blue. Priest figured he had a few minutes at the most to turn the tables. On an even footing, a confrontation would have had only one outcome. The fake copper was under six foot and didn't look like he was carrying much underneath the uniform. Priest was six foot three and weighed fifteen and half stone, most of which was muscle. Knocking him out had been more luck than judgement, too.

He sat, immobilised, for what seemed like an age, although he guessed it was only a few minutes. A few minutes in which Priest couldn't think of anything but the buzzing in his head and the bastard smell of fish.

The towel was suddenly whipped away and Priest's kitchen came into view, spoilt by the figure of the grinning policeman.

'Gotcha!' the fake copper announced.

Priest didn't say anything, just stared at the intruder as neutrally as he could.

'Why so upset, Priest? Should have seen it coming?' The fake copper threw the towel aside and took a few steps back, folding his arms and grinning. 'This uniform cost me two grand. So don't feel too bad.'

He was probably telling the truth about the price. Getting hold of a replica that good wasn't impossible, but it was very expensive. Priest started to wonder about his chances.

The fake copper continued, 'Ah, it was worth it. Guessed you wouldn't open the door to any other type of visitor. The concierge downstairs was also very helpful.'

'What do you want?' Priest asked.

'Just a chat. For now. Little chat. So you can get to know me a bit better.'

'And *you* know *me*?'

The fake copper smiled. 'You're Charles Priest but everyone calls you Charlie. Divorced. No children. Forty-three years old. Cambridge first. Joined the Met in ninety-four, did two years on the beat. Fast-tracked through CID to DS in ninety-seven and then DI in two thousand and one. In two thousand and four you left the Force under a cloud and retrained to become a lawyer. You worked in the commercial litigation department of an international firm before setting up your own practice in the City specialising in fraud investigation. Now you earn half a million a year and rank pretty highly in the Legal 500 as one of the most respected solicitor-advocates in the UK. Your parents are dead but you have one sister, Sarah Boatman, thirty-nine years old, a co-owner of a PR agency, and one brother, William

Priest, forty-six years old, currently residing at Her Majesty's pleasure in a secure psychiatric hospital outside the city having been declared criminally insane five years ago. You suffer from dissociative disorder, which means you constantly feel detached from reality, occasionally experiencing fits in which you descend into a state of complete dissociation, much like an out-of-body experience. Shall I go on?'

Priest sniffed. He'd earned more than half a million last year but the rest was accurate enough.

'You've clearly been reading my Facebook profile.'

The intruder's pallid skin and dilated pupils suggested there was more to his charm than just a natural swagger, but Priest had seen something in his eyes other than coke. Something that troubled him more than the cable ties around his wrists and legs. Something dead.

The fake copper started digging through a pile of papers on the work surface. They weren't much – bills, lists, receipts. An instruction manual for the expensive coffee machine his sister Sarah had bought for him last Christmas that he still hadn't got around to using. But *his* stuff, nonetheless.

'Priest and Co,' the fake copper muttered. He was examining a business card. 'Course he would have sent it to you.' He pocketed the card and turned back to Priest.

'Are you going to tell me what all of this is about?' Priest was surprised by how calm he sounded, despite the anger swelling in his chest.

'You've come into possession of something of mine,' the man said slowly. 'Something very important to me.'

'Your dermatologist's address? You should sue the bastard.'

'No, Mr Priest. Something infinitely more valuable.'

Priest did the best impression of a guy shrugging while strapped to a chair that he could.

When he didn't say anything, the fake copper carried on. 'Well, then, let me help you a little. I'm looking for a flash drive. A data stick. I want it back. Then I'm going to burn your house down, Mr Priest. Whether you give me the drive voluntarily or not determines whether you'll still be strapped to that chair when I strike the match.'

Priest said nothing but kept on watching. Watched the guy walk over to the box on the kitchen table. Watched him rummage around inside. Watched him take out a drill.

'You're here to put up some shelves?' Priest quipped.

The intruder's smile didn't materialise this time.

'I have all night, Mr Priest. And you're not going anywhere. Know how many holes I can drill in you before you pass out?'

'No.'

'Neither do I. Perhaps we can find out together.'

The fake copper took a drill piece out of the box and screwed it in. Pulled the trigger a few times, watching the barrel whirl. A rising sense of panic washed over Priest. *I wasted those few precious minutes.* He swallowed but his throat was still dry. He started jolting his arms, trying to find some movement, but he was helpless.

The intruder took the drill and pressed the flat of the barrel to Priest's ear. Priest kept his mouth shut, tried to control the overflow of oxygen he was taking in through his nose. It didn't seem real – nothing ever did. But it *felt* real, this time. He needed to avoid hyperventilating. At least while he was conscious, he had half a chance of talking his way out of this. Although that prospect seemed to be fading by the second.

Fake Copper pulled the trigger. Priest threw his head sideways and grimaced as the barrel burnt the side of his face. He heard the maniac laugh. *The fucker's enjoying this!* Priest was running short of ideas so he decided to stall.

'OK. OK. The data is through there.' He nodded towards the dimly lit lounge.

The visitor pulled back reluctantly. 'Where?'

'I downloaded the data on to the computer in the corner of the room and destroyed the flash drive.'

'Why?'

Good question. 'I just did.'

Priest's visitor looked at him. Rubbed his hand across the drill. Leant in close. Priest could smell stale smoke and alcohol.

'If you're lying, I'll take your fucking eyes out first.'

4

Priest figured it would take the fake copper at least three minutes to work out that he was bluffing. In Priest's world, second chances were like gold dust. *Just ask my ex-wife.* This one wasn't going to be squandered.

He couldn't lean forward, but he could bend his neck. Enough to crane over to where his lighter was nestled in the top pocket of his shirt. He scrunched his stomach muscles and hunched his back until he heard something crack, which gave him enough leverage to get his tongue around the metal end of the lighter and extract it from his pocket into his mouth. When he had a good hold, he lifted his head. He wrenched his right wrist round so his hand was palm up. The cable tie worked like a cheese cutter, searing into the soft flesh around his wrist. He bit down hard on the lighter to control the pain. Then he steadied himself and spat.

For a moment, the red Clipper seemed to hang in the air, as if caught in an invisible spider's web. The trajectory looked all wrong. Gravity seemed too strong. It was going to fall short. Priest blinked and in that split second the scene changed again.

His fingers closed around the plastic cylinder, but his grip was tenuous. He held his breath. He manoeuvred the Clipper, manipulated it between forefinger and thumb. Finally, it sat bolt upright in his hand. He breathed out heavily. Twenty-five seconds gone, maybe thirty. He flicked the control switch to the plus sign and snapped down on the spark wheel. It ground against the stone, igniting the gas. The flame danced uncertainly, then settled. More finger manipulation and he was able to push the lighter slowly across his palm towards his wrist before nudging the top down with his first finger and then easing the flame slowly across his hand.

The burning sensation was instant. His arm tensed up. Pain shot through his body, signals flashed to his brain telling him to drop the lighter. It was excruciating, but he held on.

At last the flame met the plastic. Priest bit down hard on his lip, only letting the occasional gasp escape. His arm was going crazy. At first, the plastic didn't seem to be responding. The flame just wrapped around it, burning the skin on either side. A tremor started in his upper arm, sweeping down to his wrist. He realised he could only withstand so much. He spat and cursed; his body was taking over, the urge to pull away was irresistible. There was a faint smell of meat cooking slowly on a barbecue.

He thought he might have to abandon his plan for escape, but just as he decided he couldn't stand it any longer, he saw the chemical change happening in the composition of the plastic. It was softening; slowly, agonisingly. His eyes were streaming; it felt as if his body were melting along with the plastic.

He could bear it no longer. His shirt sleeve was starting to smoulder. If it caught fire, he stood little chance of extinguishing himself. *Now I know what my lemon sole felt like . . .*

At last the binding snapped and the plastic tie fell to the floor. The broken ends glowed, a little trail of smoke drifted upwards. He didn't dare look at the damage done to his wrist. It felt as though there was a knife wedged through it.

The lighter had also fallen on the floor, but it didn't matter. With his free hand he was able to reach a small drawer in the kitchen table and pull out a letter knife. It was his late father's – a straight blade with his father's initials, FP, carved into the curved, bone handle.

He slipped the knife in between his wrist and the cable tie, making short work of cutting himself loose. Same for his legs, then the duct tape round his chest. When he was finished, he stumbled off the chair, gasping and wheezing, and then bent double over the kitchen table. Two minutes had passed, maybe less. *Not bad, Houdini. Although you'll probably never play the piano again.* He had time to spare. His eyes narrowed. The room was spinning. It occurred to him that he must also be concussed. He didn't feel *there*, in the room. Nothing new about that, though. *Fifteen seconds.* He would allow himself fifteen seconds of slow, controlled breathing before he made his next move.

Fifteen seconds later he was moving.

The box was still on the table, as was the T-baton. Priest picked up the weapon. Pain shot down his arm as his hand curled around the grip but he clung on. He briefly considered the letter knife, or something bigger from the kitchen drawer. *No.* Knives caused mess and rarely disabled a determined opponent quickly. The T-baton could end it with one well-aimed blow.

He held it by the side handle, so the butt covered his forearm and the main shaft extended outwards. It was more accurate this way and the base acted as a shield. Held by the butt, it was just like any other blunt weapon. This way, it was an extension of his own arm.

He stood still for a moment, listening. No tap of a keyboard or click of a mouse. Nor the whirr of the old fan. Was the intruder still in the flat?

He slipped his shoes off so he could move silently across the kitchen floor. Shoes would have made a lot of noise, even if he was careful. The door to the living room was ajar. Priest got a view of a slice of the room but not enough of an angle to see the desk. There was no way of knowing if the intruder was still sitting there. He listened hard again but heard nothing.

The door didn't squeak as he slowly opened it outwards, using the end of the baton. A little more of the room was revealed. Red leather reclining sofa curving around a glass coffee table. A fifty-two-inch plasma TV hung on the wall over a fake hearth. Bookshelves spanning the whole of one wall, filled from floor to ceiling with various books. Crime thrillers, horrors, classics. Academic texts on psychology and hypnosis, the art of war. Biographies of great leaders, the odd graphic novel. A diverse and seemingly arbitrary collection.

The only light came from a constellation of spotlights over the sofa and the fish tank – designed for mood, not for illumination. Opposite the bookshelves, the other wall was entirely glass. The curtains were drawn, veiling the cityscape behind. There were doors that led off to the other rooms. Two bedrooms, a cloakroom, a study and set of stairs that accessed a private roof garden overlooking Covent Garden. Fake Copper could be anywhere.

Priest pushed the door a little wider. He was tense, every muscle in his body coiled like a spring, ready to run the baton right through the bastard's head. Every heartbeat felt like the noise of an army, crunching in unison over the hardened earth. It wasn't the only noise. Nine storeys up, even the reinforced glass couldn't block out the hum of the crowds below, the people weaving in and out of department stores and coffee houses, the rumble of traffic and street musicians striking up their discordant tune. At night, Priest would sit in the roof garden and listen to the consorting sounds, like the purring of some giant machine turning over endlessly in the street below.

The desk was unmanned. The computer was untouched. The room was completely still. For a few seconds, Priest felt as though he was caught in a vacuum. He took a couple of steps forward into the room, the T-baton held out to shield him from an attack. The doors were all shut. Priest straightened. It had been a long time since he had walked the beat in uniform but the transitions he had undertaken from policeman to detective and then to lawyer hadn't diminished him physically. He was still a natural athlete, broad-shouldered and lean. But right now, he was concussed and carrying an arm so wracked with pain that he was struggling to keep a solid grip on the T-bat. Perhaps it was not totally unexpected, then, that not for the first time that evening, he reacted just a fraction of a second too late.

He lifted the baton to protect his face but he was knocked sideways as the fake copper leapt on to his back and slipped a cord around his neck. He gasped for breath but found with horror that his windpipe was being crushed. Panic washed through him as the oxygen was turned off. He choked. His gag reflex kicked in. It didn't help but made it worse. Much worse. The two men pirouetted in a violent embrace as Priest tried to throw his attacker off. They hit the bookshelf. Priest rammed his aggressor into it, but he held on tightly, increasing the intensity of the chokehold.

Priest felt hot breath on his neck, the grunt of triumph in his ear. He saw flashes in front of his eyes as his brain, fatigued and starved of air, started to shut down. His struggling lessened as one by one his muscles began to surrender. He thought about his father for a moment. His brilliant smile and deep blue eyes. Blue eyes like his. Defiantly staring at him, calling to him. Telling him he was not to give in. *Never retreat. Never submit. Never let them push you around, Charlie. No matter what.*

He thrust the T-bat's butt into his assailant's ribs. Felt the metal penetrate the tissue and the fake copper's momentary loss of grip on the cord. It was enough to give him a gulp of air. He struck again, harder this time, in the same spot. This time the man yelped with pain. He jolted sideways, hung on, but Priest had leverage; enough to force the baton hard into the intruder's side. Finally he heard the satisfying crack of bone.

In one movement, Priest managed to turn, leading with his right arm, and lever the fake copper's arms down using the T-bat, leaving his head exposed. Then he punched with his left as hard as he'd ever punched a man. Priest flipped the baton up and caught it neatly again so he was holding just the butt. No need for subtlety now. He hovered over the man for a moment. He was bleeding – it looked like the baton had taken a chunk of his face away. It would have been easy enough to finish him off, to ram the bat across his head so it split open like a watermelon. He raised the bat, but something stopped him. He wavered.

Enough, Charlie, his father said. *You're not your brother.*

Priest let his arm drop. *You're not your brother, Charlie.* William Priest wouldn't have hesitated – William would have opened up the intruder's head to see what was inside.

That was why William would never get out of Fen Marsh Secure Hospital.

'Who are you?' Priest asked.

'What does it matter?'

'I lied to you. I don't have any flash drive belonging to you.'

'Fuck!' The intruder coughed up a ball of red-stained saliva. 'He said it was here.'

'Who's *he*?'

When the fake copper didn't answer, Priest took a step towards him. He intended to pick him up and stick him against the wall to get some answers. But it didn't work out like that; the intruder still had some fight left in him. As he stepped forward again, the intruder lunged and took hold of Priest's leg, sinking his teeth into Priest's ankle. For a moment, Priest thought he'd bitten right through it as a shockwave of pain rippled up his leg. It was enough to unbalance him. As he hit the floor, the intruder took off back through the kitchen and, moments later Priest heard the sound of the front door bursting open. Outside, the street musicians were still piping out their bluesy melody.

5

24th March, 1946
A remote farm in middle England

They sat the Nazi butcher down across the table from Ruck. Two
Tommies, Lewis guns hung over their shoulders, pressed him
firmly into the wooden chair. They cuffed his hands behind his
back and whipped the bag off his head. Then they retreated, as
though their captive was diseased.

Ruck watched his guest appraise his surroundings – a twenty-
five foot barn, void of the ploughs and machinery that once
would have been stored there. A sterile, empty space, save for
the table at which Ruck and his prisoner sat and the chains that
hung from the rafters, swaying eerily in the breeze blowing
through the cracks in the walls.

Ruck swept his hair from his eyes. It was cut immaculately,
although a few loose blond strands still fell across his face. His
suit was pristine, Savile Row, bespoke. In the shabby barn, partially illuminated by blades of light cutting across the floor, he
looked utterly out of place.

The Nazi wore the rags of a POW, more of a sack than a gar-
ment, but he sat bolt upright, head up, as dignified as anyone
could be in his situation, staring Ruck straight in the eyes. Ruck

wondered how many people had looked into those blue eyes, pleading for mercy. He knew what that kind of desperation looked like – he'd seen it before.

Kurt Schneider was taller than Ruck, but desperately thin. He didn't resemble the skeletal wreckages they had emancipated from the concentration camp, but Ruck had deprived him of sleep and food for several weeks and the strain was seeping out of his etiolated skin. That said, it seemed Schneider wasn't done yet. The deep crevices running down his face and the wisps of silvery hair that started well above his creased forehead had aged him, but not in a way that nature ordinarily permitted. One piercing eye looked at Ruck defiantly while the other wandered to the side. Ruck lit a cigarette. *I am looking at madness.* He avoided prolonged eye contact – it made him look as though he was concerned about breaking it. He offered the packet to Schneider then looked at the doctor's constrained hands. Ruck shrugged his shoulders and withdrew the offer. He'd sit and wait a short while to see if Schneider would speak first. He suspected he wouldn't.

No, not madness. Evil.

As it happened, he was wrong. Schneider moved suddenly, lifting his whole body up out of the chair before sitting back down heavily. Not an attempt to escape. Frustration. Anger. A sign of protest perhaps. Ruck raised an eyebrow.

'You think bringing me to a barn intimidates me, pig?' Schneider demanded. His English was as good as Ruck had expected, but his accent was unmistakable.

The coarse tone of the master race. The Devil's tongue.

Ruck let the silence that followed linger.

'Where are we?' Schneider asked.

'On a farm. A long way from London. A very long way from Berlin.'

'I never had any particular liking for either city.'

'Good. Both are crippled beyond recognition, anyway. Although one burns a little brighter than the other.' Ruck picked up on Schneider's look of interest. 'Didn't you know, Doctor? The war is over. Hitler is dead. Russia remains a communist backwater state.'

'That is of little consequence. If you are lying, then unless an invasion happens very shortly, I will be killed. If you are telling the truth, I will be killed also.'

Ruck had noted the tiny flicker of Schneider's wandering eye when he had said Hitler was dead. He wondered if the German had somehow managed to train his eye to look the other way. He was certainly responsible for stranger perversions.

'Why didn't you follow the exodus from Buchenwald when you had the chance, Dr Schneider? You knew the Americans were coming days before Ainsworth and his boys showed up. Why not . . . save yourself?'

'If I had, then I would not have had the pleasure of meeting you.' He was still staring at Ruck. He seemed to have trained that bloody eye not to blink either.

Ruck sat back, took another drag. For two years, he had worked in the secluded detention centre in Kensington known as the Cage, a secret prison where Nazi POWs had been tortured for information. He'd reported directly to the head of the Prisoner of War Interrogation Section, a division of the Directorate of Military Intelligence that, as far as the public were concerned, did not exist. Ruck had been a special-ist in the extraction of information in the shortest conceivable time. Now the war was over, his talents had been passed to MI5 to see what useful knowledge could be salvaged from the ravaged continent. To see if there were any gemstones hidden in the ashes of war.

'My name is Ruck. I work for the British government, Military Intelligence, Section Five. My rank is Colonel, although I rarely use it. I am a specialist in interrogation, covert intelligence gathering and espionage. There will be no record that this discussion ever took place other than a report I will prepare for the eyes of a very select number of people and which will be destroyed as soon as it has been read. If during your trial, or at any other stage, you should mention our meetings, it will be denied. Do you understand?'

Schneider paused for a while and thought about it. 'You have my full attention, Herr Ruck. For now, at least.'

The barn door opened behind Schneider. Light streamed in. Ruck watched as a woman was ushered in by two soldiers. Another two men carried a small desk and chair. They set this up near the barn door, ten yards away from Ruck's table. On the desk, they placed a stenograph machine. The woman sat down. Throughout the whole thing, Schneider hadn't moved.

'Perfume,' the doctor said, inhaling deeply and closing his eyes. 'Something French.' He opened his eyes and looked at Ruck with excitement. 'Our personal record keeper. To write up your report, Herr Ruck! I am right, no?'

Ruck said nothing. The woman looked up. She was far younger than Ruck had expected – no more than twenty. He had wanted her to be inconspicuous but he found himself glancing back to check that his first impression had been fair. In seconds, he had taken everything in. Shimmering brown hair and glasses with thick, black frames. A petite, heart-shaped face. Pretty. Pearls dangling from her neck. Straight skirt. Completely ill-prepared, like everyone else they'd sent him. She looked as though she should be strutting down Oxford Street to a bank, not transcribing interrogation in a barn.

Ruck nodded at her and she began to type.

'What were you assigned to do at Buchenwald, Dr Schneider?'

'I was a house doctor at the hospital there.'

'Hospital? Is that what you call it?'

Schneider was silent.

'They have assembled a court, Dr Schneider. At Nuremberg. They're calling it the first true international military tribunal. In October this year an indictment will be published. It will bear your name. How do you feel about that?'

'Nuremberg? Have you seen Nuremberg, Herr Ruck? It is a scrapyard. Churchill's war engines have destroyed it.'

'It has been rebuilt by the Americans. You should see the Palace of Justice now.'

Schneider scoffed. 'I have committed no crimes. I have nothing to fear.'

'Your membership of the SS will be sufficient to earn you the death penalty.'

'I was never a member of the SS.'

'Suit yourself, Doctor. Your political affiliation is of little consequence to me, anyway. They've declared the SS an illegal organisation, by the way. Perhaps you are wise to deny your connection to it, although it won't take the Americans long to tie a few pieces of paper together and build a case.'

Schneider was thoughtful for a moment, or perhaps he was letting the typist catch up. Either way, the only noise for the next few moments was the sound of her fingers on the keys. Then he looked at Ruck with fresh interest.

'If you're looking at a dead man, Herr Ruck, then why do you not grant him a final request and let him know what it is you actually want?'

Ruck nodded and allowed a smile to play at the corners of his mouth. The Nazi was unsettled. That was good enough for a morning's work. He produced a set of papers from a bag and placed them on the table.

'Although you say, Dr Schneider, that you were a house doctor at the hospital, we both know that you engaged in various forms of human experimentation. Do you disagree?'

'Not at all.'

'Good.'

Ruck lined up photographs neatly in front of Schneider. They showed a black-and-white room from different angles. A metal operating table in the centre. Leather straps hung at the sides. Instruments scattered everywhere. The room was a mess. Dark stains covered the floor.

'This was your surgery. Do you disagree?'

'No.'

'These are the Hell Rooms. So the Americans call them, anyway. A good name, I think. None of your victims gave their consent to the torture you subjected them to. What are you going to tell the Nuremberg court, by the way? That your work was for the good of mankind?'

'Will they let me have a lawyer, Herr Ruck, do you think? And what evidence do you think they will consider at this trial of yours?'

'You destroyed the paper records of your experiments before the exodus from Buchenwald, Doctor. You personally stayed behind, on Himmler's orders, to destroy the paperwork. I think that's why you were still there when the camp was liberated. Am I right?'

The air outside whipped up, causing the barn doors to shudder. Ruck noticed the typist pull her jacket tighter around her shoulders. There was something about her he could not place his finger on. Perhaps it was the way she was sitting, or the look of concentration on her face. Whatever it was, she made him uncomfortable.

'There were three Hell Rooms,' Ruck continued. Schneider remained impassive. 'In the first two, we found evidence of surgical operations carried out on camp inmates – primarily by you, but by others under your stewardship as well. You removed limbs, although for what purpose I have never ascertained. There were other experiments with mustard gas and various poisons. In one case, we found evidence of a woman being shot in the thigh at point-blank range so you could observe the efficacy of different treatments for bullet wounds. Most people who were led into those rooms never came out.'

'You're beginning to bore me, Herr Ruck.'

'You're anxious not to talk about your work, Doctor? An unusual trait for such a pioneer, wouldn't you say?'

Schneider waved Ruck away as though he were swatting a fly.

'You asked me to indulge you, Herr Ruck. Why should I? The Americans will try me and condemn me to death. But what I have achieved will live on for centuries. I don't know what history will remember me as. A murderer? A scientist? A revolutionist? I suppose it depends who writes the textbook you're reading. But history *will* remember me. And my work. What more important thing is there? I wonder how history will remember *you*, Herr Ruck. As a name? A number? A rank? Or as nothing at all. Just a speck of dust on the pages belonging to me. Nothing more. So have your say while you can. Have your moment. Make it last. Take me through every procedure I carried out. Go through them one by one, if you will. I don't care. And in a few years from now, neither will anyone else.'

There was a moment's silence, except for the stenograph machine. Ruck stroked his chin thoughtfully. 'As I said, Doctor, there were *three* Hell Rooms.'

Schneider opened his mouth, but aborted whatever it was he had planned to say.

Ruck noticed the Nazi's change in posture.

'You know something, Herr Ruck?' Schneider leant forward, as far as the restraints wrapped around his wrists would allow him. 'I recall one day I scanned the lines of newcomers. They thought I didn't care. That I thought they weren't human. That's not true, or fair. I looked at each one with a pedant's eye. Looked at every scar, every mole, every curve. I was meticulous about the patients I picked. *Loving* even, in the way I went about it. They knew who I was, of course. I allowed rumours of my work to ripple through the camp, like a stone thrown into a pond. They'd shrink at the very sight of me sweeping up the line, selecting the chosen few.'

Ruck tapped the ash from his cigarette and took a heavy drag. He noticed the typist had slowed down, the keys pressed with absolute precision. Ruck wondered what was going through her mind. Was that what troubled Ruck about her? Yes, there it was. The thing that was out of place: *she isn't scared. Not nearly enough.*

'Tell me about your poison experiments, Dr Schneider. That was your specialism, wasn't it?' Ruck said, tearing his eyes away from the woman in the corner.

'Ah, so you're a chemist, Herr Ruck?'

Ruck took another drag. 'We heard some intriguing rumours. That you were experimenting with poison, something so powerful that victims would mutilate themselves just to stop the pain from spreading through their bodies.'

Schneider didn't respond but fixed Ruck with an expression of mild indifference.

'Further evidence was found that other SS officers and camp guards would gather to watch the administration of this drug. Now why would that be?'

'You would not understand.'

'Try me.'

Schneider laughed. 'Herr Ruck, you flatter yourself. How could you possibly comprehend something you have never witnessed?'

'What was it, Doctor?' Ruck taunted. 'What was your audience deriving from the proceedings? Pleasure? Entertainment? Enlightenment?'

'You want to know how to make the poison, Herr Ruck? Fine – I will show you. Give me your pen. And, Scribe, a piece of your writing paper.'

Schneider turned his head as far as he could and motioned towards the woman. Ruck waited a moment, chewing on his cigarette. He wasn't going to unshackle his prisoner and arm him with a pen without careful thought. After a short while, he nodded at the two guards. The first covered Schneider with his Lewis gun while the second undid the cuffs and placed a piece of paper on the desk. Schneider expectantly looked up at Ruck, who hesitated before tossing it in the doctor's direction. Schneider took it and scribbled something on the page, then threw the pen back.

Ruck took the paper and examined it. 'You're modifying strychnine. Why? It is already an efficient killer, is it not?'

'Perhaps too efficient.'

Ruck grimaced. He had had the misfortune of witnessing death by strychnine, a naturally occurring alkaloid extracted from the seeds of the native Indian strychnine tree. The poison worked quickly but death was agonising – the victims would spasm and contort grotesquely as though they were possessed.

'What was the purpose of these modifications?'

'Quite simply to keep death at the door without opening it and letting him in.'

'A poor way to carry out interrogation,' Ruck observed. 'If that was the intention.'

'It was not.'

'Then what? What was the point?'

Schneider looked vaguely amused. 'For God so loved the world, that he gave his only begotten Son, that whoever believes in him should not perish but have eternal life.'

'John 3:16.'

'You know your Bible, Herr Ruck. How quaint.'

'My father was a rector. A good, honest man. Right up until the Nazi bomb exploded in his face and killed him.'

Schneider shrugged. His face was a mask. The skin around his eyes and mouth was drawn so taut there was little room for expression.

He leant forward and said in a low tone, 'How familiar are you, Herr Ruck, with Him?' He pointed upwards.

'God?'

'Of course. God.'

'Well enough to know that He was absent from Buchenwald during your reign.'

'No.' Schneider shook his head emphatically. 'That is naive. What I achieved offered those who believed in His existence the opportunity to leave this world temporarily and look upon the Holy Trinity.'

'You saw God? Through the torture of a human being?'

'A useless eater – not a human being.'

Ruck sat back in his chair, thoughtful. He glanced over at the typist. For the first time, her fingers slipped on the keys. The guards shuffled their feet. Outside, a gust of wind rattled the barn doors – a storm was approaching.

6

The offices of Priest & Co took up four floors of a narrow seg-
ment of a Grade II listed building less than fifteen minutes' walk
from the Royal Courts of Justice on a street aptly named The
Nook. The road served no purpose other than as an append-
age to the Strand and Charlie Priest's office represented the
only apparent point of interest, other than the absurdly small
establishment opposite known as Piccolo Café, which Priest
regularly frequented. He tended only to order tea, much to the
disgust of the incumbent barista.

Priest took the office steps two at a time, bounding past the
small bronze placard affixed to the wall, which was the only
way of identifying the building's occupants, and into a plush
reception area. The smell of old leather hung in the air. The fur-
nishings were dark mahogany and oak. One wall was entirely
occupied by ink-pen caricatures of famous lawyers and judges,
the other by an old bookshelf filled from floor to ceiling with
law reports. There was a faded poster advertising the famous
Carbolic Smoke Ball.

Priest hated it – right down to the fake flowers on the mantelpiece – but the look was for clients, not for him.

Maureen looked up from behind the front desk. Gave him a
where-the-hell-have-you-been look. He had had a meeting with

the bank this morning, which he had asked her to rearrange. They weren't happy, apparently. Having said that, Priest had no borrowings over the building, had never touched the overdraft and ran only a very limited client account. He was hardly the bank's number one concern.

He threw Maureen a sorry-it's-been-a-complicated-morning look in return and swept into his office before she could speak, then closed the door behind him.

Priest's was the biggest room in the building, although this had come about by chance rather than design. It just so happened that he had the most files to store.

He collapsed into the chair behind a large, modern desk on which sat two computer screens and a jumble of papers. There was a flat-screen TV on the wall to his left showing a muted Sky News broadcast. He examined a mug hiding between the two monitors and found it to have become home to a foamy layer of unidentifiable fungus.

Must have a word with the cleaner. Perhaps introduce a pay-by-results incentive scheme.

He flicked the mouse. Both monitors clicked and whirred and he was presented with lockout screens. He tapped in the password idly but his fingers were on autopilot. He needed thinking time. Somebody had gone to an awful lot of trouble last night to try to kill him in order to recover something that he didn't have. Or wasn't aware he had. That constituted a bad night. Moreover, his assailant was still out there somewhere, lurking in the metropolis. Priest shivered. He could hardly move his incinerated wrist.

He should call the police, of course. He knew that. But he wouldn't. Priest had spent eight years of his life excelling as a policeman before he had committed what his former colleagues judged to be the ultimate betrayal by becoming a lawyer. As if the natural mistrust that existed between law enforcers and law manipulators wasn't enough, Priest had rubbed salt in the wound by making an awful lot of money in the process.

Lucky I don't care about what people think about me. Those that aren't trying to kill me, at least.

Priest doubted that being assigned a crime reference number would help much. Besides, he had far better resources at his disposal than the local blue. If he needed someone found, he would do it himself. *A matter which the pain in my head is seriously impeding, although a hot cup of tea in a clean cup might be a good starting point.*

A curt knock preceded the door opening. An enormous black man filled the doorway. Glossy grey suit, no tie. Custom lime-green shirt matching the handkerchief protruding from the breast pocket. The flash of a Rolex.

The career of Vincent Okoro, Priest & Co's in-house counsel, was as big and impressive as he was. Admitted to the Bar in 1995, the Nigerian-born barrister had, like Priest, come to the law late, having run his own development company for ten years before retraining and eventually accepting a tenancy at an upcoming Lincoln's Inn chambers. There he had thrived, specialising in complex commercial litigation and gaining a reputation as a ruthless cross-examiner and a savvy tactical thinker.

Okoro shut the door behind him and took the seat opposite Priest. It groaned under his weight. Not fat but muscle – a lot of muscle. Priest often speculated that Okoro was just one big muscle. And this morning, he was one big, grim-looking muscle.

'I've spent the last hour on the phone to Monroe,' Okoro said. His voice was as exquisite as his suit – majestic – the growl of a king, each word perfectly pronounced in soft Nigerian tones.

'Who?'

'Monroe. He's our bank manager.' Okoro nodded patiently.

'Oh, him.'

'They want another cash-flow forecast.'

'What was wrong with the last one I did?'

'You haven't done one, Priest. In fact, in all the years I've known you, you've never done one.'

'So they don't want *another* one then. They just want . . . *one*.'

Okoro smiled and nodded slowly, as though he was listening to some soft music that pleased him. 'You look like shit, Priest.'

'Bad night.'

Okoro raised an inquisitive eyebrow. 'A bad *weekday* night. Wow. So, it's come to this?'

'Is it past twelve yet?' Priest asked, glancing at his wrist and seeing only the horrific burn marks. He hastily covered them up.

'What?'

Priest fished around in the bottom drawer and eventually picked out a bottle of blended malt Scotch. He wasn't sure how it had ended up in his drawer – probably a gift from a grateful client – but he was pleased he'd remembered it was there. He poured two glasses and pushed one across the desk to Okoro. Downed his and poured another one. Downed that and then looked up at Okoro expectantly.

Okoro regarded the glass suspiciously. 'Is this a new firm policy? Midday drinking?'

Priest took another shot. Drinking wasn't a habit or a hobby for him. In all likelihood, a thirteen-year-old girl could drink him under the table, but right now he felt like he needed something to dull his anxiety.

'Is something bothering you, Priest?'

Priest shook his head, but kept his hand on the bottle.

'What happened last night?'

'Nothing much. Usual kind of night. Repeats of *The Saint*, KFC, fed the fish, played the piano a bit. Then someone tried to bust my head open. Next thing I know, I'm strapped to my own fucking chair and there's this guy waving a drill in my face.'

There was a moment of silence while Priest rubbed the back of his head where the T-baton had made contact. There were two lumps the size of golf balls – it was a miracle his head had held together.

'You don't play the piano, Priest.'

'Does that detail matter?'

'Want to tell me what you're babbling on about properly? I'm in court next week.'

Priest sighed and took another shot of whisky. The amber liquid burnt his throat and a thought struck him. *I hate whisky.* He shook that thought away and launched into last night's events, scene by scene, careful not to omit a single detail. After he'd finished, there was another silence.

Okoro breathed heavily. 'And you didn't know this gentleman?'

'Nope.'

'Never seen him before?'

Priest shook his head. 'No.'

'No idea what he wanted?' Okoro raised an eyebrow and Priest sensed his scepticism.

'A flash drive.'

'Containing what?'

'No idea.'

'Uh-huh. Why did he think *you* had it?' Okoro rubbed his bald head as if he was in pain.

'He mumbled something about somebody else telling him I had it, but he didn't say who.'

'Did you recognise him?'

'No.'

Okoro kept on nodding slowly.

Okoro's big break had come in 2003 when he'd been offered the role of Deputy Prosecutor of the then newly established International Criminal Court, the international tribunal founded so that, for the first time, cases against the perpetrators of genocide, war crimes and crimes against humanity could be heard where national courts lacked jurisdiction or, more likely, the stomach for it. Okoro had found himself in the midst of an elite company of lawyers whose job it was to uphold the rule of law in territories that recognised no such notion, and to impose it on individuals who held the rest of humanity in nothing but the lowest form of contempt.

He was hardly a stranger to ruthlessness.

'Are you OK?' Okoro finally asked.

'I can barely move my wrist and my head feels like a travelling circus just moved into my frontal lobe. My eyes are sore. I've had two random nose bleeds this morning. Things feel funny when I taste them.'

'But are you *OK*?' Okoro pressed for confirmation.

Priest looked at Okoro for a few moments. Behind the half-smile, he saw genuine concern in the barrister's eyes. Okoro was putting on a front – staying calm, maintaining eye contact, not moving around too much. Priest always found it strangely relaxing to be in the gentle giant's company, and today of all days, he was grateful to have Okoro's counsel.

'Yeah, I'm fine,' he said, eventually. 'Bit annoyed that I didn't see it coming. It was a bullshit story. Good replica suit, mind. I wonder where he got it.'

'You can get anything if you know the right people, Priest. You know that. But it means he's well connected. Which means you have to be careful. You might want to revise your decision not to contact the police.'

'How do you know I've made that decision?'

'Because I know the great Charlie Priest better than he knows himself.'

'Mm.' Priest looked reflective but he had no intention of changing his mind. 'I'll think about it.'

Okoro nodded.

The computer pinged, hailing the arrival of another email behind the lockout screen. Luckily, it was a quiet week. Priest & Co worked for only a few very select and very lucrative clients: transnational companies trying to identify corruption in their ranks of middle management, dot-com companies with a rogue director taking backhanders, firms accusing their competitors of illegal practices, bribery, anti-competitive cartels. The occasional bent MP.

The key to Priest & Co's business model was results. Deliver what you say you're going to deliver, when you say you're going to deliver it. And the key to the one hundred per cent success record was simple, too. Careful case selection. There might only be one or two cases running at one particular time. Allocation of resources was critical. So Priest only took on what he thought he could handle and what he thought he could win.

In some ways, Priest had been lucky. The fake policeman's visit had coincided with the lull that comes about between the mopping up after a major trial and the start of the next one. The deep breath before the plunge. The previous success had been Theramere International Plc, a FTSE 100 listed company. They sold experience packages – track days, balloon rides, dinners cooked by celebrity chefs. The company had grown and mutated so quickly that the founders had lost their way, pledging their faith to a CEO poached from a competitor then wondering why he'd become richer than they'd been paying him. Three weeks in front of a red-robed judge and Priest & Co had shown that the reason was because the CEO had had control of three other companies offering similar services in Morocco, Germany and Holland and he'd been playing them off against each other for his own gain. Now he was paying his secret profit back to Theramere and it would take him the rest of his life.

Okoro stirred in his chair, shifting his gigantic weight to one side. The chair complained audibly underneath him. He mused, 'So this guy spent a lot of money and invested a lot of time into setting up an operation designed to recover something from you – electronic data of an unknown nature – and he executes his plan but he doesn't get what he wants . . .'

'Yes.' Priest nodded, completing Okoro's assumption. 'So he's going to try again.'

'You need to be careful.'

'*We* need to be careful.' Priest reiterated.

'What do you mean, *we*?'

'He knew a lot about me, Okoro. Probably knows who you are too.'

Okoro chuckled. 'I can look after me. It's you I'm worried about. Are you going to let the others in on what's happening?'

Priest let the question hang in the air. By 'the others', Okoro meant Priest & Co's two other associates – Simon 'Solly' Solomon and Georgie Someday. Priest had already decided he would tell Georgie. At twenty-five, she was the youngest of the team but what she lacked in age she made up for in mental agility; rarely had Priest encountered a legal brain as fine as Georgie's.

Solly, Priest & Co's in-house accountant, was a more complicated question. Socially impotent, a hopeless conversationalist and probably autistic, Solly was a numbers man and, as he was fond of saying in rare moments of lucidity, 'People are not numbers, Priest.' It's a good job they weren't, too – Solly could spot a pound moving between eight different accounts across four different jurisdictions hidden in six hundred pages of audit.

If people *were* numbers, then Simon Solomon would be the world's greatest psychologist; but since they weren't, Priest didn't like to worry him about things like drill-wielding maniacs.

'I'll mention it to Georgie. We'll think about Solly later.'

'You'll *mention it*? Like you just thought of a new recipe for lemon drizzle cake?'

Priest shrugged. Okoro rose to his feet, a vast storm cloud suddenly filling Priest's office.

'I'll start digging around for you. In the meantime, if you need a place to stay . . .'

Priest waved him away.

'No, no. I'll be fine. Besides, your wife hates me.'

'My wife hates your social awkwardness, your poor table manners and your intellectual arrogance. She doesn't hate *you*, per se.'

'It's a long list of hate.'

'Yeah, it's *my* damn list, too. Watch your back, Priest.' Okoro loped out.

Priest turned around to the window behind him and stared at the doorway of the Piccolo Café. He had been thinking he needed a holiday. Somewhere warm, but not burning. A golden beach, crystal-clear ocean. Cocktails served by scantily clad maidens. Maybe once he had managed to ensure, somehow, that his nocturnal visitor wasn't coming back for another drilling session, he'd swing by the travel agents and pick up a few brochures. *That's what a near-death experience does. Makes you think of all the things you've missed in life.*

The alcohol swam around his head. He hadn't felt this confused since his divorce. Dee Auckland seemed like a lifetime ago now, but it had been for the best. Mainly because he was socially retarded and she was a fucking nutter.

It wasn't cold, but he found himself shivering.

From beneath some papers in the drawer where the whisky bottle had been stashed, Priest took out an old photograph. It was torn at the edges and creased across the middle. He should take better care of it, he thought. The three Priests – William, himself and Sarah. So much potential, faces full of naive wonder. It had all ended when William pleaded guilty to serial murder and they read the headlines the morning after the trial: *Senior policeman's brother modern-day Jack the Ripper.*

That was when the questions had started. How had William, with his PhD in psychology, metamorphosed into such a vicious killer? How had he evaded detection for so long? Why had he killed? Why were none of the expert profiles right? What drove him to madness? Was he abused as a child or did he suffer a serious blow to the head?

Or was there evil in his blood?

Priest looked at his wrists where the flame had burnt him; a black, purulent mess that had started to blister and hurt every time he moved his hand. But underneath it, a network of veins carrying blood – the same blood that . . .

There was another knock at the door. Priest slipped the picture back into the drawer. Okoro's bald head reappeared.

'Priest. There's a guy here to see you.'

'Who?'

'Don't know. But he's got a pretty mean-looking badge.'

7

Neville McEwen was fatter than Priest remembered. The red-haired Scot bulged in every direction and was barely contained inside his ill-fitting suit. He had aged, too: years of alcohol and fags had turned his face a deep shade of purple.

Okoro showed him to the chair opposite Priest and took a seat in the corner of the room. Priest winced as the Scot sat down heavily. *There's only so much stress that chair can take.*

Despite the extra pounds, Priest had recognised McEwen immediately. He'd been a detective sergeant when Priest had been fast-tracked to detective inspector. It had been no secret that McEwen had wanted the DI job and he'd been waiting an awful long time for it. Watching a man ten years younger and with only a quarter of the experience leapfrog him must have been upsetting for McEwen. Priest expected hostility – he'd probably put the fat bastard's career back five or six years.

'Charlie Priest,' McEwen muttered. 'Well I'll be damned.'

Priest leant across the desk so he could hear better. The combination of sleep deprivation, whisky and probable concussion was starting to make his head spin and he recalled that McEwen had an unfortunate habit of slurring his words.

'DS McEwen.'

'It's D*I* McEwen now.'

'Oh. Well done, old chap.'

'How long has it been?' McEwen growled.

'Long time.'

'Aye. Long time.'

'What can we do for you, Detective Inspector McEwen?' asked Okoro from his sentry position behind the policeman.

McEwen didn't look around. 'I'm here to speak to the organ grinder. Not the monkey.'

Priest saw the choice of words register with Okoro. Twenty years ago, Priest suspected he might have reacted but Okoro had heard it all before. Priest clicked his tongue in the silence that followed.

'You don't look so good, Priest. Late night?' asked McEwen.

'I have difficult skin. Sometimes I look tired.'

'Aye. Tired. Right. I'd like to ask you a few questions, if I may, Priest. Where were you last night?'

'There's no sergeant with you,' Priest observed.

'So?'

'Just seems strange. That's all.'

McEwen inhaled deeply. Sounded like a wind turbine starting up. 'Where were you last night, Priest?'

'At home.'

'Any company?'

'What's this all about, Inspector?' interrupted Okoro.

McEwen ignored him. 'Have you heard of Ellinder Pharmaceuticals International?'

'Drug company?' Priest suggested.

'Aye. Clue's in the title, right? The CEO – Kenneth Ellinder – ever heard of him?'

'Nope.'

'His son, Miles, was found dead last night in one of the company's warehouses.'

'OK.'

'The name Miles Ellinder mean anything to you, Priest?'

'Not a thing.'

'Uh-huh.' McEwen sniffed loudly again and wiped his nose on his sleeve. He finished by clearing his throat, hacking up a ball of phlegm and swallowing it back down. He placed a photograph on the table – a headshot of a man in his thirties with slicked black hair and dead eyes.

Priest swallowed. The man in the picture wasn't wearing a policeman's uniform but he did resemble his visitor from last night.

'This is Miles Ellinder,' McEwen said. 'Does his face mean anything to you?'

'Afraid not. Are we through?'

'No, far from it. Miles Ellinder's body was found by a caretaker early this morning. Purely by chance. He found a door leading to a basement open and followed it down. And there he was, dead. We're treating the death as suspicious.'

Priest shrugged. 'OK.'

'Know why we're treating the death as suspicious?'

'No.'

'Sure you don't.'

McEwen produced another picture from the inside pocket of his suit jacket. He slapped it down on the table. Priest stared long and hard. It took a while for the image to make sense, like a magic eye puzzle. Then it dawned on him that what he had registered the first time around was exactly what the picture showed. *Sweet Jesus.* Priest was vaguely aware of Okoro getting up and leaning over the desk to look. He wanted it to change. He wanted the true image to reveal itself, but the more he looked, the more the scene crystallised. The reality was inescapable. For a moment, he thought he might be sick.

'Any further thoughts, Priest?' McEwen said with a sneer.

'That's no way for a man to die,' Okoro said quietly.

McEwen picked up the photograph. It had been on the table for only a few moments but it was enough to burn the image into Priest's mind.

'How do you know it's Miles Ellinder?' Priest asked. The picture was clear but the body was a good ten feet away from the camera and the head was turned slightly to the side. Priest hadn't been able to tell whether or not this man was the same as the fake copper, or even if he was the man in the first picture McEwen had produced.

'The family identified him. There's no doubt,' McEwen grunted. 'He was impaled. There was a metal shaft welded to the warehouse floor. Purpose built. Thrust up his rectum to the nape of his neck, although they probably only partially lowered him on to the shaft, which they'd greased up first. Then gravity did the rest. He might have died quickly if he was lucky. But he wasn't lucky. Pathologist said he was probably writhing around for up to an hour. The pole missed most of the vital organs. It was pretty carefully planned. Quite a show.'

McEwen leant as far forward as a man his size could and fixed Priest with a penetrating stare.

'Does his face look familiar to you, Priest? Huh? The pole up his arse, maybe? *That* familiar?'

Priest didn't reply.

McEwen looked unimpressed. 'If you don't know Mr Ellinder, then perhaps you can tell me how he came about one of your business cards?'

McEwen took out a clear plastic evidence bag and threw it at Priest, who only needed to glance at the blue script to know it was his. He remembered the fake copper had picked up one of his business cards and pocketed it before producing the drill.

'No idea.' Priest shook his head.

'You've no idea?'

'I do a lot of business, Inspector. I give out a lot of cards.'

'A client of yours, maybe? Of one of your associates?'

'I know all the practice's clients. This man wasn't one of them.'

'You're not being particularly helpful, Priest.'

'I'm answering your questions. How do you know he had it on him?'

'His clothes were dumped in a corner. Looked like he was wearing a copper's beat outfit. Probably a replica. Nothing else – no wallet, no phone. The caretaker who found him recognised him. Right now the only lead I've got is you.'

'I'm sorry, Inspector, there's nothing I can help you with.'

'You know it won't take me long to get a warrant for this place, Priest. Little piece of paper that lets me look through every file, every drawer, every safe and every toilet bowl. Shame to have to do it. It would leave a fuck of a mess.'

'Come on, Inspector, we both know this is a waste of time,' said Okoro. 'You're ahead of the game right now but how long will it be until the media gets hold of this? A matter of hours, probably. Perhaps you should be pursuing a more tangible line of enquiry?'

'That's interesting advice.' McEwen turned round to Okoro for the first time. 'But the new assistant commissioner was keen for me to pursue *this* line of enquiry.'

Priest sighed. 'McEwen, the AC isn't going to be interested in me, I can assure you.'

'That depends on who the AC is.' McEwen's face contorted into a half-smile. It was a disturbing sight. There was something reptilian about his thin lips.

'McEwen, I haven't been in touch with Met politics for a decade. I don't know who the current AC is.'

McEwen actually laughed. 'She knows you very well, Priest. In fact, she told me personally to get over here and put you through the grill. I guess the last thing you knew, she was in Manchester. But now she's back. One rank higher and I bet still with no love lost. Dee Auckland.'

Priest felt something attach itself to the inside of his throat. 'I'm happy for her promotion,' he said. It was a problem. There was rarely a good outcome involved where his ex-wife was concerned.

'Aye. And she's happy to be back. She's taking a personal interest in this. For PR reasons, of course. I'm sure you understand.'

'Perfectly.'

'Anyway' – McEwen rose to his feet – 'best be off. I've got a magistrate to see about a warrant. You boys take care of yourselves.'

Okoro stood up as well and, as McEwen turned to leave, there was a brief moment when the two heavyweights stared at each other before Okoro opened the door and motioned for McEwen to negotiate his way through it. 'Thank for your time, McEwen,' he said pleasantly.

Priest stayed rigid in his chair. If he got up, his legs might not support him properly.

McEwen was halfway through the open door before he turned back to Priest. 'What do you know about mayflies?' he said.

Priest blinked, twice. 'Little bugs, aren't they?'

'They don't live very long. Not long at all.'

Priest considered letting it go but it was too obscure to ignore. 'Why do you mention mayflies?' he asked reluctantly.

McEwen's face broke into the toadlike grin of self-satisfaction again. 'They made him swallow one before they stuck a pole up his arse.'

❧

From the window, Priest watched McEwen fall into his Volvo and set off down The Nook towards the river. In the distance, he could hear the traffic building along the Strand – the drone of idle engines punctuated with the horns of anxious Londoners and the blare of sirens. He could feel himself slipping. It was as if the ghosts in his head were converging upon him all at once, their hollow screams echoing in the void. *I'm not part of the real world. I'm one of the ghosts.* He tried to ground himself, but his head was throbbing.

Okoro had taken the seat in front of Priest's desk again.

'You didn't tell him, then,' Okoro pointed out.

'No.'

'A little risky, Priest.'

'Why?'

'Something about perverting the course of justice.'

'Mm. It's bought us time. He won't get a warrant request past the local bench so we've slowed him down. That might give us a few days' head start.'

'To do what?'

'To find out what the bloody hell is going on.'

'It'll be nice to reacquaint yourself with your ex-wife.'

'No it won't, Okoro.'

'She still pissed at you?'

'I'd imagine so.'

'They'll track your movements from here.'

Priest nodded. He'd already factored that in. He felt tired, drained to the point of depletion. He was worried about Sarah. He wasn't sure why, but he felt like he should pay her a visit. Even if just to mention that his psycho ex-wife was back in town. It wasn't a surprise to him that she'd been promoted and transferred again. *I wonder who she's pissed off now.*

Until a few minutes ago, Priest had assumed Dee was still a commander at the Manchester Met, the position she had left him for when she had walked out five years earlier. At that point she had declared him 'mentally ill', which Priest couldn't argue with. He did, after all, have dissociative disorder, which was a pathological condition. He had tried to explain it to her; the feeling of detachment that could descend on him at any moment. At best, it was like a sudden twist to his surroundings – like the onset of a migraine in which reality holds more or less firm but in a distorted, disconnected way. A dream in which the dreamer knows full well he is actually asleep. At worst, he could experience moments of complete derealisation, as if he was catapulted out of his body into a strange, alien world in which he would view himself, or a twisted parody of himself, trying hopelessly to interact with his surroundings. Moments like those, although rare, could last for minutes or hours; a nightmare in which the dreamer has no idea whether he is asleep, awake or even alive.

It was hard to function in a world that was often only semi-real and sometimes completely *un*real. And so what if he was habitually inappropriate, flippant and occasionally downright rude? He didn't mean to offend. Huge chunks of his existence could cruise by like the blurry moving images of an old slide-show; sometimes it was only the reactions he provoked in others that made him feel properly human.

Not that Dee had been able to relate to any of that. Priest had met earwigs with more empathy.

Her final taunt – *you're mentally ill* – had stuck with him and made him realise what he had secretly always known: *people with dissociative disorder make rotten husbands, but sociopathic control freaks make even worse wives.*

A polite cough alerted Priest to the fact that Georgie was standing in the doorway. How long had she been standing there? By the look on Okoro's face – who was used to indulging Priest's silent moments of internal contemplation – a few minutes at least. She was wearing a pleated skirt and white blouse, her ginger hair tied back. She stood a little gawkily, her uncertainty obvious.

'I'm sorry,' she said. 'I knocked but I wasn't sure if you'd invited me in or –'

'It's OK, Georgie,' said Okoro. 'Come in. Priest was away with the fairies again.'

'Thanks.' She stepped into the office and looked at Priest. 'Oh. You don't look so good, Charlie.'

Priest nodded slowly. He supposed she was right. He hadn't showered this morning. His suit was crumpled and he wasn't wearing a tie. He probably resembled an extra from a zombie film.

'Yes, well, it's been a busy morning. Now, Georgie, you know how good you are at assimilating large quantities of disturbing information quickly? Well, it's a quality you're going to need over the next five minutes.'

'Great!' She produced a counsel's notepad and pen and looked up eagerly.

She's far too keen. Priest gave her an edited account of the last twenty-four hours, including the drill and McEwen's visit but excluding the nature of Miles Ellinder's death. There were certain details that she didn't need to know right now. When he had finished, there was a short pause during which he was unable to distinguish the hum of the traffic outside from the blood rushing past his ears.

After a short moment, Georgie put her pen down. 'Oh my God!' she said. She was shocked, obviously, but she couldn't hide an underlying sense of excitement.

He looked at her and, for the first time in several days, smiled. Georgie had stood head and shoulders above the other candidates he had interviewed for the associate's position a year before. On paper, she hadn't been much different to the other hopefuls. Solid first degree from Oxford, a masters in philosophy

from King's – like Priest – a distinction in her professional quali-
fications. In practice she was resourceful and dedicated. But there
was something that set her apart that Priest had latched on to; a
reservoir of energy hidden behind her emerald eyes.

'For obvious reasons, Georgie, this is currently on a need-to-
know basis. OK with that?'

'Of course! Top secret.' She paused and he could see her
struggling with the question. 'But how did you escape from the
chair?'

'I burnt through the binding with a cigarette lighter.' Priest
held up his wrist, which resembled a badly barbecued kebab.

'Does it hurt?' asked Georgie with genuine concern.

'Yes, it hurts like fuck, Georgie. As perhaps you might expect.'

Georgie nodded and made another note in her book. '*Hurts
like fuck*', *presumably*.

'OK, now that we've established that burning your own skin to
escape a drill-wielding madman is a distressing experience, down
to business. What do we know about Ellinder Pharmaceuticals
International?'

'They make antidepressants, mostly,' said Okoro. 'I hear
there's a lot of money in drugs and a lot of money floating
around the Ellinder family, too. As you might imagine.'

'Ellinder,' Georgie mused. 'Ellinder.' She produced an iPhone
from her pocket and started playing with the screen.

Priest waited patiently for her to find whatever it was she was
looking for. His head was still pounding but at least his thoughts
were beginning to order themselves.

Finally, she looked up, evidently pleased with what she had
found.

'There was a Competition Appeal Tribunal case in 2011 involving the Ellinder Group of companies. They had discovered an antidepressant called Meilopain, which they had packaged and branded and sold to the NHS for tens of millions. The patent was due to run out after fifteen years. After that, the other drug companies would start to make their own Meilopain much cheaper. It's not an unusual cycle because, after all, the drug is just the drug. Ellinder's version of Meilopain was no more effective than the cheaper versions, except it cost six times more. Flooding the market with cheap Meilopain would cut Ellinder's margins by anything up to seventy-five per cent, so the Ellinder parent company paid the other drug companies to delay release of their cheaper versions by a few years so Ellinder could milk the NHS a little longer.'

'What happened?' asked Priest.

'They were fined fifteen million pounds.'

'Did the family feature in the case?'

'I don't know. I've got the transcript here so I'll look it over and find out.'

'Good. Have we been paid yet by Theramere?' Priest addressed Okoro.

'We had a tranche of a hundred yesterday and we're due a final payment of two fifty at the end of the month.'

The total fees were close to a million. Not bad for two years' work. The rogue CEO had been ordered to pay most of Theramere's costs but Priest & Co's terms had allowed them to recover their fees from the company directly. There was no way Priest would have wanted to try to enforce his bill against an individual whose assets were hidden offshore.

'Shall I go now?' asked Georgie.

'Yes. And, Georgie, McEwen mentioned something about mayflies.'

'What about mayflies?'

'They feature in this. Somehow. General research, please.'

'OK. Got it.' She smiled broadly.

Priest waited until she had left before releasing a long and heavy alcohol-laced breath. *I can trust her.* He looked over at Okoro who had also risen and was standing with his arms folded, looming over the desk.

'Are you sure she can handle this?' Okoro asked.

Priest waved his hand dismissively. 'Georgie? Not an issue. She's the best.'

'She's pretty, too.'

'I hadn't noticed.'

Okoro chuckled. 'Of course. So, what's your next move?'

Priest sat back and looked at the ceiling. It seemed to be slowly spinning around. 'Sit here and think for a bit,' he said at last.

'OK. That's healthy. Then what?'

Priest considered this. 'Let's assume for now that McEwen was telling us the truth. That leaves us with me having been visited by a deranged but clearly desperate individual who believed I have in my possession a flash drive containing data of an unknown nature. Said deranged individual is later tortured and killed in a grotesque and theatrical way. So, why was he killed?'

'Maybe because he failed to dispossess you of the data, or because he lost it in the first place.'

'Both admirable suggestions but I sense a more Byzantine plot, Okoro.'

'What do you mean?'

Priest opened his mouth but found himself unable to answer. He looked at his hand. It didn't seem to belong to him. *So it begins.* He was conscious that Okoro was looking at him but he seemed out of focus and blurred. Inside his head, a familiar conversation was playing out.

'Did you feel it?'

'Feel what?'

'The disconnection, Charlie.'

'I don't know what you're talking about, Wills.'

'I doubt that. You are my brother, my blood. When I see you staring vacantly into a mirror I know it's hardly a daydream you're experiencing.'

'It's nothing.'

'We are the same, Charlie. I know what you're thinking when you look into the mirror.'

'Stop it, William.'

'You're thinking, who the fuck is that staring back at me?'

Priest understood perfectly what was wrong with him. Most of the time, he functioned as an ordinary human being. The remainder of his time was spent in a different world. Derealisation – an alternative manifestation of dissociative disorder – occurred when Priest's perception distorted and he existed in a foggy parody of his usual perception. Such episodes, or *disconnections*, could last anywhere from a few moments to a number of days.

'Priest?' He suddenly became aware of Okoro's concerned face. 'Are you having one of your . . . special moments?'

Priest shook his head. 'No. I'm fine.'

'As usual, your inability to lie is quite striking.' Okoro sighed heavily. 'I'm going to make some discreet enquiries on your behalf. In the meantime, go home and sort yourself out, OK?'

Priest nodded and Okoro left. There was a dripping noise, like a leaking tap. Priest looked down and saw a small splatter of sticky, dark liquid on the desk in front of him.

His nose was bleeding again.

8

It was still cold. The fog was heavier now – a damp shroud hanging in the air – but it didn't deter Priest from walking the two and a half miles to Sarah's house. There were joggers out – health freaks doing their lungs more damage by breathing in the smog than the exercise was benefiting them. Priest checked their faces carefully. Miles's death didn't mean he was no longer in danger. The fresh air helped clear his head a little but he didn't enjoy the walk.

The photograph of Miles Ellinder stuck on a pole was nightmarish. He hadn't had the opportunity to study it closely but he had registered the network of rigging on the warehouse ceiling that must have been used somehow to restrain Ellinder while they forced his contorting body down over the greasy shaft. He shuddered.

And yet something troubled him about the picture that went beyond the horror of the image. Something he couldn't quite place.

He tried to think rationally; to break the questions down to their simplest forms. What was on the flash drive that Miles Ellinder was looking for? *It's important, clearly. Important enough to kill for.* Who had suggested to him that Priest had it? *Ellinder had said 'he would have sent it to you'.* Who would *have sent it to me and why?* Why was Ellinder subsequently tortured and ritualistically killed? What was the purpose of such an elaborate murder? What were the killers trying to say? Who killed him? *There must have been more than one person involved to pull off that stunt.* And finally, why would my ex-wife turn up again now?

Priest rounded a corner of a residential street lined with cars on one side. The road was bordered by Victorian terraces with black iron railings and half a floor below pavement level. The house was rented and Sarah's landlord was a profiteer of the vilest kind. Priest had offered on countless occasions to foot the cost of a deposit somewhere else but she always declined, with genuine appreciation and dignity in equal amounts. Matters were complicated by Sarah's husband. Ryan Boatman was still unemployed and, in all likelihood, would remain so for the foreseeable future. His latest get-rich-quick scheme had recently flopped as spectacularly as Priest had predicted. All in all, Priest regarded his brother-in-law with the same level of affection as he might have regarded a stomach ulcer, and although he hoped that didn't affect his relationship with his sister, he knew that it did.

Priest knocked and, shortly afterwards, Sarah opened the door. A look of pleasant surprise flashed in the family blue eyes.

'This is a little spontaneous for you,' she remarked.

'What do you mean by that?'

'You know very well what I mean. Do you need money?' She laughed and kissed him on the cheek as he walked into the hallway. Priest considered that the house was too small but it was pristinely kept. Shoes were neatly arranged underneath coats on pegs labelled for each family member, the carpet had recently been vacuumed, but there was a scent of something artificial in the air. *Hiding the smell of the idiot husband, maybe.*

'Ryan's out.'

'Oh, right. Another long board meeting, eh?'

'That was low,' she said, showing him through to the kitchen where a percolator was bubbling in the corner. 'I'm afraid I don't have any of that weird tea you drink.'

'Coffee's fine, Sarah.'

He took the mug she handed him and sat at the breakfast bar. Watched her for a moment or two while she cleared away Tilly's drawings from the worktop and bundled them into a folder she kept of her daughter's creations. He smiled inwardly – everything had its place in Sarah's world. Priest had always admired his sister's sense of style, her smart suit and blonde hair short and ruffled. Sarah co-managed a newly established city PR company which specialised in disaster management. Her work ranged from copywriting statements for adulterous boy band members to planning comeback campaigns for discredited businesses. Being the boss gave her the freedom to work from home, too, whenever it suited.

'So why the impromptu visit?' she asked, taking the seat opposite him.

'Just making sure you're OK.'

'The great Charlie Priest doesn't just drop by to see if people are OK. Even if it *is* his sister. Anyway, it happens to be quite fortuitous that my *single,* older brother visits me upon this day.' She smiled mischievously.

He didn't reply but raised an eyebrow in mock curiosity. He knew what was coming.

'I've got this friend . . .'

'Oh, Sarah, not this again.'

'No, hear me out.'

'Sarah –'

'No, you'll like this, I'm sure. She's right up your street.' It was a familiar routine that usually ended with Priest telling her he was fine and she should stop fussing, but right now he was too exhausted to argue.

'So,' she was carrying on despite his pleading look, 'She's thirty-six, single, obviously. A messy divorce a couple of years ago. She's an accountant, partner in a good firm. Likes tennis, films, indie music, theatre. Very cultured. Like you, really.'

'I'm not cultured. I like zombie films.'

'She's a great cook.'

'Which I'm not.'

'Precisely. You're a complementary match.'

'I can watch zombie films while she cooks me dinner.'

Sarah sighed. 'You're really not entering into the spirit of this, are you?'

He smiled as best he could, but he couldn't hide the feeling of unease.

'What's bothering you, Charlie?' she said, narrowing her eyes. She saw everything, of course, just like their late mother.

'This idea of yours, Sarah. This match dating thing that I don't understand. Why don't you just do it?'

She looked at him, puzzled for a moment. 'You've changed your tune.'

'Well, you know. Come on, it's a great idea.'

'Last time we spoke about it you said it was – what was it now? – ill-conceived, over-romantic poppycock,' Sarah chided.

Priest cringed. *I did say that.* 'Yeah, yeah. But you could make it work.' Sarah had floated the idea of a new dating website a few months earlier. There was a twist to it, although, to his shame, Priest couldn't remember what it was. All he could remember was his unenthusiastic reaction. In light of recent events, he felt compelled to try to correct it. *Another response to a near-death experience. First there was self-indulgence, now atonement. Perhaps there's a third stage. Enlightenment, maybe, although that seems a very elusive notion right now.*

'You said you should never try and turn a hobby into a business,' Sarah pointed out.

'OK, maybe I was a little rash,' he admitted.

'And harsh, too.'

'Perhaps. But what was it? Ten per cent of all relationships start online?'

'Twenty.'

'OK, twenty. So you have a captive market, a bespoke service that people want. And you have *you*.'

'Wow, you're complimenting me! Are you ill?'

'I have a bit of a headache.'

She shook her head and got up to pour more coffee. The sound of some cartoon channel was coming from upstairs. He assumed Tilly was up there.

'You're looking after yourself, Charlie, aren't you? You know what happens if –'

'I'll fund it,' he interrupted.

'Charlie –'

'No. I'll fund it. What do you need to start it? You can build the website but you'll need some help with the coding and the search engine optimisation. You'll need a marketing guy. We'll do the legals. A little office somewhere in town. A hundred thousand enough for the first year?'

'Charlie, it's not that I'm not grateful. Really. But that's a lot of money.'

'A hundred and fifty?'

She looked down, reached out and put her hand on his shoulder. Suddenly she had morphed into their mother again.

'Ryan isn't so keen,' she explained.

'So?'

'*So?* So, we make decisions like that together.' She folded her arms defensively.

'You're the breadwinner. You call the shots.'

'That's not how a marriage works, Charlie. You should know that. It's why your first one failed.'

'What's his problem with it?'

'He has his reasons.'

They were silent for a while. Priest's head was still pounding. He thought about recounting the last twenty-four hours to Sarah, unburdening himself, but it wasn't fair on her. So he swallowed the thought back and channelled his anger towards Ryan, whose reasons for not wanting Sarah to give up her well-paid job were obvious. He spent the money she made on what he called *corporate hospitality*. In truth it amounted to betting and drinking with his halfwit mates. He wouldn't want that income risked by a start-up business.

'You know what, Sarah? This isn't about him. It's about *you*.'

'It's about *us*. It's *our* decision,' she protested.

'It's some stupid control thing.'

'No . . .' She faltered. 'You just . . . just leave it, Charlie. Please.'

'Well maybe if he didn't need your income to feed his gambling habits . . .'

'Please, Charlie.'

'I'm just making sure you're OK.'

'And how do you think that makes me feel?' Sarah demanded.

'What?'

'The "I'm only making sure you're OK" bullshit.'

'I don't know what you mean.'

'Yes, you do. I don't need protecting and your obvious dislike of Ryan – actually, Charlie – really upsets me. Did you ever think about that? What it does to me to have my brother constantly slag off my husband?'

'Well, if he wasn't an arsehole . . .'

'He looks after us.'

'He looks after himself, Sarah. Always has.'

'You don't have to do this, Charlie.'

'What?'

'Act out the part of father.'

'I'm not. I'm just saying your husband is an arsehole.'

'Charlie –'

'And a drunk and a layabout.'

'Charlie –'

'With less charisma than a vegetable.'

'Charlie!'

She slammed her cup down and stared at him with a mixture of amazement and anger. She nodded at the doorway. Priest followed her motion and his shoulders sank. Tilly stood staring at him. She looked confused underneath her mass of tangled, ungovernable hair.

Priest made to say something but it came out as a barely audible noise. At least the tone was apologetic.

'Uncle Charlie's here, sweetheart,' Sarah said, forcing a smile. 'He doesn't normally come round on a school night, does he? Say hi.'

'Hi, Uncle Charlie.'

'Hi, Tilly. Did you have a good day at school?'

She trotted over to him and put some pictures on the table for him to look at. He picked them up carefully, as though they might crumble to dust in his hand.

'Wow, these are great,' he said to Tilly as he helped her climb on to his knee. Sarah mumbled something about some washing that needed attention and disappeared out of the kitchen. Priest hoped she wouldn't be long. He needed to apologise. Suddenly, he felt very stupid.

'That's Mummy.' Tilly pointed to what appeared to be an assortment of arbitrarily chosen colours layered on top of each other.

'Yes, I can see that. Isn't Mummy pretty?'

'Mmm. Yes.' Tilly took out a set of colouring pens from a Hello Kitty pencil case and started working on the picture some more, gently humming to herself. Priest watched over her shoulder.

'Are these clouds?' he asked.

'They're birds, silly.'

'Oh.'

He was pleased Ryan wasn't around. He wouldn't have let Tilly sit on his knee. Ryan would have scooped her up quickly and ushered her out of the room as if Priest posed some sort of threat to her. He supposed making Priest out to be inadequate with children was Ryan's way of asserting what little control he had over him. Probably something to do with his limited understanding of dissociation disorder. 'That thing that William the Ripper has', as he was fond of saying.

'And what about this? Is this a scarecrow?'

'No, that's Mummy.'

She giggled and he laughed, too.

'I like Mummy's hair,' he remarked. 'Can I help colour with you?'

She nodded and passed him a blue crayon, and then indicated that he should start work on the sky.

'Mummy says we should all have a blue sky,' Tilly sang, while she started to draw red apples on one of the trees.

'Mummy's right, sweetheart,' Priest whispered, remembering the phrase from his own mother. Sarah must have remembered it, too.

'Where's your blue sky, Uncle Charlie?' Tilly asked after a while.

Priest pursed his lips and carried on colouring in. *Where's my blue sky?* He watched as Tilly moved to a different part of the page.

'I think it's behind a few black clouds right now, sweetheart,' he said. 'Maybe I'll find it tomorrow.'

9

It was getting dark already. He flicked a switch on at the wall. An hour of heating just to take the chill out of the air. Then he attended to locking the door, rattling the knob a few times to make sure it was fast. It didn't look like *his* hand again but that didn't bother him.

The sensation, which the psychiatrist called *derealisation*, was familiar. The world dissolves into a foggy dreamland – a nirvana. Objects can lose their size and shape; people can morph into distorted human parodies or, worse, robots. It makes the onset of a migraine feel like a walk in the park, the psychiatrist had warned. Incurable, untreatable and unpredictable.

Priest had only been to the psychiatrist once. That was enough.

He had said a slightly sheepish apology to Sarah when she had finally emerged from the utility room. She had accepted it, kissed him and promised not to contact her accountant friend about a date if he wasn't ready yet. Whatever that meant.

Priest wasn't sure what angered him the most – his propensity for upsetting Sarah or his sister's limitless capacity to forgive him. He didn't deserve it: her forgiveness, her endless love in spite of his faults. But since she had disconnected William from her life – unplugged and discarded him – she didn't seem capable of being angry with Priest for long, even when he deserved it.

On the way home, he had considered whether he had been rash to turn down Sarah's offer to put him in contact with her friend. He had been on his own for five years, but he hadn't lost his sexual appetite. Sarah's choice of potential companion was probably going to be much better than his own. She had been adamant from the start that Dee was a bad choice. So what was the problem? Fear of failure? Hardly. He had enough experience of that when it came to women to be an expert at it.

No, it's more complicated than that. Fear of myself. Fear of the ghosts in my head.

Priest's parents had died in 2002. Their flight from Berlin had been delayed and they had needed to return to England urgently. They had ended up taking a private jet at the expense of a business acquaintance. The little plane had hit a storm over the Channel and never made it through. The wreckage was still at the bottom of the sea somewhere. Ever since, Priest had been trying – and failing – to fill the void his parents had left in Sarah's life.

William had been tried in 2010, a year after Tilly was born. Eight people were dead by his hand. Eight that they knew of, anyway. He was declared not culpable for his crimes due to insanity; the so-called 'special verdict'. Since that day, William had languished in a secure psychiatric hospital, dead to Sarah – a vile stain on the family name. No wonder she had been so keen to rid herself of it. Tilly had never heard of her Uncle William and that was the way it would stay. Sarah had eradicated him from her life – shredding photographs, burning his unopened letters to her, throwing out presents he had bought her and things that reminded her of him. Purging him absolutely.

She had expected Priest to do the same, and not unreasonably, either. But he could not. A malignant seed of doubt had been planted in his mind about his own disposition and the mental defect he shared with his brother, the brother that killed. Priest was haunted by the ghosts of doubt.

No, I'm not ready for a date. Not until the ghosts have been exorcised.

He took a can of sweetcorn from the kitchen cupboard and opened it. He thought about making something but decided it was too much hassle, so he ate straight from the can.

He flicked the news on. There was something about Miles's death so he turned up the volume and the Sky News presenter's voice filled the room.

Early this morning, the body of Miles Ellinder – son of the millionaire businessman Kenneth Ellinder and believed to be one of the heirs to the Ellinder Group of companies – was found dead in the basement of a warehouse in south London, thought to be owned by one of his father's companies. Police have revealed relatively few details concerning Ellinder's death, other than they are treating it as suspicious.

Kenneth Ellinder, chairman of Ellinder International, released a statement a few hours ago saying that Miles was a much loved son and a well-respected entrepreneur in his own right, and asking that the public respect the family's wish to grieve with dignity. Very little has been said regarding the circumstances of Ellinder's death but

> there is speculation from sources close to the Ellinder
> family that Miles Ellinder was a much troubled man who
> hadn't made a public appearance in over a year . . .

Priest shut the sound off. He didn't want to hear any more. He turned on the kettle and poured the boiling water over an Earl Grey teabag in a mug before going into his bedroom while it brewed. From under the bed, he retrieved a shoebox. He removed the lid and fished around in amongst the packaging. Eventually he pulled out the Glock and checked the cartridge was full. He cocked it and made sure the safety was on – made sure three times. He left the box out on the bed, retrieved the steaming mug of tea after discarding the teabag in the bin, and wandered through to the lounge. The room was moving. Not spinning, but gently tipping back and forth like a ship at sea. He sipped the tea. The burning sensation felt good – made everything seem real again, if only for a moment. He fed the *Pterois* and then felt a sudden urge to sit down.

Laboriously, he hauled a red leather armchair away from the plasma TV so he could sit looking through the lounge doorway to the kitchen. He sat down heavily. The room was spinning quickly now. He placed the gun on his knee. After an hour, he tumbled into a dreamless sleep.

∽

Priest awoke to the sound of a mobile phone. He didn't recognise the ringtone at first but, after a few moments, he realised it was his. He found the phone lying on the floor in front of him. He picked it up and answered.

'Priest?' said a familiar voice.

'Okoro.'

'Sleep well?'

Priest rubbed the bridge of his nose. 'No.'

'Too bad. Will you be in the office later?'

'Perhaps. What time is it?' Priest got up and the gun clattered to the floor. He braced himself but the safety was still on. He breathed out heavily.

'Nine thirty,' Okoro was saying. 'Will you be in the office later or not?'

'I refer you to my previous answer.'

'Two people here to see you. They look important.'

'Fine – I'll get a shower. I'll be an hour.'

'I'll tell them you'll be twenty minutes.'

⸺

Priest vaguely registered the two people in reception. An old man and a woman in her early forties. He groaned inwardly. The man had already risen to greet him as he entered the reception area. They were dressed smartly, which meant they were probably from the bank.

He did his best to pretend he hadn't seen the old man get up. Maureen cast him a disapproving look as he skipped by. He managed to look as though he hadn't seen that either. He made a bad job of both deceptions and carried on up the stairs towards his office.

'Charlie –' Maureen called after him.

'Good morning!' Priest called back down. His office door slammed shut behind him.

He unlocked the computer and scanned his inbox. A hundred and seven unread messages. A new record. He started forwarding them to Solly. That seemed a little unfair, given that Priest knew Solly would act on each email so his inbox wasn't clogged up. He would then run the anti-virus software eight times followed by a full defragmentation, and then take the RAM out and clean it with an antiseptic wipe. But needs must.

He dialled Georgie's number and asked her to come through. She appeared at his doorway almost instantly. Her hair was down, cascading over her shoulders; he thought he preferred it tied back.

'There's a guy called Ryan Boatman,' he began, before she could even say hello. He gave the address. 'Find out all you can.'

'OK. Is this connected with Ellinder?'

'No.'

'What sort of stuff do you need?'

He thought about it before saying, eventually, 'You know. Just stuff.'

She looked puzzled for a moment. Priest burrowed his head in some papers on his desk in order to deter her from asking any more questions. She had disappeared when he next looked up.

The phone rang. He glanced at the caller ID. Waited a few rings and then picked it up.

'Hi, Maureen.'

'There are two people here to see you.'

'I know.'

He hung up and immediately picked up the phone again – dialled a number he read from his iPhone. It rang for ages until a surly voice spoke.

'Charlie *fucking* Priest.'

'Giles. I need a favour,' said Priest matter-of-factly.

'Come again?'

'I need a favour.'

'*You* need a favour from *me*?' Giles sounded both suspicious and slightly drunk.

'Yes.'

'Fuck off, Priest.'

'Giles, be reasonable.'

'Reasonable? The last time I did you a favour you hung me out to dry and I ended up doing three months in a Russian prison,' Giles retorted through gritted teeth.

'It was a holding cell in a Russian police station, Giles, and it was a few days, tops.'

'It stank of vodka.'

'In which case it was hardly a taxing few days. So, what d'ya say?'

There was silence for a while. Priest couldn't work out whether the humming noise was a bad line or the whirring of the cogs in Giles's head.

'All right,' Giles said at last.

'Good. A man called Miles Ellinder was apparently murdered last night in London. Do you know anything about it?'

'I heard a rumour. Sounds like some freaky shit is going on. So what?'

'I need whatever documents you can lay your hands on. Witness statements, post-mortem reports, file notes. Anything and everything.'

'What? You know I can't get that, even for you, Priest.'

'It's important.'

'So's my job.'

Giles was part of SO15 – the Met's Counter Terrorism Command. When Priest had first met Giles twenty years ago, he was a small-time smack dealer. Amazing to think that he was now one of the few good people that stood between London and ISIS. They had history, Priest and Giles, and Priest was pretty sure Giles was in arrears in terms of favours.

'Just see what you can do for me, OK?'

'Priest!' Giles sounded irritated. 'Give me one reason why –'

'Because I can still tell the Russians the truth,' Priest interjected.

There was a short pause on the other end of the line before Giles relented. 'All right, I'll see what I can do.'

Click.

An email popped up from Maureen. The heading read 'People in reception for you!' He didn't read the rest. *The bank can wait. Everybody can fucking wait.* He found some painkillers in the desk drawer and took three. Probably made by Ellinder's company. He felt worse than he had yesterday and he hadn't even had a cup of tea yet, but he was focused and surprisingly energised for a man who'd had less than eight hours sleep in the last forty-eight. He wasn't sure what it was but something was overriding the crippling ache that was developing at the back of his head. Whatever it was, it was time to stop sitting around feeling sorry for himself.

The phone rang again. This time it was Solly. He sounded panicked, but then Solly always sounded panicked.

'Priest. All these emails!'

'I know, Solly, I'm sorry.' Priest was as patient as he could be.

'How many are there?'

'A few more.'

'Can you space them out, at least? Maybe I can deal with them one at a time.'

'Of course I can, Solly.'

'Thank God.'

Priest replaced the receiver and sent the whole lot in one go. He waited for the phone to ring again but it didn't. *Good. That will keep Solly busy for the rest of the day.*

He rang Georgie.

'Hello?' She answered the phone within half a ring.

'Georgie,' he said casually. 'The chap who was killed yesterday – Miles Ellinder – did I mention he was impaled?'

'As in – you know – stuck on a pole?'

'Yes.'

'*Really*?' She sounded strangely excited. 'You want me to check out the significance of that?'

'I think so. I think that's why I'm ringing.'

'Sure!'

Click.

Priest looked at the phone for a few moments before putting it back down. She was enthusiastic. That was probably a good thing.

Okoro was suddenly seated opposite him. Priest jumped. He hadn't seen or heard him come in.

'Did you . . .?'

'Knock? Yes. I've been knocking since you got here, Priest. In the end, I got fed up with it and just walked right in.'

'Sorry. Little distracted,' Priest conceded.

'Evidently.'

'Is there a tea going, or –'

'The people in reception.'

'The bank, I assume. Okoro, we don't have an overdraft facility. We have cash reserves of over a million pounds and we own the building outright. What's the big problem?'

'It's not the bank.'

'PI insurance?'

'Miles Ellinder's father and sister.'

Priest rubbed his chin. It reminded him that he hadn't shaved in a few days, which in turn reminded him he had probably looked terrible *yesterday* and he doubted there would be much improvement today.

Miles Ellinder's father and sister. Here to see me. A seriously unexpected turn of events. Shit. Did I feed the fish before I came out?

'Say something,' Okoro invited.

'Oh.'

'So far I've managed to explain that, since you weren't expecting them, you've been busy rescheduling meetings so you can see them this morning, but they're not going to wait much longer. I strongly suspect this is the longest Kenneth Ellinder has waited for anyone in his life.'

'Yes. That's probably got something to do with all that money he has.'

'Probably.' Okoro stretched out. 'I'm going to get up now. Then, I'm going to lead them in here and shut the door. That gives you about half a minute to make yourself look vaguely like a man who *wasn't* one of the last people to see Ellinder's son alive.'

10

Up close, Kenneth Ellinder had more of the university professor look about him than a bank manager. From the wispy strands of thin, silver hair falling down past his shoulders to the tweed jacket complete with elbow patches – he just needed a pair of round glasses to complete the ensemble.

The tall and elegant woman accompanying Ellinder met Priest's gaze briefly before taking a seat, uninvited, in front of him. She hadn't so much entered the room as acquired it, such was the regal manner with which she presented herself. The family resemblance to Miles Ellinder was not immediately apparent. She had rich, auburn hair that fell around an ascetic face which conveyed the displeasure of a woman who had been kept waiting far too long. She was evidently her father's daughter.

Georgie sat to Priest's left, legs crossed. Priest didn't want to seem heavy-handed so Georgie sat in while Okoro retired to his office.

'Thank you for eventually seeing us, Mr Priest,' the old man said. 'This is my daughter, Jessica.'

She didn't smile – she didn't look capable of it, although she was undeniably attractive underneath the sour expression.

Priest cleared his throat uncomfortably. He started to offer some words of condolence but they stuck in his throat.

'You are very welcome,' he said instead. 'This is my associate, Miss Someday. I hope you don't mind her sitting in with us.'

'Of course not.'

Georgie smiled but didn't receive anything by way of a response.

'I'll get straight to the point, if I may,' said Ellinder. 'It appears an unfortunate incident has befallen my son, Mr Priest. You're no doubt aware.'

Priest nodded, slowly. *An unfortunate incident.* Kenneth Ellinder had the gift of understatement.

'I'm very sorry for what has happened. It is truly shocking. You must be going through hell.' For a moment, Priest thought someone else was in the room but then he realised the words were his.

'In hell, Mr Priest, at least there is the consolation of knowing you're not the only damned soul to suffer,' said Ellinder.

'Yes, I . . . Yes.' It was a difficult line to follow, so Priest didn't try. He realised that Kenneth and Jessica Ellinder would have been told the grotesque nature of Miles's death, but did they know he knew? *I'll assume not for now.*

'It makes one very uneasy, to have one's dirty laundry aired in such a public way,' continued Ellinder. He looked at Priest expectantly, although what he was expecting was not clear.

'You don't need to worry about that in this room, Mr Ellinder,' said Priest softly.

'I'm sure.'

'We understand that the police came to visit you yesterday, Mr Priest.'

Priest let Jessica Ellinder's words swirl around in his head for a few moments, judging the tone and sensing the danger lurking there. She had an extraordinary rasp to her voice.

'Yes,' Priest confirmed.

'In connection with my brother's murder?'

'Yes.'

'A business card of yours was found in the inside pocket of Miles's coat.'

'No, I was told it was found in his clothes, which were dumped in the corner of the warehouse.'

Jessica Ellinder frowned. It was enough to suggest to Priest that McEwen had lied about the location of the card. Probably to make it sound more significant than it was. Besides him, he sensed Georgie shifting her weight on the chair.

'Detective Inspector McEwen said that you weren't very helpful,' she remarked. She was difficult to read but not so difficult that Priest didn't recognise that he was being appraised very carefully.

'I answered his questions.'

'Economically, I gather.'

Priest clicked his tongue. 'I prefer *succinctly*.'

'In their trade, they call it evasive.'

'You would make a very good detective, Miss Ellinder.'

No ring on those willowy fingers meant she *was Miss* Ellinder and, indeed, she made no effort to correct him.

'She probably would,' Ellinder agreed. 'My daughter is my most trusted aide. The eyes and ears of an old, failing man. I am confident that the Group will be left in safe hands.'

'You're retiring, Mr Ellinder?'

'A retirement of sorts, Mr Priest. But one driven by necessity of circumstances rather than choice. If my physicians are correct – and they are rarely wrong – I have six months to live, twelve at best.'

Georgie let out a small gasp of air. Priest looked long and hard at Kenneth Ellinder. He didn't look ill but that didn't mean much. His watery eyes were resolute though. He was probably speaking the truth.

'I'm sorry to hear that, Mr Ellinder,' Priest offered.

'Don't be. I have grown weary of life and my affairs are generally in order. Until yesterday, I would have died a relatively contented man. But things change. Priorities change. People change. Perhaps, given my life so far, I am unsurprised that God has seen it expedient to deal me one final hand.'

'I cannot begin to imagine what a loss Miles is.'

Ellinder dismissed the comment with a wave of his hand. 'Not at all. For a start, Miles is not my son. He is my *step*son. My wife's child from a previous relationship; the price I paid for her love. He is – *was* – a failure in almost every venture he was involved in. I could hand him the most stable of companies and he could wreck it in weeks. He was a walking disaster.'

'Miles and I were not close, Mr Priest,' Jessica Ellinder said.

Priest nodded. *Not close. Got it.*

'In the last six months,' Ellinder said, with a heavy sigh, 'I had not seen Miles once. Jessica neither. He disappeared without trace. We assumed he was dead.'

It seemed an odd assumption.

'You've no idea where he went?' Priest asked.

'My half-brother was involved in something unsavoury, Mr Priest,' said Jessica. 'We don't know what. But it was dangerous. And it got him killed.'

'Miles was never able to concentrate on anything for long,' explained Ellinder. 'He would spend weeks on end living like a hermit, festering inside his house. Squirrelled away from the world. He was almost certainly on something, and the irony of being the head of a pharmaceuticals company and having a drug addict for a son is not lost on me, but there was something else too. A more fundamental change set in a few years ago.'

Priest thought back to the grinning lunatic hunched over him and ramming the barrel of a drill in his ear. *Pinprick pupils, dead eyes. Addict's eyes*. It made sense.

'How long had he been an addict?' Priest asked.

'Since he was eighteen,' Ellinder said, rubbing his head with his hand. 'He didn't have the constitution to deal with the privileges he was handed, you see. Some of us are just made like that. Money is corrosive and that corrosion can eat away at a younger mind much more destructively than an older one. I tried to wean him off the drugs. I spent a small fortune on therapy, practically built a rehab centre for him. He wasn't interested. Just cash and women, booze and pills. That was Miles.'

'That must have been very hard for you both to deal with.'

'Naturally. But all families have a black sheep, don't they, Mr Priest?'

Priest nodded. The old man was setting the ground rules. Letting him know that he knew about William, perhaps? Establishing a point to negotiate from by making it personal. *Well, it's hardly a social call, is it?*

'You said Miles changed fundamentally a few years ago?' Priest prompted.

'Indeed. Before he was loud, eccentric – an embarrassment. Then he withdrew from us all. He retreated *into* himself. He cut ties with us, even his mother, and while given his general contempt for the family, that may not seem strange in itself, he also cut himself off financially. I was supporting him, of course. My daughter believes I was feeding his habit. No doubt she is right. But what else could I do? When he cut himself off, I tried to reconnect but I found nothing but brick walls and barricades.'

'There's just the four of you?'

'I have a sister, too,' Jessica replied. 'Scarlett. She works abroad and has almost nothing to do with Miles.'

'Why would Miles cut ties with you?' Priest asked.

Ellinder did not immediately reply; but then, 'I believe Miles was scared of something and it certainly wasn't death. It was something far worse. He had got himself involved with something extremely dangerous. Something that went far beyond his sordid world of drugs and prostitution.'

'You've no idea what?'

'That it was criminal, I have no doubt, but we are talking about a millionaire drug addict, Mr Priest. People engage in criminal behaviour for only a limited number of reasons. Money is the most common motive. Miles didn't need money, which must rule out a great number of high-risk crimes – drug trafficking, pimping, organ trafficking, fraud – since they all have money as a primary motivation. His motivation must have been far more complicated.'

'Something more personal. Enjoyment, perhaps?'

Ellinder breathed deeply and ran his hand through his silver hair. He looked at his daughter.

'As much as it troubles us, Mr Priest,' she said, 'that *is* possible. We still don't know what and we're tired of speculating. Whatever it was, it killed him.'

'In a quite spectacular fashion,' Priest ventured.

Jessica fixed Priest with an icy stare. 'Quite.'

'I've had the details recounted to me,' said Ellinder, looking down at the table with a vacant stare. 'I understand that my stepson's death was slow and undignified. Miles was a rogue, but no one deserved to die in the manner he did.'

'There's a limit to your intolerance of Miles, then?' asked Priest. He wondered if his question might have come across as impertinent but Ellinder brushed it off.

'He was my family. Like it or not.'

Priest nodded. William was family. *Like it or not.* 'Anyway,' Ellinder continued, 'my personal feelings on the matter are not important. For the sake of my family's business, I need a swift resolution to this fiasco. And my wife, Lucia. For her sake, too.'

'You have months to live. Your stepson was found impaled in one of your warehouses yesterday, in what appeared to be an assassination. The media are treating his death as a big story. When they find out the circumstances of his death – and eventually they will – it'll be the biggest story of the year. Your share price has already crashed; your companies are collapsing. But you're here, talking to us.'

'You have a way with words, Mr Priest,' the old man replied. 'And you are quite right. However, this meeting is of the utmost importance to us.'

By the look on her face, this was apparently not a view Jessica shared.

'You may be disappointed –' Priest began.

Ellinder raised his hand, closed his eyes. He seemed to be concentrating very hard on something. 'The officer in charge of Miles's murder case – McEwen – do you know of him?'

'Yes. We worked together briefly when I was in the Force a long time ago.'

'Then you know he is intellectually impotent, incompetent and backward-thinking. A bumbling buffoon whose only achievement so far is managing not to pass wind at each press conference.'

Kenneth Ellinder went up a few notches in Priest's estimation.

'This is a big case for anyone to handle,' said Priest carefully.

'Very diplomatic, but we both know the man is a moron. I have tried to arrange for McEwen to be removed from the case but without success . . . I have limits, as you observe. Like all public servants, the police are under-resourced and heavily unionised. The entire future of my family and business legacy sits on the edge of a knife, and do you know where DI McEwen is now?'

Priest shook his head.

'Applying for a warrant to search your offices. What a total waste of time! It will tell him nothing. No, Mr Priest. I will not rely on a man like McEwen to save us. I need someone far more capable. Someone with a brain, balls, guile. Someone like you, Mr Priest.'

'Me?' Priest was taken aback, but something in those watery eyes suggested Ellinder was deadly serious. 'Why?'

'Good question. It was my wife Lucia's idea in the first place. There are three reasons. First, and most important, you are already involved. If you had any inclination that your involvement would be peripheral, think again. McEwen will see to that. Maybe you've met Miles, maybe you haven't. That's your business. But there's a reason why he had your card on him when he died. You need to find that out, Mr Priest, and you will do. I only ask that, whilst you do so, you also find out what the hell happened to my son.'

Priest felt sick. Rather like he imagined Atlas felt as he stared at the sky, wondering which way to approach picking it up.

'Second,' Ellinder went on, 'you have a reputation for ruthlessness. And for being clever. You are resourceful and multi-skilled. You have a respected team to aid you. You are used to investigation – it's what you do. You go into companies and tear them apart from the inside. Find the bit that's rotting and extract it. That is what fraud investigation is all about. This is just another manifestation of that technique, except that it may not be fraud that you are exposing.'

'And the third?'

'I knew your father, Mr Priest. We were friends. You may not have known that; there are certain clubs in London where alliances are not shouted about. There's nothing sinister about that; it's the way it is. Way it was, anyway. And if Felix were alive, then I would have him find *my* son's killer in a second. But he is not. And that makes you the next best thing.'

Priest sat back in his chair. The Ellinders hadn't been on any family party guest list that he could recall but that didn't mean the old man was trying to deceive him. Priest's parents had been away on business for months at a time when he was a young man. It was perfectly plausible that they had known the Ellinders.

'Their death was a tragedy, Mr Priest,' said Kenneth Ellinder softly. 'But I know they would have been proud of what you achieved after they were gone.'

Priest wondered if they would have been proud of his divorce, or the time he'd spent working in a bar just to regain control of his life. Still, he had never murdered anyone, which meant he was doing marginally better than William.

'We realise this is a lot to take in, Mr Priest,' said Jessica. She didn't look at him. There was an eerie formality to the way she conducted herself, but where anybody else might have made such rigidity appear uncomfortable, she somehow retained a quiet dignity. 'But my father is keen to enlist your help.'

'You'll have complete access to everything you'll need, Mr Priest,' Kenneth Ellinder assured him. 'My business will be opened out to you. Jessica will assist you, of course. She is a very accomplished businesswoman in her own right.'

'Indeed,' replied Priest. *She's also someone who I'm struggling to stop staring at, although I'm not sure why.*

'We'll pay you, of course.'

Of that, Priest had no doubt, although he rather wished the old man hadn't mentioned money. He'd known it was coming but sitting in his office looking into the desperate eyes of a dying man offering to pay him to find out why his son had been impaled on a shaft in a warehouse made him feel . . . unclean.

Priest considered his response. 'I'm not sure I can help,' he said eventually.

Ellinder put up his hand, presumably a gesture designed to deter Priest from being hasty. 'I'm sure it is something you need to consider.'

'I'm not sure I can help,' Priest repeated. 'I'm sorry.'

'What's your hourly rate?'

Priest hesitated. 'Five hundred.'

'We'll double it. Triple it if you tell me what happened to my son.'

Georgie exhaled sharply.

'It isn't a financial issue, I assure you.'

'Then what?' Jessica cut in sharply, and Priest found himself stumbling for a convincing reply.

What's the real issue, here? I can hardly tell them I'm committed to the race but not sure which horse to back. Priest was kneading his unshaven chin and the motion must have prompted something in Kenneth Ellinder because he got up suddenly and offered his hand.

'I appreciate this is a lot to take in, even for a man of your capabilities, Mr Priest. I trust we have achieved enough to at least procure your agreement to think about it. Felix, I am sure, would also have reserved his decision.'

Priest got up and shook Ellinder's hand. 'Of course. I'll think about it.'

The old man managed a smile before withdrawing his hand. 'Please call me in the morning with your answer.'

As the door closed behind them, Priest realised that not once had Jessica Ellinder looked him in the eye.

11

25th March, 1946
A remote farm in middle England

Bertie Ruck was eating eggs. Two of them. Poached. That was about all he could find the morning after his first interview with Dr Schneider. He had arrived at the farmhouse the previous week and spent the first couple of days reviewing notes, documents, photographs, reports. Anything that might help him deconstruct the subject.

The German had been here for months, hidden away from the world. For his own protection more than anything else. The farm buildings had been adapted for his containment. Bars on the windows, heavy bolts and locks on the doors. It hadn't taken much to turn the farm into a prison. There was an assignment of six soldiers but their job was not a difficult one. Schneider had shown little interest in escapology. What was the point of being a German fugitive in England after the war was lost? They had worried about him taking his own life initially – just as Himmler had – but Schneider had not shown much interest in that pursuit either.

Ruck's sleep had been sporadic. It was cold still, the winter was refusing to retreat. The bed was lumpy and damp but the farmhouse kitchen had at least lived up to his expectations. Stone floor, hot stove, pots and pans hung from every shelf. Everything was bathed in sunlight.

Lance Corporal Fitzgerald was leaning up against the open door puffing on a roll-up cigarette. His body was so extraordinarily long and lanky that he never seemed to fit anywhere properly. He was permanently bent out of shape. So far Ruck had managed to ignore him, although Fitzgerald's squeaky voice was starting to grate.

'Well, c'mon then,' Fitzgerald said gleefully, looking at Ruck as if expecting him to perform a magic trick. 'What was it like?'

Ruck sighed heavily. *Only a week more of this nonsense and then back to London and away from Nazis and simpletons.*

'As you know, Lance Corporal, I'm not permitted to disclose anything of my conversations with Dr Schneider . . .'

'Schneider?' Fitzgerald sounded genuinely baffled. 'Nah. I meant Eva!'

Ruck finished his mouthful before looking up. 'Who?'

'Eva! Eva Miller. The totty with the botty!'

Fitzgerald grinned stupidly. His teeth were as long and bent as his body. Every part of him annoyed Ruck incessantly. He ought not to let the cocky bastard speak to him like that; he ought to command respect, keep discipline. But Ruck was tired of that system, and what did it matter out here, in an operation that officially didn't even exist?

'You mean the scribe?' Ruck sighed.

'Yeah. That's the one. Now, ain't she a fine-looking woman! Dunno how you can cope with her around. She's staying here, you know. Across the way. Own quarters, near me. Arrived yesterday. Driven in a private car.'

'Quite.'

'Nice, isn't it? Havin' a bird around, I mean. Something to think about when it's cold at night. Bet it's warm between those big titties of hers.' Fitzgerald stopped at the sound of the polite cough behind him. He jumped away from the door as if he had been burnt.

To Eva's credit, she showed neither embarrassment nor annoyance as she strode past him. Fitzgerald tried to say something but the only noise he made was a strange wheeze of surprise. Ruck carried on eating his eggs. Eventually, Fitzgerald mumbled something, and loped off.

Ruck glanced up at Eva. She had the most extraordinarily beautiful face. White, translucent skin, deep red lipstick. Brown hair immaculately curled. But something else. He had seen it yesterday, but only from afar. An air of something he could not quite place. He saw it even in the way she stood, a little uncertainly, across the table from him. She was elegant, graceful. Every crease in the blouse beneath her blue coat was pristine. Every pleat in her skirt perfectly aligned. She looked like a doll freshly removed from its packaging.

'Colonel Ruck.' She nodded at him, politely.

'You're American.'

'Partly. How can you tell?'

Ruck looked up again, made sure he was right. 'Way you dress.'

Eva looked down at herself. 'Boston,' she conceded. 'Although my mother was from Cheltenham.'

She produced a cigarette from her purse. 'Do you have a match, Colonel Ruck?'

He fumbled around in his inside coat pocket, produced a box of matches and struck one for her. She cupped her hand around the flame as she lit up. The smoke glistened in the dawn sun.

'You're not much of a conversationalist,' she observed.

'No,' Ruck agreed.

She sat down, crossed one leg over the other. Ruck turned back to his eggs, but they were looking unappetising all of a sudden. He shifted his weight in the chair and drank from the cup of tea on the table, although it was stone cold. Nazis were one thing, but *women* were a different species. He thought about saying something but a sensible remark or observation eluded him temporarily. In the end, he settled for a question. 'How is your accommodation?'

'Fine,' she reported. 'A little cold at night but I found that the linen was clean. They did a good job of making us comfortable, although to what end I am not sure.'

'Indeed.'

'Why are you drinking cold tea?'

Ruck glanced over at the cup. It was freezing outside and not much warmer in the farmhouse kitchen despite the brilliance of the sunshine. Nonetheless, there was no steam wafting from the cup. *Very well observed, Miss Miller.*

'Isn't it an American habit?' he asked. 'To take drinks that are traditionally served hot and drink them cold?'

This brought a smile to Eva's lips, which transformed her face. She was the personification of elegance and class but there was something behind her green eyes. Something unsettling. He took another sip of the tea.

After a while she said, 'They told me, Colonel, when they assigned me here, that I was not to ask any questions about . . . what we're doing. They told me about you, also. They said I shouldn't burden you with my curiosity.'

'Then do not.'

Eva nodded.

'Very well,' she said. 'I believe a further interview commences in an hour.'

She left the room. Ruck looked about – the kitchen seemed a lot duller without her.

⁑

Ruck made his way across the courtyard to the barn where Schneider was ready for him. He'd made the doctor wait a while and ordered the men to make sure he was tied to the chair as uncomfortably as possible; not because he took any particular pleasure from seeing the Nazi in pain but because it might help him open up a bit, if only because he wanted to be put back in his cell.

He had intended to call London and ask them to send another scribe but something had stopped him. It seemed like an extravagance – demanding a replacement because . . . why? Because Eva unnerved him? It was ridiculous.

He was within reach of the barn door when he realised he had left his pen back in the makeshift office they had installed for him above the kitchen. Cursing under his breath, he turned around and marched back to the farmhouse. As he crossed the courtyard, he saw the outline of Fitzgerald's gangly figure lurking in the kitchen doorway and a mist of cigarette smoke swirling upwards before being swept away in the breeze.

He waited until the cigarette was tossed on to the cobbles and Fitzgerald had retreated inside. The man grated on Ruck; the last thing he wanted was to hear him whining again. Fortunately, by the time Ruck reached the kitchen, he was gone.

Ruck climbed the stairs silently. He had registered each creaky floorboard of the farmhouse on the first day so he could move around more or less unheard. It was an unnecessary precaution – the farmhouse's location was secret and heavily guarded – but Ruck's default disposition was to be cautious. Years of patrolling the corridors of the Cage had conditioned him to assume the worst.

When he reached the office door, he found it ajar. He stopped, listened; his hand involuntarily moved to where his pistol nestled in its holster. He *could* have heard a noise on the other side of the door, but he wasn't sure.

Cautiously, he pushed the door open and peered in.

Eva was standing in the middle of the room, hands behind her back. She didn't look shocked or concerned at being caught. Her expression was neutral as she stared at him. Just waiting.

'What are you doing here?' Ruck demanded. He pulled the door closed behind him and folded his arms.

'I need typewriter ribbon.'

Ruck glanced over her shoulder at his desk, quickly scanning the surface. Everything seemed in place. Drawers as they were, the middle one slightly open.

Typewriter ribbon.

'There's some in the store. Across the courtyard.' Ruck nodded to the window behind the desk.

'Of course,' she said, without turning around to look.

He took a step towards her. She stood still, hands still wedged behind her back, obediently. It infuriated him. Her compliance was a facade – he saw straight through her, past the feigned pout, red lips and curves to her eyes, wherein lay the undeniable spark of intelligence.

Far too much curiosity for a scribe.

'You're young, for a colonel,' she remarked.

'And you're very forward for a scribe.'

'I'm sorry.' She was watching him with a clinical interest so intimate it made his skin crawl. 'I meant no offence, but you don't . . . I'm not sure. You don't seem like the type of person who enjoys interrogation.'

'We all do what we need to for our country,' Ruck countered, although with little conviction. She was out of line and he should point that out, but he didn't. Maybe she had a point.

She stepped towards him, close enough that he could smell her. It had been a long time since he had smelt a woman. He stiffened, trying not to react to her closeness or her overfamiliarity, but something stirred in the pit of his stomach – a sudden awareness of his vulnerability, the feeling that somehow she had managed to open his head and see straight through to his thoughts, his private space. She could see everything, he was certain of it; every intimate notion, every illegitimate desire.

'Stop it,' he demanded, turning away from her.

'What?'

'This. We have work to do.'

She put her hand out, her intention clear. It would have been so easy for him, to take her hand and lead her . . . where? Towards the desk? The floor? Flustered, he pulled himself together, opened the door and ushered her out, locking it behind him.

As she went down the stairs she called up after him, her voice as smooth as silk: 'I'm sorry, Colonel Ruck. But we can't escape who we are, can we?'

12

Priest went home early. There didn't seem much to be gained from sitting around in the office watching his inbox flash up more messages warning him it was full.

He had thrown a ready-meal into the microwave and waited while the plate revolved. It was like watching his problems slowly cooking. The end result was not encouraging: it looked like a cross between dog food and the dry stuff that astronauts kept in silver packages, but it stopped him from passing out.

He fed the fish and then smoked a cigarette outside on the roof garden. He had thought that the nicotine might dull the sense of sickening dread festering inside him but it just gave him another headache. He went back inside and gave a bottle of beer languishing at the back of the fridge brief consideration but in the end rejected it in favour of a cup of Earl Grey tea. He took this to the lounge and collapsed into an armchair next to the fish tank. *What the hell am I going to do next?* One of the lionfish drifted down to look at him enquiringly. Priest stared back.

'You're no fucking help.'

The doorbell buzzed.

Priest retrieved the Glock and tucked it into the back of his belt. He clicked a button on the intercom. The image was grainy but unmistakable.

'You know where I live?' he said, after opening the door.

'Yes. I do,' replied Jessica Ellinder.

She offered him no explanation – just walked past him and stood expectantly in his kitchen.

'Would you like a drink?' he asked, closing the door behind him.

'Yes,' she replied after a short pause. 'Black coffee.'

There was a percolator in the corner, although Priest rarely used it. He subtly ran a J-cloth round the rim to remove the dust before filling it.

A strange silence lingered while he made the coffee. Priest found it uncomfortable but Jessica didn't seem concerned. Eventually, he handed her a mug, which she carefully examined. *Shit. She isn't a mug person. Should have gone with a cup and saucer.*

'You're wondering why I'm here,' she observed.

'I'm wondering many things right now,' said Priest. 'But let's start with that one.'

'I'm here to prevent a travesty.'

Priest raised an eyebrow. 'Okay.'

'You've already decided not to take my father's commission. I'm here to persuade you to change your mind.'

'How do you know I'm not taking the job?'

'You didn't say *yes*,' said Jessica.

'I didn't say *no*, either,' he pointed out.

'More tellingly, you didn't say *yes*.'

'Were you legally trained?'

Jessica snorted, blew across the top of the coffee and took a gulp. It must have been very hot, but she didn't seem fazed.

Priest was coming around to the idea that it was going to be a long night. He changed his mind about the beer and salvaged it from the fridge. By the time he'd turned back, she was in the lounge.

'*Pterois*,' she called through. He found her gazing into the fish tank. 'Lionfish. Or to some, the devil firefish.' She moved her hand across the fish tank from one end to the other. The fish didn't seem interested.

By way of explanation he said, 'I stepped on one in Gordon's Bay when I was twelve. Nearly killed me.'

'South Africa,' she confirmed.

Priest nodded, impressed. 'Family holiday.'

'So now you have three of them, incarcerated in a glass cage in your living room. You've mastered your fear. The hunted becomes the captor. Congratulations.'

Priest shrugged. 'I just like the colours.'

Jessica turned to him and fixed him with a fierce stare. It was the first time she had looked at him directly.

'I get the feeling,' he said, 'that your father wants me to take this job. But that is not what *you* want.'

'What my father wants *is* what I want.'

'No, no. I don't think so.' He paused. 'Did you see what they did to your brother? Whoever *they* are.' Priest waited for her to reply. He wanted to gauge her reaction. Something about the way Miles Ellinder had been killed troubled him, beyond its extreme cruelty.

She seemed to give her answer some thought before she said, 'It hardly matters. In six months, Mr Priest, maybe less, my father will be gone. The cancer is in his blood. It was agony just to come and see you this morning. He is obsessed with knowing the truth and why we had to lose Miles . . . *in that way*. Personally, Miles has given us nothing but unimaginable suffering since he could first hold a crack pipe. What happened to him was only what he deserved. But for six months, I can play my father's game. I owe him that much. He thinks you're important. Ergo, so do I.'

Priest had thought about offering her a biscuit, but the moment seemed to have past. His beer tasted funny. A quick glance at the label told him it was four months out of date. He took another small swig and placed the bottle on the table, near the fish.

She hasn't seen any photographs, nor has her father, who said the details were recounted to him. By McEwen, presumably. Priest dismissed the thought as irrelevant. In his experience, most people wanted to see the body, not the crime-scene shots. *They must really have cared very little about him.*

He was conscious that Jessica was watching him cautiously, as if he might suddenly sprout wings and lay an egg at her feet. He took a few steps towards her and she took one back. He leant around her. He could smell her perfume. It was nice, mellow and light, although he didn't recognise it. She was stylishly dressed in an autumn-coloured coat, long and elegant, and a simple blouse, open at the top revealing a patch of beautiful white skin.

'What are you doing?' Jessica demanded.

He flicked a switch behind her. There was a whirring noise and the curtains opened to reveal a damp, foggy, metropolitan afternoon. He went to the middle of the window and stared out at London.

'I'm sorry,' he said.

'There is no need,' she replied, although her tone suggested otherwise. 'I have no regrets about Miles. He won't be missed, except by my mother, perhaps.'

He stopped her. 'About your father, I mean.'

When Jessica didn't reply, he turned and looked at her. She wasn't the only one with a searching gaze.

'You said you were here to prevent a travesty. How had you planned on achieving this?'

'For a start, I know you've lied to both my father, McEwen and me about not ever meeting my brother.'

Not for the first time in the last twenty-four hours, Priest found himself wrong-footed.

'How do you know this?'

'I know he visited you recently. Maybe even the night before his death. Maybe you were one of the last people to see him alive.' She told him what she knew matter-of-factly, without any suggestion of accusation.

'How so?'

'Because he told me,' she said. 'Or at least, he told me he was going to see you. We had a brief discussion, over the telephone. We were angry, both of us. I was angry at him for disappearing and not giving a shit that our father is dying, and he was angry because I had managed to find him. His final words were that he intended to go and see a priest. I thought he meant to confess. Now, knowing that your business card was found on him, I don't think he meant *a priest*. I think he meant *Priest*.'

'He was Catholic?'

'Good grief, no.'

'But you never told your father about this conversation,' he guessed.

'No.'

Priest smiled. 'Then that makes us both *very* naughty.'

She folded her arms, not sharing the joke. Priest noticed a light rash had spread across her chest – her stress seeping through her skin. Priest wondered how much of Jessica Ellinder was an act.

'This isn't a game, Mr Priest. Why did Miles come to see you?'

Now it certainly *was* an accusation. Priest chewed it over. The pretence didn't seem to be serving any further purpose and there was something about the way she stood in his lounge, watching him reproachfully without ever making eye contact. She wasn't going to leave until she had the truth.

'He was looking for something,' Priest conceded eventually. 'Something that he believed I had. A flash drive, a USB stick. Containing, presumably, computer data. He didn't elaborate on what the data was.'

She looked thoughtful. He had expected her to make a fuss about his having kept this information from her earlier that morning, but she seemed surprisingly unperturbed.

'Why did he believe you had this data?'

'I have no idea.'

'How did he seem?'

'Agitated. I think it was when he strapped me to a chair and put a drill to my eye that I worked out that he was a little on edge.'

Priest had expected that this might provoke a reaction but he was disappointed. Instead, she made for the door.

'Thank you for the coffee,' she said.

'That's it?'

'Yes. You'll rethink your position regarding my father's offer?'

'I'll think it through, Miss Ellinder, but I'm really not sure I can take it.'

'I think otherwise, Mr Priest,' she said, opening the door and stepping out into the corridor. 'You're in far too deep now, and you need our help as much as we need yours.'

13

The security guard's face was familiar but Priest couldn't put a name to it. He wanted to say Karl or Conrad, or Percy. It probably didn't matter. The guy never spoke anyway and Priest had stopped trying to get anything other than a curt smile out of him months ago.

Karl, Conrad or Percy watched as Priest deposited his phone and wallet in a transparent locker and pocketed the key. No such contraband was allowed past the security checkpoint. Priest was led through a heavy metal door, which was shut unceremoniously behind him. For a moment, it was just him and the grim guard in a cupboard-sized, airless room until the sound of a click and another heavy door swung open into the main hospital complex.

It was another world on this side of the door – a quiet wilderness. The sense of threat enveloped him. The air seemed different somehow, stale and heavy. He had heard the wardens call it the 'Twilight Zone'. He could see why. The visitor's room was situated in a block on the other side of a yard interspersed with patches of grass and dirt – small allotments for the inmates to grow vegetables.

At the door to the block Priest was greeted with a firm handshake.

'Dr Wheatcroft,' Priest said warmly.

'Mr Priest. Nice to see you.'

'Likewise.'

For a man who spent his days caring for serial killers, rapists and lunatics, Wheatcroft projected extraordinary calm.

'How's he been, Doc?'

Wheatcroft sighed and ran his hand through his hair. It was the sort of hair that no amount of ruffling could dislodge.

'Not too bad. Not too bad. A little more distracted this week. He's missed a number of sessions, too. He claims he finds mingling with the other patients stultifying.'

'Back to his old self again,' Priest remarked.

'I'm afraid so. Progress is slow but not immeasurable. No doubt your visit will perk him up.' Wheatcroft touched Priest's arm and stepped aside to allow him through.

∞

Dr William Priest wore the expression of a man captivated by some baffling thought. Two male nurses led him through to the table where Priest stood waiting and sat him down. Priest sat opposite his older brother on a plastic chair. The family resemblance was unmistakable – the same thick, mousy-brown hair and glassy-blue eyes. But five years as a patient at Fen Marsh Secure Hospital had taken the shine off William Priest's striking features. There were dark circles around his eyes. His skin was ashen white. Priest felt that every time he visited, he saw a little more of his brother's humanity ebb away.

'My brother,' said William, barely looking at Priest. 'How reassuring for you to visit me.'

'How have you been, Wills?'

Their eyes met as William considered this; then he reached out, his hand finding Priest's face. Obviously alarmed, one of the attendants leapt forward, grabbed William's arm and held the back of his neck. It happened so quickly that Priest hadn't even had time to move.

'Wait!' Priest demanded. The attendant stopped, looked at Priest and released his hold. William seemed oblivious to the intervention. 'Let him be.'

'You cut yourself shaving, brother,' William observed, gently running his finger under the tiny scratch on Priest's jaw. 'Two days ago and you haven't shaved since. What has caused you to abandon your morning ritual?'

Priest nodded at the attendant, who withdrew, exchanging an uneasy glance with his colleague.

'A rough few days,' Priest said, by way of explanation.

'How exhilarating the outside world must be.'   ·

'Do you miss it?'

'Parts of it.' William's head was cocked to the side like a curious wren. 'Something troubles you, brother. Something more than *a rough few days*.'

'Because I haven't shaved?'

'Because your eyes betray you.'

Priest sighed heavily. 'You were always the best at reading people, Wills.'

William gave a triumphant coo. 'Indeed! And this visit is two days earlier than our planned rendezvous. There are bags under your eyes. That is the second day you have worn that shirt. You smell of coffee, which you only drink in rare instances when there is no Earl Grey tea available, so either you have run out – which is not likely – or you left in a hurry this morning and needed to procure a caffeine fix on the go. You chose that jacket in a hurry, too.'

'How do you know that?'

'Your pen – the expensive fountain pen our sister bought you for your thirty-second birthday – is absent from the inside pocket,' announced William. 'I noticed as you moved the chair back to sit down. You carry that pen everywhere, meaning that it has been left in the pocket of whatever jacket you wore *last week*. Unusually, you omitted to transfer it over to *this suit*, which suggests a carelessness created not by your fatigue, because that would have ultimately ended with you remembering to correct the error later, but by the haste with which you prepared this morning.'

'And the fact that we're meeting two days earlier than usual is significant because . . .?'

'Simple. Two days ago, something traumatic happened to you and you are about to embark on something of a campaign to remedy some breakage or discover some secret, so you're getting our engagement out of the way before you drop out of circulation for a short while.'

Priest noticed the smaller of the two attendants shift his weight from one foot to the other. Behind him, the red light on a CCTV camera stood out against the gleaming white walls.

'Now you,' prompted William excitedly.

Priest sighed again; he found the game tedious but they had played it since they were old enough to talk. He examined William up and down, then glanced beyond him at the nurse who had been shuffling his feet. 'That guy there is new. His name is Harry Clarke and he recently acquired a new cat, probably from a rescue home. He has no children, although he's recently divorced. He plays golf regularly but probably not very well and he's type 1 diabetic.'

Priest looked across at the nurse. The man's mouth was open in astonishment. Eventually he nodded his head and turned to look at his colleague for some sort of explanation.

William turned and gave the nurse the same curt inspection. 'Bravo, Charles. All fairly elementary, though. Let me see. He's new because you've never seen him before. The new cat because of the scratches on his arm, which you saw when he intervened just now, much too deep for a juvenile feline. That also explains no children, or it would have been more likely to have been a kitten. Adult cat so probably from a home rather than a pet store. Divorced because of the faint mark around the index finger, the wedding ring having only been recently discarded. Golf because one hand is slightly less tanned than the other, the hand upon which the glove would be worn, and not very good because the mere fact that you can see the difference suggests he wears the glove a lot and of course that would only be the case when taking a shot. The more shots one is taking, the poorer the player. Type 1 diabetic was a stretch but there's a chain around his neck. The nurses here aren't allowed jewellery unless it's for some good reason, such as the pendant a diabetic might wear with instructions in case he falls into a coma. But how did you get the name?'

Priest shrugged his shoulders. 'It's on his name badge.'

'Ah, exemplary.' William clapped enthusiastically. 'So clever of you, brother.'

The change was quick – a frightening thing to witness for the first time but something Priest was used to. Five years of visiting once a month had desensitised him to William's sudden changes of mood. So when William placed his hands on the edge of the table and leant forward conspiratorially, whispering words in a voice that had descended almost an entire octave, Priest didn't even flinch.

'I'm on to him, brother. The Director. He observes me at night. He thinks I am slumbering but it is an illusion. I have avoided REM sleep for months so that I am alert for his nocturnal visits. He believes he has subdued me but he has underestimated his lab rat's conviction.'

Priest sighed inwardly. It pained him to hear his brother's delusions. 'The Director' was William's pet name for Dr Wheatcroft. He harboured the fantasy that Wheatcroft was somehow responsible for his madness and that he spent his time testing his *creation*.

'Dr Wheatcroft is a good man –'

'*Do not* utter his name!' William seethed. 'He's probing me, Charles. Trying to push me to the brink of my mental limits. He's trying to make me *kill* again!'

'They're dreams, Wills. Just silly dreams.'

'Do not make the mistake of assuming my incarceration in this institution means that I cannot tell the difference between apparition and reality.' William was working himself up and the two attendants shuffled forward a few feet, ready to put a quick end to any trouble. Priest didn't move a muscle.

'I have deficiencies, Charles,' William went on. 'A malfunction of the brain. But it is not organic. It was a seed planted there by the Director. A seed that *he* now waters. He's seeing if he can push me to the edge again.'

The older of the two nurses put a hand on William's shoulder. Visiting time was over. 'Come on, William. Let's not keep your brother.'

'He'll come for me eventually, Charles! You'll see!'

'*Come on*, William,' said the attendant.

Priest watched with sadness as they took William by the arms. Five years ago William Priest would have thrown the two men off like sacks of potatoes. Now, dishevelled and confused, he was easily subdued.

'See you next month, Wills,' Priest said quietly.

'He is a great manipulator, Charles. We must not let him win!'

The two nurses picked William up. He barely struggled as they carried him to the door.

'I haven't finished!' he protested. 'Charles *must* know the truth. Let me say one final word.'

The older nurse raised an eyebrow at Priest, who nodded. They stopped at the door and allowed William enough movement to turn his head to face Priest.

'In 1971, Soviet scientists discovered a field of natural gas in Turkmenistan. Fearing it was poisonous, they decided to burn off the gas. They lit it, thinking it would burn out in a few days. Forty years on, it is still burning. The locals call it the Door to Hell – a great pit of fire in the desert. The mind is like that pit, Charles. Set it alight . . . and it burns. And burns. *And burns.*'

14

William was right. Priest had called in on his monthly visit early to get it over with. The encounter had stirred a familiar cocktail of emotions – guilt, sadness, disgust. Guilt because he didn't go often enough and because Sarah didn't go at all. Sadness because he loved his brother. His *brother* – not the serial killer, William Priest, the feral creature his brother had become. And disgust. With himself. For letting him down.

He'd googled the Door to Hell on the way to the office just to see if it was real – it was.

Maureen raised an eyebrow as he walked past; it seemed his recent behaviour hadn't gone unnoticed. She had gone heavy on the foundation this morning and wore a deep red lipstick that didn't suit her. In fact, it wouldn't have suited anyone. Priest decided he couldn't slip past her another time. She was too much of a perceptive old bat.

'Good morning,' he offered, slowing but not quite stopping.

'Remind me,' she grunted, 'it's *Mr Priest*, isn't it?'

'Yes. Your generous employer.'

'Hm, right.'

He smiled as he neared the stairs but, glancing down at his arms, noticed that his jacket sleeve had ridden up and the angry burn mark shone out like a beacon across his wrist. Hastily, he pulled his sleeve down but he knew she would have seen.

Maureen sighed. 'You know, Charlie, you're going to have to sort yourself out.'

Priest stopped for a moment, the words lingering in the air, then carried on up the stairs.

∽

Vincent Okoro presented himself in Priest's office wearing a cream suit that had been measured so perfectly it fitted like a second skin. There were fewer items of jewellery about his person today and Priest could only identify one modestly sized diamond earring.

'A hearing later?' Priest asked.

'Oral application for permission to appeal,' Okoro explained. He took the seat opposite Priest as usual.

'Your application?'

'My opponent's.'

'Any chance?'

'None. He's a simpleton. But his client's pissed I beat his arse.'

'Understandable.'

'Enough chit-chat. What's the latest? Anyone try to kill you last night?'

Priest mentioned Jessica Ellinder's visit. Okoro nodded thoughtfully but didn't interrupt. When Priest had finished, he handed over a letter.

'This was couriered over this morning,' Okoro said. 'I signed for you. Looks important. Better open it.'

As Priest studied the envelope the door opened and Georgie came in. Her hair was tied back again in a ponytail. She wore a black, knee-length suit skirt and a jacket with a deep red lining. The thick-rimmed glasses would have looked hideous on any other face but they somehow suited Georgie Someday.

'Hi,' she said, motioning in a sort of wave. 'I was just wondering . . .'

'What I want you to do next?' finished Priest.

'Yes!'

Priest clicked his tongue. 'I want you to look into the use of impalement as an execution method. Religious and social significance, history, conceptual meaning – that sort of thing.'

'I did that already,' Georgie said. She cleared her throat. 'Impalement is most commonly associated with the fifteenth-century Romanian tyrant, Vlad the Impaler. You might know him better as Dracula.'

'Dracula? As in, Bram Stoker?' asked Okoro.

'Yes, Stoker's Dracula was based on a real person whose favourite method of execution was impalement. I read a lot of Gothic horror,' she added.

'Pretty unpleasant way to die,' said Priest.

'Yes, Vlad was one of the most brutal dictators in history. He would sit by firelight eating and drinking while his impaled enemies writhed in agony around him. He favoured the spike penetrating the anus or, in the case of women, vagina.'

'As opposed to . . .?' Priest found himself cringing not so much at Georgie's description as at the enthusiasm with which she was delivering it.

'Hanging the victim upside down and inserting the spike down the throat, of course,' said Georgie, brightly. 'It kills quicker.'

Priest nodded. 'Of course. Why didn't I think of that?'

Georgie continued, apparently oblivious. 'So I guess there are two reasons why impalement might be used to kill someone. First, it's a very painful and degrading way to die. Second, it's associated with a man who took great enjoyment from torture and death.'

'He got a kick out of it?' asked Okoro.

'According to most sources. Especially women. He would mutilate their sexual organs and force mothers to eat their own babies. He really wasn't very nice.'

Priest swallowed hard. If he had been given the chance, he would have gladly put his fist through Miles Ellinder's face. But it was difficult to conceive the level of sadistic evil necessary to commit the atrocities Georgie had described.

Priest looked back down at the envelope in his hand. It was unmarked, no frank or stamp. One word was inscribed in pen on an otherwise blank white envelope.

Priest.

'Who delivered this?' he asked Okoro.

'Fastlink. They're a private courier.'

Priest held the envelope for a few more moments before tearing it open and pulling out a letter written by hand on thick, cream paper. He read it. Read it again. Then looked up at the other two.

'This letter is from the Attorney General,' he told them.

'As in . . .?' said Okoro, slowly.

'Yes. Sir Philip Wren. My godfather.'

15

Hayley Wren slumped down heavily in front of the vanity mirror and examined her tired face. There were bags under her eyes and her skin looked blotchy and dry. She grimaced.

She considered the small array of products in front of her, stacked up neatly along the dressing table. Most of them were gifts from her mother – perfumes and creams endorsed by celebrities she had never heard of, that sort of thing. All part of her parents' futile attempts to encourage her to join the real world.

Get your head out of the clouds, Hayley.

Her father's voice rang in her ears. But how could she ever live up to his expectations? She was the daughter of the great Philip Wren, Attorney General. The lawyer's lawyer. She had enrolled on a law degree, as he had directed, but had never made it past freshers' week. That was almost eighteen years ago. In three years' time she would be forty, and she had nothing to celebrate except for two unfinished graphic novels and a job in a charity shop.

And that was it. Her whole life summed up in one pathetic incident, when she had walked away from full-time education. A life full of 'not quites'. The girl who was not quite pretty, not quite clever, not quite the same as the rest. *Not quite what Daddy wanted. Not quite male enough, maybe.* Her father had been particularly short with her the last time they had spoken. He had urged her to come home. Perhaps he wanted to have another go at trying to prise her away from Jesus. He hated her involvement with the Creation Church but she didn't care. She had finally found something tangible in the Reverend Matthew's little gathering. Something she could hold on to.

Which was why she had found herself drawn to Reverend Matthew's counsel like a magnet when, the week before, an envelope had dropped on her doormat. There was no note inside, no letter, no address, just her name inscribed on the envelope. *Somebody walked right up to my door and fed it through my letterbox.* She shuddered just thinking about it.

When she had tipped the contents out on to her bed she had nearly been sick.

Within an hour of opening it, she was sitting, shaking, at the table in the back room of the community hall where services were shared with line-dancing classes and AA meetings.

'Does it mean anything to you?' Reverend Matthews had asked. He was kind and gentle but the way he'd looked at her, the way he'd put his hand over hers – he'd been just as troubled as she was.

She had shaken her head. She had no idea why anyone would send her . . . *that.*

'Leave the envelope with me,' he had advised, and she had gratefully thrust it across the table at him.

Hayley had tried to forget about the envelope but she hadn't been able to. She had thrown away the bedding on which its contents had fallen – it felt defiled, unclean. But the image still haunted her and, worse, the dreadful misgiving that that last conversation she had had with her father and the envelope were somehow connected.

Perhaps I should have gone home when he told me to.

She ran a brush through her hair and stared at the mirror. Behind her, she saw her room, everything neat and tidy as always.

Except something felt different.

She slowed the gentle tug of the brush and examined the reflection in the mirror further. Nothing seemed out of place. But there was something not quite right.

It was the door to the hallway.

It had been open, but it was now closing, hinges groaning slightly with the motion. By itself.

She felt her blood freeze instantly.

Oh, Jesus, be with me now.

In front of the door stood a man, arms held stiffly at his sides, face hidden behind a white hood through which all she could see were two dark eyes watching her.

16

'Your godfather is the Attorney General?' Georgie looked excited.

'Philip Wren was a family friend,' Priest explained. 'He and my father went back a long way. Old boys' network. That sort of thing.'

Lunches at the Wrens had always been a tedious affair. Priest had never really taken to Philip Wren. He was one of those over-confident men who had every right to be overconfident. Sarah had once referred to him as a 'vile, self-indulgent pig'. To his face, too. William had been indifferent about him.

The Attorney General's wife, Terri, was a small, delicate creature – the opposite of her husband. They had one daughter, Hayley, who was even more introverted than her mother. Priest was a year in to his fourth decade. He thought Hayley might be a few years younger than he was, but she was one of those people who always seemed to stay the same age; she had never crawled out of her early twenties. Perhaps that was one of the reasons why Sarah had never had much time for her – but then again, Sarah was a tomboy and had spent her youth in bare feet climbing trees. Hayley had spent her youth reading in her room. It was obvious that Hayley wasn't what her father had wished for, which was hardly her fault.

'It must be really cool,' said Georgie.

'What must?'

'Having the Attorney General as your godfather.'

'Why?'

She faltered. 'Well . . . my godfather's the local vicar . . .'

Priest watched her fiddle with her hair. If she was wearing any make-up at all, it was understated and applied sparingly. He liked that.

'Will you read the bloody letter out, Priest,' Okoro prompted.

Dear Charlie,

I write in haste and with a heavy heart. There are few men to whom I could reasonably turn in this dark hour. Unforgivably, I have turned to you.

Please excuse the brevity of this note. Time is short. Lives are at stake. I make that last statement quite consciously, knowing that my next actions may endanger you. For this, I can do nothing more than offer my apologies, which I do not expect you to accept.

I have dispatched under separate consignment a small parcel containing electronic data to your home. It is my only hope that you will know what to do with it.

For me, all is lost.

I am sorry.

Yours sincerely,

Philip Wren

For a while, no one spoke.

'But no such consignment was received by you,' Okoro pointed out, breaking the silence.

'No. But the electronic data Wren refers to must surely be on the flash drive Miles Ellinder was looking for.'

'He says he knows he may be putting you in danger?' said Georgie, bemused.

'A man tried to drill my eyes out. He was right.'

Priest picked up the phone.

'Can you just *phone* the Attorney General?' Georgie asked.

'You can phone anyone if you have their number.' The phone was ringing, but no one was picking up. He tried a different number.

He vaguely registered Georgie saying timidly, 'I was never sure what the Attorney General actually does.'

It wasn't a stupid question in Priest's view. In matters of legal constitution, there was no such thing.

'Think of him as the government's main lawyer,' Okoro explained. 'The Treasury solicitors act for and represent the government in court. The AG is the head guy, so to speak. Philip Wren has held the position for years now. He must be nearing retirement age.'

'No, I won't hold,' Priest was insisting. 'I'm trying to reach Philip Wren. It's urgent . . . tell him Charlie Priest wants to speak to him. Now.'

After a while he threw the phone back down.

'No one at home,' he reported indignantly. 'Office don't know where he is. Solicitor General isn't available either.'

'The Solicitor General is effectively Wren's deputy,' Okoro whispered to Georgie. 'I met him in court once. Don't remember his name but he had bad taste in ties.'

Priest considered the letter again. *A dark hour*, Wren had announced in a letter written *in haste*, but scripted in ink, and with some care, too. Every character painstakingly formed to perfection. No evidence of haste at all. None of it made sense.

And the flash drive that Miles Ellinder was so keen to procure. *It is my only hope that you will know what to do with it.*

'This could be a suicide note,' Priest remarked, examining the letter closely, as if the paper itself might hold the answer.

Okoro opened his mouth but whether it was in agreement or objection Priest would never know. Just then the door was thrown open with such force that it shook a picture off its hook and sent it crashing to the ground.

A familiar figure filled the doorway. Beyond him, Maureen was trying to push her way past.

'I'm sorry, Charlie,' she croaked. 'But this gentleman wouldn't let me call up for you. He insisted –'

'It's all right, Maureen.' Priest held up his hand. 'What can we do for you, Detective Inspector McEwen?'

McEwen was agitated. His neck was wrapped in an ugly-looking rash and his forehead was damp with sweat, despite the cold outside. He looked as if he had run all the way.

'You'd better take a seat, McEwen,' said Okoro, rising to his feet. 'I would hate to see you passing out on the rug.'

McEwen ignored Okoro and Georgie and went straight to Priest's desk. He leant over Priest. His body odour was over-powering.

'Jessica and Kenneth Ellinder were here yesterday, Priest.'

'Yes,' Priest said casually.

'Well? What did they want?' McEwen demanded.

'Why don't you ask them?'

McEwen whirled away from the desk, insofar as a man of his size could whirl. He grabbed the seat Okoro had offered and threw his fat frame into the plush leather. Okoro held up his hands.

'Don't play games with me, Priest. Your involvement in this mess is already attracting considerable attention from higher sources than me. Do yourself a favour and start helping me out.'

Priest assumed McEwen was referring to Assistant Commissioner Auckland. No doubt she was looking for her own form of retribution and his connection to the Ellinder affair must have provided the perfect opportunity.

Not that Priest felt Dee deserved much by way of revenge. It was hardly his fault his brother was a serial killer, but the connection had been extremely inconvenient for his ambitious wife. *She'd have never made AC by hanging out with me.* Admittedly, the matter was compounded by his social awkwardness and tendency to hallucinate at parties; it was a toxic mixture that eventually detonated in a brutal ending to a short, childless marriage.

Priest said, 'You know what, McEwen? You're boring me. There's a killer out there. A pretty messed-up one. Why don't you try to find him?'

McEwen ignored him. 'What did they want, Priest? Did they just happen to pop in to renew their wills or did you invite them?'

'They're the family of the victim and they're powerful people. They have a right to visit whomever they see fit.'

'But why *you*? Did they want legal advice?'

'If they did, I wouldn't tell you.'

'Oh!' McEwen clapped mockingly. He seemed to be having some difficulty keeping all of the spit he was chewing up in his mouth from occasionally dripping down his chin. 'Client confidentiality. So now the lawyer falls behind his precious rule book.'

'Nothing to do with client confidentiality, McEwen, because they're not my clients. I wouldn't tell you because it's nothing to do with your investigation and you are, candidly, a tool.' Priest knew the comment would earn him a whole heap of trouble, but it felt good. He was conscious that Georgie's jaw had dropped so low it was in danger of detaching.

It turned out that McEwen was able to recognise when he was on a hiding to nothing after all. He got up and glared at Priest unpleasantly through his squinty eyes.

'This is far from over, Priest. Involved – not involved. I don't care. Either way, I *will* find a way to drag your name through so much mud you won't be recognisable even to your dead parents.' He pushed past Okoro and turned, just before he got to the door. 'How's your brother, by the way? Still a fucked-up serial killer?'

Priest said nothing. Mention of his family had touched a nerve.

'Maybe you'll be seeing a lot more of him in the future, Priest.' McEwen spat as he left.

Nobody spoke for a while. The only sound was that of Priest grinding his teeth.

∞

An hour or so after McEwen stormed out, Priest went down to his car. He needed to go home to think undisturbed. He was about to get in when he saw someone approaching him from the far side of the parking area beneath the office. The stride was confident, purposeful. The mid-morning sun was pushing through the mist and casting shafts of yellow light across the concrete through slits at ground level above his head. As the footsteps grew closer, the streaks of light were punctured by the shadow of a figure.

He stopped and waited for her to walk to the other side of the car, where she leant over the roof. He wondered how long he would have to stare into her eyes before he turned to stone.

'Is this really your car?' Jessica Ellinder asked with a tone of unexpected amusement.

'Yes' – Priest looked at the old Volvo and suddenly felt very defensive about it – 'it's cheap to run.'

She nodded and even offered him a wry smile. 'Do they still make parts for these?'

'It has its charms,' he said, shrugging. 'What do you drive?'

She didn't answer. He felt determined not to feel awkward but it wasn't easy.

When it was apparent that she wasn't going to speak, he said, 'This morning I received this.' He reached inside his jacket pocket and handed her Wren's letter, which she read.

'The parcel Wren sent to your home. The flash drive?' she queried, returning the paper.

'Undoubtedly.'

He got in the car and shut the door, then waited a few moments for her to climb in the passenger side. When she was finally seated, she looked at the dashboard curiously. 'This car has a beige interior,' she remarked.

He started the engine – which, to his relief, actually fired up first time.

'Why would the Attorney General send you this letter?'

'He's my godfather,' he explained as he pulled out into the morning traffic.

'But you haven't actually received a package, otherwise Miles would have found it.'

'No.'

'Curious that he would send you a letter to your office saying he sent a package to your home,' she mused.

Priest shrugged, but he was also troubled by it. 'Maybe he just wanted to make sure I was looking out for the package,' he said, although that sounded unconvincing even to him.

'When was the last time you saw your godfather?'

'At William's trial, I think,' Priest said softly.

'Your brother is William Priest. The serial killer.' It seemed to be a statement rather than a question.

'Yes, he is.'

'That must be tough.'

He looked at her sideways. 'How perceptive of you.'

'What . . . motivated him?'

Priest sighed. Unlike Sarah, Priest didn't object in principle to having to explain about his brother when he came up in conversation. However, right now, he couldn't work out whether or not he was being patronised. Indeed, he couldn't work Jessica Ellinder out, full stop.

'He thought that –' Priest rubbed his chin, trying to find the right words. 'He thought that he had lost his soul and by taking other people's lives –'

'He might take part of their soul to replace his own?' she suggested.

Priest nodded in surprise. 'Yes. You seemed to get that – quite quickly.'

She shrugged. 'It wasn't hard.'

'I see. And you? Any murderers in your family?'

They headed south-east through the city until they reached a frost-covered playing field peppered with couples walking their dogs and runners, their breath clearly visible in the chill. On the other side of the street loomed rows of Georgian townhouses. Lines of white sash windows watched their progress like rectangular eyes sunk into the red stucco-finished brickwork.

'Do you have any other family?' Jessica asked after a while.

'Sarah, my sister. My parents died in 2002.'

'I'm sorry. How?'

He paused. For a moment he wondered why he should tell her but couldn't think of a good reason not to.

'It was a plane crash. My father was high up in the police but it was Mum who made the money. They were on business in Germany and flew home in a private jet, with a business partner. They hit a storm and never made it over the Channel. William blamed the pilot – I blamed fate.'

She nodded gravely. They didn't speak for several minutes.

'Here we are,' Priest said, at last. 'You never asked where we were going, by the way.'

'The Attorney General's house. Obviously.'

Eden Park was the kind of place where high brick walls bordered plots of perfectly mown grass around which generously sized homes were placed complete with fake marble pillars at the entranceway. The sort of artificial haven where nobody spoke to each other but everyone knew everyone else's business.

The sort of place Priest hated. The old Volvo had never looked so out of place as it did next to the Maseratis and Range Rovers that lined the streets.

The Volvo crunched over a gravel drive flanked by leafless trees. Wren's home was like all the rest – oversized and characterless – although it was distinguishable by several salient features; namely, blue-and-white crime-scene tape surrounding the inner perimeter of the garden, four squad cars abandoned haphazardly in the courtyard, lights still whirling, and a SOCO van near the stable block.

A uniformed policeman clutching his cap waved them down. He looked a few months short of eighteen. Priest swore under his breath and pulled over at a gap in the trees where the driveway widened out into the courtyard. He exchanged a glance with Jessica before winding down his window.

'Sorry, sir,' said the uniform. 'You can't go any further. Can I ask you what you're doing here?'

'I was hoping to speak to Sir Philip Wren,' said Priest.

The sentry scanned the car's interior. The back seat was covered with files and papers. His eyes lingered over Jessica for a moment.

'That's not going to be possible,' he said eventually. 'Maybe you should be on your way.'

'What's happened?'

'I'm sorry, sir. Police business. Perhaps you ought to leave.'

Priest opened his mouth but stopped. Jessica suddenly leant across him, her hand on his knee for support.

'My name is Jessica Ellinder. Who is in charge here?'

Whatever the uniform had by way of response, Priest would never know. Just then the boy's skinny body was replaced, rather suddenly, by a much larger figure.

'That'll do, laddie!' McEwen's face filled the window and he glared at Priest. The rash hadn't improved. Nor had the smell. 'Well, well. If it isn't the Scarlet Pimpernel popping up again. How fascinating. Don't you just turn up everywhere!'

'The Scarlet Pimpernel was famous for *not* turning up everywhere but somehow still managing to rescue French aristocrats from the guillotine, you moron,' said Priest blandly.

'What are you doing here, Priest?'

'I'm here to trim the leylandii.'

'How about you get out of this rust bucket you're driving and we'll have a chat under caution, you fucking ponce?'

'That won't be necessary,' Jessica told him. She had got out of the car and was standing feet away from McEwen.

Priest raised an eyebrow.

'Miss Ellinder?' McEwen was taken aback.

'Yes. Now what's happening here, Inspector?'

17

Priest was impressed. It took a tremendous effort, but McEwen was forced not only to escort them up to the house but also to explain what was going on, although every word seemed to cause him excruciating pain.

'Sir Philip is Mr Priest's godfather,' Jessica explained. 'Perhaps I can call my father and you can explain to him why we aren't allowed through?'

Evidently, Kenneth Ellinder had friends in high places.

They were taken through a stone-floored kitchen to a luxurious study furnished with a beautifully handcrafted writing desk as its centrepiece. A magnificent circular window looked out on to an orchard leading down to a beck, the trickle of water just visible in the gloomy haze.

Wren was hanging from one of the oak beams that supported the ceiling.

'His wife was out last night,' McEwen explained. 'She came back late but didn't think anything of the fact that the bed was empty. That wasn't unusual, apparently. She found him here this morning. Didn't report it straight away. Quite a shock, I'd imagine, seeing him just hanging around in the study.'

'Lady Wren is here?' Priest asked, ignoring McEwen's attempt at humour.

'Aye. There's a family liaison officer with her making tea and handing her tissues so none of your concern, Priest.'

Priest glanced at Jessica. She was staring at the limp body, watching it sway, mesmerised.

'First time with a corpse?' he whispered to her. She nodded slowly. He touched her arm. 'Come on. We don't need to linger.'

'No,' she said. Turning to look at McEwen, she demanded, 'What is this?'

'Suicide. Obviously,' said McEwen.

'Where's the note?' asked Priest. 'There's always a note.'

McEwen shrugged.

Wren's letter was burning a hole in Priest's pocket. *Was that your suicide note, Philip? I think not. I was wrong about that. Things aren't what they seem here.*

'For me, all is lost,' the letter had said. *Yet there's something fundamentally wrong with this scene.*

'Suicide. Period.' McEwen repeated. He was chewing on something. It was beginning to grate on Priest.

Wait, that's it. 'How'd he get up there?' Priest asked McEwen.

McEwen shrugged again. 'Climbed up on the desk and hooked the rope around the fan unit.'

'He came in from outside first?' Priest asked, glancing over at the French windows.

'How do you know that?' asked McEwen suspiciously.

'His shoes have mud on them.' Priest drew McEwen's attention to the soles. They were filthy. 'And the key is in the door leading outside. A man like Philip Wren wouldn't keep the key in the door when it's locked because that makes it easier to break in. All a burglar would have to do is smash the glass to get the key. So it stands to reason that the door is unlocked.'

'That's just . . .'

'Try it.'

McEwen hesitated before trying the handle. The door opened without difficulty.

'So what if he came in from outside?' grumbled McEwen.

'The desk. Where's the footprint? Not one grain of dirt, anywhere. He didn't climb on the desk.'

McEwen paused. 'Priest, why don't you leave the detecting to the detectives?' His red face had darkened.

'Are you saying this wasn't suicide?' Jessica asked.

'Over half of all suicides in the UK are carried out by hanging or suffocation,' Priest told her, 'and it's more common among men than women. Although it's cumbersome, it's popular because it is the cleanest and most pain-free way to die and most people don't have access to firearms. But hanging seems an odd choice when there is a perfectly well-stocked gun rack in the corner.'

Priest gestured to the glass gun cabinet behind Wren's swaying body. While McEwen went over to examine the shotguns inside, Priest managed to take a couple of quick photographs of the scene.

'Where's Lady Wren?' Priest asked, pocketing his phone just as McEwen turned around. 'I want to see Terri.'

∽

In the oak-panelled library, Priest found Terri Wren sitting with a shawl over her knees in a large leather chair. He knelt down so his head was level with hers. He couldn't remember the last time he had seen her, but her hair, once a sandy colour, was now streaked with grey.

'Terri,' Priest murmured.

Her eyes were wet and dark. She barely glanced at him but seemed to know who he was. 'Charlie. What are you –'

'I'm with the police. It's complicated . . . but I'm helping out.'

'That's good. They need all the help they can get.'

'I'm so sorry . . .'

She held up her hand and turned away. His words fell short instantly.

'There's no need, Charlie. It's Hayley I'm crying for. Not me.'

He nodded. 'I know.'

She turned towards him. He resisted the temptation to look away. He knew that was what people would do to her for the rest of her life – look away. So he did her the courtesy of holding her gaze.

'I don't know what Philip had got himself into, Charlie. Maybe if your father had still been alive he might have been able to save him. He was a wonderful man. Even Philip, as pig-headed as he was sometimes, saw that.'

Priest touched her hand gently. 'What happened here, Terri?' he asked softly.

'I don't know,' she said, pulling her shawl tight around her. There was a quiver in her voice. She seemed so fragile that she might shatter into a thousand pieces at any moment.

Priest found himself holding his breath when she spoke.

'You know Philip. He had his work, his precious work. It took him so far away from here – away from me – that I barely knew him. But for him to . . . do this? I just can't believe it.'

'My father once mentioned an old Japanese proverb that Philip told him about.'

'Yes! I know it well. *Fall seven times, stand up eight.*' Terri paused. 'You see. Philip wasn't the sort to . . . you know.'

Priest bowed his head. 'Where's Hayley, Terri?'

'I don't know,' she whispered. 'She hasn't been in touch for a week or so but that isn't unusual. I tried ringing earlier but she didn't answer. I'm sure she's just out, or at that church of hers. Or maybe she has a man she doesn't want me to know about.'

Priest nodded. Something was nagging at him – something more than the body in the study.

'Is someone coming to be with you, Terri?'

'My sister. She lives in Wiltshire. On a farm.'

Priest nodded. 'And Hayley?'

'She'll turn up. She always does.'

'Terri, did Philip –' Priest hesitated. *Did Philip what?* This wasn't the time, nor was it fair to say anything to Terri that might suggest there was anything for her to be worried about above and beyond the death of her husband.

'Charlie? Did Philip what?' She looked at him, alarm registering in her eyes.

'I'm sorry,' he said, giving her hand a squeeze. 'It's nothing.'

Priest could hear the floorboards creaking in the next room. McEwen was pacing the hallway. Counting down the five minutes he had allowed Priest.

'One minute more, Priest, that's all,' he called into the room.

'Terri, if there's anything I can do . . .'

She smiled, although her watery eyes looked straight through him. 'You were always a good boy, Charlie. I know Philip thought so much of you. He had this crazy notion, you know. About you and Hayley . . .'

'Terri . . .'

'I'm sorry. I shouldn't have said that. I'll be fine. You should go.'

'Perhaps you could ask your sister to contact me when Hayley turns up.'

'Of course.'

Priest got up slowly. When he got to the doorway, Terri called after him.

'Charlie?'

He turned.

'Thank you for coming.'

He nodded. His head was pounding.

Priest closed the door on Terri Wren.

'Did she –' Jessica was waiting outside, just out of McEwen's earshot.

'No. She doesn't know anything.'

She nodded, disappointed. 'We ought to go. I think we've outstayed our welcome.'

She was right. McEwen had spotted Priest emerging from the library and was bustling up the corridor with a thunderous glare. A couple of his men lurked in the background – they looked shambolic, loitering in the corridor without direction or purpose. Priest swallowed back the urge to shout at them.

'OK, enough, Priest. I'm not playing your game anymore. You clearly know more about this than you're letting on,' McEwen spluttered.

'Has anyone contacted Wren's daughter, Hayley?'

'What's that got to do with you?' McEwen demanded.

'Have you contacted her? Terri said she hadn't been in touch in a week or so and now she can't get hold of her.'

'If it hasn't escaped your attention, Priest, you're not a copper anymore. You're an ambulance chaser.'

'McEwen, listen. Philip Wren did *not* kill himself. You need to be taking this seriously –'

'You need to learn to keep your fucking nose out of my business, Priest,' the Scot growled.

Priest clenched his fists. He was a good head taller than McEwen and the thought of punching him in the face was tempting. He buried the feeling quickly. The boundary between reality and the unreal void that disassociation sufferers inhabit was a thin veil and some days Priest was never quite sure which side of the veil he was on. He wondered if William had ever had the same thought. The idea scared him. *Was that all that separates us? A thin veil?*

'Priest?' Jessica prompted.

He shook off the mist that was enveloping him. Jessica was looking at him – her dark eyes curious and sharp.

He turned back to McEwen. 'It's not about *your business*, McEwen,' he said, calmly. 'Finding Hayley Wren should be your priority.'

McEwen waved his hand dismissively. 'Fuck off, Priest. We'll do our job. Which right now might involve arresting you for obstruction.'

'You need to act on fact, not assumption, McEwen. Hayley Wren . . .'

'Are you telling me how to do my job?'

'Yes, I am,' said Priest, feeling his anger start to gain control.

The purple veins in McEwen's neck stood out angrily. He had removed his jacket and, despite the chill in the air, there were large patches of moisture under his arms. He made to say something but the words appeared to stick in his throat. Priest felt a hand around his arm as Jessica led him to the door.

'As I said, we've outstayed our welcome,' she breathed in his ear.

❧

Priest drove Jessica back to pick up her Range Rover. She had reverted to avoiding his eyes. He spent the journey turning occasionally, trying to remember what her face looked like when it wasn't obscured by her hair.

They had exchanged a few disjointed sentences.

'Do you know Hayley well?' Jessica asked.

'Not really. From my childhood mainly, and a few meetings when I was in my early teens. She was nice enough,' Priest replied.

'Not your type?'

'My colleague Okoro says I don't have a type.'

By the time they got back to the underground car park, the temperature had dropped to close to freezing. Priest expected Jessica to get out of the car as soon as they had stopped but she stayed put, pulling her coat tightly around her when he turned the engine off.

'Does this change anything?' she asked.

He thought for a moment. 'Philip Wren sent me a letter to my office saying that he had sent a package to my home containing a flash drive which your brother, who later turns up murdered, was looking for. Our chances of finding out what Philip has to do with this have diminished considerably.'

'I meant my father's instructions to you, to your firm.'

'Ah, I see.' Priest scratched his head.

She shuffled in her seat. She had her hands clasped over her lap, her eyes fixed on the dashboard.

'No. It changes nothing,' he said, finally.

She nodded and he watched her walk away across the car park. He had no idea whether she was disappointed or not.

18

The bar was not the sort of establishment that Priest habitually frequented. For one thing it was too loud. They were playing the Beastie Boys' 'Sabotage'. It was bad enough that the choice of background music arbitrarily switched from Shania Twain to Placebo in a heartbeat. Having to listen to it at over a hundred decibels was unforgivable.

It was their monthly catch-up and Sarah's turn to choose the venue. To try to stimulate his enthusiasm she had referred to it as a 'trendy wine bar', but this had turned out to be a disappointing misrepresentation.

'It's a student dive,' he complained on arrival.

'They do two-for-one on shots.'

'Sarah, I haven't had a shot since my last tetanus jab.'

She laughed and sat him down in a booth with a couple of bottles of beer. As usual, she talked and he listened. He liked that – it meant he didn't have to put much effort in himself and he liked to hear about her life. It reminded him how dysfunctional he was, but that was good – he needed to hear that sometimes. Her monologue, or at any rate as much of it as he could hear, drifted pleasantly: Tilly was doing well at school, her company had had a decent quarter but they might have to shed one of the agents next month as part of the cutbacks. Ryan was still a job-less deadbeat.

'Have you seen William recently, Charlie?'

'A little. He asks about you.'

'How is he?'

'You know. Mental.'

That was the extent of any discussion regarding William and, although Priest had no objection to talking about it, he knew that Sarah was asking for his benefit, not because she had any genuine interest. Through this ritual, Sarah afforded Priest the courtesy of acknowledging William's existence, and Priest afforded her the courtesy of a brief reply.

Sarah bought the next round and pushed a bottle of San Miguel across the table towards him. She had settled for a tall glass of some green liquid that he didn't recognise. She took the cocktail umbrella out of her drink and slotted it into the top of his beer bottle.

'Remember that girl I mentioned the other day?'

'No, Sarah. I don't remember,' he lied.

'Don't be facetious, Charlie. You're an awful bore when you're like that.'

He laughed and took a swig of the beer, poking himself in the forehead with the cocktail umbrella. 'I'm not interested.'

'Charlie, I've forgotten how long ago your divorce was but it seems like decades. Have you seen *any* girls since?'

He shrugged. 'A few.' Another lie of course, but she didn't question it.

'I just don't get you.' Sarah sighed.

'What do you mean?'

'Well, you're wealthy, charming, a successful professional. Not as good-looking as me but not *that* ugly, either.' She smiled mischievously, sipping her green drink through a straw.

'I'm a social retard. *Charming* is quite an overstatement.'

She weighed it up. 'That's true. And you have that thing that sometimes makes you see people with fish heads and shit.'

'Mm. You're right, Sarah. My bachelor status is the single most baffling question since the discovery of dark matter. With my painful antisocialism, lack of cultural awareness, mental illness and obsession with old zombie films, I'm quite a catch.'

Sarah laughed their mother's wonderfully warm laugh. 'OK. Nobody's perfect but, for the record, can you let me know what the actual problem is?'

'You really want to know?'

She leant across the table with her chin resting on her hands. 'Please.'

'Well, it's just that . . . a lot of your friends suck.'

She kicked him under the table and they burst into fits of giggles. For a moment it was as if they were children again and all the problems of the world suddenly evaporated. It might have gone on, had so many things not been playing on Priest's mind.

'Do you remember Philip Wren?' he asked, suddenly.

She screwed up her face as if she had sucked a lemon. 'Yes. I remember he was a pig. Why are you changing the subject?'

'He's dead.'

She swallowed a little too much green drink and had to swallow twice to gulp it down. 'Oh. I'm sorry. How?'

Priest clicked his tongue. 'He hanged himself.'

He had thought she might have been shocked, but she just looked away, running her hand across her chin. 'That's awful.' She said it more to herself than him.

'You're not still in contact with Hayley, are you?'

'We have a Facebook relationship, I guess. I don't meet up with her.'

That didn't mean much. Sarah knew almost *everyone* through Facebook. Something else they didn't share.

'Been in touch with her recently?'

'No. Her page is weird. Lots of references from the Bible. I think she found Jesus at some point. You know what I mean? You drift around a bit. Hate your parents. Get used to not fitting in. Never have any luck with boys. Then you're sucked into a dogma that you kind of know is flawed but it gives you a little comfort and before you know it, you're singing hallelujah with the God Squad.'

'Wow, what happened to my sister? The non-judgemental one?'

'Mm. Do *you* believe in God?'

'I used to be indifferent, I suppose. If there was a God, then he was just as likely to be a very talented computer programmer as an omnipresent super-being. But then I thought about the victims and, somehow, it seemed wrong of me to believe in God.'

The victims. Priest meant the people William had killed. He knew who they were, their faces, everything about them. He had spent months studying them, trying to make sense of it all. But he had never once been able to utter their names out loud. They were just . . . the victims.

'Why aren't you allowed to believe in God?' Sarah asked, intrigued.

'Because if there is a God, and he or she stood back and did nothing while William did what he did, then that's fucking scary. So it's probably better just to not believe.'

She nodded, reached across and gave his hand a squeeze. 'Amen, Reverend.'

The music changed again. Feeder, 'Feeling a Moment'. His hand was cold from clinging to the beer bottle.

'Why did Philip hang himself, do you think?' she asked him.

'I don't know. Pressure of the job, maybe.'

'So sad.'

'Mm. Well, if there is a God, I doubt he has space for another lawyer in Paradise.'

'What do you mean *another* lawyer?' Sarah grinned.

19

26th March, 1946
A remote farm in middle England

Heavy blobs of rain pelted down the Austin's windshield. It was almost too much for the flimsy wipers to cope with and Ruck had to lean forward with his nose as close to the glass as he could get it just to see a few yards ahead. Tyres crunched over the courtyard gravel. He intended to leave the farm behind him for the evening. Schneider might be a prisoner there but *he* certainly wasn't. There was a town a few miles south. Perhaps a chip shop, or a pub maybe.

The figure came out of nowhere. A flash of red. He hit the brakes. The Austin's wheels lost traction for a moment before coming to a stop. Ruck grabbed his hat and got out. The wind blew the rain into his face. He cursed under his breath as the icy water hit him. He had to half shout to be heard over the noise.

'Hey, what!'

'I'm so sorry, Colonel Ruck,' Eva Miller shouted back. She was soaked from head to toe. Her hair, which had been immaculately curled earlier, now fell limply around her shoulders. The red coat she was wearing – which did not look cheap – seemed to have shrivelled up.

'What on earth are you doing out here in this weather?' Ruck asked.

Perhaps a gentleman would have rushed round, taken his coat off, flung it over her. Ushered her inside. The thought crossed Ruck's mind but he just stood there, getting as drenched as she was.

'I was trying to find the kitchen,' she explained. 'Now I'm afraid I can't find which door leads me to my room. They're all locked.'

Ruck faltered: it was unlikely she had already lost her bearings but the rain was relentless and she was soaked to the skin.

'Get in,' he instructed.

They both climbed into the Austin. Eva closed the door and threw her head back against the seat in relief. Ruck flung his hat on the back seat. Patting his soaking coat, he pulled out the piece of paper hidden in the inside pocket to check it was undamaged. Fortunately, Schneider's formula was still legible. He had considered where to keep the paper but he didn't trust the guards not to snoop, and there was no safe in his room. The most secure place for the formula was with him.

Seeing Eva watching, he hastily stuffed it back in his pocket.

As he drove round to the back of the farm, it crossed his mind that she must have known how to get to her room – they had been here two nights now. Perhaps the storm and the dark had disorientated her. 'Here.' He stopped the car. 'The door will be locked. Fitzgerald will let you in. Just knock and call for him.'

Eva made a noise as if she understood, but didn't move. He turned to look at her. She was staring at him.

'Where were you going, Colonel Ruck?'

Even in her bedraggled state, she looked beautiful. He tried not to think about that.

'To the town down the road. A warm pub, if I can find one. Anywhere as long as it's away from this detestable place.'

'Sounds wonderful. Although I imagine anywhere other than here would seem wonderful.'

'There could be worse places.'

'Perhaps it is the proximity to Schneider that disturbs me?' Eva smiled a wonderful, radiant smile. With her eyes, too.

In Ruck's experience, people never did anything without some reason. Especially smiling. He turned to face her and found himself tensing up again. She was still staring at him with those big, green eyes.

'I agree this is not the most pleasant of assignments,' he said. 'But it is an important one, nonetheless.'

'You have a charming way of understating things, Colonel Ruck. Now let's go to this pub of yours, shall we?'

∞

They drove in silence down the miles of waterlogged roads that wound through the valley. The Austin bumped along, the suspension shuddering and the frame rattling over every pothole. After a while they saw houses. Little red-brick cottages set back from the road, boundaries marked with low walls made from moss-covered stone, and tall trees dancing in the wind. There was a sign marking the entrance to a village. Ruck didn't catch the name. It wasn't what he was expecting but it would suffice.

He should have thrown her out of the car back at the farm. Dragged her out in the rain if necessary. She had no right, demanding to be taken to a bloody pub. He hadn't, though. The green eyes. The way her rain-sodden blouse clung to her chest after she had removed her coat.

Ruck gripped the Austin's wheel tighter.

A few more corners and they saw a larger building – an old mill converted into a public house. The sails had been removed and an extension had been bolted on.

The rain had eased to a gentle patter, although as they got out of the car there was a low rumble of thunder in the distance. Inside, the pub was pleasant enough. A fire burned in the corner and a black Labrador dozed on the hearth. Hops hung from the low ceiling above wooden beams and tired chairs. The only other customers were an old man apparently asleep at the bar and a gentleman engrossed in *The Times* sitting in the corner.

'Not seen you before,' remarked the barman, a man so wide that he took up a good proportion of the bar. He eyed them suspiciously, his gaze falling on Eva for longer than Ruck found acceptable.

'A whisky,' Ruck ordered. 'Miss Miller?'

'We don't allow women in the public bar, I'm afraid, sir. We have no lounge bar, either.'

Ruck felt a flush of annoyance. A quiet night away from the farm, that was all he wanted.

'I feel sure that an exception will not bring the walls caving in on their foundations,' he said dangerously.

'A gin, please,' said Eva.

'Some tonic water to accompany it?' asked Ruck, ignoring the barman's disapproving stare.

'No. Straight. On the rocks. Please.'

'I'm sorry, sir,' growled the barman. 'I can't serve her.' He stood, rubbing the pint glass with a cloth.

Ruck glanced around. No one was paying attention. He leant across the bar, grabbed the barman by his collar and pulled the man's head down so it was level with his. The barman uttered a strangled protest but Ruck's grip was immovable.

'Will you pour the lady a drink, or shall I do it for you?' Ruck hissed.

A few minutes later, Ruck placed the gin on the table in front of Eva. She took it and swallowed a surprisingly large mouthful. Taking off his wet coat, Ruck sat down next to her and took a sip of his own drink. The whisky was single malt, cheap and musty, but it did the job.

'How did you get this assignment?' Ruck asked, studying her. Her movements were purposeful. Everything Eva Miller did seemed to be calculated for effect. The way she touched her cheek when his eyes were upon her suggested an understanding of the world far beyond her years.

'I was a secretary to General Warrington. When the war was over I thought, like many others, that I would have to leave. But then a man came, a man like you. There were ten of us girls. He said that one of us would be selected for a very important assignment. That the pay was good but it was subject to extreme secrecy.'

'This man picked you.'

'He picked Rose. Not me.'

'And you're here because . . .?'

'Because Rose is dead.'

Ruck took another sip of the whisky. Out of the corner of his eye he could see the barman leaning on the corner of the bar nearest to them, straining to eavesdrop. He was about to ask how Rose had died, but Eva put her hand up.

'Colonel Ruck,' she said. 'The doctor you are interrogating . . .'

'Lower your voice, girl.'

'Of course. I'm sorry.'

Eva shuffled along the bench so she could speak in barely a whisper. Her shoulder brushed against his and he could smell the perfume Schneider had noticed. He stiffened, unsure. He felt as though he should shift to make an appropriate distance between them but he let her touch him.

She continued, 'Schneider said that he saw God.'

'Yes.'

'Do you think that is true?'

Ruck thought about it. 'No. Not for one minute.'

'What if you are wrong? I mean . . . there has to be a reason for it all, doesn't there? I mean what happened in Europe.'

Ruck put the whisky glass down slowly, not taking his eyes off her. 'The reason was not God.' He found the words sticking to the back of his throat. The hairs on the back of his neck were rising but he couldn't explain why – other than it was her doing. Somehow he could feel her, underneath his skin.

'No,' she whispered. 'You're right. How silly of me.'

Ruck swallowed the last of the whisky.

'We ought to be getting back,' he announced, standing.

'Yes. Of course.' Eva drank down the rest of the gin and stood up.

Ruck made his way across to the bar. As he opened the door, a gust of icy wind greeted him.

'Your coat!' Eva called. She picked it up from the bench and walked over to him, holding it out. It had been surprisingly easy to lift the piece of paper from the inside pocket. As easy as dropping the cyanide capsules into Rose's tea.

It was her flatmate's birthday, but Georgie Someday hadn't felt like going out. Not that this was unusual – she rarely felt like going out. In fact, she never felt like going out, least of all with her flatmates, of whom there were four – Mira, the birthday girl, Li, Fergus and Martin. However, in a moment of poor judgement, she had agreed to come along, having mistaken Mira's invitation to come to 'the theatre' as the prospect of an evening of civilised culture, whereas Mira had actually been referring to The Theatre, a sticky-floored bar downtown.

Georgie looked around her. It was freezing cold outside and every time the door opened to allow another scantily clad patron to stumble in, she was blasted by cold air that Captain Scott would have winced at. So why was she the only one who had brought a coat, gloves, scarf and hat? Were they all crazy?

Earlier that evening, she had watched Mira knock back another small glass of something that resembled washing-up liquid, so perhaps she should have guessed that her birthday wasn't going to be spent watching the RSC's interpretation of *Don Quixote*. Equally, Mira might have known that, given Georgie's love of Wagner, she might not enjoy an evening listening to Pearl Jam, but then despite the fact that they had all been at Oxford together, with the exception of Li, whom Georgie found tolerable, she didn't really know her flatmates all that well.

Martin was now shuffling up closer to Mira. He put his mouth to her ear, and she burst out in flirtatious fits of laughter. Georgie registered the look he had cast her, and the little smile playing at the corners of his mouth. He liked her watching him, she noticed. Liked her wariness of him, her embarrassment at what had happened. She wore her shame like a coat that only he could see.

Georgie pulled that coat tightly around her and looked away. Something knotted in her stomach.

They were huddled around the bar. Fergus was negotiating a round of drinks. They'd have one more, he had said, then head to Dojos, a dark, smoky and seedy local club. She planned to slip off home before they joined the queue. She'd shown her face. That was enough.

Fergus returned with a tray of shots. He placed the tray on the table and collapsed next to Georgie, then took one of the drinks and offered it to her. It was an unappealing shade of bright blue.

'How's work going?' he enquired in his deep Irish brogue.

'Fine,' said Georgie, inspecting the drink. It was a reply that was designed to discourage conversation.

As it happened, the last six months at Priest & Co had been the best of her life. She had finally found a place, a sense of worth, and an escape route from the people she had sat next to in law lectures. Mira was a paralegal at a high-street practice in

Sutton. She claimed she was in the tax department but in reality she was making tea and taking minutes. Fergus was a bum. Li was temping, probably through an agency. Martin had achieved nothing.

Georgie was one of the most successful students in her year at Oxford, and the only one out of her flatmates not to have squandered the opportunities that had been set out for her. And she had done it without Mummy and Daddy's help, too, unlike Mira, whose mother was the CEO of some trade body and whose father was a GP. Together, they were an interest-free bank. Georgie had a far humbler background. Her mother had had Georgie late and was now retired. Her father had died when she was twelve. They had known poverty – Georgie had negotiated with bailiffs on the doorstep on more than one occasion – but her mother had had a stroke of good luck last year. She had won a competition – fifteen hundred pounds per month for the rest of her life, increasing with inflation each year. Not much, but enough to sustain her when added to a couple of modest pensions.

Georgie's mother had never entered a competition in her life, something she had apparently put to the back of her mind. The reference on the direct debit was *Competition UK – Congratulations!* Georgie had not seen her mother so excited since her graduation. Georgie had set up a separate account so her mother couldn't trace the money back to her and she fed part of her wages through each month on a standing order. She didn't miss the money.

'It's a Blended Smurf,' Fergus explained.

'I'm sorry?' said Georgie, coming back to the present.

'The drink. It's called Blended Smurf.'

'Because it's blue or because it tastes like a mutilated ferret?'

Fergus laughed and downed his drink.

Georgie stared out across the bar to where a group of under-dressed girls were giggling stupidly over a phone, the glow of the screen throwing a faint artificial light on their feigned grins. She was vaguely aware that Fergus was attempting to tell her a joke – something about a vicar and a dildo – but she wasn't listening. She had noticed a broad-shouldered man near the door who, in designer jeans and a suit jacket, looked almost as out of place as she did. He was saying goodbye to an attractive blonde. She said something as she turned to leave and he smiled in return. She didn't think she had ever seen Charlie Priest smile like that. His whole face changed – he radiated affection for this woman. *Who can she be?* She was slim, stylish and she kissed him on the cheek with absolute self-assurance and confident familiarity, too. Georgie had understood – from Okoro – that Priest was single, but now she wasn't so sure.

She looked over at Martin. He had his arm around Mira. How ordinary he looked. How pathetic. Strange how he seemed so unthreatening; how relaxed Mira was. Did she know what he was really like?

Martin was a fraud. Not half the man her boss was. As Priest turned back towards the bar, their eyes met. Georgie held up her hand and waved awkwardly. To her delight, he smiled. Not the smile he had shared with the mysterious blonde woman, but a nice smile nonetheless.

'Hi, Georgie,' Priest breathed in her ear after making his way through the crowd. Martin had decided that now was a good time to show some interest in her and was leaning across the table. Fergus looked crestfallen but took the hint and slid away to talk to Li.

'This doesn't seem like your kind of place,' Georgie said.

'What kind of place would you expect to see me in?' Priest replied, cocking his head to one side.

She blushed. He had this infuriating habit of forcing her to say stupid things. *I have to think before I open my mouth.* He seemed to find her amusing.

'Well, you know . . . somewhere a bit more –'

'Quiet?' he suggested.

She grimaced, trying to find the right description. 'Less *studenty*.'

'Ah. I see. You're right. This isn't the sort of place for an old man,' said Priest with a mischievous smile.

'No, I didn't mean that!' Georgie could feel another blush rising.

'Georgie, relax. And you're right – this *isn't* my kind of place. The music I recognise involves a lot of heavily distorted synthesisers. The music I don't recognise appears to be just bass and devoid of any identifiable tune.'

'I know what you mean.' Martin was leaning in, trying to eavesdrop. 'Did you have any luck with the Attorney General?'

'No. He's dead.'

'Dead?' Georgie put her hand to her mouth. 'The Attorney General is *dead*?'

'Yes. Dead.'

She leant towards him. Maybe it was the bass, but she suddenly became aware that her heart was pounding in her chest.

'What happened?' she asked. 'This is a major thing, isn't it?'

'Not really. They'll just hire a new one.'

'No. I mean for you. My goodness! Did you find the computer data he sent you? He said it was sent to your home. When does your post come? I can't believe this is happening and we're just here in this awful place. Did you know this drink is called a Blended Smurf?'

'Georgie,' he held out his hands to slow her down. 'You need to breathe in more when you speak.'

'I'm sorry. I get ahead of myself when I'm . . . you know . . . nervous.' She paused. 'Was he impaled, like Miles Ellinder?'

'He hanged himself.'

'Oh – really? Why? I bet there's foul play. This is *so* extraordinary!' She stopped, realising that perhaps her enthusiasm might be coming across as insensitive. 'I mean – you know . . .' she tailed off.

'Don't worry, Georgie.'

Priest was looking at her sideways the way a parent might watch an overexcitable child. She wasn't sure that was a good thing. 'Listen, I've got an early start.'

'Oh, of course! Actually, we were just going to Dojos.' When he looked at her blankly, she explained, 'It's a club down the road. It's awful but you're welcome to come.'

'You're inviting me to an awful place?'

'Yes. No. I mean, yes.'

The party was indeed moving on to Dojos. Fergus was fiddling with the zip of his jacket and the others were standing up and collecting bags and phones from around the table.

'We're going, Georgie,' Li shouted across the table. 'You can bring your friend with you!' She winked and laughed. Beside her, Martin stood watching Georgie, straight-faced. Perhaps her chance to slip away quietly had been squandered.

'It's a very kind offer,' Priest was talking in her ear just to be heard, touching her shoulder with his hand. 'But I do have an early start in the morning. I'm going to head back.'

She knew there was no possibility that he would have agreed to join them, but she felt disappointed nonetheless.

They got up awkwardly at the same time. The others were starting to move towards the door; Mira was already staggering out into the maelstrom of night-time London. Georgie looked at Priest. He had the most extraordinary blue eyes, like crystals. She kissed him on the cheek and, by the look on his face he was as surprised as she was. Perhaps it was the spontaneity of the moment, or the fact that she hadn't caught his cheek square on and their lips had touched lightly; either way, it was clumsy. But clumsy as it was, by the time her flatmates had drunkenly marched her to the door of Dojos, the taste of Charlie Priest's kiss was still with her.

∽

Priest watched Georgie disappear into the crowd of people meandering past the bar. When he looked a second time to make sure she was all right, she had already vanished into the street. He liked Georgie – he liked her abrasiveness, her lack of tact, her innocence. It reminded him of himself, a long time ago.

The bar was getting noisier. The social-drinking students were beginning to be replaced with hordes of locals with their own agenda. Priest was about to leave his empty glass on the table where Georgie and her friends had gathered but there was a reasonable prospect it would be swept on the floor by some overenthusiastic dancer or, worse, smashed across somebody's skull. So he made his way through the ruckus to put his glass on the bar. The gril behind the bar looked over as he deposited the glass by the sink and smiled. Then he heard a familiar voice in his ear and his heart sank. *Oh, this isn't my night.*

'Didn't know you drank in these sorts of places, Charlie,' said the familiar voice. 'Come to think of it, didn't know you drank at all.'

Priest turned around. His brother-in-law, Ryan, was staring straight ahead, his fingers wrapped around an empty shot glass, an inane grin notched into his face. It was the chin that did it, Priest had decided a long time ago. A chin that jutted out so far you could sunbathe on it.

'Hello, Ryan,' Priest said.

Ryan was with friends. There was a bald guy with earrings, propped up against the bar facing him. He was a foot and half taller than Ryan. His thick lips were pursed threateningly and his eyes, unlike Ryan's, were firmly locked on Priest. He looked like he might be a handful. There were at least two others with him. One of them kept glancing over and laughing. They were all Ryan's age or thereabouts. In their late thirties – along with their IQs.

'Nice jacket, Charlie,' Ryan jibed.

This brought a howl of laughter from the third man, who was now leaning across the bald man to hear what was being said.

'Sarah said she had to be home early. You here to check up on her?'

'No. Didn't know she was here at all. Pure coincidence,' said Ryan, the grin widening.

'You're not looking after Tilly, then?'

'No. Someone else is.'

The problem was that someone else always was. Priest hated men who were lucky enough to have kids but shirked their responsibilities. The fact that it was his brother-in-law, his niece's father, made it much worse. Ryan was a joker, a fraud, undeserving of the gift of parenthood. Priest gritted his teeth. There was alcohol in his veins. Not a lot but, combined with his disassociation, enough to blur the edges of reality.

'*You* should be looking after her,' Priest told him.

'Why? That's what Sarah's for, isn't it? Lighten up, Charlie. Have a drink on me.'

'No. I'm just leaving.'

Ryan still hadn't looked at Priest, and he still hadn't removed his stupid grin. He got up, and as he did he struck Priest on the back of the shoulder, just hard enough to be less than playful.

'Mind how you go, brother,' Ryan sang. 'I've got some more drinking to do before I go back and nail your sister.' The third guy gave a bark of drunken mirth.

Priest glanced across at the big, bald man. He was the complication but also the key. Take him out, the rest would crumble.

Priest saw it play out. Saw himself take Ryan by the collar, ram him into the bar and then plunge his elbow into the big, bald man's abdomen, deep into the solar plexus. One well-judged strike destabilised the diaphragm, sending it into spasm, incapacitating him instantly. Next Priest slammed his palm into the back of Ryan's head, broke his jaw, dislodged a row of teeth on the bar. There was blood, lots of blood. People were screaming, running towards the door. The third man, Laughing Boy, was falling backwards, Priest's fist arching away from his limp body. The lights . . .

'Hey!'

Ryan was staring at him, clicking his fingers in front of his face. Priest blinked. Ryan looked perplexed and a little amused, but undamaged. Relief washed over Priest.

'What the fuck is wrong with you, Priest? You just pass out or something?' Ryan laughed.

Priest rubbed his hand over his face. He turned and left and the cold air outside hit him like a club.

Priest leant back in his office chair and watched a Sky News anchor with dimples report that the body of the Attorney General, Sir Philip Wren, had been found at his home yesterday morning and that the death was being treated as suicide. The reporter was standing at the bottom of Wren's driveway but it could have been anywhere.

It was morning, and raining. Priest had emailed Solly and asked him to prepare a detailed report on the Ellinder company structure and the financial strength of the group. Kenneth had said that money wasn't a motivation for his son's misadventures; it was time to test that theory. Moreover, if there was something unusual going on at Ellinder International then Solly would find it. Family businesses hid family secrets. After a moment he received a pithy response from Solly.

Yes.

The problem was getting into the Ellinder empire without Jessica interfering. And McEwen. He needed circumnavigating, too. He picked up the phone. Time to put the cat among the pigeons.

'Switchboard,' said a nasal voice.

Priest didn't hesitate. 'Dee Auckland, please.'

'Assistant Commissioner Auckland?'

'You have two Dee Aucklands?'

'Putting you through to her PA.'

A pause, followed by clicks and other encouraging telecom noises.

'Miranda Coleman,' said a new voice, higher-pitched than the first.

'I'd like to speak to Dee Auckland, please,' said Priest.

'Assistant Commissioner Auckland?'

'You have t— Oh, it doesn't matter. Can you please just put me through?'

'She's in an internal meeting at the minute.'

'Tell her it's Captain Kirk.'

Suddenly, the PA seemed less certain of herself. 'Captain K—'

'Kirk, yes. Captain Kirk,' said Priest pleasantly.

Pause.

'Wait one moment, please.'

Lengthy pause. Three minutes and sixteen seconds of pause, filled with some classical music. Tchaikovsky, *Swan Lake*. An odd choice. Even odder when interrupted with reminders of the Crimestoppers number.

Finally, 'What do you want, Charlie?' growled his ex-wife. She had an extraordinarily deep voice.

'Hi, Dee.' *It's so lovely to speak to you again after all these years. You sound as if you might not have given up smoking like we discussed in 2008.*

'What do you want?'

'Call off McEwen. I've got some shit to clear up and he keeps stealing my shovel.'

His ex-wife actually laughed. There had been a time, a very long time ago, when Priest had liked that laugh. The huskiness had been sexy, the depth of it intriguing – a laugh that had promised a future and had offered him solace. Now it sounded like nails on a schoolroom blackboard.

'Detective Inspector McEwen is performing his role admirably, Charlie,' said Dee slowly, as if she had to spell out the words to enable him to understand her.

You've lost none of your old charm, Lieutenant Uhura.

She began to rant in his ear, presumably for old time's sake. 'And this phone call is out of order and your request will be denied, as you well know. If there's nothing else . . .'

'McEwen's a prick, Dee. We both know that. He's got Wren's death all wrong. It wasn't suicide.'

'That's enough, Charlie.'

'Listen to me, Dee!'

'No, you listen to me. You pulled me out of a meeting whose attendees are right now sitting around a transparent board featuring pictures of your ugly mug on it next to a whole host of other unsavoury characters. You're a fucking person of interest, Charlie, in Miles Ellinder's death, and bugger me if I'm going to stand in the way of McEwen and his team as they dismantle you piece by piece.'

'Don't you think you should perhaps mention our brief but unforgettable marriage to your new buddies, Dee?'

'Fuck off, Charlie.'

'Dee, listen. Just cut me some slack, that's all I'm saying. You owe me that.'

'I owe you *nothing*, Charlie.'

When she hung up, the room was eerily quiet.

∽

Priest knocked and waited. He considered for a moment how many other principals knocked and waited patiently at the doors of those they employed. Very few, he supposed – but then there weren't many people who would even consider employing an accountant with severe OCD, let alone accommodate his peculiar little rituals.

After a while the door opened and Priest was permitted to shuffle in. He walked straight to the desk – which was completely clear of any of the usual paraphernalia one might associate with an office – and sat down, making sure that the chair didn't move from the grooves it had already cut into the carpet.

He glanced around quickly. The office wasn't clean – it was *immaculate*. It radiated orderly perfection. There were seven filing cabinets squeezed around two walls of the room, with one drawer for each letter and two drawers marked 'not used'. Priest knew that some of the drawers – X and Z, for instance – would be empty but, importantly, all of the files were alphabetised and separated. Books were categorised according to genre and size, pens dependent on size and colour. Behind the clear desk was another workspace with a laptop and a tape measure to make sure that it was set dead square in the middle of the desk surface. Everything was completely symmetrical. The two desks took up the central floor space with two bookcases facing each other on opposite sides of the room. It was freezing cold, to the point where Priest's breath was misting in front of his eyes. Solly had arranged for the radiator – which had been off-centre – to be removed. Priest knew that the blind was lowered by six hundred and fifteen millimetres because that meant the view from the desk was only of buildings, uncontaminated by patches of sky.

'Hello, Charlie,' said Solly.

The room might have been immaculate but, paradoxically, the occupant was not. Solly was in his early thirties but he had a blotchy skin complexion that made him look like a teenager. His hair was a receding, wiry mass of brown curls. He sat at the desk with his hands crossed over – the only breaches of the symmetry were the three identical red pens protruding from his blazer pocket.

'Hi, Solly.'

'I understand that Sir Philip Wren is dead,' Solly remarked, without the slightest trace of emotion.

'Yes. Very dead.'

'You and he knew each other?'

'He was my godfather.'

Solly nodded in what he presumably thought was an appropriate gesture. 'I've always wondered what it would be like to know someone who dies. How do you feel?'

'I have a headache.'

'Yes. Of course. I understand.'

It was clear to Priest that Simon Solomon did not understand in the slightest, but the effort was touching.

'The Ellinder Group?' Priest prompted.

'Ah, yes. The Ellinder Group. Most intriguing. There are three holding companies owned by various trusts that belong to the Ellinder family. Twenty-four subsidiaries in England, all registered to the same address. Accountants in Kensington. Associated companies in eight other countries including the UAE but it's mainly a domestic operation. The foreign ventures are relatively new, last five years. Looks like they felt they had cracked the UK drug market and they were looking to expand internationally. The operation is very internalised. They do everything themselves – research, manufacture, packaging, branding, distribution – hardly anything is farmed out.'

'Profitable?'

'Last year the group made ninety-four million, eight hundred and sixty-two thousand, four hundred and nine pounds after tax.'

Priest whistled. 'A hundred million pounds for chewable paracetamol.'

'Sorry?' Solly frowned and shook his head. 'What did you say?'

Priest didn't follow. 'I said, a hundred million pounds for chewable paracetamol.'

'No, that's quite wrong.'

'What?'

'It's not a hundred million. It's ninety-four million, eight hundred and sixty-two thousand, four hundred and nine. Also, this is not a company that specialises in the production of chewable paracetamol. In fact, chewable paracetamol accounted for less than point two per cent of global sales in the second quarter of –'

'OK, enough.' Priest held up his hands.

Solly blinked twice, as if he had just had dust thrown in his eyes. 'I have to finish my sentence,' Solly pointed out.

'Fine, but do so quickly.'

'I have to start from the beginning.'

It was true to say that Solly would have struggled in most high-street practices. He was, essentially, dysfunctional. But his ability to disseminate information, analyse figures and remember unfathomably large wads of data and text outweighed his social awkwardness.

As it happened, Solly never got to restart his sentence because the door opened. Without a knock.

'Please!' Solly protested. 'My door must not be opened more than forty-five degrees . . .'

His plea fell on deaf ears.

'Priest,' said Okoro. 'You'd better come downstairs.'

∽

Priest had never seen his waiting room so packed full of people. An untidy mixture of uniforms and suits were clustered around the low table that Maureen regularly adorned with copies of *The Times* and a few law periodicals to keep up appearances. McEwen had taken up a position at the back of the room, leaning arrogantly on the inside of the doorframe. His massive weight looked as though it might be enough to crack the wood and send him sprawling down the side of the building.

Maureen was getting on with some typing. When Priest arrived, she barely looked up.

'I've asked the gentlemen nicely to at least shut the door,' she told him, her old fingers not slowing even momentarily as they danced across the keyboard. 'They're letting the cold in.'

Okoro stood behind Priest, arms folded.

A small, wiry man with a light blue suit presented himself to Priest and held out a hand. Priest took it and shook firmly. The man announced that his name was Evans and he was a representative of the Crown Prosecution Service. He was in his early forties, maybe younger, with square glasses perched on a large, aquiline nose and prematurely grey hair that started halfway over the crown of his head and descended chaotically down the back of his neck. He looked as if he was experienced, but the little tremble in his voice betrayed his nervousness.

'This is a search warrant,' Evans explained before handing Priest a familiar-looking document. 'It entitles these officers to conduct a thorough search of these premises as part of the ongoing investigation into the death of Miles Ellinder.'

Priest glanced at the paper. No need to read – he knew what it said. It would be useful to know which district judge had signed it off, though.

He addressed Evans pleasantly. 'What are the grounds for suspecting that there is anything in these premises connected with the death of Miles Ellinder?'

'It is understood that you are acting for Kenneth and Jessica Ellinder, the father and sister of the deceased. There is reason to believe that either or both of these individuals – your clients – are involved in Mr Ellinder's death.'

Priest sniffed. The warrant had been signed off by District Judge Fearnly. Last year, Priest had taken one of Fearnly's decisions to the Court of Appeal. He had been successful and the higher court had been particularly scathing of the judge's handling of the case. Fearnly must have thought it was Christmas when Evans had come in front of him this morning and applied for a search warrant for Priest & Co's offices.

Priest looked up. Apparently, Evans was talking.

'Mr Priest? Are you hearing me?'

'Yes.' He caught McEwen's eye and the Scot nodded curtly. Priest returned the gesture. 'Where do you want to start?'

Evans raised an eyebrow. Priest guessed that most people put up more of a protest when presented with a document that entitled the police and anyone else they thought reasonably necessary to turn their places upside down.

'You heard the man,' McEwen barked gleefully from the back. 'Now do try not to leave Mr Priest's establishment in a complete mess, won't you?'

There was a general hum of approval from the crowd of officers occupying Priest's waiting room. They started to file forwards. Priest and Okoro didn't move. Evans turned away, satisfied or relieved – it wasn't clear which.

Priest said quietly to Okoro, 'We're not acting for the Ellinders. This is a fishing expedition. Get on to your friend in listing and get in front of a judge who doesn't dislike us and get this bloody thing rescinded.'

'I'll do my best, Priest, but I don't know how quickly I can do that.'

'I'll stall.'

Okoro looked sceptical. The police were conferring, obviously splitting up the task of dismantling the inside of the building. He made a quick phone call. When he finished, he whispered in Priest's ear, 'In front of Burrows. Twenty minutes. Can you buy me that?'

Priest nodded. Okoro was already out of the door. McEwen noticed him leave but didn't object.

Priest turned back to Evans. 'Can I have a copy of the notice, please?' he asked mildly.

Evans frowned, wrinkling his forehead. 'I gave you a copy of the warrant.'

'Yes. You did. But I'm also entitled to a copy of the Notice of Rights and Entitlements. It's a document that sets out my rights as a person subject to a search . . .'

'I *know* what it is,' spluttered Evans. 'You are a solicitor of the Supreme Court. You must surely *know* what your rights are?'

'A brush up now and again would do no harm.'

Priest smiled. Evans rubbed his face. He turned away. McEwen was breathing down his neck. Priest had guessed right. He hadn't brought a copy of the notice with him.

'Well?' growled McEwen.

'He's entitled to a copy of the notice,' Priest heard Evans explain reluctantly. 'I'll have to go back to the office to get one.'

'How long will that take?' McEwen demanded.

'In this traffic? Half an hour?'

McEwen grunted and nodded to the rest of the group to tell them to stand down and wait. He took up a seat opposite the reception desk while Evans scurried off. It was now a race to see who would come back first – and it would be tight. The court listing office had said twenty minutes, but that was assuming Burrows had finished whatever sorrowful case was in front of him.

'Anything from Hayley Wren?' Priest said to McEwen. The DI was slouched with Priest's waiting room chair wrapped around his backside. He was sweating again.

'What about her?' said McEwen irritably.

'Has she turned up?'

'Give it a rest, Priest. Wren committed suicide. The daughter's shacked up with some bastard somewhere and doesn't even know yet. Nothing to do with you. I'd be more worried about what my boys will turf out of your filing cabinets when Evans gets back, if I were you.'

Priest had nothing to hide, but it would be rather inconvenient to have the police tear his office apart. It would also be bad for business. And time was ticking away. McEwen had confirmed Hayley hadn't shown up, which meant she was still missing. It didn't bode well.

Priest wandered back to the reception desk and leant on the counter. Maureen looked at him sternly.

'What have you got yourself into this time, Charlie?'

'Nothing I can't handle.' When she looked at him incredulously he added, 'It's fine, Maureen. Honest.'

'You're an awful liar,' she said, turning back to her typing.

∽

Disappointingly, Evans won the race. He not so much entered as fell through the door to reception clutching a bundle of papers in his hand. He was out of breath and red-faced but still managed to thrust the papers into Priest's hand.

'Enjoy brushing up,' he wheezed.

McEwen rose from his seat. 'Don't think we can be that tidy now, Priest. Not now we've been made to wait.'

'Where are your files kept?' Evans demanded. He was annoyed, clearly, but the tremble in his voice was still evident.

Priest hadn't heard from Okoro and it was looking like he might have to give over to McEwen. He thought about Solly not allowing anyone to open his door more than forty-five degrees. He was up there now, probably sterilising the seat Priest had used. Solly wasn't going to cope with this. Priest needed to stall some more but his head had emptied itself of ideas.

'Which one of you is Evans?' Maureen shouted from behind the front desk.

'I am.'

'Phone call for you.' Without looking up, Maureen offered the receiver. Priest raised an eyebrow.

Evans looked baffled. McEwen halted his troops for a second time.

The CPS lawyer took the phone and placed it to his ear. 'This is Evans. Who . . .? Yes . . . Yes, sir. Good morning . . . Yes . . . As you know, I represent the Crown . . . yes. Yes. The order was granted earlier by District Judge Fearnly in circumstances where . . . yes? Yes, I see, sir. Indeed . . . Good morning, sir.'

He handed the receiver back to Maureen. The colour had drained from his face and he seemed to have aged ten years. He glanced at Priest, appeared to think about saying something but then sidled over to McEwen instead.

'That was District Judge Burrows,' Evans said weakly. 'The search warrant has been rescinded.'

'What does that mean?' growled McEwen.

'It means we go home. The basis for the warrant was establishing a solicitor–client relationship between Charlie Priest and Jessica or Kenneth Ellinder. That is apparently factually inaccurate –'

Evans never got to finish his explanation. McEwen was already out of the door.

22

Slowly, excruciatingly, Hayley Wren opened her eyes. For a moment, all she could see was intense white light.

She was lying down on a firm table, arms by her side. A breeze gently caressed her down one side. She might have been on a beach, somewhere warm, with the sea lapping at her feet and the gulls squawking overhead.

She closed her eyes again. The impression of the beach drifted away and was replaced by the terrifying image of a hooded face coming for her, tearing through the darkness, screaming her name.

She opened her eyes. The figure vanished. A slowly turning ceiling fan came into view. Her mouth felt hot and acidy – she guessed she had been sick at one point.

She tried to lift her arm to touch her face, make sure everything was intact, but her arm didn't move. She was strapped down to the table. She shifted from one side to the other. Her arms and legs were held fast, and a strap was across her midriff, too.

Panic seized her. *Where am I?* She remembered the hooded figure taking hold of her from behind. She had tried to break free but he had overpowered her easily and had held a handkerchief over her face that stank of . . . she wasn't sure. Fuel?

She had fought with all her strength. She had prayed, too. She remembered praying to Jesus to help her. *Why did He not come?*

A room came into focus. White-washed walls and a naked bulb swinging over her head, underneath the ceiling fan. The table was raised, maybe four feet off the floor. She couldn't turn her head all the way round but the room appeared to be windowless and the only form of light came from the harsh bulb above her.

Maybe I'm already dead. Maybe this is Purgatory and I am awaiting judgement.

She looked down her body to her feet. She was naked, covered only by a thin white sheet from shoulders to knees.

This is not Purgatory!

She tried to scream but the sound stuck in her throat – she felt like her own fear was suffocating her.

My God, what's happening to me? What has already happened to me?

From the corner of her eye she saw a movement. A figure was gliding around the back of her. She felt the hair on the back of her neck rise as a hand moved over her shoulder, stopping just above her breast – where her heart was threatening to explode inside her chest.

Her throat constricted and she closed her eyes again. Tried to think of something, anything, to distract herself from what was happening. She tried to remember the beach again, and the gulls overhead, the hot sand on her back and the sun on her face, but the vision was blurred and, in the end, the sun was blotted out by a cloud. A white hood with two black eye sockets.

A voice rumbled in her ear.

'Hello, Hayley.'

23

The little wooden tables were covered with easy-wipe plastic sheets patterned with fading strawberries and raspberries. The cutlery was thick and heavy, the mugs were mismatching and stained slightly yellow.

Jessica sat with her hands on her lap. She seemed to be trying to avoid touching anything. Priest was studying the menu; every now and again he glanced at her. He found her discomfort mildly amusing.

'I'm not hungry,' she announced all of a sudden.

'Are you sure?' He looked up, surprised. 'The breakfast here is like nothing you've ever tasted.'

'I don't normally have breakfast at one o'clock and I don't like fry-ups.'

Priest was disappointed. 'There are other things. Bacon butty? Black pudding tower?'

'Do they have anything vegetarian?' Jessica asked.

Priest mulled it over. 'I think they replace the bacon with extra mushrooms, the black pudding with a tomato and the sausage with . . . well, I think they just remove the sausage.'

Jessica made a face. An old woman wearing an apron hovered over them, pencil poised expectantly. She had two large front teeth that looked like playing cards jammed precariously in her gums.

'Yes, duck?' she croaked.

Priest looked at Jessica pleasantly. She shook her head.

'Two specials, please,' he said.

The waitress bustled off. She passed the slip of paper through a hatch on the far wall where it was collected by a very hairy hand. Priest had never seen the owner of that hairy hand. He had no desire to. He just knew that, for some reason, that hairy hand knew how to make very good scrambled egg.

'The invitation to eat was kind,' she remarked in a way that suggested otherwise.

Priest nodded while he poured the tea. There was a ring on her middle finger today. It was understated – a simple design, but, even to Priest's untrained eye, the stone sparkled with affluence – much like its owner.

'We had a little visit this morning,' Priest told her. 'Our friendly neighbourhood policeman popped in to see me.'

'Ah. McEwen. A pleasure for you, no doubt.'

'Quite. He is working under the apprehension that you and your father are somehow involved in Miles's death.'

He had expected her to react violently to this but she just shrugged and added two sachets of sugar to her tea.

'My father and I have already identified DI McEwen's inadequacies. Hence our approach to you.'

'That was your father's idea, though. Not yours.'

'Perhaps. But I trust his judgement.' She stirred her tea rather too vigorously.

'You intimated that you and your brother didn't get on?' Priest suggested.

'Yes,' she admitted. 'Miles didn't really get on with anyone. Daddy paid a lot of money to prevent him from destroying the business.'

'He was the black sheep?'

'Mr Priest, my family is one big flock of black sheep.' She gave a thin smile.

'Your father is concerned that Miles had become entangled in something dangerous.'

She fixed him with a penetrating stare. 'Isn't that obvious? Someone impaled him.'

Priest poured a drop of milk into his own cup and stirred. 'Have you heard of Vlad the Impaler?' he asked.

'Yes. I understand he was the source for Dracula.'

'Do you think somebody was trying to make a point by murdering Miles in such a barbaric way?'

'I have no doubt, but the point eludes me.'

'No vampires in the family, then?'

She took a sip of tea, glancing at him from behind the mug. He couldn't help thinking that somewhere deep down she had a sense of humour. At least he hoped so. If there wasn't, then he had genuinely offended her several times already and they hadn't even started the food.

'They tell me you're a horror film buff, Mr Priest,' she said shortly.

'I wasn't aware that your research on me extended to my personal habits.'

'You think we would entrust a matter that threatens my family's survival without first finding out everything we can about our preferred champion?'

Priest smiled. *So she does have a sense of humour.*

When he didn't say anything further, she went on. 'Can you tell me who the creator of the modern vampire myth is?'

'That's easy. Some people attribute it to Lord Byron but in fact it was his personal physician, John Polidori. Byron may have been Polidori's original source, but he was not the begetter of the creature who would later be refined by Stoker.'

'Indeed,' she said. 'How fascinating that literature's two greatest monsters – the vampire and Shelley's reanimated fiend – were conceived at the same time, in the same house, no less.' She paused.

'Some still say it was Byron,' Priest pointed out.

'What do you like about horror films?'

Priest hesitated before he replied. He was used to conducting the cross-examination, not being the witness. 'Connection, I guess. In other film genres, you generally laugh at funny things, cry at sad things, but you're detached, an observer. In horror, you feel the fear that the character feels. You are connected to the story in a completely different way. You're part of the production.' He might have added that feeling a connection to anything when you have disassociation disorder was an achievement.

The waitress returned with two plates of prime English breakfast dripping with grease, and deposited them on the table.

Priest cleared his throat. 'We need to find Hayley,' he said.

Jessica looked up from her inspection of the plate. 'Why?'

'Because she's been missing for a week and no one else cares.'

'No, that's why *you* have to find her. I'm asking, why do *we* have to find her?'

Priest started to cut up a very thick sausage. It had the diameter of the truncheon Miles Ellinder had used to cosh him. 'Her father has most likely just been murdered and now she's missing. Maybe that's a coincidence, maybe it isn't.'

'Is this your way of saying that you would now like to reconsider my father's commission?'

Priest examined the sausage. There had probably been more meat in the truncheon.

'We have a common goal, Jessica,' Priest said gravely. 'Might as well work together.'

'Apparently, we don't. My goal is to find my brother's killer and put this nasty business to bed. Yours seems to be to find the Attorney General's daughter and have someone keep the police off your back while you look.'

'They're connected, inescapably. Wren wrote to me saying that he had sent me a flash drive containing computer data. Your brother turns up at my flat looking for – lo and behold – a flash drive containing computer data. Chances are, they were referring to the same flash drive which, incidentally, I haven't found.'

'That's highly inconvenient.'

It was clear she didn't believe him. He didn't blame her – it wasn't the first time he would have held back information from her.

'It's a fact that rather underlines the limitations of our investigatory routes,' he pointed out.

'And finding Hayley helps us how?'

'I don't know until we find her.'

Jessica continued her examination of the breakfast, prodding the beans with her fork. She looked as if she was making sure it wasn't alive.

'You going to eat that black pudding?' Priest asked, his mouth full.

Without speaking, she slid the black pudding on to his plate, making an obvious effort to keep her hands as far away from the food as possible. He mixed everything up. It dawned on Priest that this was the first proper meal he had eaten since Miles had visited him.

'Tell your father I'll take the job,' he said.

Jessica got up. She picked up a Radley handbag and put on a pair of large sunglasses. It was still cold outside, but the rain had relented and the sun was streaming in through the cafe window.

'I'll see if the offer is still open for acceptance,' she announced before leaving.

∞

Priest was heading home. He had planned to go to the office after his late breakfast with Jessica but he realised that wasn't a good idea. He studied his hand carefully. It looked like a rubber accessory attached to an animatronic arm, like something out of a puppet show. *Fuck. Not now.* He glanced out of the black cab window to the world beyond with a growing sense of dread, knowing that his perception was already beginning to warp. *I am a ghost. A cursed ghost.*

There was still time. Time, he thought, during which he could function properly, although the boundaries were blurring quickly, quicker than usual. He'd taken a taxi – unusual but the easiest way to secure a safe arrival to his flat, but they'd been forced to take a detour because Oxford Circus was littered with hippies bearing billboards.

'Bloody anti-capitalists!' the cabbie exclaimed. 'They stomp around London all day complaining about making money and then Tweet about it all evening on their bloody iPhones. Talk about hypocrites.'

Priest barely heard him. His phone was ringing. Had he called someone? Okoro's deep voice vibrated in his ear.

'You OK, Priest?'

'Fine,' Priest said uncertainly.

'That's good. How can I help you?'

'What?'

'Priest?'

Priest clicked his tongue. 'Just popping home for an hour or so. I'll be fine.'

'I see. Quite some result this morning.'

'What?'

'This morning,' repeated Okoro. 'My audience with District Judge Burrows during which the learned judge made some interesting observations about the warrant. Said it should never have been granted in the first place.'

'Yeah,' said Priest, detached.

'I bet the CPS lawyer's face was a picture when Burrows telephoned him.'

'Yeah.'

Okoro paused. 'Priest, are you with me?'

'Not really.'

'Mm. Well, goodnight, sweetheart. I'll send someone to come and find you if you don't check in by the end of the day.'

The phone went dead.

∽

Priest stumbled towards the front door of his apartment with no recollection of exiting the taxi, or paying for it. He searched for his keys. He was vaguely aware of people walking past him, laughing and jostling for space on the busy pavement. He looked away quickly. One of them had a dog's head with a big wet tongue flapping down the side.

Not again . . .

The door was moving, swaying in and out of focus. The path felt like it was a ship's galley and he was struggling to fit the key into the lock. It didn't seem the right size, or the lock was the wrong size. Or both. He couldn't tell.

He examined the key carefully. He recognised it, but not the hand holding it. Worried, he looked around. There was a set of steps near the door that led down to the basement area. *There are bins down there.* Again, it was familiar, but he had the disturbing sensation that it wasn't his.

He half fell down the steps.

There was a bin, as he suspected. It was an old one – round and made of steel. Not one of those new ones on wheels that were colour-coded. The colours denoted something but he couldn't remember what. There was a horrible distorted noise coming from inside the bin. After a moment, he realised it was the sound of his own laughter.

He thought about Jessica Ellinder and her half-hidden eyes staring at him through waves of thick, auburn hair.

'Charlie?'

He recognised the voice. Or was it just that he recognised his name? Then there was more noise. The sound of someone else descending the stone steps quickly and rounding the corner.

A fleeting thought entered his mind – he was trapped.

'Charlie?' The voice was soft and sweet, like silk. 'What the fuck are you doing in my bin?'

∞

Priest was looking through a frosty window at a scene playing out. A woman was standing at a kitchen counter, pasting butter on to toast. She seemed worried; something was bothering her. A man sat hunched over the kitchen table, head resting on an outstretched arm. Priest recognised himself and he felt a flush of shame. He was staring out of the window, not at himself looking in, but beyond, into the middle distance. The kitchen was small but neat with a matching red kettle and toaster. There was the smell of coffee in the air – a smell he thought he should like but that now seemed nauseous and oppressive.

After a while, he felt his hand burning on the cup. It hurt and he examined it to see if it was damaged. There was no label on it to tell him how to fix it if it was damaged. He should be concerned – but he wasn't. It didn't matter. It was definitely his hand, just somewhat distorted.

She was talking to him. The woman who had been making toast. She was concerned, perhaps even a little annoyed at something.

He had a vague feeling of unease. He knew the man at the table and the woman by the counter, who was now tending to his burnt hand.

His hand throbbed.

'Jesus, Charlie,' said the woman. He was surprised he could hear her so well through the window. He noticed that the kettle was black. *Had it not been red earlier?* 'You need to stop doing this. Can you hear me?'

Priest heard her, but the voice was now muffled, like a train platform announcement.

There was a black spot in the corner of his eye moving slowly across his vision. A darkness descending. A pain ran down the right-hand side of his face, enough to make him check if he was bleeding. His stomach felt like a giant hand had taken hold of his gut and was twisting and wrenching it out of place.

'I'm worried about you, Charlie,' the woman was saying. 'It's getting worse. It's just – you know – I don't want ... I don't know. I'm just worried.'

'What worries you?' he said.

'You swear you never remember what happens. You just live for hours in like a vacuum. Doesn't that scare you?'

'Yes.'

'And what is it? A dream?'

Priest thought about it. No, it wasn't like a dream. In a dream – especially a vivid one – reality is fabricated. There is no sense in a dream that anything is wrong. The stage is set, the backdrop complete. But, critically, when consciousness returns, so does reality and you are left with a sense of relief or disappointment that what preceded wakefulness was only a dream. In *this* world, reality bleeds away slowly and is replaced by a hollow, colourless world utterly distinguishable from a dream.

He was aware that time was passing.

'No,' he said. 'It's not a dream.'

'Do you know who I am? Right now?'

She was sitting very close to him.

'Yes. You're Sarah. My sister.'

'Good.'

He blacked out.

When the darkness subsided Priest found himself lying fully clothed on an unknown bed surrounded by crimson-coloured walls holding shelves covered with books.

Fuck.

He had no idea what time it was and the light hurt his eyes. William's description of emerging from a disassociation episode rang in his ears. *Take the worst hangover you've ever had, multiply it tenfold and then imagine downing a bottle of vodka in one.* The last thing he remembered was phoning Okoro in a taxi but he couldn't remember the conversation. He vaguely recalled drinking coffee in Sarah's kitchen. That probably happened, although derealisation warped his memory.

Jesus. I really don't like coffee.

The last few hours were like trying to remember a place he had only been to once in the fog.

He hoped he wasn't at Sarah's house but the marketing textbooks suggested he was. He held his head in his hands, trying to focus. He tried to sit up but a pain had taken hold in the back of his head and he fell back down on to a lumpy pillow. He stank of sweat, his legs felt heavy. He felt ashamed, again.

'*We are the same, brother,*' said William in his head.

'Hi, Uncle Charlie.'

He had no idea how long Tilly had been standing at the doorway. Despite the pain, he forced his head up and managed a smile, which she didn't return. She had a beaker of something in one hand and her bunny in the other.

'Hi, sweetheart. Hope I didn't scare you.'

She came through and placed the beaker delicately on the bedside table. She seemed to fade in and out of focus as she walked across the room like an apparition. Priest had to concentrate to keep her in one piece.

'I got you juice,' she explained. 'Mummy said don't bother you but you might be thirsty, right?'

'That's very kind of you and, as it happens, I'm *really* thirsty.'

She giggled as he drank greedily from the beaker, sloshing it down purposefully to draw more laughter. He relaxed a little. And he *was* thirsty, too – parched. It felt as though he had eaten nothing but salt since breakfast. Seemingly, Tilly had made the juice herself from cordial mixed with two or three teaspoonfuls of water at best. It tasted of syrup but he didn't mind.

When he had finished, she hopped up on the bed next to him. He wondered if Ryan was in the house. Probably not if Tilly had come through to see him, which was a relief. He could hear the gentle clash of dishes downstairs – Sarah making dinner for them.

'Mummy said you were poorly. Are you OK now?' Tilly asked with genuine concern beyond her six years.

'I'm much better, thank you, darling. I think your juice made the poorly go away.'

'That's good. Would you like to come bowling with us later?'

'Oh, that's very kind but no, thank you. I have to get back home.'

Tilly looked disappointed. 'We're not going bowling anyway.'

'Then why did you ask?'

'I thought maybe if *you* wanted to go then Mummy would take us.'

He laughed and kissed her on the forehead. She wrinkled it and giggled. For a moment, he saw Sarah staring back at him. And William, before he had started killing people.

'Welcome back,' said Sarah. She was standing in the doorway, although Priest had no idea how long she had been there either.

'Sorry,' Priest groaned. 'I think I –'

'Vincent Okoro phoned. He was worried about you.'

'I was talking to him before –'

'Yes. Funny how the whole world runs around worrying about you, Charlie, and what do they get in return?'

Priest bit his lip but didn't reply. He couldn't work out what to say. Sarah rolled her eyes and motioned for Tilly to come out of the room. The little girl hesitated but, seeing the look on her mother's face, scurried out.

'I'll make you a sandwich.' Sarah sighed. She turned to leave.

'I don't deserve you, Sarah,' Priest managed to call after her.

She looked back over her shoulder and grinned. 'You're damn right, you don't.'

24

Hayley was finding it difficult to breathe. Her lungs had deflated and her windpipe had contracted dangerously so she had to resort to snatching short gulps of air in between agonising periods of stillness. The hooded figure was standing over her, his hand massaging her naked shoulder.

'I'm sorry for scaring you earlier,' he said.

Hayley closed her eyes. She wanted to scream until her throat burnt away, but she couldn't move. She was still lying flat on a metal table with a white sheet draped over her naked body. Her stomach hurt and she could taste blood in her mouth. How long had she been here? She had drifted in and out of consciousness for hours, occasionally waking to find the hooded man staring over her, murmuring softly. Now she was fully awake, he stayed in the room.

'What do you want?' she gasped.

His hand was under the sheet now, moving further down to the top of her breast. She tensed every muscle in her body, forced herself to writhe as much as she could, to fight against the straps holding her down. Anything to stop what was happening.

But her efforts were futile.

'I want you to help me, Hayley,' the hooded man explained.

To her horror, he gently peeled the sheet down to her waist, exposing her top half to the cold air of the room. He leant across her, the hood against her neck. Even through the material she could feel his hot breath on her skin.

Jesus? She opened her eyes, the brightness of the artificial lighting momentarily blinded her. *Jesus, are you there?* She had never doubted that before. So why, in this desperate moment, did she doubt it now? *Please help me, Jesus. I . . .*

She was light-headed, the room was spinning. She realised that she was hyperventilating, her brain swimming with excess oxygen. Much more and she would drown.

She wheezed. Every word was excruciating. Her lungs felt as if they were going to explode. 'Are you . . . going to rape me?'

The hooded man laughed gently in her ear. *My God!* His hand was on her breast, his fingers digging into her skin.

'No. That would be most unbecoming of me.'

Then what? Her stomach convulsed and she thought she might retch. *What do you want from me? Jesus! What does he want from me?*

He removed his hand and stood upright beside her. From behind his back, he produced a metal tin and positioned it at the end of the bed. He was humming tunelessly to himself.

Hopelessness suddenly overwhelmed her; her stomach churned again. She turned her head to the side and vomited. *Jesus, why have you abandoned me!* The warm, acid fluid spilled out over the table and down her chin and neck. She gasped for air.

The hooded man did not move. He just watched her through the two slits in the hood until she had finished before moving around to her other side and examining her arm. He reached down and took out something from the metal tin at the end of the bed. Something that made her blood freeze.

I'm going to die. Jesus, I'm going to die.

The hooded man held the needle up to the light and checked it carefully. Gently, he squeezed the syringe. A clear liquid dropped on to the bed.

'What's that?' she panted.

'Something very special, Hayley.'

'*No!*' Hayley cried out in pain and anguish, fighting against the straps around her ankles and wrists. It was no good.

He pressed the needle into her arm.

There was nothing at first. Then she saw it. Her veins, engorged from the stress of trying to resist, blackened. A dark shadow began to spread across her arm from the point where the needle had penetrated her. Something was taking control of her, consuming her. Swallowing her whole. *The Devil is inside of me!* It crept across her like a black vine wrapping itself around her arm, right up to her shoulder.

Then every nerve in Hayley's body erupted in inconceivable pain.

25

Georgie reflected on the previous evening out while getting ready for work. Following Fergus's altercation with one of the bouncers, they had been ejected from Dojos prematurely and found themselves in the corner of a bar down the street. She hadn't enjoyed any of it; the evening had served as a reminder of how detached she had become from her so-called friends.

Martin had largely ignored her. Until Charlie had turned up, that was. Was he worried that their secret wasn't as secure as he thought? She pinched the bridge of her nose; her eyes were still stinging.

She decided to let her hair fall over her shoulders today. She wasn't sure that tying it back was sending out the right message. Too much *I'm in control.* But wasn't that what she was supposed to be doing? Taking back control?

Georgie resolved to do two things after work – first, find another house, by herself. Her income wouldn't enable her to buy anything, not when a one-bed flat the size of a shoebox cost half a million pounds locally, but she might be able to lodge or maybe even rent somewhere just outside the city's central zone. And Charlie was a generous employer. Forty-five grand a year plus bonuses for a newly qualified and inexperienced solicitor was well above the average. Second, she would confront Martin. *Let's talk about what happened that night, one year ago.*

There was a knock at the door.

Li was half dressed, garbed luxuriously in a silk teal dressing-gown embroidered with a red-and-gold dragon down the side. It had probably cost more than Georgie's whole wardrobe. Her hair was wet. Georgie wondered if she had woken up alone.

'Good morning,' Li said brightly. She looked perfect, as always. Certainly not the way someone who had only had two hours sleep should look. 'Can I borrow your straighteners? Mine are on the blink.'

Whatever she did, Li's hair would dry perfectly. She hardly needed straighteners. But Georgie was prepared to indulge her. If she moved, she might even miss Li. A fleeting thought crossed her mind – *would Li like to move in with me?* Together, with Georgie's salary from Priest & Co and Li's income from escorting and her father's credit card, they could probably afford somewhere more central.

'Sure. They're over there,' Georgie said, gesturing to a chest of drawers covered in books.

Li fumbled around in the drawers for a moment. 'They're still in the box. Do you use these?'

'Not really. I don't have many – you know – girly things.'

Li laughed good-naturedly. 'I don't know how you survive, Georgie.'

Georgie shrugged. 'Somehow, I guess.'

'Mm. So what about Martin and Mira, then?'

Georgie carried on getting ready. Perhaps that way Li would get the message and the conversation would be short.

'Yeah. It's something, eh?' Georgie said without enthusiasm.

'I heard them. His room's above mine. Fuck, made even *me* blush!'

'Wow.'

Georgie collected a pilot's bag full of papers and books. Her guide to the Civil Procedure Rules, two spare counsel's notepads, a copy of Archibald and a copy of Chitty. One of the reasons why she had taken the job at Priest & Co had been the opportunity to work in both civil and criminal law. Li stood around for a moment, evidently not sure what to do next.

'You're not . . . you know?' Li was watching her reaction carefully.

'Not what?' asked Georgie curtly.

'You know! Bothered or anything?'

'About what?'

'Oh, Georgie. About Martin and Mira getting together. About them spending the whole night fucking like rabbits in the room down the hall?'

'Li!'

'I'm just looking out for you.'

This was probably true, but Georgie knew full well that Li was also very keen to satisfy her own curiosity.

'It doesn't bother me in the slightest,' Georgie said. It didn't sound particularly convincing, even to herself.

'You're not . . . *jealous*?'

Georgie hesitated, trying to gauge Li's expression. Did she know? 'It's . . . more complicated than that.'

Li smiled, but her eyes were disbelieving. Georgie thought better of saying anything else on the subject. She put on her glasses and made for the door.

'Sorry, Li. Got to dash. Busy day.'

'Busy day with that very handsome boss of yours?'

'Hm?'

'The guy you spoke to last night? That was your boss, right?'

'That was Charlie Priest.'

'Fuck. How do you manage to stay so cool all the time around *him*?'

'I – I've never –'

'Thought about it? Oh, come on, Georgie. Even you . . .'

'Even me what?'

Georgie glared at Li. She could be such a nosy busybody sometimes. Georgie resolved not to ask whether she was interested in sharing a flat. *This is why I'm not a people person. People annoy me too easily.*

'Sorry,' said Li. She at least had the decency to look a little sheepish.

26

Jessica Ellinder was waiting by her car when Priest stumbled out of his apartment block and into the frost-covered road. Even in the weak, Sunday morning light, she looked impatient. Her breath misted in front of her.

'You're late,' she said as he approached.

'Sorry. I'm not good with mornings.'

Jessica looked him up and down. 'You're wearing a suit jacket over a T-shirt.'

He looked down. 'Apparently.'

Jessica climbed in the driver's side. Priest paused before opening the car door and taking the passenger seat. It was bolt upright.

'How do you –' Priest looked around for some way to adjust the seat.

'It's the one above the lumbar support. Sorry, Wilfred usually likes it like that.'

She had insisted on driving. The precaution was entirely justified – Priest's old Volvo had never travelled further north than Watford and he doubted its capability to get them safely to Cambridge.

'Wilfred's your dog?'

'What led you to that conclusion?' Jessica asked.

'You're single, and Wilfred's a lousy name for a horse. And horses prefer their seats reclined.'

She sighed. 'I'm single?'

'No ring,' he explained.

'I could very well not be single but have no desire to wear a ring, or indeed any reason to.'

'You're single,' Priest grunted. *I note that you didn't take offence at the presumption that you have a horse, too.* 'I checked with Terri Wren this morning. Hayley still hasn't shown up. That was why I was late.'

'I heard the news. Philip Wren's death is being announced as suicide. He suffered from severe depression. There'll be a service after the body is released. The family will be setting up a trust fund for mental illness.'

'Bullshit.'

'Maybe. But whoever killed Miles did it in spectacular fashion. Why switch MO and fake a suicide?'

Priest had already calculated the possibilities. All of them seemed as unlikely as each other.

'You and Wilfred often take drives together?' he said eventually.

'If you stick your head out of the window and yelp at the postman on the way it'll be like any other road trip for me,' she said venomously.

They stopped to refuel and Priest resisted the temptation to buy a packet of cigarettes. He made do with a Coke. She had coffee. He had offered to operate the pump and she had looked at him strangely as if to say, 'You think I can't refuel my own car?' After that they had sat in silence until they reached the outskirts of Cambridge and entered the maze of sandy, baroque buildings and narrow, car-repelling streets. Students in skinny jeans wobbled dangerously on bicycles around them as they drove slowly into the centre.

'I had Solly build up a profile of Hayley based on her social media activity,' said Priest.

'That doesn't seem like a very accurate way of profiling someone,' she mused.

'It isn't.'

'And what has he deduced?'

Priest took a deep breath. 'She's introverted, religious, intelligent but socially naive. She has a very small group of friends but none of them apparently know her particularly well and I suspect, apart from her various blogs – which are probably written for her own self-preservation rather than for anyone else's benefit – she keeps herself to herself. And, like you, she's single.'

Jessica scowled.

∽

The Creation Church was identified by a sign promising free entry to the Kingdom of Heaven for people who spread the Word. In reality, it was less of a church and more of a community centre. According to the pinboard in the foyer, the last event of any significance had been the Women's Institute race night, two weeks ago.

'This is it?' Jessica asked.

'Solly says this church is mentioned a number of times in Hayley's blogs.'

'I was expecting something more –'

'Not all religions have the resources to build cathedrals, Jessica.'

She turned up her nose. 'A church with an IPA beer pump strapped to the reception desk?'

'I bet Holy Communion is a most fulfilling experience here.'

The interior was as tired as the exterior. A room of reasonable proportions, plastic chairs stacked in one corner, peeling white lines on the floor loosely delineating a badminton court. At the unmanned reception desk, one could pick up a copy of the Creation order of service or a pint of dark, sediment-filled ale – the choice was yours.

A voice hailed them from across the room. They turned and saw a man in a dark suit standing in a doorway that led through to a small kitchen. He was younger than Priest, with a beard as dark as his clothes and heavy glasses. He was good-looking, slim and wouldn't have looked out of place in a courtroom, were it not for the worried expression and awkward stance. Priest doubted that the Creation Church saw many unfamiliar faces, especially not ones dressed as stylishly as Jessica Ellinder. Priest hadn't shaved, and probably looked as though he was more likely to be here for the beer than the homily.

'Hello? Can I help you?' the man asked.

'My name is Charlie Priest; this is my associate, Jessica Ellinder.' Priest held out his hand.

The bearded man took it firmly. 'Reverend Matthew,' he offered.

'Reverend?' Jessica gestured to her throat, where the dog collar should be.

He laughed nervously. 'Oh, we don't go in for that sort of thing round here, Ms Ellinder. We're all equals, preacher and flock.'

Jessica smiled and he relaxed a little.

'We wonder whether you could help us, Reverend?' said Priest.

'Yes?' Reverend Matthew narrowed his eyes a little, the first sign of defensiveness.

'We're private investigators,' Priest explained. This was not a complete lie – essentially that was what many civil lawyers were.

Matthew frowned. 'I see.'

'We're looking for a young woman. Mid-thirties, long wavy blonde hair, reserved. A member of this church,' Priest explained.

'We have lots of those, Mr Priest.'

'Her name is Hayley Wren.'

'Yes,' he said without hesitation. 'Yes, Hayley is one of our regular attendants. One of our flock. Is she in some kind of trouble?'

'No,' said Jessica. 'But it's important we find her.'

Reverend Matthew faltered. He seemed to be debating something internally.

Priest picked up on it. 'As my colleague says, Reverend Matthew, it's important we find Hayley as soon as possible. Can you help us with that?'

'Who hired you?' he asked. His cheeks were flushed and he looked more troubled than when he had first appeared at the kitchen door.

'Hayley's mother,' Priest said.

'Hayley – Hayley had no parents that I am aware of. They died in a car crash. That's what she said.' Reverend Matthew looked worried.

'No,' Priest corrected. 'Her father is – was – the Attorney General.'

'To be honest, I thought as much,' Reverend Matthew said, as much to himself as to Priest or Jessica. 'I suspected she had family ties. She was a very private person. Very *inward*. She would rather lie about her kin than admit to anything that might lead to questions being asked.'

'Where is she, Reverend?' Priest was beginning to feel uneasy. He took a step forward.

Matthew glanced at Jessica and then back at Priest. He seemed to make a decision. 'Come through,' he invited.

He ushered them into the kitchen, then through a locked door and into an office of sorts. There was an old cash register on the side next to a gambling machine, and a table took up most of the space. Cigarette trays lined every surface. Evidently, the smoking ban hadn't quite penetrated the back room of the Creation Church. The stench was overpowering.

'I'm afraid rates in the city centre are high,' Matthew said. 'This is the best we can do. We are hardly the Church of Scientology when it comes to fiscal resources.'

'You don't have to be apologetic, Reverend,' Priest told him. They took seats – Priest and Jessica on one side of the table, Matthew on the other.

'Sometimes we use this room for cleansing rituals,' Matthew said.

'Cleansing rituals?' Jessica queried.

'The Catholics call it confession,' Matthew continued. 'Although our version is more like an informal therapy. Come in and lift the weight of the world off your shoulders. In here, we give out advice and support to those who need it. We do not offer the hollow concept of *forgiveness*. We don't promote guilt as a good thing.'

Priest nodded. For a cleric, Matthew seemed pretty down to earth. And there was an integrity in his eyes that was impossible to dismiss but something else too – a fervent disquiet.

'Was Hayley ever cleansed in this room?' Priest asked.

Matthew talked earnestly. 'Yes. I heard her. It was about a week ago, I think. That was one of the first times I had really spoken to Hayley. I knew who she was, of course. She was here every week. I'd tried to communicate with her, tried to get her to engage, but she made it clear that she was happy sitting at the back. She just wanted to be part of the furniture. Sometimes it's like that.

'So I was surprised when she approached me. I might be able to pinpoint the exact day for you if I had my calendar with me. It was snowing outside, I think. Not heavily, but a sprinkling. The service was about conversion – always a tricky subject. It's one that we handle very sensitively around here, you see. I used to be Catholic. And then I heard a sermon one day about how they hoped that terrorists would see the light of God and how Jesus would guide them to righteousness and I realised how stupid I had been. They were no different than the extremists – those middle-aged, self-congratulatory worshippers. They believed in something. They wanted others to believe in the same thing. They pitied people who didn't. So, I left the Catholic Church and God guided me here. And what better place to start my campaign against the Devil? Amongst such squalor! Point is . . . we deal with conversion carefully. We don't shove our religion down other people's throats.

'So that's how I remember Hayley came to me after that sermon, because it was so unexpected. Usually I get a dribble of well-wishers followed by a larger dribble of busybodies saying we aren't doing enough to bring new faces to the church after I had stood up for an hour and told them that it was not their prerogative to recruit new followers. That prerogative is His and His alone. But Hayley took me aside and asked if I would see her – cleanse her – there and then.'

'How did she seem?' Priest asked.

'Agitated, upset. Something was bothering her enough to break her silence. So I got rid of everyone else and we came here, to this office, to talk.'

'And what did she say?'

'Not an awful lot, as it turned out.' He paused and pinched his nose, trying to remember. 'Let me see now. She asked me if I believed in evil. I said *yes*. She asked me whether there will be judgement over those that do wrong. I said, of course. God will bring every deed into judgement, with every secret thing, whether good or evil.'

'Ecclesiastes,' murmured Priest.

'Yes! Very few recognise this particular verse,' Matthew exclaimed. 'You must be a student of God.'

Priest grimaced. 'Not exactly.'

'Go on, Reverend,' Jessica prompted.

'Anyway, that was how it was,' Matthew continued. 'She wanted reassurance about *something* and of course I don't think it was anything to do with wanting reassurance about God's will. I was being tested, to see if I could be trusted, perhaps. I'm not sure, but we went on like this for a while. Did I understand fear? To fear the Lord is to hate evil, I told her. Eventually I stopped her and asked what this was all about? Was she OK? Was she in any kind of trouble? She didn't answer me but she did hand me something – an envelope – and explain that it had been posted through her door. It was significant to her, although she didn't understand what it was. Did I? I'm afraid not. But I know one thing: what I saw in her eyes that day, and detected in her voice, was a terror unlike any other that I have borne witness to, and I'm sorry to say that I have not seen her since.'

'You haven't seen her since the meeting you spoke of?' asked Jessica. 'You said she attended every week.'

'Yes,' said Matthew uneasily. 'Without fail. Until now.'

'What have you done to try and find her?'

'What could I do? Nobody knows anything about her. I don't even know where she lives.'

Jessica shook her head, dissatisfied.

'What was in the envelope?' Priest asked.

'I'll show you.' Matthew got up and went to a sideboard piled with papers. He rummaged around and, after a while, produced a small envelope, which he placed on the table in front of Priest. There was something inside. A bulge. Priest took the envelope in his hands and carefully opened the top, allowing the contents to fall out on to the table.

His body stiffened and a chill ran through him.

'I confess I didn't immediately recognise it,' said Matthew, 'but I carried out some research and I believe it's what is commonly known as a March brown mayfly.'

27

The promising sunlight that had welcomed them to Cambridge was fading fast and the first spots of rain began to splash on the pavement. The students running the river trips were busily covering their punts with tarpaulins. It wasn't the season for punting anyway, and even the lightest of showers would dissuade the last few remaining visitors from a trip down the Cam. This time of year, Starbucks did a hell of a lot better trade than they did.

Sarah had been wrong, Priest concluded. Hayley hadn't been sucked into a dark world of apocalyptic Bible bashers. She had found peace in that ramshackle community centre. And the Reverend Matthew was the real deal. Priest had met too many profiteers, fraudsters and criminals to not recognise legitimacy when he saw it. Jessica, who had been ashen ever since the dead bug had hit the table, held a different view.

'He did nothing. She was clearly in trouble and he did nothing!' she declared.

'He was as scared as she was,' Priest pointed out. 'Not everyone is a hero, Jessica.'

'If this is the only community in which Hayley had any involvement, then she's been missing for a week at least.

Reverend Matthew and his made-up church could have done something.'

'What could he have done?'

'At the very least he could have filed a missing person report with the local police.' She was becoming agitated, fiddling with the key to get the Range Rover started. Giant droplets of rain were bouncing off the roof now. They had to keep their voices raised just to be heard over the noise. 'I'm sorry,' she said. 'This situation is stressful.'

Priest shrugged as if it was nothing. And it was. His head was elsewhere, trying to process more new information and deal with the residual distraction of yesterday's blackout. Trying to piece together the last forty-eight hours was like trying to reconstruct a bag of shredding but with half the pieces missing.

After a while, Jessica said, 'The mayfly –'

'They found the same thing in Miles's throat, according to McEwen,' Priest said.

'I don't understand,' she confessed.

'It's a symbol.'

'A symbol for what?'

Priest clicked his tongue. 'I don't know.'

What was it that Reverend Matthew had said? *God will bring every deed into judgement, with every secret thing, whether good or evil.*

Priest plucked his phone out of his pocket and started filing through the numbers. He pressed one.

'What are you doing?' Jessica asked, her voice quivering slightly.

'She lived round here. We need to find out where.'

'This is awful . . .'

For an extraordinary moment, Priest thought she might be crying. He placed a hand on hers. Her body stiffened at his touch. He removed his hand.

There was a muffled voice. Priest had forgotten about the phone call. He put it to his ear.

'Priest?'

'Solly.'

'Hello, Priest.'

'Can you get the IP address for the Facebook entries that Hayley Wren posted?'

Solly laughed, although there was no genuine amusement in his tone. Solly never *really* laughed. He just made the noises that he heard other people emit when they found something humorous. Solly might be a genius, but he was incapable of understanding human emotion. He was a living android.

'I already did.' Solly gave an address. 'I got the street and Land Registry office copies for all the houses on that street. One of them is registered to Sir Philip and Lady Wren.'

Jessica fed the address into the Range Rover's GPS and they headed east through the suburbs. There was a burning sensation in Priest's stomach. He had a bad feeling about Hayley.

'Don't do that,' Jessica complained. At first he didn't see what she was talking about until she nodded at his foot, which was tapping against the side of the car door. 'It's bloody annoying.'

'Sorry, I do that, sometimes.'

Fifteen minutes later they were ringing the doorbell of a mid-terrace, late-Victorian house on a street comprising mainly of student digs. With its high railings and bay windows, it was vaguely reminiscent of Sarah's house.

There was no answer. A look through the keyhole revealed a mountain of post heaped up against the door. A smell of scented candles drifted through the hallway. Priest tried the door. It was locked.

'Did you ever knock down a door when you were with the police?' Jessica asked.

'One or two.'

Priest looked up and down the street, No one around. He inspected the door. The wood was old; the lock original. He knew where the stress points on the door were and that a well-aimed kick would take the lock off with not too much trouble.

'Stand back,' he instructed.

With one final glance up the street, and gripping the protruding wall for balance, he was about to kick when a voice cut through the rain.

'She's not in!'

Priest and Jessica both swung around and looked up. A fellow in his thirties was hanging out of the second-floor window of the house next door. He was grinning inanely from ear to ear. With his body concealed by the old Victorian brickwork around the window, he looked like the Cheshire Cat.

'She's not in,' he repeated.

Priest didn't need to stare into his eyes close up to recognise Hayley's next-door neighbour was a junkie.

'Have you seen her recently?' Jessica called.

'You police?' The junkie was shouting to be heard above the rain.

'Salvation Army,' Priest replied.

The junkie sniffed. Rain was now running down his greasy, black hair and into the empty flower box on the sill. He didn't seem to mind, or even notice. Then he was gone.

Jessica swept her wet hair out of her eyes. She looked tired. 'Salvation Army?' she said sceptically.

Priest shrugged.

There was a sound of a door opening. The junkie was standing in his doorway, the grin still carved across his face. He wore a sleeveless vest that had seen better days and a pair of baggy chinos tucked into a pair of brown boots.

'Sally Army, you said?' He beckoned them in. 'You lot gave me these boots last year.'

∽

The junkie's lounge looked as if a bomb had hit it. The floor was strewn with balls of tinfoil that Priest doubted had been used to wrap baked potatoes.

Priest perched himself on a footstool. Jessica declined the bean bag offered to her and elected to stand at the side of the room. She peered around suspiciously, as if the room was haunted.

Shortly, they were handed mugs of herbal tea – camomile for Jessica, green for Priest in the absence of Earl Grey – and were drying themselves in front of an old electric fire.

Their host had identified himself as Binny. It was fortunate that he seemed to hold the Salvation Army in high regard.

''Ave we met before, then?' Binny enquired. From underneath his chair he pulled a tray, out of which he began to roll himself a joint.

'I think we have,' said Priest smiling. 'But it was a long time ago. How are you doing?'

'Oh, yeah, better,' Binny said. 'Got myself a little job at the recycling centre, you know.'

'I hear and I'm told you're doing a very good job, too.'

Binny smiled broadly and lit the spliff. The smell of marijuana took hold almost immediately.

'So, what d'you want with that woman next door, then?' asked Binny through a haze of intoxicating mist.

'Hayley?'

'Yeah. Her.'

'She expressed an interest in becoming a Soldier.'

'Really? You kiddin' me.' Binny wiped his nose on the back of his hand.

'Don't you think she would make a good recruit?'

Binny thought about this in between drags. 'Suppose so. Keeps herself to herself. You lot have to be talkative, don't you?'

'When did you last see Hayley?' asked Jessica.

'When did I last see Hayley?' Binny said thoughtfully. 'Let me sees. D'you want some green, by the way? It's Purple Haze, or something. Not very strong but does the trick.'

'No, thank you,' said Jessica flatly.

'Suit yourself. Now then. Hayley. When did I last see Hayley? Ah . . . a week ago, maybe.'

'What was she like when you saw her? Notice anything unusual?'

Binny pulled a face as he struggled to recall, although given the way he was burning through the spliff, it was doubtful his recollection could be trusted. 'She left in a car. I watched her from the window. I like to hang out there when I do my smokin'. Let the wind flap about me face.'

'Do you remember anything about the car?'

Binny considered this for a while. 'Not really. Didn't seem important.'

'What sort of time of day was it? Morning? Evening?' Jessica asked.

'Well if I was up to see it, then that could mean any time of day, I guess.'

'Was it dark?' Jessica asked impatiently.

'Gettin' dark.' Binny took another long drag. 'It was after someone left a message for her.'

'What do you mean?' said Priest slowly. 'Left a message how?'

'He left a message.'

'Who?'

'Dunno. Her dad, I think. On her answerphone.'

Priest and Jessica exchanged looks.

'How do you know that, Binny?' Priest said gently.

'It's on my answerphone.' Binny seemed to realise that this might seem curious, so he added somewhat sheepishly, 'Not so easy to afford a phone line. Foreigners got all the good jobs, don't they? So I, you know, tap into next door's phone. And electricity. And gas. Long and short, I get her messages on my machine.'

'Can you play the message for us, Binny?' asked Jessica.

Binny seemed surprised that this revelation hadn't been met with disapproval and flashed Jessica a toothless grin. He got up and staggered off. Jessica and Priest followed him through an uncarpeted hallway scattered with pizza delivery leaflets and old Avon catalogues. Binny located the answerphone hidden under a pile of yellowing newspapers.

Solemnly, Binny clicked a few buttons. 'Here we go.'

After several moments, the tape whirred. Priest leant in to listen. A voice groaned from the machine, spectral and desperate.

'Hayley. It's Dad. Pick up if you're there . . . Hayley? I told you to answer your phone if I called you! Your mobile isn't ringing, either. Listen to me, get a taxi to the station and come back home. Now. Don't pack any things; come right away. It's not safe where you are. I – I need to know you're OK. Call me when you're in the taxi. I'm sorry. I've failed you.'

28

26th March, 1946
A remote farm in middle England

Colonel Bertie Ruck couldn't sleep.

He had become accustomed to the rattle of the door as the wind swept down the chimney and out through the fireplace and the gentle call of the owl that visited the barn at night. It wasn't that. It was him, he realised. Or her, maybe.

Ruck sat up and rubbed his head, dropped his legs over the side of the bed and pulled his coat over his nightshirt. A walk would loosen up his churning head.

He took an oil lantern and strolled out on to the landing. The stairway led down to the pantry and from there, an oak door gave access to the courtyard. Across the way, they had converted one of the old outhouses into a small prison. Schneider was chained to the walls but, other than that inconvenience, he slept in better conditions than his physician colleagues at Nuremburg.

Ruck was about to descend the staircase when he saw a light framing the doorway at the other end of the corridor.

Eva's room.

Curious, he waited, listened. There was a noise coming from the room. The sound of low whispers, scuffling. More than one person.

Alarmed, Ruck hung the lantern in the corridor and slipped quietly back into his own room where he retrieved a pistol from its holster. He made his way towards the source of the disturbance but he was halted abruptly by a scream cutting across the landing, a scream loud enough to be heard on the other side of the courtyard.

'Eva!' he shouted.

Ruck bolted the last ten yards, put his shoulder hard against the door and the hinges splintered. He fell into the room, pistol outstretched.

The sight that met him rendered him speechless.

Eva was standing in the corner of the room, her face ashen. Her nightdress was torn down one side, her body partially exposed from breast to hip. On the floor near the foot of the bed, Lance Corporal Fitzgerald was thrashing around like he was possessed, clutching at a wound in his chest. His rifle had been abandoned next to him.

It took Ruck a moment to register what he was seeing. Fitzgerald was screaming, his body convulsing.

'Colonel!' he spat. 'She –' He pointed.

Ruck saw the knife in her hand, the blade stained with the soldier's blood. 'What have you done?' Ruck demanded, turning to Eva.

She looked at him. He could see nothing in her green eyes. Not distress, not fear. Nothing.

'He tried to rape me,' she said coldly.

'That's a bloody lie!' Fitzgerald roared. 'Colonel! She's lying!'

Ruck gripped the pistol tightly but kept it down. He didn't know who to point it at even if he did find the fortitude to raise it.

'Eva?' he said uncertainly.

'He came into my room. I was asleep. He held a knife to my throat and tried to rape me.'

Ruck hesitated.

'Look!' she screamed, taking the torn dress in her hand and pulling it open, revealing her nakedness underneath.

'She *told me* to come here,' Fitzgerald gasped. 'She said *I should come* here. Colonel, you have to believe me!'

Fitzgerald started to crawl across the room towards Ruck. Blood was oozing from the wound. He was clutching his chest where the bayonet's knife blade had penetrated him, desperately trying to stop the bleeding, but it was no use. Ruck knew a fatal wound when he saw one.

'Eva, look at me,' he instructed. When she didn't respond, he bellowed, 'Look at me!'

She looked. There were spots of blood on her face; her eyes were wet with tears.

'He placed his arm across my chest and pinned me down. He said if I screamed he would kill me. Then he said I had to open my legs.'

'You lying bitch!' Fitzgerald roared.

With one final effort, Fitzgerald launched himself at the rifle. He grabbed the butt and hauled the weapon around so that the barrel was pointing at Eva.

A gunshot rang out.

Fitzgerald slumped down against the wall of the bedroom. Ruck lowered the pistol.

Outside, an owl took flight from the barn.

∞

Some time later, they sat in silence. Eva was hunched up on Ruck's bed, her arms folded around her knees. He sat at the desk, staring out of the window, smoking a cigarette.

He tried not to think about the curve of her midriff, exposed by the tear in her nightdress. She made no effort to hide it. He should cover her with his coat. A gentleman would.

The two soldiers guarding Schneider had sprinted across the courtyard on hearing the gunshot, rifles at the ready. Ruck had ordered them to remove Fitzgerald's body and bury it in the woods half a mile from the farm.

'You will not breathe a word of what you have seen here tonight.' Ruck had forestalled any questions. 'The man we knew as Fitzgerald did not exist. This place does not exist. *You* do not exist. Is that clear?' The men had nodded. 'Do not in any way consider that ignoring this instruction will not have consequences for you.'

Consequences. Yes, there would be many, but that was a worry for another day.

He inhaled the smoke deeply, the heat burning the back of his throat. It felt good and helped numb the sensation of uneasiness building in his gut.

'Thank you.' Eva spoke, suddenly and softly. A voice that was barely audible, even in the stillness of the night.

He turned to look at her. She had her head half buried in her knees, one eye appraising him carefully. If he didn't know any better, he could have sworn she was smiling. He felt sickened by her.

'You said he attacked you,' he remarked.

'He tried to rape me,' she said in the same detached voice she had used when she had first made the accusation. When Fitzgerald had still been alive.

'I see. And you were able to disarm him and stab him with the knife he held to your throat?'

'Yes.'

'Some achievement.' Ruck did not believe a word of it. Not one word. But he had shot Fitzgerald anyway. *What spell am I under?*

'I don't know how I managed it.'

Ruck felt sickened by the lie.

'I'm sorry,' she whispered.

'For what?'

'You're doing important work here. I'm a distraction.'

Ruck narrowed his eyes. Eva was teasing him, seeing how far he would go. And he was all too familiar with the limits of his own endurance. When she sensed she had his attention she unhooked her arms from around her knees, put one leg down and shuffled down the bed. He should have told her to stop but he watched silently.

Eva lifted one arm and draped it over her head, linking her fingers around the bedpost. The tear in her dress was just enough for him to see her as she really was. Her slender body, undulating across his bed.

As Eva turned her head he tried to register her expression. Whatever it was, it was not the look of a woman who had just seen a man die.

'Did you see Him?' Ruck said through gritted teeth.

'Who?'

'God?'

'Whatever do you mean, Colonel Ruck?' she said in a coquettish voice. It sounded wrong.

Ruck felt the grip he had on his control loosening. 'When you put the knife into Fitzgerald's chest and twisted it. When he screamed as he saw his blood escape his body. Did you see God?'

'Oh, what a silly notion, Colonel Ruck.' Eva moved her hand down her body, exhaling softly.

There was something feral about her.

'It isn't real, Miss Miller,' he murmured thickly, barely able to speak. 'None of it is real. Schneider's ridiculous idea that one can create a channel to God through suffering. It was a rant, a perversion, something malignant spewing from the mouth of evil.'

'Oh, Colonel Ruck,' she said again. 'You say the silliest of things.' She had her hand on her pelvis. Her green eyes were boring into him.

'You must listen to me, Eva. Don't let him in.'

'Who?' she asked, running her tongue around her lips.

'Schneider.'

She laughed. 'I'm always very careful, Colonel Ruck, about *who I let in.*'

He swallowed, then stubbed out his cigarette. He thought he might burst.

She rose from the bed, wrapping her torn dress around her before walking to the door. She placed her hand on the handle. 'Good night, Colonel Ruck. I am sure I will be reassigned in the morning. I hope I have not caused you too much inconvenience.'

The latch clicked, and so did something inside Ruck. Something he did not know was within him. He crossed the distance between them like a storm, descending on her with such force that she tumbled backwards, crashing into the door. He felt her fight back. She took hold of his wrists, wrenched them around but, whether she was pulling him in or trying to throw him off, he could not tell and did not care.

He tore at the nightdress, found her skin soft and warm underneath.

'Colonel Ruck,' she gasped. 'Wait – no!'

Her hand gripped tightly around his right arm with an almost unnatural strength. Her other hand was wrapped around his left wrist, twisting it downwards until he thought it might break, until he felt the warm sanctuary between her legs.

She snatched at his belt buckle and he fell on top of her. The pained gasp from the sudden escape of air from her lungs as she hit the floor only maddened him further.

'No –' She bit his shoulder.

The pain rippled down his body like a shock wave. 'I know you lied to me about what happened,' Ruck hissed.

She took hold of his hair, moaned as he entered her. He could taste her moist skin in his mouth, smell her sweat.

'You want to see God?' he panted.

'Show me –' She took hold of his collar, tore at his neck. 'Show me –'

She pulled him in deeper.

29

Georgie sat at her desk at home and sniffed the steaming hot mug of Cup-a-Soup she had made herself. *Cream of Asparagus.* Or so the packet had promised. She had spent the day at the office catching up on admin and sorting through a few smaller cases Priest & Co had taken on. They could have waited but she needed something to fill her time other than reading about fifteenth-century tyrants. *Sorry, Vlad, but I've had enough of you for the moment.*

It had been another day of strange revelations. When she had been stirring sugar into her third latte, Charlie had called her from Cambridge, of all places. He had been with Jessica Ellinder; and the thought of them together was a little discomfiting. *Although, of course, that's nothing to do with me.* She doubted Jessica was his type anyway. They hadn't found Hayley, but they had found a link between her disappearance and Miles Ellinder's death. She had been sent a mayfly in the post, the same insect that McEwen had said had been found lodged in Ellinder's throat.

'A killer's calling card?' suggested Georgie. She tried hard to keep the excitement out of her voice.

'Maybe something like that, Georgie,' Charlie had said. 'Could you at least *try* and act concerned?'

Undoubtedly, Georgie *was* concerned. A girl was in trouble. The police, and particularly DI McEwen, weren't interested. A man had been ritualistically murdered. And Charlie Priest was now travelling back with Jessica Ellinder to her family home outside London.

She hoped he wouldn't be spending the night.

Georgie's room on the top floor was the smallest but she owned the least things and, by way of compensation, her window overlooked the Thames. In the summer, she could watch the river traffic chug by – converted fishing boats ferrying tourists, teams of rowers heaving their way through the water at astonishing speed, low barges piled high with rubbish. Georgie liked the way the sunlight danced across the water, and the way the reflection was disturbed by passing ships, like a painter running his brush across the face of the canvas.

Georgie's cheeks had reddened as she sat poised at her desk furiously scribbling notes as Charlie spoke in her ear. She had a new assignment. She was to go and speak to Lady Wren and, if she could, take some photos of Sir Philip Wren's office, although Charlie had been a little vague on why. He had relayed the plan to her; it wasn't going to be straightforward because the police were no doubt still in attendance at the Wren household, but he was going to phone ahead and brief Terri. The importance of the task sent a shiver down her spine. This was her moment.

She needed something to carry her things in but she didn't own a handbag. Georgie was the only woman she knew who didn't own at least one handbag. She had pockets. Pockets were for carrying things in. Handbags were for *fitting in*, which Georgie didn't do. Mira had a whole wardrobe full of them. Li probably had a lock-up garage somewhere for her collection. She could borrow one – from Li, of course, not Mira – but talking to any one of her flatmates right now didn't appeal.

She took a counsel's notepad, a fountain pen and an extra cartridge, fifty pounds in cash and her mobile.

In the corridor, she noticed Martin's door was shut. The gentle thud of music was seeping through. Something not quite his style – a drum-and-bass rhythm. Fast and repetitive. Not him but Mira, maybe – probably. It really didn't matter, she told herself.

'Georgie!'

For one awful moment, she thought it was Mira.

'My hairdryer's broken,' said Li, making a sad face.

'I have one but it's not very good,' Georgie admitted. 'At least it's out of the box.'

'Can I use it? I'm sorry, I probably owe you rent for the stuff I keep borrowing.'

'It's in the bedside table drawer.' Georgie tossed her the key.

'Thanks, Georgie.' Li smiled again.

'I'll pick the key up later. Will you be in this evening?' asked Georgie.

'Might have a guy but don't worry, just knock first. Are you out all evening? A date or something?'

'Do you think I take notes on dates?'

'Actually, I do.'

'Hm. It's not a bad idea. See you later.'

Georgie waved then ran down the stairs and out of the front door without giving Li the chance to reply. Outside, the river looked dark and less friendly than on other days.

∽

Li watched Georgie disappear down the stairs and waited until she heard the front door close.

She has a very awkward gait. It struck Li that Georgie Some-day wasn't quite sure how to walk properly. *That girl has con-fidence issues*, she thought. Unnecessarily, as it happened. She was really quite pretty, if she stopped dressing like a Christian missionary. She could certainly do a whole lot better than that idiot Martin. Why Georgie had ever shown any interest in him was a mystery; although Li suspected something more compli-cated was at play.

It had been two years since Martin had tried to stick his tongue down Li's throat. He hadn't tried to repeat the opera-tion – he had nearly lost his tongue. Li had accepted many years ago that her English father and Japanese mother had left her confused, straddling two cultures with a tenuous grip on neither. She could have been like Georgie, if she had chosen to be: ambitious, career-driven, intuitive. She could have started in a local firm as a paralegal and made partner by the age of thirty – and her parents would have put in some equity, too. But instead, she was an escort.

She had met Mrs White at a party before the Oxford class of 2013 had moved to London. Come to think of it, perhaps it was even the same night on which Li had sent Martin off to the out-of-hours GP to get his mouth patched up. Mrs White was an extraordinary woman. She was in her late fifties, with a curve down her hips that most models would have been proud of. She had been wearing an exquisite, white Jovani dress that had stood in stark contrast to the mahogany tone of her perfect skin. Li remembered the encounter well.

'My, my,' Mrs White had remarked as the barman had pushed a cocktail in Li's direction. 'What a beautiful outfit.'

'Thank you.'

'Tell me, dear, are you one of the students or a very young lecturer?'

Mrs White was used to getting what she wanted. And what she wanted was Li. In turn, Li had discovered that she was the sort of girl who, for five hundred pounds a time, was quite happy to let the odd forty-something businessman come on her tits. And for that sort of money, it didn't have to be every night, not even every week. Just as long as whenever Mrs White rang her to say she had a client – 'this one's a lovely chap, dear. He's sixty-two and probably can't even get an erection but if you let him finger you he'll pay double' – Li made herself available.

'You've always been one of my best girls, Li,' Mrs White had once said to her with a wry smile. 'It's that Oriental look, and the freckles. Drives the poor sods wild. If you had three vaginas and could hold your breath for an hour I wouldn't need anyone else!'

Li smiled as she walked back up the stairs to Georgie's room. She was surprised Georgie had given her the key. Where was she off to in such a hurry this evening? Perhaps she was giving it to that dishy boss of hers. Li had seen the way that red rash had spread across Georgie's face when he had showed up at the bar the other night – and why not? He was very handsome and, judging by the size of his arms, it looked like he spent a lot of time in the gym.

'Good for her,' Li said to herself as she unlocked Georgie's door.

The room smelt of Georgie. Not an unpleasant smell but a human smell. Not like Li's room, or Mira's, which smelt like a nail bar. There was a laptop in the corner but Li wasn't here to snoop around. She needed a hairdryer, genuinely. But she would walk slowly to get it – there was no rush.

There were four shelves of books. Li recognised most of them from their university days. Some of them were even hers – gifts that Georgie had eagerly accepted after Li had decided that soliciting paid better than solicitors. Multiple subjects, no apparent specialism. But then again, Li knew the only brain with more capacity for knowledge than hers was Georgie's.

There was no shrine to Martin. That was a shame. Not that Li got off on watching someone pine, but she had hoped at least for a clump of his hair, a few nail clippings, maybe the odd sock. So Georgie's weirdness did have a limit.

There was some post discarded on the side. Three letters – two obvious circulars and something else.

You're here for the hairdryer, girl. But Li was already feeling the crinkles of the envelopes. *Is that an Avon invoice? Does she use Avon? Really? How old is she, fifty?*

Something else, too. An envelope with Georgie's name and address printed on it in faded blue ink, but no postmark. Some-one must have shoved it in the pigeonholes at the entrance to the building. Intrigued, Li studied the envelope further. There was something inside, something lumpy. One end of the sealed lip was riding up, the adhesive not sticking all the way across. Li shook the envelope and a little more of the lip detached from the waxy strip.

Something fell out and on to the table.

Li frowned. She didn't pick up what fell out. She put the enve-lope down in disgust. *Why the hell has someone sent Georgie a dead insect?*

30

The Dower House fulfilled every part of Priest's expectations to the point where it was disappointing. The driveway meandered through clusters of dormant trees, curving sharply for no reason other than to ensure the front of the house wasn't visible from the road. White pillars stood either side of an oak door intricately carved with leaves and intertwining vines. The pediment bore a red-and-blue shield above the entrance – presumably the family crest. The house was early Georgian. Rows of white-framed sash windows punctuated the red brickwork giving the impression that there were more rooms than there actually were.

The rain had let up but Priest pulled his jacket tightly around himself as they trudged across the gravel to the front door. As they approached the steps Jessica turned to him, her hair partially covering her face, making it difficult for him to read her expression.

'I should warn you,' she said gravely. 'My sister's back from the States. She came as soon as she got the news about Miles.'

'Why must I be warned about this?'

Jessica coughed and shivered in the cold before taking hold of the handle and pushing the front door open. The warm rush of air that met them was welcoming. She turned to him and they went in. 'She's a corporate lawyer advising American businesses on UK law. She's a handful.'

A few moments later, Priest stood in a spacious kitchen, gleaming with new appliances. There was a farmhouse feel to it but, on closer inspection, the rustic finish was an expensive imitation.

'You could have called earlier.' A tall, frail-looking woman rose from the kitchen table. She kissed Jessica on both cheeks. For Priest, she offered a curt nod of the head before averting her eyes.

'I'm sorry, Mummy, there wasn't time. May I present –'

'I know who this is, Jessica. Tea, Mr Priest?'

Priest accepted the cup she poured and shuffled his weight uncomfortably. Grief hung in the air. He had no right to be here. This family was in mourning.

'I'm sorry to intrude, Mrs Ellinder,' he offered. 'I know this is a difficult time for you.'

'Lucia, please,' she replied dully.

He opened his mouth, not sure what combination of words would emerge, but any potential embarrassment was prevented by the arrival of Kenneth Ellinder.

'Jessie!' The old man embraced his daughter momentarily. 'How wonderful. And Mr Priest, too. You are both very welcome.'

'We wanted to update you, Daddy.'

'Of course, of course. But it is late and you must be starving. Will you join us for dinner, Mr Priest?'

It was the last thing in the world that Priest wanted right now. He felt as if he was drowning. Overwhelmed by a sick feeling of helplessness, desperate to claw his way to the surface. But Jessica looked tired and her father was paying his bill, and so he relented. As Kenneth Ellinder led him through a set of double doors, Priest caught Lucia Ellinder's eye. Her look made something clear: He wasn't welcome here.

∽

The dining room was dimly lit but even in the gloom Priest could make out a dozen or so sets of eyes bearing down on him – various dead members of the Ellinder family, immortalised with varying degrees of merit, on canvas.

'This is a ninety-three,' Kenneth explained as he peered at the bottle of wine. 'The ninety-five is arguably superior but I cannot trace a single drop of it in the cellar.' He poured a crimson liquid into Priest's glass.

'Thank you. I wouldn't know the difference anyway,' Priest admitted.

Priest felt movement from somewhere behind before the seat next to him was very gracefully taken.

'You're late, Scarlett,' Kenneth observed, although he didn't appear to be too annoyed.

'Sorry, Daddy.'

Scarlett Ellinder was a few years younger than Jessica. Like her mother, she was tall and elegant with striking brown eyes. She moved with extraordinary precision – as if every manoeuvre was pre-planned. She also had her mother's looks, and her sharp features, more so than Jessica in many ways. But Scarlett lacked the hardness that Jessica and her mother exuded. Her eyes were bright and playful, her smile genuine – the way she rested her hands on the table and leant forwards suggested she might have more of an intuitive understanding of people than her older sister.

'You must be Charlie Priest,' Scarlett said, offering her hand.

'And you must be Scarlett.' Priest returned the smile. He felt Jessica's scowl burning into the back of his head. He noticed the sisters didn't appear to acknowledge each other.

'May I say, Mr Priest,' said Kenneth Ellinder, pouring Scarlett a glass of wine, 'how pleased I am that you finally agreed to accept our instructions in the matter of Miles's death.'

'Your daughter is most persuasive, Mr Ellinder,' replied Priest.

'The matter of Miles's murder, Daddy,' said Jessica quietly. 'Not his *death*.'

'And so, please do not prolong an old man's woe any longer. What progress has been made?' Kenneth asked, ignoring Jessica's remark.

Priest considered his reply. What progress *had* been made? He flashed a look at Jessica. Kenneth Ellinder still didn't know that Miles had visited Priest the night before his murder. How much did Jessica want her father to know?

'It's too early to say,' said Priest carefully. 'I have several leads, but . . .'

'Give them a chance, Daddy,' said Scarlett. 'It's quite unreasonable for you to demand a progress report about an investigation at such an early stage. Let's be realistic. It could be years before we know what really happened to Miles.'

Scarlett looked at Priest and smiled again. He nodded in gratitude.

'The Attorney General is dead, Daddy,' Jessica announced.

Kenneth bowed his head. 'I am aware. Very sad. But what has that to do with –'

'Did you know Sir Philip, Mr Ellinder?' Priest interrupted.

'I did, as did your father of course, although he perhaps knew Wren better than I did. Philip Wren was an honourable man. I gather he was under considerable stress, although I had no idea the burden was great enough to result in him taking his own life.'

'I don't think Philip Wren killed himself.' Priest took another sip – the wine tasted of almost nothing to him.

Ellinder frowned. 'What are you saying?'

'Just that. Philip Wren's death was not suicide.'

'How do you know?' asked Scarlett, leaning forward, holding his gaze.

'We were there, Scarlett,' said Jessica in a warning tone.

'The police –' Ellinder began.

'Are being led by Detective Inspector McEwen,' Priest interjected.

Ellinder hit the table with his fist. 'That man is an incompetent buffoon! Why on earth is he involved with Philip Wren's death? He should be finding out what happened to my son!'

'Moreover,' Priest added, 'there is another connection between what happened to Miles and Sir Philip's death.'

'Surely not!' Kenneth exclaimed.

At the end of the table, Lucia Ellinder shuffled in her seat and let out a groan.

'Sir Philip has a daughter called Hayley,' Priest continued. 'She seems to be missing, driven away in an unknown car several nights ago. We have just returned from Cambridge in an effort to trace her.'

Ellinder narrowed his eyes. 'And this is connected to Miles because . . .?'

'In Cambridge, we made contact with a reverend in Hayley's church. Prior to her disappearance, Hayley had been sent a dead insect in the post. The same sort of insect that was found lodged in Miles's throat. A mayfly.'

Kenneth Ellinder placed his wine glass carefully back down on the table. Priest could feel disapproving eyes on him, both living and dead.

'Does this mean anything to you, Mr Ellinder?'

The old man sat grimly for a moment, rubbing his fingers up and down the wine glass. Priest held his breath.

'No,' he said in the end. 'It means nothing to me.'

There was silence for a while until Lucia pushed her chair back violently, upturning her glass and spilling wine across the table.

'I'm sorry!' she declared. 'I cannot stand this.'

She swept away from the table. Her husband rose to his feet but she was out of the door before he could do anything to stop her.

'Lucia!' Ellinder called after her.

Priest heard the sound of a door slamming shut.

31

In the taxi Georgie had worked out what she was going to say when she knocked on the Wrens' door, but now, standing at the top of the driveway with a policeman approaching, her plan didn't seem all that great. *The plan involves lying. I'm really no good at lying . . .*

'Can I help, madam?' asked the policeman, positioning himself between her and the house.

'Yes,' Georgie replied.

There was a moment's silence; then the policeman shrugged. 'And?'

'Oh, sorry.' Georgie could sense her face flush. Even in the bitter cold she was starting to feel hot. 'I should have said. I'm from Pipes and Cooper. The funeral directors?'

The policeman looked her up and down suspiciously and said, 'You don't look like you're from the funeral directors.'

Georgie hesitated. 'I'm an apprentice,' she tried.

This seemed to strike a chord with the policeman, who scratched his beard and led her up to the front door. He rang the bell.

'Sorry about that,' he said sheepishly. 'Got to be careful nowadays. You'd be surprised at the number of news reporters who say they're one thing just to get a good story.'

'It's quite all right,' said Georgie.

A few moments later, the door opened and a stern-looking face appeared. Georgie smiled as pleasantly as she could.

'This lady is from Pipes and Cooper,' the policeman explained. The face didn't flinch, or respond. 'The funeral directors.'

'Not due for another week,' retorted the face jutting out from the side of the door. Georgie was starting to feel her confidence melt away. The policeman shot her an accusing look. *I did say I was bad at lying.*

'Lady Wren asked us to come early,' Georgie offered. It was her last roll of the dice and from the sour look, it hadn't scored high. Georgie was just wondering whether she could outrun the policeman when she heard a voice from somewhere inside.

'It's all right, Sissy. Let her in.'

∞

Georgie understood loss. She remembered how her house had felt when it was permeated with the grief of her father's death. How still everything was. How it seemed as if everything was made from ash, ready to crumble at the slightest breeze. This was how the room felt in which she found Terri Wren hunched up in a leather armchair, a woollen blanket trailed over her knee.

Sissy scowled as she ushered Georgie through and sat her down. She was a stern-looking woman in her late fifties with the air of a strict schoolteacher about her. She introduced herself as Terri's sister.

'Shall I stay?' asked Sissy, casting Georgie a disapproving look.

Terri was looking apprehensively out of the window, as if she had seen something approaching. Or someone, perhaps. Sissy coughed and Terri looked up, straight through Georgie.

'No, Sissy. Thank you.'

Sissy nodded but made a point of whispering in Georgie's ear before withdrawing from the room. 'Five minutes, dear. No more.'

Georgie crossed and uncrossed her legs, trying to wriggle into a comfy position on the sofa. 'I'm grateful for you agreeing to speak to me, Lady Wren. I know this is a very difficult time for you.'

'Do you?' The side of her mouth inched upwards but there was no hint in Terri Wren's sad eyes that she was actually smiling. 'I doubt that, dear.'

'Charlie sent me,' Georgie told her.

'I know. He phoned me and told me to expect you. Were it not for the fact that Charlie had sent you, I wouldn't have let you in.'

'Thank you. I really am truly sorry to intrude.'

Terri furrowed her brow as if she was in pain. 'What is it you want?'

Georgie wondered whether she should take out her notepad, or whether Terri would see it as disrespectful. In the end, she left it where it was. Behind her, she heard the floorboards creak. Most likely Sissy, prowling the hallway.

'Has there been any sign of Hayley?' Georgie began.

Terri sighed. 'No. But she will turn up – she always does.'

'Are you sure?'

'Quite sure, dear.'

'Before he died –' Georgie swallowed. She suddenly felt very inadequate. 'Before he died, Sir Philip sent Charlie a letter telling him that he had sent a flash drive containing computer data to Charlie's home. Do you know anything about this?'

'No,' Terri said pitifully.

'You weren't asked to post anything for him?'

'I just said, no.'

'Sorry.'

Terri had pursed her lips, folded her arms. She was staring, mesmerised, at the floor.

This isn't going well. After a moment's hesitation, Georgie said, 'I wonder whether –'

'You could see his office?' Terri asked.

'Yes.'

Sissy appeared, as if from nowhere, and led Georgie to the Attorney General's office.

'Two minutes this time, dear,' Sissy whispered. 'I'm counting. And do not under any circumstances touch anything.'

Georgie stepped cautiously into the room. The office was like any other. Desk, filing cabinets, fan. She took shots on her phone from different angles, trying to capture everything. She had no idea what she was looking for, so tried to document as much of the room as possible. Charlie would do the rest.

Sissy had disappeared from sight but Georgie doubted she had gone far. The desk was bare. Just blotting paper and a few pens. No computer. She guessed that had been seized as part of the evidence. She took pictures of the desk anyway and particularly of the partial footprint across the edge. It struck her as curious; it was so perfectly aligned as if . . . *No, it doesn't matter.*

She stopped and listened. Silence. No footsteps outside. She tugged at one of the desk drawers. Locked. Another. Also locked. This one made a rattling noise rather more loudly than Georgie would have hoped. She tried the third drawer down but found that also locked. The filing cabinet didn't look any more accessible.

Her heart sank. Pictures and a fifteen-second interview. Rather unimpressive considering the risk Charlie had taken getting her in here. The thought of letting him down made her feel sick.

She stared at the desk – willed it to bequeath her a secret. Then she noticed something odd – there were three drawers but four handles. It took her a second to register that the top handle was attached to a sliding surface which wasn't a drawer but which opened outwards to make another surface. She pulled the handle and it slid out. Tucked in the narrow gap beneath the underside of the desktop was a thin bundle of papers. At first glance, a police report.

A movement in the hallway. Georgie's heart skipped a beat.

'Time's up, dear,' called Sissy.

Georgie stuffed the papers into her coat pocket. 'Coming,' she called.

32

In one respect, dinner at the Dower House had been modestly successful, in that Priest had been convinced that Kenneth Ellinder's reactions to the revelations concerning the mayfly found at Hayley Wren's church were genuine. In another respect, the meat had been overcooked and experiencing the domestic politics of the Ellinder family at first hand had been decidedly awkward.

I wonder if the old man knows more than he's letting on?

Priest stepped out of the shower and wrapped a towel around his waist. He had been allocated a room in a guest wing, tucked around the back of the house and comprising a small office, a dressing room, a double bedroom boasting a fine-looking four-poster bed and a bathroom. The shower had provided a welcome reprieve – for the first time in days, Priest felt he might be able to sleep properly.

Scarlett Ellinder is a turn up for the books. She and Jessica really are chalk and cheese.

Priest took a piss, borrowed some mouthwash he found in a cabinet above the sink and stared at himself in the mirror. There were bags under his eyes and his stubble was more beard-like now.

He stopped when he heard the noise of a latch softly clicking behind him. The bedroom was on the ground floor, with bay windows looking out on to a terrace. Had the latch belonged to the window or the door?

The bathroom door was ajar. Priest made his way across the tiles as quietly as he could and peered through the gap between the door and the frame. He could see less than half of the room but no intruder. He tensed up and looked around for something he could use as a weapon. There was no T-baton conveniently lying on a table this time around.

Priest pushed the door open a little further, holding his arm up in case someone was standing behind it. It turned out he was right. He *had* heard the latch click, but to the door, not the window.

She stood leaning with her back against the door to the corridor draped in a black silk dressing-gown, her eyes fixed on a point behind him.

'Jessica,' he said softly.

She didn't say anything but crossed the room and for a moment he thought that she might walk straight through him, like a ghost straying briefly into the material world only to dissipate into nothing, but she stopped short. Their eyes met, briefly. She smelt of lavender.

'I'm sorry that my mother left like that.'

'It's nothing, of course. You're all under incalculable stress.'

'She's normally quite ... unemotional. It's difficult – seeing her like this.'

'I'm sure.'

She was examining his body, unperturbed by his near nakedness. Suddenly, she reached across and took his hand, examining the burn mark across his wrist. She held his hand in hers for a moment, occasionally changing the angle, checking every detail around the wound.

'Did it hurt?'

Priest swallowed. He could already feel his heart rate increase, his body reacting to her touch, but there was something strange about the way she asked the question, the answer to which should have been obvious. *Did it hurt?* His gaze followed her arm up to her own shoulders, her neck. The dressing-gown accentuated her curves. It fell low across her chest and revealed enough for him to realise that there was nothing else underneath except her exquisite skin. He felt a warm sensation creep over him as he stiffened underneath the towel.

'Jessica –' he began. He had intended to stop her, to take her hands away, but he was electrified by the touch of her fingers on his. She wrapped her hand around his wrist, creating a jolt of pain, which she must have known would happen, and drew his arm towards her so that his hand was on her bare chest.

'Jessica, wait.'

She breathed out heavily as his skin made contact with hers, and pulled him in closer, guiding him down underneath her dressing-gown. It gave way and he took her breast in his hand before their lips met, tentatively at first, then harder. They kissed hungrily and Priest felt the grip on his self-control loosen as she pushed her tongue further into his mouth, then took the back of the towel with her free hand, casting it aside. A wave of intoxication flushed through him as his blood surged south while she wrapped her leg around his hip.

'This is *not* what I came here for,' she gasped, biting hard into his neck and pushing him towards the bed.

'You're a fucking awful liar,' he breathed.

'No! I don't want you.'

Priest's heart was racing. For a moment, he thought she might be telling the truth as she suddenly pushed him away, digging her nails into the tops of his arms and cutting into his skin. He tried to kiss her again but she ducked underneath his advance and pulled him down on to the bed on top of her.

'Jessica, wait!'

The next manoeuvre was as graceful as any expert combat move he had seen. She positioned him sideways and, using her new-found leverage, twisted his body around so she was on top. He quickly hauled himself further up the bed and she followed, straddling him and tearing the dressing-gown away. She had him pinned, her body was in complete control of him.

'Are you sure you know what you want?' he asked, panting.

She smiled a remarkable, mesmerising smile before she took hold of his erect penis and slid it inside her, letting out a groan of pleasure and pressing herself down over him, forcing him into her as deeply as possible. She writhed on top of him, moaning softly as she pleasured herself. He concentrated on her face, which was turned up to the ceiling, eyes closed, and let his hands skim over her hips, her midriff to her breasts.

As the rhythm of her movement quickened and the sounds of her moans intensified, he guided her head down over him so he could kiss her face. He could feel the crescendo building to the point where their symphony would erupt into orgasm.

'Are you sure you know what you want?' he whispered breathlessly.

There was a moment where she grunted, frustrated and animal-like. A few more glorious thrusts brought Priest right to the edge before she groaned in his ear.

'Yes.'

～∞～

Priest awoke in the early hours of the morning. On average, he slept for less than five hours, three if he was working on a big case. He wasn't an insomniac, he just didn't need as much sleep to function as most people did, so he was unsurprised to find himself in a dark room that was illuminated only by a sliver of moonlight creeping through the gaps in the heavy curtains.

Beside him, Jessica's warm body rose and fell gently with the rhythmic breathing that deep sleep precipitates. Careful not to disturb her, he got out of bed and found his clothes using the display on his phone to light his surroundings. His jacket had been slung on the floor. He didn't bother with his shoes. Most of the Dower House floors were carpeted anyway.

The corridor was lit, maybe for his benefit, or perhaps it was always lit. He felt apprehensive. Priest hated intruding into other people's private spaces. He had no idea where he was going but he couldn't expect anyone to be up for another few hours and he was sure he had seen a small study with a television at the end of the hallway. When he got there, he stood listening at the door. The television was on. There was banging, commotion, panic. Then splintering of wood and blood-curdling screams. He recognised the scene. He opened the door.

'There was nothing else on,' she explained.

'Night of the Living Dead,' he remarked.

'Very apt for this old, still house shrouded in darkness, isn't it?' Scarlett was draped over a small sofa that looked like it had been looted from a French chateau – its frayed fabric a hideous clash of gold and blue.

She didn't make any effort to move when he came in, clicking the door shut behind him. She was wearing short, pink pyjamas that clung tightly to her athlete's body. Her arms were stretched back and around to support her head. She had contorted herself perfectly to fit inside the awkward shape of the old sofa.

'Did you know George Romero appears as a zombie in every one of his films?' he said. On the screen, a woman screamed as hands burst through the window and took hold of her, trying to drag her outside.

'Mm. I can never work out which one he is.'

Scarlett turned and looked at him and Priest felt obliged to sit down.

'All zombie films are about class struggle,' she mused. 'Did you know that? What happens when the peasants revolt.'

'I just like the relentless violence.'

Scarlett laughed in a way that was very different to Jessica. Come to think of it, had he ever heard Jessica properly laugh?

For a few moments, they watched the scene develop. There was a desperate attempt to board up the broken window but it seemed inevitable that the slow, cumbersome, badly made-up extras would eventually break through.

'Do you normally spend the early hours watching B-movies?' he asked.

'Couldn't sleep,' she replied, yawning. 'Think I still have jetlag.'

'I'm sorry you had to come home in such circumstances.'

She made a dismissive noise. Her eyes were still locked on the black-and-white screen. 'Don't be. It's the coming back that's annoyed me, not the circumstances.'

'Your brother was found impaled on a metal pole in one of your father's warehouses,' Priest pointed out. It wasn't meant to be a criticism, but Priest held his breath while he waited for her reply.

'Miles is not my brother,' she said eventually. 'He came with my mother.'

'Of course, I'm sorry. Was your mother married previously?' He thought about Lucia Ellinder and imagined a string of bankrupt ex-husbands.

'Not married, no. But she came with baggage.'

'Baggage you didn't approve of?'

She shrugged. 'Miles was nothing to me. A spoilt drug addict who squandered every penny Daddy spoon-fed him. The ungrateful shit got what he deserved.'

Priest was about to open his mouth when she turned to look at him.

'And don't think for one moment that I was stupid enough to tell the police that.'

'Although you were in the States at the time of his death.'

'What if I had orchestrated it from afar? Conspiracy to murder by Skype, perhaps.'

'I'll bear that in mind. But what about your mother?'

Scarlett looked up, as if trying to find some inspiration from the ceiling. 'You may find this very unacceptable, Mr Priest, but neither Jessie nor I really know much about our mother. Of course we love her. She brought us up in the right way. We tolerated Miles, for her sake. But we're not a close family.'

'You can love someone without connecting with them,' Priest suggested, thinking of William.

Scarlett nodded.

'So, what do you think happened?'

'You want my opinion?'

'Your father's paying me handsomely to procure it.'

She turned back to the television. It looked as though things weren't going well at the zombie-infested cabin. She was much more conventionally attractive than Jessica. He wondered how many lesser mortals were wrapped around those slender fingers.

She leant forward. 'I think there's something very dangerous out there, Mr Priest.'

'You mean aside from George Romero dressed as a zombie?' Priest asked.

She ignored him, serious now. 'I think Miles was engaged with some cult or other that's gone horribly wrong. That in itself would hardly be unusual. There are plenty of secret societies recruiting people of my brother's disposition – vulnerable, stupid and rich. Skull and Bones, the Golden Dawn, the Masons . . .'

'None of those are well known for impaling people this side of the twenty-first century,' Priest pointed out.

Scarlett shrugged. 'Bram Stoker was a member of the Golden Dawn. The main source for Dracula was –'

'Vlad the Impaler.'

'Very good,' she said. 'You know your useless junk occult stuff.'

'Thank you, although I have very open-minded and resourceful staff to tell me these things. Do you really think Miles was a member of some sort of cult?'

'His death was ritualised, clearly.'

'Do you know of any cults or societies operating today that have the resources and capacity to pull this off?'

'I can think of one.'

He waited but she didn't expand.

Instead Scarlett sat up with a swift movement. 'I want to show you something, Mr Priest.' At the door, she stopped and looked over her shoulder at him. He checked the zombie situation. It looked pretty dire. He followed her down the corridor.

At the far end of the house, Scarlett stopped. 'What's your favourite film, Mr Priest?' she asked.

Priest thought for a moment. '*Freaks.*'

'What do you like about it?'

'I like the strapline: *Can a full-grown woman truly love a midget?*'

'Genius,' she said with a smile.

'We walked a long way to discuss film interests.'

She turned to a door at the end of the hall.

'There's a detail you're missing, Mr Priest.'

'Hm. I'm toying with the possibility that your father was being selective about what he tells me.'

'He doesn't mean to deceive. He is trying to deal with this situation with as much dignity as possible, although I fear it is a futile exercise. The group share price has already halved since details of what happened to Miles leaked out.'

The door was locked. Scarlett took a key from the top of the doorframe. Priest wondered how much of this had been set up. Perhaps the whole thing, from the moment Jessica had announced they were going to the Dower House. Just one big production, including her seduction of him.

The latch clicked. The room was dark. As he followed her into the gloom, anxiety began to settle in. The floorboards groaned under his weight. The walls were textured, covered with something. Books. A library, perhaps.

She flicked a switch behind him and everything illuminated in glorious multicolour. His eyes adjusted. Not books. Display cabinets fixed wall to wall. At first, the light bounced off the glass, obscuring what was behind. He shifted position; the reflection subsided.

He swallowed but his throat was taut with dryness. 'Jesus Christ.'

Tiny insects – their delicate, papery wings glistening lightly, nails driven through their torsos fixing them to their mounts. Hundreds of them.

A collage of flying insects: butterflies, dragonflies, moths . . .

'Your father –' Priest began.

'Collects dead bugs. Yes.'

'Including, coincidently, the same insect that was found in Miles's throat and sent in the post to Hayley Wren?'

Scarlett was looking at the floor. She seemed to be in a trance. Priest wondered if she regretted showing him.

'Will you confront him about it?' she asked quietly.

'What will I gain if I do?'

'Probably nothing.'

Priest quickly scanned the cases, rapidly assimilating each display. They varied in size and colour from tiny, yellow butterflies to brown moths the size of a man's hand. Other winged insects he didn't recognise. But no empty pins – they were all apparently present and correct.

He turned to Scarlett. 'You said you could think of one contemporary society capable of carrying out what happened to Miles.' She didn't answer at first. 'Scarlett?'

'Isn't it obvious?'

'Help me out.'

'The Nazis.'

Priest stood in the insect room and allowed the words to swill around his head. *Nazis.* He had calculated the possibility, even likelihood of some sort of cult being involved in Miles's death but although neo-Nazism permeated much of Europe and parts of Asia, as far as Mongolia, there was no significant resurgence of the movement in the UK. There was nothing about Miles's death that suggested it was politically motivated. It didn't seem to fit. Priest turned to ask Scarlett what she meant.

His words would have been wasted. Scarlett Ellinder had gone and he was alone with the insects.

33

For the second time that morning, Priest awoke, this time with a headache. He experienced a few moments of disorientation before, slowly, the room came into focus and he remembered where he was.

His phone was ringing.

'Hello?'

'Charlie? Are you OK?'

'Fine.'

Priest rubbed the back of his neck and found a goose feather from the pillow tangled in his hair. His wrists were still marked from the cable ties Miles Ellinder had used to restrain him and his arm was still sore from the burn. The underside of his forearm had blistered horribly.

He'd crept back into the room after spending some time considering Kenneth Ellinder's insect collection and managed to slip back into bed without disturbing Jessica. She must have left at some point after he fell asleep because when he turned over he found nothing but a warm indent in the mattress.

'Charlie?' said the voice down the phone.

'Sorry. Georgie. How are you?'

'I'm great. Better than you sound.'

Priest climbed out of bed and opened the door to the en suite. There was no sign of Jessica. Disappointed, he cupped the phone to his ear with his shoulder and used the toilet.

'I'm not good with mornings. What time is it?'

'Seven thirty. Are you pouring tea?'

'It's not tea anymore. How did it go last night?'

'I tried to ring you when I got back but your phone was off.'

Yes, I was in the middle of something . . .

'I got pictures of the room, like you asked. But nothing useful out of Terri Wren.'

'That's good. Can you send me a picture of the desk?'

Georgie paused. 'Just the desk?'

Priest flushed and loped back into the bedroom.

'Just the desk,' he repeated.

'There's more,' Georgie urged.

'What more?'

'I found a classified file, tucked in the top of the desk. The papers were out of order, as if they'd been put back in haste.'

'And?'

'And I'm sending you the files along with the picture of the desk.'

∽

Downstairs, the kitchen was cold. In a cupboard, he found a cereal he didn't recognise but which promised to fulfil his need for a wholesome, sugar-coated breakfast. He sat near the Aga, the only source of heat in the room.

He flicked through the contacts in his phone and found Jessica's name. He dialled. The signal was weak, barely enough for a conversation, but it didn't matter – the phone went straight through to her voicemail. Her phone's generic message, of course. Nothing personal.

There was a long pause. He realised he had absolutely no idea what to say.

'Jessica,' Priest said at last. 'It's me. Obviously. Just wondered how you were? Where you were? That sort of thing. Oh, and McEwen's bent. Don't go near him. Georgie sent me a picture of Philip Wren's desk, as of last night. There's a nice big muddy footprint on it, for the coroner's benefit, placed delicately post-mortem by McEwen using Wren's shoe before he was cut down. As we thought, his suicide was faked. Call me when you get this. It would be . . . you know, nice to hear from you.'

He was about to shovel in a spoonful of the unknown cereal when he looked up, sensing someone standing at the doorway.

'How long have you been there?' he asked.

'Long enough. Is there something going on between you and Jessica?' asked Scarlett. Her arms were folded, her brow furrowed.

Priest tried not to react. 'You haven't seen her this morning?' he asked.

'She left. Early.'

'I see.'

'I hope you know what you're doing, Mr Priest.'

'I didn't plan to –'

'I don't mean that.' She sat opposite him, a red dressing-gown draped around her shoulders. If she had spent the whole of last night awake watching black-and-white horror films, she looked pretty good for it. 'I mean Miles.'

Priest raised an eyebrow. 'You care about what happened to Miles?'

'I care about the group.' Scarlett narrowed her eyes. 'In three weeks' time, Mr Priest, the Health Minister is going to issue another statement urging GPs to stop prescribing antibiotics; antibiotics that we produce. I care, Mr Priest, about our share price. And starting something with Jessie right now in our family home is beginning to look like fucking up.'

'I'm . . .' He was about to reply, about to let her know, gently, that he also cared. About Jessica, not the share price. But that didn't seem appropriate. It also seemed like a big thing to admit to. And there was something else. 'What did you call this place?'

'What?'

'This house. You called it . . .?'

'Our family home.' Scarlett looked bemused. 'Priest? What's wrong?'

Our family home. Priest thrust a heaped spoonful of the cereal in his mouth before getting up and rushing past her.

34

27th March, 1946
A remote farm in middle England

Ruck awoke in the early hours of the morning with a throbbing head and the stain of guilt splashed across the bed-sheets.

He reached out but he knew she had already gone. He recalled her getting up in the middle of the night. He cursed himself for not waking up fully, but he'd thought she had just been going to the bathroom.

He sat up and rubbed his aching head. Somewhere outside a cockerel was crowing. If he ever found it, he'd shoot the bloody thing. He ran a hand across his chest before getting out of bed. He glanced at his skin in the mirror: a constellation of bruises and scratches. It looked like the work of a wild animal. He dressed – trousers, shirt and tie. A new beige pinstriped jacket bearing the CC41 logo: rationed utility clothing. All neatly pressed.

He'd locked the pistol away in a drawer when Eva had finally fallen asleep, a precaution he would have taken anyway but one that he had executed with particular care last night. He tried not to think about what they had done, about the violence he had unleashed on her, but he could not get the images out of his head. Nor could he exorcise the notion that Eva Miller brought something out in him; something he was afraid of.

Ruck swallowed hard. Fitzgerald was dead. His lover was a murderess.

Three urgent knocks at the door. Before Ruck could respond, it was thrust open. Outside was a soldier, red-faced and sweating, despite the cold. His bayonet was fixed on the rifle that hung over his shoulder. Ruck struggled to recall his name. Paris. That was it. Private Paris.

'Sir, you need to come.' The man was shaking.

'What?' Ruck retrieved the pistol. Thank God it was still there.

'It's Doctor Schneider . . .'

Private Paris turned on his heels, shot back along the corridor, and clattering down the stairs.

Ruck had to run to keep up. He followed Paris across the courtyard, all the time checking around him for Eva. *Where was she?* He looked back at the house. The kitchen was in darkness. There was no sign of movement in any of the upstairs windows. Everything was still.

Except for that blasted cockerel.

Paris threw open the door to one of the outbuildings to reveal two other soldiers, faces partially illuminated by the naked bulb above them. They shrank back from Ruck; they were the two he had ordered to bury Fitzgerald.

'What's going on?' Ruck demanded.

The two soldiers exchanged nervous glances. Ruck could feel his patience wearing thin.

'Well?'

The one on the right lifted the latch on the door to Schneider's cell. Evidently it had already been unlocked. The door swung open and he stepped aside, motioning Ruck past him.

Ruck took out the pistol; Paris followed, rifle ready. The other two lingered outside, peering in.

As it happened, guns were not necessary. Schneider was on the floor slumped up against the bed but he posed no threat. His face bore little resemblance to the sharp features of the man Ruck had interrogated the day before; it was bloody and swollen, with a nose bent horribly to the side. There were wounds on his body, too; his tunic was stained with blood. His feet seemed to have suffered the most – they were a mangled bundle of blood and pulp.

'We found this, Colonel,' said one of the soldiers. Ruck turned. He was holding a claw hammer dripping with blood.

Ruck stepped forward and knelt down. Schneider's eyes were locked shut by the swelling; his breathing was laboured. His injuries were terrible. Ruck's heart was pounding. He didn't feel any remorse for this Nazi – justice was often a rough path to tread – but first Fitzgerald, and now this . . . Something felt malevolent.

'Who made you this pretty?' Ruck whispered softly. Schneider turned his head, exhaled painfully. When he spoke, the arrogance in his voice was gone – it was nothing more than the wheeze of a dying man.

'Would you believe, your little scribe?'

'You couldn't protect yourself against a mere woman, doctor?'

Ruck took out a handkerchief and dabbed at the laceration that ran down the Nazi's right cheek. She had taken the claw of the hammer and tried to open his face up.

'She is full of surprises, Herr Ruck. Best be careful with that one.'

'What did she want?'

'To hurt me.'

Ruck moved his hand fast, reached across and took Schneider by the throat. The doctor winced with pain but didn't cry out.

'No, doctor. What did she want?'

Schneider spluttered and for a moment Ruck thought he might be through but it turned out to be laughter, or the best attempt at laughter Schneider could manage.

'Sharp as always,' Schneider choked. 'Yes, this wasn't just for pleasure. Not entirely. I had to give up certain information to save my life.'

'What information?'

'It appears that your little scribe has a keen interest in chemistry.'

'She wanted the formula?'

'She already has that.'

Ruck's eyes widened with horror. 'She has it?' he began. 'What –'

'What she wanted was more detail. Where to find the ingredients, for instance.'

'And you refused to tell her?'

'She felt I was holding out, yes.'

'But in the end you told her.'

Schneider nodded, but whether he was disappointed or pleased, Ruck couldn't tell.

'Everything.'

Ruck pushed Schneider away – this time he did cry out in pain – and marched out of the cell.

'What should we do with him, Colonel?' Paris called after him.

Ruck called back over his shoulder without breaking stride: 'When he dies, bury him next to Fitzgerald.'

He bolted across the courtyard, through to his bedroom, and rifled through the pockets of yesterday's jacket. Nothing. He tossed the jacket down, checked the pockets of the rest of his clothes, but he knew he hadn't misplaced the piece of paper. Through suffering, Schneider had claimed he could see God. Ruck remembered the way Eva had spoken, the way she had turned the words over on her tongue. Now he was sure she was gone.

Eva. His murderess.

Ruck looked out of the window. The sun had breached the line of trees surrounding the farm, casting long shadows across the grass. Nothing moved but it was sterile rather than still. Beyond the tree line the terrain undulated, a grey pastel sheet peppered with farmhouses.

She was out there somewhere, a fury unleashed on the world. Dark and beautiful, the doctor's secrets travelling with her.

A harbinger of death.

Ruck knew above all – beyond whatever cursed duty he owed to his country, to Operation Mayfly – only one thing.

She must be stopped.

35

The Priest family home remained in the sole ownership of Felix and Esther's middle child. Set in two acres of overgrown woodland, it was more a hotchpotch of small buildings awkwardly fused together than it was a house.

It was an inadequate family home. The original bungalow had been added to, extended, moulded and bent over decades as Felix and Esther had fought for space to raise their children in. They could have moved. It wasn't as if money had been an issue. But for Esther in particular, the Vyre had held such precious and fragile memories that no one had had the heart to sell up. After both Felix and Esther had died, Priest had bought out his siblings to ensure the property remained in the family.

On days like these, he wished he'd had the damn thing condemned.

Just over two hours had passed since he had been sitting at the Ellinder breakfast table. He'd taken a taxi back to collect the Volvo, which he had now parked on the side of the driveway. A fog had settled over the hills. He couldn't see more than fifty yards past the house on either side, not that there was much to see. A flock of starlings lining a telegraph wire watched him as he trudged up the path to the front door.

The Vyre's gardener, a brusque old man Priest simply knew as Fagin, had trimmed back the weeds but the exterior was choked with ivy and in places it was hard to see where the greenery ended and the house began. Priest fished out a key; the lock turned surprisingly easily.

The house was empty, more or less. A few tables pushed carelessly back against the walls. The odd chair here and there. A Welsh dresser in the hallway. Things he couldn't be bothered to sell on eBay. The air was heavy, stale. At the back of the entrance hall, he stopped to look at the copy of *The Funeral* by George Grosz that had hung there as long as he could remember. He smiled at the faded colours, predominantly red and black. The painting was a rebellion against humanity by an artist who saw people as ugly, immoral, fear-driven cattle. A procession of grotesque and weird characters crammed through the corridor of a dark modern city, frenzied and drunk, swarming desperately around Death, who drinks from a bottle, indifferent to the suffering and madness around him.

It had been one of William's favourites.

There was a noise from the kitchen.

Priest made his way softly across the hall and pushed open the door to the kitchen. For one brief moment, he thought he would see his mother turning to smile at him, her hands busying themselves over the stove.

But of course it wasn't her.

Priest quickly assessed the situation. The intruder wasn't a threat. First, because he was smaller and lighter than Priest. Second, because he had his back turned and hadn't seen Priest. Third, he was on his own.

The kitchen was at the end of the house. There had been plans to build out even further, to create a summer house, or at least install a door to the garden. They had never been put into place. The trespasser was trapped.

'Hello,' said Priest, walking out in full view, his hands thrust deep into the pockets of his mac.

It was the second time in a week that he had come across an unwanted stranger in his house. The odds were a lot better this time round, though. Scarlett's reference to her 'family home' had triggered the thought that perhaps Wren might have sent the flash drive not to Priest's apartment but here, to his family home.

The intruder was rifling through a bundle of old post on the countertop.

'Did you find it?' Priest asked casually. 'The flash drive?'

The stranger looked up, shock and panic registering across his face – an animal caught in the headlights. There was nothing controlled about his movements. He wasn't even, apparently, a particularly good burglar, judging by the state of the window he had smashed.

'Cat got your tongue, Burglar Bill?'

Priest took the intruder by the collar, hit him hard in the side of the stomach where the damage would be minimal but the pain intense and lingering. Air burst from Burglar Bill's lungs. *Good.* For a moment, Priest thought he might have inflicted more damage than he had intended but there was an eventual agonising noise as Bill gasped to replace the lost oxygen.

'Fucking hell!' the man wheezed.

Priest was in control. His punch had incapacitated Bill instantly. He had an urge to take his head and slam it into the side of the kitchen cupboard. He resisted, but his rage was held in check by a thread.

'I said, *did you find it*?' Priest hissed in the intruder's ear.

'I don't know wha—'

Well. If he was going to play that game, the reasons for holding back seemed less persuasive. Priest smashed Bill's head into the side of his mother's cupboard, pulled it back and saw a small and satisfying splash of red on the door.

'Try again,' Priest suggested.

'No! I didn't find it! C'mon, man. I'm just an errand boy!' Bill whimpered.

'Errand boy for whom?'

'I can't . . . they'd kill me.'

'*They'd* kill you? *I'll* fucking kill you!'

Priest marked the cupboard door again. This time the sound of the thud was accompanied by a howl.

'Wait! Please!' begged the intruder.

'Talk then.'

'Some guy sent me, to get one of those memory stick things. Said it would be in the post. I don't know why! He didn't tell me nothing. Just that it was in this fucking house, somewhere. Gave me four hundred quid. You know how many houses I have to go through to get four hundred quid's worth of stuff?'

'Who sent you?'

'I don't know his name!'

Priest pulled Bill's head back, once more positioning it level with the side of the top cupboard. He wanted to see that red mark splashed across the face of the old wood. 'Try again,' he suggested.

The intruder was whimpering. His nose was squashed and bent – the ridge had snapped. 'I don't know his name.'

'Then how do you know who to thank for your four hundred quid?'

Priest kept him held close to the edge of the cupboard, a foot or so away. Sufficient distance to create enough force to slice his head open if he was so inclined. As it happened, he wasn't. He'd done sufficient damage to make the guy spill. Sarah wouldn't be impressed if he ended up sharing a padded cell with William. He doubted Jessica would be, either.

'The Bagman.'

'Who's the Bagman?'

'I don't fucking know! He wears a bag on his head. That's why I call him the Bagman. I swear, fella. I don't know his fucking name!' Bill swallowed and ran a dry tongue over his fat lips, opening and shutting his mouth like a dying fish.

Just as Priest was about to grab him again, there was an explosion and part of Burglar Bill's head tore away and splattered on the cupboard door.

Priest dropped the body instantly. Turned round as it fell to the floor.

The Bagman trained the gun on Priest without the slightest tremor, apparently unperturbed by the shattered body lying between them. He was broad-shouldered but a little shorter than Priest. He wore a long, brown trench coat pulled tightly around him, cut-off gloves and heavy boots, but the most striking feature was the white hood covering his head, with slits for eyes.

Priest waited. He was shaking; his breath was short. There was a crippling tightness around his chest.

'I guess you're the Bagman.'

'Some would know me as this.' The Bagman's voice was a rumble, a low, throaty growl. Nothing was genuine, except the expertise with which he held the gun and where he stood. Close enough to let Priest know there was no prospect of missing; far enough away to deter him from making any sudden moves.

Priest was no longer in control. What he said next might keep him alive.

'You were watching the house,' Priest said.

'Yes.'

'And you saw me come in.'

'That was your misfortune, Mr Priest.'

'Where's Hayley?'

The Bagman chuckled. 'Safe. For now. At our special house. Please don't worry about her, Mr Priest. I'm afraid your involvement in this pursuit is now over. You have only one task left to perform.'

Priest was taking in more oxygen than his brain could cope with. 'Which is?'

'To open that envelope.'

The Bagman motioned to the stack of envelopes on the counter. The top one bore Priest's name. Priest recognised the writing. He reached for it. It was padded, sealed with parcel tape and with an unmistakable bulge in the middle.

Without taking his eyes off the gun, Priest opened the envelope and reached in to pull out a flash drive.

'Ah. Good. Would you mind throwing it to me?' the Bagman asked.

'What is it?'

'Does it matter? The data is important to me. What else do you need to know?'

Priest tossed the flash drive over and the Bagman caught it neatly.

'It's nothing personal, Priest,' said the Bagman, a hint of amusement in his voice.

'It feels that way to me,' Priest murmured.

'Then you will have to die with that thought and let it follow you all the way to Hell.' The Bagman laughed, a ringing, haunting sound. 'Hell. Isn't that where all lawyers go?'

'Better to reign in Hell than serve in Heaven,' Priest whispered. He was standing on the edge of a giant precipice. He felt a great weight lifting.

'Milton,' the Bagman said. He sounded impressed.

'Yes.'

Priest heard the hammer snap back. He waited, wondering if he would hear the sound of the bullet from this range. He hoped not. He hoped death would be silent.

The gun exploded and Charlie Priest found out that death was anything but silent.

36

Hayley gasped for breath. Her lungs felt as if they were on fire and she could taste blood, lots of blood.

She was alive.

She didn't want to be alive.

Hayley remembered the pain. The unspeakable pain. The pain of Hell itself. She couldn't go through that again. She would rather die. Yes – she would kill herself rather than face the prospect of the evil the hooded man had injected into her.

She crawled to the corner of the room. Every inch of her progress was agony. She couldn't use her right arm, the arm in which he had injected the poison. It wouldn't respond and when she had dared to look at it she couldn't see any flesh she recognised as her own. Just a withered black stump – more like the branch of a tree than an arm.

'A taster,' the man with the hood had explained. 'A small dose to allow immunity to build. Nothing to worry about.'

I want to die.

She collapsed in the corner of the room where she curled up as tightly as her naked body would allow.

He was gone, for now.

She thought about her father and his warning to her. A warning she had ignored. She had known something was wrong for weeks and she had ignored him. But it had been obvious, hadn't it? Her father had hardly seemed to know she existed when she was growing up, but then, all of sudden, he wanted to see her.

He had taken her to a cafe a mile or so away from her house. A small, dingy place, partially underground where the coffee tasted burnt. He had talked about his work, his obsession. He was involved in something secret, something complicated. He had mentioned something called the House of Mayfly. She wouldn't understand the details, but she needed to know about it.

'I'm just saying, Hayley, there's a lot going on right now and we may not see much of each other,' he had said, although that was hardly anything new. 'I just want you to look after yourself. Find a friend to move in with; I hate you living alone.'

She had protested. She enjoyed not having someone else to worry about. But there was more advice.

'Take a different route home each time. Don't be predictable. Have your phone on you at all times. Call me if you feel that you need to. Any time.'

None of it had registered. Not his words, not his tone. Her head was buried too deeply in the sand. Even his final warning failed to hit home.

'If I call you, you must answer straight away.'

If only she had listened.

Above her, a ceiling fan rotated unsteadily, just like the thoughts in her scrambled mind endlessly spinning, never quite coming together.

It was all there to see but you had to bury your head like you always do. Now you'll die. Alone, in this cold room.

Tears ran down her cheeks. She tasted blood in her mouth.

'Blessed are the merciful,' said Jesus. 'For they shall receive mercy.' When I die, I can forgive you, Father, if the Lord gives me the strength.

Hayley looked down at her arm. Whatever had been injected in her had taken root. The black, oily substance had spread through her body, desecrating it and defiling her mind, filling her head with filth and evil.

It was a demonic creature, she realised. Not a chemical. A Demon. Inside her.

She saw things. Images of unmentionable suffering.

What am I thinking?

She understood what was happening. She was going to be the spectacle that men paid to watch. She was in the House of Mayfly, with the Devil, and the poison was already working its magic, already taking hold. *A taster. A small dose. Nothing to worry about.*

Hayley closed her eyes and thought of God. *I'm sorry I looked.*

37

The crack of the gun catapulted Priest back to his early twenties. After four years on the beat he had been eligible to join a firearms unit and had signed up for training at the National Police Firearms Training Centre in Kent. He'd spent six weeks firing a Glock 17 at targets of ever decreasing size until one day, just as his skill with a gun had begun to be noticed, he had taken a call from Scotland Yard. There was an opening for a new detective constable. Priest had not fired a gun since.

In the fraction of a second it took for Priest to jerk himself back to the present he understood something else.

He was still alive.

The gun had fired but the bullet had lodged itself in the wall to Priest's right, missing him by several feet. The weapon itself had been sent skittering across the kitchen floor by a large figure who was attacking the Bagman with wild anger, beating him with a large wooden staff.

'What're you doin' here? Eh? What're you doin' here?' he roared.

'Fagin?'

It took Priest a few moments to recognise the Vyre's gardener. Fagin was a pensioner but forty years of working outdoors in all weathers had chiselled out a muscular frame and, with surprise on his side, he had managed to gain an advantage over the Bagman, who was frantically kicking at him with feral alarm.

The Bagman parried the first couple of blows from the staff with his arms. Another strike downward and with more luck than judgement, he jumped aside, narrowly avoiding his skull being crushed. The miss wrong-footed Fagin and tipped him off balance and the Bagman was able to use his weight to topple the gardener over into Priest. They fell backwards, Priest taking the brunt of the fall on his back and shoulder.

'Fucking hell!' Priest wheezed as the air shot from his lungs. 'Fagin, the gun!'

The gardener righted himself with surprising agility and dived for the weapon. But his lunge had been unnecessary. With defeat inevitable, the Bagman had made his exit. By the time they had both picked themselves up, he had vanished.

∞

Fagin was not his real name. His real name was Brian. His weathered features, heavy long coat and his insistence on carrying a thick wooden staff with him everywhere had earned him the Dickensian nickname, which he did nothing to disassociate himself from. Sarah had despised him as a creepy old man with a Victorian sense of status and discipline. But Priest had always had a soft spot for Fagin. He didn't exactly like him, but he accorded him a certain sense of respect, which, on the whole, was reciprocated.

Priest had kept Fagin on to look after the Vyre after he had taken over the house. He just couldn't bear seeing the place completely fall apart, nor put the old man who tended to the conifers and kept the grass short out of a job. It had turned out to be a wise investment, despite Sarah's reservations.

'What the blazes are you doing here, Charlie? And who the hell was that?' Fagin demanded.

'It's a long story,' Priest murmured.

'I don't doubt it. You back in the old kitchen with a dead man at your feet and a gun to your head doesn't sound like a short one.'

Priest was struggling for breath; his body was still electrified with adrenaline. Fagin was standing between him and the door, the staff at his side. Waiting.

'I'm in trouble, Fagin,' Priest said.

'Really? Could've fooled me.' Fagin grunted.

'I'm afraid that I've associated myself with some unpleasant business.'

'Hmm. Your father was just as bloody clear as mud. Chip off the old block, you. Well, whatever it is you're into, I don't want to know. Don't concern me. Blokes wearin' hoods for disguises are bad news in my book.' Fagin stooped down and picked up the gun, examining it closely. 'Import. Cost a lot, Charlie. A Desert Eagle. No wonder your friend here has part of his head missin.'

'How hard did you hit him, Fagin?'

'Not hard enough. He'll be back, if that's what you mean.'

Priest shrugged. He had hoped Fagin might have done enough damage for the Bagman to check into a hospital, giving Priest a chance to track him. He knelt down and inspected the dead body oozing blood on his mother's kitchen floor. He put his hand over his mouth – the smell was nauseating. It was different from the fetid smell of decomposition he remembered from crime scenes. This was the smell of fresh blood.

'Think this one's a grunt,' Fagin remarked, prodding the body with his staff. Priest fished inside the pockets but found only smoking paraphernalia. No wallet. He guessed the man was homeless, recruited to a cause for four hundred quid.

'But to what cause?' Priest muttered.

'He's not going to tell you anything, son. Dead men and tales and all that.'

'Mm.'

Priest got up and hovered by the window. A large oak in the distance caught his eye, its gnarled roots buried deep in the earth, anchoring the mighty trunk down. He knew that tree well. He'd married Dee under it.

'Charlie?' Fagin prompted.

Priest turned and the memory evaporated. 'Sorry, what?'

'Huh. Looks like you could use a rest. I'll sort this mess out for you. Nice and quiet, like.'

'Fagin, you don't need –'

The old man held up his hand. 'Wouldn't be the first time I helped a Priest move a body.'

Priest hesitated. He wasn't sure whether Fagin was being serious, but he'd hypothesised years ago that William must have had some help for one or two of the killings. Now wasn't the time to feel guilty again.

'That would be great,' he heard himself saying.

Fagin nodded. 'You OK?'

'Fine. Pity he got away. That's all.'

'Did he take something of yours?'

'Yes. Something important.'

'A little microchip,' Fagin suggested.

'A bit like that.'

'Hmm.' Fagin nodded again, solemnly. He thrust his hand deep into his seemingly bottomless pocket, swirled it around and to Priest's astonishment, produced a flash drive. 'A bit like this one?'

'Where . . .?' Priest's head felt like someone had poured hot oil into it.

'Why the hell do you think they call me Fagin?'

∞

Priest took the steps to the office three at a time.

He'd tried ringing Jessica four times on the way back from the Vyre but the phone just jumped straight to her answer message. Frustrated, he left another message. 'Jessica? It's me. Where are you? I have the flash drive. Call me as soon as you get this.'

He rushed across reception towards the stairs. Maureen opened her mouth to speak. 'Sorry! Tell them I'm on holiday.'

On the first floor, Priest flew into his office and slammed the door shut behind him. He paused. Where the hell was she?

He turned the computer on, put the stick into a USB port and waited while a little message told him that some software was being installed. *Come on!* He tapped his fingers on the desk impatiently.

'Good morning, esteemed leader.'

Priest jumped, physically pushing himself away from the desk. He hadn't heard Okoro come in. Georgie was lurking behind him. She flashed him a smile.

'Sorry,' she said. 'We knocked but . . .'

'I've retrieved the flash drive,' he told them. They took seats. Georgie had a pen poised over a notepad, as if she was at a lecture. 'You're all going on an extended holiday.'

'What?' Georgie said, surprised.

'Our present circumstances . . .' Priest began. 'This situation is very personal to me, but it's not your problem. It's dangerous, far more dangerous than I had ever imagined. And you're not paid for dangerous. Maureen will keep things ticking over here until this business is behind us.'

'It's *our* problem, too, Priest,' said Okoro.

Priest held up his hand. 'No. Really.'

Georgie looked crestfallen. 'I can't *not* be involved in this, Charlie.'

'Georgie, look at me. You see these white blobs on my coat?'

'Yes.'

'Do you know what they are?'

She leant forwards and inspected the jacket: 'Calamari?'

Priest winced. 'It's brain, Georgie. Someone's brain.'

'*What*?' She shot back in her seat.

'Let's not have this hero routine, Priest,' Okoro said, frowning. 'You're stuck with us. Period. Now, what do you mean *brain*? Whose *brain*?'

Priest tried to formulate a credible response but something made him hesitate. His guilt burned fiercely. This wasn't their fight but, then again, it wasn't his either. Someone had made it his and he had made it theirs. Maybe his best way of protecting Georgie, Okoro and Solly was to keep them in the dark.

'Priest?' Okoro demanded.

Georgie's pen was still poised, the embodiment of everything pure and innocent.

'No,' Priest said, shaking his head. 'I will not be responsible for you.' Georgie stirred in her seat, ready to protest, but he raised his hand again. 'No, Georgie. Enough. I won't patronise you.

I know you know it's not a game. Both of you. It's far from it. But there's something out there. Something so evil that people are dying to protect it, to serve it, to defy it. Whatever it is, it's bigger than us – bigger than you. Go home and take Solly with you. We're closed until this mess is sorted.'

He had thought she might try to persuade him otherwise but she just looked mournfully at the desktop. From underneath the table she produced a bundle of papers, which she laid out delicately in front of him.

'What are these?' Priest asked.

'It's a copy of the report I found in Philip Wren's office and some research I've done for you to go with it.'

He placed his finger on the papers, hesitating again. Somehow, taking the file seemed like a concession he didn't want to give but he took it anyway, flicking through the first few sheets. He looked at her and she smiled, but it didn't reach her eyes.

'Thank you.'

She shrugged.

'We'll be watching your back, Priest,' said Okoro.

'I know you will.'

They got up solemnly. It felt like a long and awkward goodbye.

'I'll tell Maureen to let your usual clients know we'll be unavailable until further notice,' said Okoro.

'Please.'

'Good luck, Charlie,' said Georgie. This time the smile reached her eyes.

He stood up and shook their hands. 'I'll keep you informed,' he promised.

They closed the door.

Priest leant back in his chair and closed his eyes but his respite was short-lived. The file had finished downloading. There on his desktop was a folder simply labelled 'Mayfly'.

He double-clicked on the file and it opened as a PDF. A database. A very long list of names and addresses. He scanned them quickly, his heart racing. *This is it? All of this hatred and bloodshed for a mailing list?*

Most of the names meant nothing to him but occasionally one jumped out. A politician he recognised, a senior planning officer he'd dealt with, a couple of barristers from chambers he knew. No apparent connection between them. But one thing was certain. *Somebody desperately wants to keep the names on this list secret.*

∽

Priest crossed the underground car park but slowed as he approached the old Volvo. A figure stood by the car, leaning back over the roof, waiting patiently. Priest stopped a few yards away, the keys held loosely by his side. The light from the high slit windows cascaded on her hair but cast her face in darkness. He couldn't see her properly but the slender features were unmistakably those of the woman he had made love to the previous night.

He paused briefly. He wanted her to think he felt nothing. He wanted himself to think he felt nothing. Wordlessly, he clicked the key fob and they both got into the car. It was several miles down the road before she spoke.

'Where are we going, Priest?'

'You don't know?' Priest asked drily.

'Obviously.'

He glanced at her sideways. 'Didn't your mother always tell you not to get into cars with strangers?'

'My mother rarely offered advice. And your insinuation is noted, but my phone battery died.'

'Where have you been?'

'Thinking.'

Priest decided not to pursue it, but as he caught a glimpse of himself in the wing mirror he was surprised to notice that he was smiling. He was pleased to see her. He thought about bringing up the previous night's encounter but by now he'd learnt enough about Jessica Ellinder to know that, if she had wanted to talk about it, she would have mentioned it. Didn't help his state of confusion over it, though. Did she regret it, he wondered? Was she ashamed?

More pertinently, was she likely to repeat the performance?

'We're going to see an old friend of mine,' he said instead. 'He's with South Wales police at the moment but right now he's on some sort of course or something nearby. It'll be an hour's drive, tops.'

'How nice,' she replied, although her tone suggested the opposite.

'You got my message about McEwen?'

'Yes.'

'And you didn't tell your father?'

Jessica paused. 'No.'

'Good. We don't need to alert McEwen at this stage.'

There was a traffic jam ahead. Red lights for as far as Priest could see, stretching up the outgoing road. A slow patter of rain tapped on the windscreen, the noise keeping time with Priest's beating heart.

He continued. 'When Georgie was searching Wren's office she came across extracts from a police file relating to a murder in a remote woodland twenty miles north of Cardiff. It was interesting because I couldn't find any reports of it in the media and yet it was a tabloid golden egg.' He stopped, suddenly conscious of her scent.

'And?' Jessica prompted.

'Sorry. Got distracted. The report is incomplete but mentioned a wooden cabin hidden in woodland. The police found the victim slumped in a chair. He'd been poisoned.'

'Poisoned?'

'Yes, but not with any ordinary poison. Something very specific. The report doesn't contain any chemical analysis but, whatever it was, it drove the victim mad.'

'What caused his death?'

Priest thought back to the contents of the report and the thumbnail picture of the victim. The second horrible parody of the human body he had seen in as many days. His stomach churned.

'He tore his own skin off.'

'I see.'

Priest waited, his head cocked. '*I see*. Is that it?'

'What would you consider the correct emotional response to that to be?'

'Anything other than "I see". Something more, you know – with a little more empathy.'

'How do you suggest I show empathy for someone who has torn their own skin off?'

'I . . .' A horn sounded from behind him; the traffic had started to move up ahead. The Volvo shuddered into life again and they began to crawl forward. Priest glanced across at Jessica. She was sitting perfectly still, her eyes on the road ahead, her hands on her lap.

Priest shuffled in his seat. What was it about her that he found so disturbing?

'You said you had recovered the flash drive,' she prompted.

'Wren had sent it to my family home, not my flat.'

'And?'

'It's a database of names and addresses.'

'That's it?'

'That's it.'

'Do the names mean anything to you?'

'Nothing. There are a few people I've heard of, but nobody of any particular significance, and some of them are dead, according to the Register.'

'So we're no further on.' He could hear the frustration in her voice.

'That database means *something* to *somebody*. Perhaps your father ought to take a look at it? See if there are any names he recognises.'

She nodded. They drove on in silence for a while.

'Your sister showed me a room in your house.' He spoke carefully. 'Where your father keeps his bugs.'

'She was always very free with her hospitality,' Jessica said sourly.

'Maybe that's something you should have mentioned to me? That your father has a collection of, among other things, mayflies. The same insect that was found in Miles's throat.'

'Does that make him a suspect?'

'Not necessarily.'

'Then why is it relevant? He's collected them all of his life.'

Priest grimaced. This wasn't going well. *While I'm about it, why don't I just chuck in a comment about the aggressive sex we had last night to make this even more awkward?* It was going to be a long trip. *Still, we're locked in a car. Can she evade the subject for the whole hour we're on the road?* Priest took a deep breath and began. 'Could I just mention –'

'The sex we had last night?' she interrupted.

'Yes, that.'

'What about it?'

'I just wondered whether you wanted to talk about it.'

She shrugged, as if the suggestion was ridiculous. 'Why? Do you want to analyse it?'

'That's not what I meant.'

'Then what do you mean?'

'I mean –' Priest hesitated. When she put it like that, he had no idea what he meant. He tried again. 'I mean – how do you . . . feel?'

'How do I *feel*?'

He couldn't tell if she was mocking him or if she had genuinely not understood what he was asking. 'Can I simplify the question for you in some way?'

'Do you mean how do I feel about *you*?' She looked at him sideways.

He cringed. The awkwardness was overbearing. 'I guess.'

She seemed to think about it, although he suspected that she was humouring him.

'The circumstances we find ourselves in,' she said after a while, 'mean that our actions last night were ill-advised.'

'Jessica –' he said, exasperated. 'Are you a robot?'

She looked back to the road. Another few minutes of agonising time passed.

'Maybe we should just talk,' he finally suggested. 'Not necessarily about last night but, you know, generally?'

She made a few meaningless hand gestures, as if she was trying to drag a conversation out of thin air. 'Fine,' she said eventually. 'How did your first marriage end?'

'That's it?' he said, aghast. 'That's your attempt at general conversation: "How did your first marriage end?"'

She shrugged.

'It's to the point,' he conceded.

Mercifully, the traffic was starting to crawl a little faster up ahead. Beyond the queue, blue lights flashed and, beyond that, Priest saw faster-moving traffic. The stagnation was finite, at least. He felt he should try harder somehow, but he couldn't find the words. Besides, she had made her position clear: she didn't want to talk about it.

He decided to change the subject. 'We're going to meet Tiff Rowlinson. Detective Chief Inspector for South Wales Police. We worked together in the Met. Tiff's an excellent policeman and also the officer who was in charge of the poisoning case near Cardiff. I want to try to establish if there's any connection between it and what happened to Philip Wren and your brother.'

'You think there might be?'

'Well there's Wren, obviously. He's a connection. So there's something.'

She nodded.

Priest kept his hands firmly on the wheel. He could smell her scent. He thought of the soft, raspy moans she had emitted the night before, the way her fingers dug into the base of his skull, the way her body shuddered with pleasure under his touch. He shook the image from his mind. There was work to do.

'My wife walked out,' he said after half an hour of silence. They had long since left London behind.

'Why?'

Priest thought about it. 'Probably because she had developed a deep-rooted hatred of me.'

She nodded. And at last she smiled.

38

Georgie didn't purchase a first-class ticket. She could have afforded it but didn't, on principle. The down side was that she only had thirty minutes free Wi-Fi. After that, the saving she'd made on the ticket would be wiped out by the premium for Internet access.

She wasn't annoyed with Charlie. She understood why he would want to take on the burden alone, why he wouldn't want any of them in danger, but she wasn't impressed with him either. She didn't need protecting! Georgie had put her past behind her. She was a survivor, not a victim. And she didn't trust Jessica Ellinder. There was something about her. She was cold, emotionless, a mannequin. But Charlie Priest seemed unable to see it. He was under stress, so perhaps that was excusable. Having said that, she hadn't ruled out the possibility that he was allowing Jessica Ellinder's undoubted attractions to sway his judgement.

The thought grated on her as sharply as the biting cold wind that swept across the platform. She checked her watch. Fifteen minutes until the train was due; if it was on time. The platform was almost deserted. A few students huddled near the cafe. A family on the other side of the tracks. The only other people in close proximity were two men in suits, sitting on the next bench along. Out of the corner of her eye she noticed one of them glance at her. They weren't speaking, just sitting. She pulled her coat more tightly around her.

Her mind wandered. She tried not to think of Martin. Tried not to let him seep into her consciousness, contaminate this quiet moment that, were it not for the cold and the suspicious-looking men in suits, she might have enjoyed. The train drew in, only a few minutes past its scheduled departure time. At the last minute she took the door to the carriage furthest away from the men in suits. Obviously, going to Cambridge to check out Hayley Wren's house was not necessarily consistent with Charlie's order that she go home and not get involved anymore, but she couldn't let it go.

Because after all there was Hayley. Who was out looking for her? Wherever she was.

She checked her phone: a number of messages about cases she was working on and a missed call from Li, but that could wait. She spent some time replying to the emails, and by the time her inbox had been emptied London was far behind her. She stared out of the window: the countryside was rolling past quickly and she realised she couldn't remember pulling away from the platform. Then suddenly there was a voice in her ear.

'Shit!' Georgie exclaimed.

The guard made a face. 'Sorry, love. I said tickets.'

'Oh – oh. Of course. Sorry for, you know, saying *shit*.'

She produced her ticket and the guard, a woman with arms thicker than Georgie's waist, and mountainous buttocks, waddled on down the carriage.

She wondered what she might say to Charlie if he ever challenged her about her little excursion. She could lie but she wasn't a very accomplished liar and Charlie had a particular aptitude for truth-gathering. Perhaps she could . . . Something made her glance around. She froze. The two men in suits had entered the carriage.

Georgie closed her eyes and counted to ten. From behind her, she heard the sound of luggage scuffing across the holding bay at the back of the carriage – and breathing. She could hear them breathing, she was sure of it.

The train was slowing. An automated voice announced that the next stop was Cambridge. Slowly, Georgie rose from her seat, not daring to look round. Inside her coat pockets, her hands were balled into fists. There was something sharp, too. *A bunch of keys.* She curled her fingers around them and positioned one of the more jagged-edged keys so that the shank protruded between her second and third fingers. Not by much, but enough to take an eye out if needs be.

She began to make her way down the carriage towards the exit. Behind her, she heard the shuffle of feet. Someone coughed. As she moved, so did they. She felt a burning sensation spread across her chest and up her neck. Charlie had been right. She should have stayed at home. Her grip on the key tightened. She was half-way down the carriage and moving quicker, trying not to run in case they gave chase.

She thought about Miles Ellinder and Vlad the Impaler, the Prince of Wallachia. The key was cutting into her hand.

The train was taking for ever to slow. Out of the window, she caught a glimpse of an industrial estate. Boxlike buildings bearing brands she didn't recognise. A low wall adorned with tags and graffiti.

The door at the end of the carriage should have opened automatically as she reached it, but it didn't. There was a pounding in her head, mixed with the sound of footsteps marching roboti-cally behind her. Georgie closed her eyes again. She had been here before. She had known then that she could scratch and bite and use the keys if she had to. But last time there had just been one man; this time there were two. Tears filled her eyes; she wished the floor would swallow her.

She saw Hayley in her mind's eye – or at least what she thought Hayley might look like. Perhaps Hayley had faced this, perhaps she had cowered in a corner, gripped with terror, perhaps she had been as scared as Georgie was right now. Well, that would not be her; *it would not be her. I am a survivor, not a victim.*

Georgie spun around. From her coat pocket she produced the keys, ready to tear the flesh of whoever had stalked her down the carriage, ready to stick the blade right through their eyes.

The burning sensation was still there. She gasped for air. Every muscle in her body tensed.

Her arm dropped to her side. Her breathing slowed. The carriage was empty.

39

Tiff Rowlinson had not changed. He seemed to be stuck in a time warp, immune to the ageing process. His hair was still a strawberry blond, still fell longer on one side so it was just above his eye line. He looked like a slightly older member of a boy band.

They found him sitting on a wooden bench staring absently over the countryside into a valley, through which a few isolated farmhouses were scattered. Were it not for the wind turbines punctuating the horizon, the scene might have been unchanged for hundreds of years.

Rowlinson turned briefly to greet them. He had his arm spread across the back of the bench and a coffee mug in his hand. When he saw Jessica, he got up and offered his hand.

'How do you do. I thought that it was just you and me, Priest. Not that three is any way close to a crowd, Miss . . .?'

'Ellinder. Jessica Ellinder.'

They shook hands. Priest could tell that, like most people, Jessica was instantly reassured by Rowlinson's gentle nature. He felt a twinge of annoyance.

'How's William, by the way?' said Rowlinson.

'Still fucking mad.'

'And you're still fucking ugly, Priest.' Rowlinson grinned. 'Too ugly to be keeping such exquisite company. If Miss Ellinder is your associate then your fees must have increased substantially.'

'Client. And it's nice to see you, too, Tiff.'

'Client?' Rowlinson raised an eyebrow. 'On a business trip this far out? I hope you're not charging Miss Ellinder an hourly rate.'

They sat on the bench, Priest in the middle, and admired the rolling hillside. Jessica was resting her knee against his, and Priest needed something to distract him. There was a pack of cigarettes in his inside jacket pocket. He thought about taking one out but remembered he'd lost his lighter after he'd used it to burn half his wrist off.

'So, tell me, Priest,' Rowlinson said. 'I don't hear from you for – what – a year? Then you ring demanding to see me this afternoon in a discreet location to talk about something so secret that you can't even mention it over the phone. And you bring a client with you. I assume you haven't come to declare your undying love for me.'

'It's been a rough few days, Tiff.' Priest blinked, eyes scanning the horizon.

'Tell me more.'

Priest handed him the extract from the police file Georgie had found in Wren's office. Rowlinson thumbed through it before handing it back. His expression had darkened.

'Where did you get that?' he asked quietly.

'In the office of the late Attorney General,' Priest replied.

'Well, well.'

'I need some help, Tiff.'

A chill blew across the valley, ruffling the grass. The deep green was patched here and there with purple moss. Jessica pulled her jacket around her. Priest wondered about offering her his coat but he doubted his attempt at chivalry would be well received.

After a while Rowlinson said, 'I'm guessing that this isn't a peripheral enquiry for you, Priest.'

'Fuck, no. We're caught up right in the eye of the storm.'

'I see. Consequentially, I recommend you bring out your most sturdy umbrella.'

Priest turned and looked at Rowlinson. 'What's going on?'

'I wish I knew,' the DCI murmured.

'This is your case, Tiff. You're the senior investigating officer.'

'*Was. Was* the SIO.'

Priest was perplexed. Rowlinson was a first-class copper. What DSI in their right mind would take him off a case?

'So who is?' Priest enquired.

'No idea,' said Rowlinson, leaning back on the bench and stretching out his legs. 'All I know is, it's not me.'

'Who took it away from you?'

'I don't even know that. My super didn't know either. All he told me was that the order came directly from the Home Office.'

'The Home Office doesn't . . .'

'Meddle in police domestics? Come on, Priest. Where have you been the last decade?' Rowlinson sighed and hunched his shoulders. 'Look,' he said, 'the word on the street is that Sir Philip Wren was orchestrating some sort of secret task force to investigate cases like the one I was on.'

Priest felt Jessica shuffle in her seat next to him.

'Wren was a lawyer, not a police strategist,' Priest pointed out.

'He had a military background. Maybe he was diversifying.'

Priest winced. It seemed unlikely. 'What can you tell me about the homicide?'

Rowlinson shook his head. 'I was on the scene with SOCO. That's all. Then our late friend showed up.'

'Wren?'

'The very same.'

'Go on.'

Rowlinson sighed. 'The victim was strapped to a chair and injected with various chemicals, the effect of which was, over a prolonged period of time, to drive him mad and induce him to mutilate himself. His suffering was unimaginable.'

'What chemicals?'

'I don't know for sure but one of the SOCO team had previous experience with poisonings. He told me that he was only aware of one poison capable of causing so much devastation. A genetically modified version of a naturally occurring compound known as strychnine.'

'Which is what, exactly?'

'There is a tree that grows mainly in India known as the strychnine tree. The seeds contain strychnine, a highly toxic alkaloid probably best known as the poison of choice of Nazi doctors during the Holocaust.'

'Nazis?' Priest's ears pricked up.

'Yes,' continued Rowlinson, not appearing to notice Priest's heightened interest. 'The poison was given to inmates at various concentration camps, notably Buchenwald in Germany. Usually it was introduced into their food. The doctors observed the effects and measured how long different strains took to kill them. But in fact it turned out that these alkaloids weren't very effective.'

'Seemed pretty effective to me,' Priest remarked.

'Not as a killing device.'

'What do you mean?'

'Well, the average dose of poison from a Golden Dart Frog contains enough venom to kill about ten thousand mice or between ten and twenty humans in less than a few minutes. Those wonderful lionfish in your apartment, Priest, assuming you've been feeding them, might kill you after a day or so if you're unlucky enough to have an allergic reaction to them. The poison fed to the victim in this case falls somewhere between those two extremes, but the aim here seemed not to be to kill, or, if it was, it's a secondary aim.'

'So what is the aim?' Priest felt a chill run through him. He already knew the answer.

'They wanted to see the poor bastard suffer,' said Rowlinson, so quietly that Priest had to lean towards him to hear. 'The poison attacks the nerves in the spine. It produces unimaginable pain, but the neurotoxins prevent the brain from shutting the body down, which is our natural defence to extreme trauma. Every muscle in the body stretches and convulses. Oxygen can't get to the extremities so hands and feet and face become cyanotic, meaning they shrivel and turn blue. The victim pukes and shits and spasms, usually by arching their backs to such an unnatural extent that they break their own spines. It's the closest thing in real life to demonic possession you'll ever see.'

'You said the strychnine was modified?' Priest prompted.

'Possibly. If it was, it is simply the most terrifying chemical ever made.'

Jessica interjected for the first time. 'What do you mean *they*? You said *they* just wanted to observe suffering.'

Rowlinson took a swig of his coffee, draining the cup.

'We found evidence of at least six people in the cabin plus the victim, and there's reason to believe they had stayed there, to watch the show.'

'How do you know?' demanded Jessica.

'Six chairs neatly set out, theatre style.'

'That's what this is,' Priest muttered. 'They get off on it. Torture porn.'

'Except they seem to enjoy a very particular type of torture. One that is based on the victim mutilating himself.'

'You said *they seem*,' Jessica observed sharply. 'Present tense.'

'I did.'

'There's more?'

Rowlinson reached down underneath the bench to a bag Priest hadn't noticed before. He produced a set of papers, which he silently handed over.

Priest skimmed through them. 'Ah,' he said. 'You knew why we were coming.'

'I guessed,' Rowlinson admitted. 'You have a habit of turning up when weird things happen.'

Priest handed the papers to Jessica. 'How did you get this?' he asked Rowlinson.

'I listened very carefully to the Super telling me this was in the hands of others and that I should forget I ever saw it. But a few phone calls later and I found other SIOs were in a similar position. You have papers there on at least two other similar incidents, but I suspect there are more.'

'This looks organised,' Priest suggested.

'Something like that.'

Jessica shivered. 'How do you –' She paused. 'How do you know they enjoy watching? How do you know it's not that . . .?'

Rowlinson turned to look at her. 'I apologise for having to say this. It's a detail I've been trying to erase from my mind ever since I set foot in that godforsaken cabin. You know how it is, Priest. I've never reacted badly at a crime scene, but for the first time ever I coughed my guts up after just a few minutes near the victim. But there's more. We found –' Rowlinson swallowed hard. 'Fluids by one of the chairs. There was blood and bile from the victim but traces of semen, too. Not from the victim.'

Priest rubbed his chin thoughtfully. Beside him, he felt Jessica move even closer. Rowlinson had resumed staring ahead into the distance.

'You said one of your guys mentioned the Nazis,' Priest prompted.

'He mentioned a Nazi doctor called Schneider who was at Buchenwald,' Rowlinson said. 'Apparently, he specialised in torturing inmates with poison. Some of the guards liked to watch. I can believe it.' He shook his head. 'The prevalence of evil never ceases to amaze and sicken me.'

∽

'Do you like music?'

It seemed an innocent enough question but it was met with a disdainful look. Priest took Jessica's wordless reply as a no and turned his attention back to the road ahead. The first ten miles of the return journey to London had been driven in near complete silence. He was disappointed. Music was important to him.

Jessica was poring over the papers Rowlinson had handed them, scanning every page two or three times, assimilating the information greedily.

'You mentioned the Nazis,' she said finally, not looking up.

'I did?'

'Scarlett mentioned it to you also.'

'You two talk?'

'That surprises you?'

'Of course not. Sorry, I didn't mean to judge.'

'Fine,' Jessica said impatiently. 'Nazis.'

'Do you think Miles was a Nazi?'

'I think it's possible.' She paused, thinking. 'His social media usernames all end in the same numbers. Eighty-eight.'

Priest thought about it. 'I don't follow.'

'The eighth letter of the alphabet is H.'

'HH. *Heil Hitler.*'

'Probably just coincidence. But these papers are extracts from police files similar to the bundle your associate found in Wren's office. There are at least three incidents under investigation in which a victim is tortured to death through poison. Each time there is evidence that a group of people gathered to watch it happen.'

'The Mayfly?'

'Maybe that's what they call themselves.'

'Impalement hardly fits with their MO,' Priest pointed out.

'From what it's possible to understand from these papers, they operate a little like a paedophile ring,' she said, ignoring his remark. 'They're well organised, clinical, careful. They make no effort to hide what they're doing because they believe themselves to be untouchable. Whoever is the ringleader sets up a show and – I guess – a bunch of sick perverts pay a lot of money to watch.'

A knot had tightened in Priest's stomach. 'Hayley . . .'

'Is the daughter of the man who was investigating this . . . what? Cult? So . . .'

'It's no coincidence that she's missing,' Priest finished.

Priest tightened his grip on the wheel and pressed the accelerator further to the floor. The old Volvo responded as he merged clumsily into the fast lane.

'There's still time,' he said, although without much conviction. 'But Hayley Wren is in great danger.'

'Where do we start?'

Priest produced the flash drive from his inside coat pocket and held it up to the failing light. 'We have the names of the audience members, remember? Names, postal addresses, dates of birth. This is the ring, right here. It must be. This is what Miles wanted so badly.'

Jessica's eyes widened. She looked pale, paler than usual. Almost alabaster.

'Is –' she started.

'No,' Priest cut in, anticipating the question. 'Miles's name isn't on the list. Nor is your father's.'

'Seems careless, don't you think?' she said. 'To keep a list of punters for these *shows*.'

'It's a good insurance policy – provided you keep it safe.'

'So was Miles trying to get the list, or was he trying to get the list *back*?'

Priest thought back to those wild eyes staring at him from behind the drill. He was almost certain that Miles had been trying to retrieve something he'd lost, not acquire something he'd never had in the first place. *Perhaps he'd been killed because of his failure to recover it. But why impale him, if that was the case? What was the significance of that?*

Priest glanced over again. Jessica was leaning mournfully away from him, her head resting against the window, her auburn hair quivering with the movement of the vehicle.

'I'm sorry,' he offered.

'For what?'

'For what's happened to you. To your family.'

'It wasn't of your doing.'

He reached across to her, but he hesitated. She made no effort to move, although she must have been aware of the gesture. He started to withdraw his hand but something stopped him. He burned to know what he meant to her, why he had caressed her naked skin with total freedom, without resistance, less than twenty-four hours ago and was now afraid to touch her.

Ridiculous.

With one hand still on the wheel, he placed his finger gently on to her shoulder. She didn't respond at first, until he moved his hand down her arm, whereupon she stirred from her mesmerised state, turned her head towards him and, eventually, cupped her hand into his.

40

14th April, 1972
Kensington, London

Detective Chief Inspector Bertie Ruck chewed on his cigarette impatiently while he waited to be escorted through the hotel lobby.

Eventually, a young detective appeared, red-faced and harassed. Ruck didn't know his name.

'Sir,' said the DC uncertainly. 'I was told you were on leave.'

'Show me.'

The DC lifted the police tape and Ruck ducked under. His old joints weren't as agile as they used to be and the motion irritated his back.

'You OK, sir?'

'Fine. Which way?'

The DC led him across a marble floor towards the main stairwell. The lift was out of action, of course, and the body was on the ninth floor. They took the stairs two at a time.

'When was the discovery made?' Ruck grunted.

'Earlier this afternoon. The resident should have checked out in the morning so the hotel manager unlocked the door with a master key. Apparently, the resident asked for a room on the ninth floor, knowing the hotel was half empty. It's low season here. Manager said she made a fuss of ensuring that there was no one occupying the rooms to the side and below. Said she liked playing the violin until the early hours and didn't want to disturb any other guests.'

'The resident that booked the room was a *she*?'

'Yes, sir. Room was booked under the name Fitzgerald, sir.'

Ruck winced as if an old wound had just been reopened.

When they reached the ninth floor they ducked under more tape and walked across the hallway to where a couple of plods stood idly, unsure as to what to do with themselves.

'You've been on the murder squad a while, sir?' asked the DC, turning to Ruck.

'I have.'

The DC nodded. 'Brace yourself, then. It's not a pleasant one.'

Ruck pushed past him.

The room was like any other hotel room. Beige walls, avocado-coloured curtains, a bed, a side table and small desk. Except everything in this room was saturated in blood. Ruck took a step further in. The victim was lying on the bed; his face was contorted horribly. He was naked but his body looked as if it had been set upon by wild animals. Great strips of flesh had been torn off one side, exposing the muscle and tissue underneath.

This wasn't a murder victim. It was a carcass.

'There's evidence of an entry wound on the arm, sir,' said the DC quietly. He was standing outside the room, his hand covering his mouth. 'There's a puncture on his arm where something was injected. I think the injuries were inflicted post mortem.'

'Wishful thinking, constable,' Ruck said.

'What's that, sir?'

Ruck's eyes narrowed and he clenched his fists. Something burned inside him. He took another small step forward and peered at the body. It was a man, or had been at some point. A young man at that.

'There's something else, sir.'

Ruck turned sharply.

The DC was holding something, his hand outstretched. 'A note. Addressed to you.'

Ruck hesitated. He moved swiftly across the hotel room and snatched the note. The DC looked shocked. Ruck unfolded the paper.

'We don't know what it means,' the DC said.

Ruck did. He passed the note back to the DC. There was nothing on it, except his name and the outline, sketched in ink, of an insect.

'Sir? Does it mean anything to you?'

Ruck paused, motionless. Operation Mayfly, the inquisition of Dr Kurt Schneider, was a lifetime ago. Nobody still alive knew the code name; nobody except him and one other.

Although Ruck had not seen Eva Miller since the night Lance Corporal Fitzgerald had died, every day that had since passed he had woken up with her scent on him. And no matter how hard he washed and scrubbed, he couldn't remove it.

He looked at the DC.

'No,' he said finally. 'It means nothing to me.'

41

Shaken but resolute, Georgie found herself staring at Hayley Wren's front door.

When the train had pulled into the station, she had alighted as quickly as she could, but there had been no sign of the two men who'd been in the carriage with her. The danger had been entirely in her own head.

Georgie produced the front door key from her pocket and let herself in.

It hadn't been difficult. Georgie had gleaned from Hayley's social media activity that she was trusting but probably quite naive. She valued her community. She was impractical, prone to forgetting things. It seemed likely that she would have left a spare key with a neighbour. Not the junkie named Binny who lived above her, but the old lady on the right, whom Priest and Jessica may have overlooked. It turned out that Mrs Mudridge, as she introduced herself, was perfectly happy to accommodate Hayley's cousin, who had come up from university to surprise her.

'Hayley said she left a spare key with you, Mrs Mudridge,' Georgie had said.

'Of course, dear! You should take it and let yourself in. I think she has tea in the top cupboard.'

And Hayley did. Herbal. A large selection, as it happened, although Georgie drew the line there. Georgie liked Wagner, and she appreciated culture, even the odd foreign film, but a cache of herbal tea that took up an entire cupboard was just creepy – and the kitchen stank of it.

It was a simple place. Original floorboards covered with a few brightly coloured rugs, Ikea furniture, a bean bag that looked like it had never been used – *probably a present* – cups neatly lined up in size order and a bookshelf full of Gothic fantasy. There was nothing personal that Georgie could detect. No family pictures or cards. An inherent loneliness permeated each room. If she didn't know any better, Georgie would have said someone had recently died in this house. She shivered.

The food was off in the fridge and the smell was nauseating. Georgie couldn't bear leaving the milk to sour any more so she threw two bottles down the sink.

Upstairs was much the same. A bathroom stocked with cheap high-street products and some clothes discarded on the floor.

In the bedroom, Georgie's eye was immediately drawn to the dressing table. The temperature seemed lower in this room than the rest of the house. Carefully, she crossed the room, stepping over a can of hairspray, a few books. She sat down at the dressing table but stopped short of touching anything. The room was freezing – her breath misted in front of the cracked mirror. A feeling of unease washed over her. The table was a mess. Perfume bottles were scattered over the surface. One of them was smashed: the clear liquid had left a trail that disappeared over the far edge and the sickly smell permeated the room. There were papers that looked as though they had once been neatly stacked but had more recently been attacked with a leaf-blower. The table was askew and the mirror cracked.

And there were fingernail marks scratched into the front edge.

Georgie instantly saw it play out as if she was watching a film. She looked over her shoulder. Hayley's assailant had been hiding in the room. She had thrown the door open, from the shower maybe. Sat herself down, not even thinking that the house was anything other than hers exclusively. He'd probably cupped his hands around her throat and mouth. Instinctively, Hayley had grabbed the table to stop herself from being wrenched away. Her hold had been weak, but the table had come away from the wall at an angle. She had panicked. Georgie looked around the room, at the chaos. Hayley had chosen fight, judging by the mess and the scratch marks. But it looked as if it was a fight that she had lost. Had the kidnapper hurt her, more than the bruises and scratches she'd have sustained from the struggle?

Georgie closed her eyes. *What else happened in this little room?*

She shivered again. Opened her eyes. She wondered if she should call Charlie. She was edgy, and the sound of his voice would be reassuring – but she shouldn't be here. She had broken a promise.

Georgie got up, fumbling around in her pocket for her phone. Behind her, the bed remained unmade, the sheets draped on the floor to one side. Had he thrown her on to the mattress as well? Forced himself on top of her? Shivering, she scrolled through the contacts in her phone until her thumb rested over Charlie's number. Something stopped her from pressing *dial*.

The front door had opened downstairs. Someone was in the hallway.

She scanned the room, her heart pounding. *This was a stupid idea.* The only hiding place she could access quickly was under the bed. Would she even fit? And what sort of assailant wouldn't think of looking under there?

Panic started to set in.

She held her breath and closed her eyes. There was no noise from downstairs. *Can someone make it across the hall to the stairs without making a sound?* Maybe they were already half way up the stairs. It was too late and Georgie couldn't move even if she wanted to. She was rooted to the spot – her fate surely sealed.

A floorboard creaked. Georgie clasped her hands over her mouth, suppressing the urge to cry out.

A few seconds ticked away agonisingly slowly.

'Hello, dear? Are you there?'

Georgie let her lungs force the air out.

'Hi, I'm just coming down,' she called back.

Mrs Mudridge smiled as Georgie met her in the hallway. She was fiddling with her hands underneath her apron. There was more lipstick on her teeth than on her lips.

'Oh, there you are!'

'Hi, Mrs Mudridge. Is everything OK?'

'Well, I just remembered, Hayley's not here, dear. She went on a long weekend. With her boyfriend, about a week ago.'

Georgie nodded encouragingly. *Boyfriend.* 'Really? She said something about doing that. I must have got the wrong date.'

'Oh, what a disappointment for you, dear. I'm so sorry.'

'I've never met Hayley's boyfriend, Mrs Mudridge. Hayley's kept him a secret from me, would you believe!'

'Really? Imagine that!'

'Did you see him at all?'

'Well . . .' Mrs Mudridge pursed her lips in concentration. 'To tell you the truth, dear, no.'

'Oh.' Georgie couldn't help but hide her disappointment. 'Are you sure it was her boyfriend, Mrs Mudridge?'

'Well maybe I was jumping to conclusions about that.' She laughed good-naturedly. 'I did see his car, though.'

'Really?'

'Yes. Parked outside, it was. I remember because I thought to myself, *oh, Hayley's got a fancy-man coming to visit!*'

'Do you remember anything about the car? Was it big, small, a four-by-four?'

'Oh, I don't know anything about those sort of things, dear. I haven't run a car since my husband died twenty years ago. You don't need one in Cambridge, you know . . .'

Georgie bit her lip as Mrs Mudridge rambled on, trying to keep the frustration from her voice. 'The car, Mrs Mudridge?'

'Oh, yes. There was one thing, dear.'

'Yes?'

'It had a very funny sign in the front windshield. One of those parking permits but with a funny symbol.'

'A funny symbol, Mrs Mudridge?'

'Yes. I'd never seen one like that before. A little silver heart.'

A chill crackled down Georgie's spine. She pulled out her phone again and googled the image she was looking for. Eventually, she found it and showed the picture of the silver heart to Mrs Mudridge, who made a fuss of putting on her glasses before staring carefully at the iPhone screen.

'Yes, dear,' she said finally. 'That's it. What is it?'

'It's the Ellinder Pharmaceuticals logo.'

∽

Georgie stepped out on to the street, her mind racing with possibilities. She had shown Mrs Mudridge some pictures of different cars on her phone but the old lady hadn't been able to give her anything to go on. Her only recollection – clear as day – was of the silver heart.

Georgie wondered if Jessica Ellinder's car had the same symbol on its windshield. She tried phoning Charlie but his phone was either engaged or out of range. Georgie left a message asking him to call her, and to forgive her for ignoring his warning. She decided to give Charlie five minutes to phone her back before trying Okoro. He wouldn't be impressed with her excursion, either.

Hayley Wren had disappeared off the face of the earth. As there was nothing more she could do in Cambridge, Georgie resolved to head back to the train station.

She walked briskly across the street and through a narrow passageway leading to the back of the Victorian housing. She studied her phone, flipping through the maps to try and work out the quickest route to the station. She was cold, and the wind was sharp. A few students cycled past, ringing their bells unnecessarily. The sound of their laughter didn't lift her; rather, it reminded her of how alone she was.

She stopped at the end of the street. Above her, the Gothic college buildings loomed up on either side and a host of warped heads carved into the stonework glared suspiciously down. She consulted her phone again, but the next section of the map was slow to load. There was some shelter from the icy wind, but the street was eerily deserted. As she tried to manipulate the digital image of Cambridge, an incoming call flashed across the screen

'Hello?'

'Georgie?'

'Li?'

'Where are you?'

'Cambridge.'

Li chuckled. 'An Oxonian in Cambridge? Why are you slumming it?'

'Is everything OK?' Georgie asked.

'Fine. I just . . . wanted to make sure you were all right.'

'Why wouldn't I be?' There was something about the way Li was speaking that made Georgie feel uncomfortable. She detected a trace of uncertainty in her friend's usually confident voice.

'I just . . . you know,' said Li.

A sense of dread crept over Georgie. On the opposite side of the road, a white van had pulled over and was sitting idle. The windows were blacked out and the van was unmarked. Georgie thought about the two men on the train, and Hayley's wrecked room. As her heart rate started to quicken for the third time that morning, Georgie stepped closer to the building next to her, trying to sink into the shadow.

'Li,' she said. 'Why did you phone me?'

'Just to say I put your hairdryer back in your drawer. Thanks for letting me borrow it.'

Something was very wrong. Over the road, Georgie heard a door slam. Someone had got out of the van on the passenger's side. She checked the street left, right and behind her. Not a soul.

'Li?' she said urgently.

'And to say that there was some post for you. It sort of fell . . . and opened.'

Georgie heard the side door of the van slide across its runners and shut. Li's words swirled around in her head but she was struggling to understand their meaning. Something told her to run and keep running but her legs wouldn't move and she was rooted to the spot.

'Georgie,' Li said and her voice was urgent. 'Georgie, there was an *insect* inside the envelope . . .'

Behind her there was a sudden burst of movement. Georgie opened her mouth but the scream welling up inside her never escaped. She felt hands on her shoulders and something around her face, wet and heavy. Her eyes lost focus. She tried to fight back but it was too late; her world had already turned to darkness.

42

Li stood with the phone to her ear, the connection dead. She redialled Georgie's number but got nothing other than her answerphone.

She felt paralysed.

She had meant well. She had paced the corridor for ages trying to work out what to do before deciding she had to make sure Georgie was all right. But the final couple of seconds of that call . . . the unmistakable noise of distress . . . Something very horrible had happened to Georgie. And it had to be connected with that insect in the envelope, she was sure of it.

She ran across the landing towards the stairs, almost knocking Martin into the wall as he emerged from his room.

'Hey!' he shouted. 'What's the hurry, Li?'

'I think something might have happened to Georgie.'

'Oh. Whatever.' He went back into his room.

She stood uncertainly on the stairway. *Shit!* Should she call the police? Mrs White would be particularly unimpressed if she involved them. And in any case, what did Li have to go on? Some muffled sounds on a phone from somewhere in Cambridge? They'd think she was wasting their time.

Should she go to Cambridge herself? Li had no idea where she would even start looking. Pulling her purse out of her pocket, she looked through the compartments. There: Georgie's card. *Georgie Someday BA (Hons) (Oxon), LLM (King's College, London) Associate Solicitor. Corporate Fraud. Priest & Co.*

Li punched the Priest & Co number into her phone. Eventually a croaky female voice answered.

'Priest and Co.'

'Charlie Priest, please,' said Li hopefully.

'I'm afraid Mr Priest is on annual leave.'

'Where can I get hold of him? It's urgent.'

'Who is this?'

Li hung up. *Waste of fucking time.*

She ran back up to Georgie's room and started rummaging through the drawers. *There must be something – anything!*

At the back of the drawer she found what she was looking for. Only someone like Georgie kept an address book anymore. She had been born a hundred years too late.

She flipped through the pages until she found Charlie Priest's number.

She rang. Another answerphone message.

'Mr Priest. I'm a friend of Georgie's. She's in trouble. Phone me back. Please.' Li hung up. She prayed it would be enough.

43

By the time Priest pulled up outside Sandra Barnsdale's legal offices in Kensington, Jessica was asleep. As the car came to a stop, she stirred, opened her eyes and put her hand to her head.

'You OK?' Priest asked gently.

Jessica nodded, sat up and looked around. As she crossed the line between the world of sleep and consciousness, Priest thought he saw a flash of the woman she really was. It vanished almost instantly.

'Where are we?' she demanded.

'Barnsdale's solicitors. Kensington.' Priest felt his phone vibrating in his pocket but decided to leave it.

'Why?'

'The metadata from the flash drive,' Priest explained.

'I don't follow.'

'The schedule on the flash drive is just a text document. From the metadata you can see when the file was created, when it was last modified and so on – and, of course, who wrote it.'

'And the person who wrote it is someone here?'

'Sandra Barnsdale – the principal solicitor in this practice.'

'You know her?'

'I've met her a few times.'

'Is there anyone involved in this that you *don't* know?'

Priest reached around behind him and collected his coat. He faltered. Jessica had turned away from him, her hands covering her face. He waited. She breathed in heavily. After a moment she moved her hands away and he saw her wipe a tear from her eye.

Suddenly every ounce of human understanding he possessed eluded him. He felt completely useless.

'I'm sorry,' she croaked.

'Don't be.'

'No! I don't . . .'

'Show emotion?'

'I must be very confusing to you,' she conceded miserably.

Priest raised an eyebrow. 'I have noticed a few inconsistencies.'

He opened his mouth to elaborate when his phone rang again. This time he reached into his coat pocket, pulled it out and glanced at the caller ID. He groaned.

'My ex-wife.'

'You'd better take it.'

He couldn't work out whether Jessica was angry or relieved.

'Hi, Dee,' said Priest, putting the phone to his ear.

'Charlie? What the fuck do you think you're playing at?'

'I take it your new friends at the Met don't know you're calling me? I hope they know what a difficult position you're in.'

'Is that a threat? Sure as hell better not be.'

'Of course not, darling.'

'Fuck you. Listen, the warrant you got set aside. Did you really think that was being clever? Innocent people let the Blue search their properties. Guilty people frustrate the process. All you did was pour petrol on a fire that's already beyond my control, you thick bastard!'

'Hey, I didn't ask for your help, Dee.'

'Yes, you did. You asked me to call off McEwen.'

Priest winced. 'Whatever. I'm not asking for it now.'

'And you're not getting it.'

'Then why phone me?'

'To give you one last chance to tell me what the hell is going on.'

'I told you – I don't know.'

'For Christ's sake, Charlie! The son of a very rich and influential man was recently killed. I've pulled every goddamn detective off from leave to cover for McEwen's team. It's a fucking miracle the press haven't cottoned on but when they do, Charlie – and they will – time will start to run out very fast for you. You ought to think about that.'

'Maybe *you* ought to think about that, too, Dee,' Priest said grimly.

He was very aware that Dee was screaming down the phone and that Jessica, who was sitting with her head cocked, could probably hear every word.

'What do you mean?' said the Assistant Commissioner, the warning in her tone obvious.

'Think about it. A high-profile victim is executed horribly in his multi-millionaire father's warehouse. It ought to be national news and yet you've managed to contain it for almost a week now. What's going on?'

It was a fact of life: tabloids paid police officers good money for stories. *You can have as many policies and disciplinary investigations as you like, but you can't plug leaks.* This story was worth at least twenty grand, thirty if it included photos.

Dee wasn't speaking. In Priest's book, that was a win.

'Your turn to listen,' he told her. 'I'm sending you a photograph of the crime scene from Philip Wren's office. I took it when I first arrived, before SOCO got there. Compare that to the photos you have on the file. Look in particular at the desktop, nearside corner. See if you can spot the difference then phone me back when you're prepared to see what's actually going on here.'

He ended the call. Jessica studied him cynically.

'You coming?' Priest said, getting out of the car.

∞

Sandra Barnsdale's office was on the top floor of a complex with a private underground car park and a gym for staff use only. It was an impressive building – a steel-framed, angular skyscraper encased in a glass facade, each pane fractionally concaved to reflect the sunlight and give the impression that the structure was made from giant ice blocks piled on top of each other.

Priest hated it.

Barnsdale & Clyde had been writing wills and administering estates for the rich and famous since the forties. They had come a long way from humble beginnings and now employed over a hundred staff and turned over close to twenty-five million annually. Sandra had been the principal since her father had died in 2003 and, to Priest's knowledge, had managed to retain one hundred per cent of the equity for herself following Bob Clyde's retirement a few years before her father's death.

The woman with bleached blonde hair barely looked up from behind the front desk when Priest coughed politely for attention. Jessica stood next to him with her arms folded. On the wall behind her was a poster: *Have you made a will yet?*

'Do you have an appointment?' Bleached Blonde asked as if she couldn't care less.

'No,' Priest admitted. 'Would you be kind enough to tell Sandra Barnsdale that Charlie Priest would like to see her?'

Bleached Blonde looked up and raised an eyebrow. 'Without an appointment?'

'That's right.'

For a moment, Bleached Blonde looked as if she might want to help, but then turned her attention back to her glossy magazine. 'Miss Barnsdale never sees people without an appointment.'

'I wonder –'

Priest was cut off by a commotion from somewhere behind them. A stylishly dressed woman bustled in carrying a box of files, which she dumped on the desk in front of Bleached Blonde.

'Jeanette, could you archive these for me, please?'

Priest leant on the front desk and turned to the woman. 'Good afternoon, Sandra.'

Sandra Barnsdale spun around, tipping the box of files over and sending them crashing over Bleached Blonde's lap. She shrieked in alarm. Sandra looked Priest up and down and her face broke out into a grin.

'Charlie fucking Priest!' she exclaimed. 'Well, aren't you a sight for sore eyes!'

44

Georgie's eyes gradually opened. The pain in her head was excruciating. For a few moments, her eyes refused to focus – everything was black.

She could sense movement and noise. The humming of an engine and the vibration of wheels rolling over tarmac.

She was lying on the cold, metal floor of a moving vehicle.

A few minutes passed and the feeling that she was going to hurl began to fade. Tentatively, she sat up and her surroundings edged into view. The space was large enough for her to be able to comfortably stand; she guessed she was in something like a Transit van. She realised with dread that it was most likely the white van she had seen across the road before someone had jumped her from behind.

The feeling of sickness returned.

She fumbled around in her pockets with shaking hands. No phone.

'Oh, Jesus.'

Georgie was not religious. Most days, God seemed a very unlikely proposition, but all of a sudden she wanted very much to believe in Him. To believe that *someone* – anyone – was watching over her.

But she could conjure up no such comforting vision. Her heart lurched. In her mind's eye, she saw Vlad the Impaler – garbed in a blood-stained tunic – driving the Transit, a callous grin etched on his wraithlike face.

Georgie had never felt so alone in the world.

∽

Priest and Jessica were shown through to a plush office in the corner of the building overlooking the river. If it hadn't been so overcast, they might have been able to see Priest's apartment from up here.

Sandra was fifty-something, tall and lean, with gym-honed biceps that zapped some of her femininity, but otherwise she was not unattractive. She was blessed with olive skin that made her look younger than she was and there was a brightness in her eyes that Priest had always liked, although not enough to have agreed to her marriage proposal many years ago. To this day, he was unsure about whether or not she had been serious.

'You look like shit, Charlie,' she observed as she showed Priest and Jessica through to a lavish office stacked with files, papers, deeds and bundles wrapped in pink ribbon.

'You're not the first one to point that out.'

'And I doubt I'll be the last until you take a shower and have a decent night's sleep.'

'I thought you liked the unkempt look?'

Sandra laughed. 'In your dreams, Priest. Now, didn't my receptionist tell you I don't accept visitors without an appointment? She better bloody have, because I pay her enough!'

'I'm sorry, Sandra. It's an intrusion, I know. I wouldn't have bothered you like this if it wasn't important.'

'You owe me one for this, big boy.' There was that glint again.

Priest wondered if Sandra was like this with all men or just him. Beside him, he sensed Jessica shift her weight.

'Oh, how rude of me,' she said suddenly, extending her hand to Jessica. 'Sandra Barnsdale.'

'Jessica Ellinder.'

'Ellinder?' Sandra paused and looked at them both. 'Punching above your weight, Priest?'

'We're not together,' Jessica said quickly.

Priest noticed a rash start to appear around her chest.

'Ah, I see,' said Sandra drily. 'All duly noted.' She motioned for them to sit down in front of her desk.

'So, what's troubling you, darling?' Sandra asked Priest, taking a seat behind her giant desk.

'Do mayflies mean anything to you, Sandra?'

Sandra Barndsdale's face didn't change expression. She rested her chin on her hand and looked at them, as if waiting for something more.

Priest placed the flash drive in front of her.

'Where did you get that?' Sandra said, her voice dropping. She picked the flash drive up, examined it with care and then set it back down.

'The Attorney General sent it to me.'

'Why?'

'I was hoping you might be able to tell me.'

Sandra Barnsdale didn't have to say anything for Priest to see she was spooked. She sat in silence for a few more moments and then pushed her chair back and strode over to a drinks machine on the table behind her desk.

'You still drink Earl Grey?' she asked Priest over her shoulder.

Priest nodded. Sandra looked over at Jessica, who asked for a black coffee. Sandra busied herself preparing drinks, poured herself some water.

'What you have there, Priest – assuming it's what I think it is – is bad news. I was hoping that I would never have to see it again.'

'I think we can safely say that this conversation is off the record, Sandra, but you need to tell me all about it.'

She turned to look at him, but it was if she was staring right through him to the wall on the other side of the room.

'Is someone in trouble, Priest?'

'Yes.'

'Is it you?'

'Partially.'

She seemed to be mulling this over. Eventually she sat back down, thrusting the drinks in front of them.

'It had better be a damn big favour I get for this, Priest,' Sandra said, adding a second spoonful of sugar to her latte.

'I can't promise anything,' he said.

'Hmm.' She smiled but her voice was serious. 'I inherited the file from my father. It was one of many little gems he left me after the cancer ate his brain away. I promised him I would keep it secret from everyone, even my own staff. It's a safe-keep file.'

'So it's not a probate file?'

'No. We get this from time to time. We're just storing data for someone.'

'Isn't that what Swiss bank accounts are for?' asked Jessica.

'Some prefer a more old-fashioned approach,' said Sandra, and if she had detected any hostility from Jessica, she hid it well. 'And why not? We have a fire-proof vault, three servers out of the city and we're all bound by client confidentiality. In many ways, we're more secure than a Swiss deposit box.'

She took a sip from her cup. She appeared calm, but Priest noticed beads of perspiration appearing around her temples. He hoped she would cut to the chase. She did.

'The instructions on the file are very simple. From time to time, we are supplied with the details of a named individual, which we upload on to a database, the most recent version of which is stored on that little flash drive there. Every upload comes with a regular payment of fifteen hundred pounds.'

'Nice little earner,' remarked Jessica.

Sandra smiled drily.

'Who supplies the information?' asked Priest.

'I don't know. It's comes via a private courier each time. Totally anonymous.'

'Do you know who your client is?'

'I don't.'

'How do you verify each update?'

'By reference to the payment, and of course the courier.'

'But for whose benefit are you keeping the information? How do you know if someone needs it?'

'There are instructions for that eventuality.'

'And you verify the authenticity of the instructions again by reference to a payment?'

'One million pounds. And a password, of course.'

Priest watched a little bead of sweat make its way down Sandra Barnsdale's temple.

'This must have started somewhere, Sandra. Someone must have given your father the first set of instructions.'

Sandra nodded. 'True. But that was his business. He didn't pass any of that information on.'

'You didn't think it was odd?' asked Jessica. 'That you were being paid large sums of money to keep a list of people and their contact details safe?'

Sandra responded sharply: 'We have a lot of strange requests here, Miss Ellinder.'

'When was the last update?' cut in Priest.

'A few months back. I forget the details but it was the same set-up. Private courier delivers the data in paper form, we upload it. Destroy the paper. Take the fee in cash. We then raise an internal invoice.'

'So how did the flash drive end up in the hands of the Attorney General?'

Sandra took a deep breath. 'Because I sent it to him.'

When she didn't offer any further explanation, Priest prompted her. 'Go on.'

'It's obvious that the data serves no legitimate purpose,' she said. 'I've known that for a long time but I've never had a clue what it's about. It's kept me awake at night too often, though. I've looked in to some of the names a few times. There's a few of note – but they all seem to have one thing in common.'

'Money?' Priest suggested.

'Quite. They're all filthy rich. Something happened a few weeks ago that meant I could no longer keep the secret I had promised my father I would.'

'Go on,' said Priest gently, willing her to continue. She was on the verge, he could tell, between deciding to tell them everything or nothing at all. He hoped Jessica could keep quiet for a few minutes.

Sandra sighed. 'Philip Wren came to see me a few weeks back. Maybe a month or so, I can't recall exactly. It was the most extraordinary conversation I have ever been privy to.' She took a moment to collect her thoughts. Drank some of the water. 'He sat down and told me that he was the head of a task force investigating a criminal organisation. His investigations were so top secret I had to sign a confidentiality undertaking. So, I want your assurance that this goes no further. You didn't hear this from me. Right?'

'You have my word, Sandra,' said Priest.

'He said that he'd established that my firm might somehow be involved with the group he was investigating. You can imagine how I felt about that. He implied that our involvement was most likely unwitting, but it was clear to me that it was still potentially ruinous if it got out.'

'He knew about the file?'

'He knew about the damn file, yes. Not the details; he just knew that we were storing data for someone. I don't know how.'

'He wanted you to hand it over,' Priest suggested.

'No. He wanted me to confirm its existence. If I could do that, he'd get a court order requiring me to hand it over. That way, I wasn't in breach of my duty of confidentiality and the evidence would be obtained legitimately.'

Priest clicked his tongue. 'But it didn't go to plan?'

Sandra hesitated. 'Are you familiar with the Nuremberg doctors' trials, Priest?'

Priest nodded. 'After the war, the Allies set up a military tribunal to hear cases against Nazi leaders accused of war crimes. After they had tried the main players they went after those accused of lesser war crimes. Twenty-three Nazi doctors were accused, inter alia, of human experimentation of the most heinous kind. Many of them were sentenced to death, although I think some were acquitted.'

'You know your history,' Sandra smiled weakly.

'Wait,' said Priest. 'What are you saying?'

'The group that Wren was chasing was established in the sixties, so he said. They're not exactly neo-Nazis. It's stranger than that. It's more like they're trying to replicate the doctors' trials from the Holocaust.'

'They're experimenting on humans?' Jessica asked, aghast. 'That's what Wren told you?'

Sandra nodded silently.

Priest took a sip of the tea. It tasted metallic. He had begun to build a mental image – a tree from which sprouted branches comprising the different pieces of information he had gathered: Nazi doctors, poison, money . . . But how did any of it fit with Miles Ellinder's death?

The doctor that Tiff had mentioned – Kurt Schneider – was credited with developing the same poison, or a version of it, used to torture and murder the man in the woods.

'I can guess what happened,' said Priest.

Sandra looked down, ashamed. 'I panicked. After he left, I couldn't sleep for days. I kept going into the office, opening the safe and looking at that file. At those names. You have to understand: if Wren had got his court order, then my firm was finished. Everyone would know.'

'So you sent him the data and destroyed the file?' Priest asked softly.

Tears welled in Sandra's eyes. 'And I'll be damned for it. But why have you got it?'

'Wren sent it to me. My guess is that the group you mentioned got to him. I think they were threatening his family, his daughter. He was in over his head. So, he sent it to me.'

Priest thought about the haunting letter Wren had written him: *Time is short. Lives are at stake. I make that last statement quite consciously, knowing that my next actions may endanger you.*

'How do you know his daughter was under threat?' asked Sandra.

'She's missing. Vanished into thin air. The last thing she heard was a voicemail from her father telling her to flee.'

Sandra swept her hair back and folded her arms, shaking her head in disbelief.

'I thought I would be saving people, not putting them in danger,' she murmured.

Priest thought about telling her she had done the right thing, but he wasn't sure he could lie convincingly enough. Maybe that was why Wren was dead. He had the names, but he wasn't ready. Maybe he'd changed his mind after coming to see Sandra, because that's when they got to him, got to Hayley.

The strain on Sandra's face was visible now – anxiety seeping through her skin.

Priest tried to think practically. 'Sandra, when you receive updates for the database, are you required to log the time and date of their input?'

'Yes. Why?'

'It may be that the names you were given are the members of this group. Perhaps it's a form of insurance.'

'So everyone is bound together,' Jessica finished.

'If someone blabs, then the list can be released and everyone goes down.'

'I don't understand,' said Sandra. 'What's the point in that?'

'Would you want to be the one who exposed the whole affair and risk the other members coming after you?' said Priest.

Sandra rubbed her hand over her face. 'Priest,' she said. 'Can you fix this?'

'That depends.' Priest folded his arms and sat back in his chair. He felt exhausted; the room was spinning. He was finding it difficult to keep his eyes focused.

'Depends on what?'

'On whether you can tell me where the file originates.'

A long silence hung in the air. Sandra pursed her lips. Priest could see defiance burning in her eyes, but he was sure that she was still holding something back.

'Priest . . . as I said –'

'Don't insult my intelligence, Sandra. Tell me where the bloody file originated. You know the name I need.'

She swallowed hard. 'I'm in danger, Priest. You must surely see that.'

'I do. So, tell me and let me put you out of danger.'

She hesitated, and Priest just sat there, arms folded, waiting.

In the end, she threw her arms in the air and got up. 'You're going to get me killed for this, Priest.' She searched through a filing cabinet over by the door and pulled out a tattered file, which she placed in front of them. Priest and Jessica leant across the desk. The name on the file was clear enough.

Miller. Eva.

'Who is she?' Priest asked, picking up the file and inspecting the contents. There was not much. A few short letters, hand-written notes and a will.

'She was a client,' Sandra admitted. 'She died some time ago. I administered the estate. She was the person who set up the keep-safe file with Dad. I kept her file just in case.'

Priest opened out the will and placed it on the table in front of them. Ran his fingers over the ageing paper stitched together with ribbon. Eva Miller was dead but a will meant that she'd had something to leave behind, and someone to leave it to.

Finally, we might be getting somewhere.

'To save you from reading any further,' Sandra said, 'There's only one beneficiary. A Colonel Albert Ruck.'

45

Priest turned on the shower. He had left the bathroom door ajar and looked through the crack to check on Jessica, who was sitting at a desk, trawling through the database of meaningless names. She seemed not to be the least bit uncomfortable occupying his bedroom; she had made herself at home with her feet tucked underneath her on his old leather chair. He thought again about the night they had spent together at the Dower House. Had it even been real? He clicked the bathroom door shut and shook the thought away. *Not now, Priest. Maybe not ever . . .*

Giles had come up trumps and had sent him a copy of Miles Ellinder's interim autopsy report. The document took an age to download on his phone but when eventually Priest was able to skim read it, it was disappointing; it simply outlined the cause of death as circulatory shock causing cardiac arrest. Mercifully, death was assessed as having taken place within a few minutes. It seemed as if McEwen's description of Miles flailing around for hours had been a deliberate embellishment.

Priest closed down the report and dialled Giles's number. He hoped the noise from the shower would drown out his conversation.

'Fucking hell, it's you again, Priest.' The irritated voice answered almost immediately. 'Did you get that PM report I sent you?'

'I did, although it wasn't particularly enlightening.'

'Devil's in the detail, Priest.'

'Mm. Giles, I need a background check.'

'You remember what happened the last time I did a background check for you?'

'Giles, the IPCC dropped that investigation pretty quickly.'

'Still on my record, you bastard.'

'Please. For old times' sake?'

There was a heavy sigh. 'Fine. What do you want?'

'Eva Miller,' said Priest.

'Did you make that up just so you could talk to me, you friendless fuck?' Giles sniggered.

'It's real.'

'Whatever. Date of birth?'

'No idea.'

'Last known address?'

Priest read out the address Sandra had given him from the file. 'Probably not her last address but this is all I've got. She died a while ago, not sure when.'

'Whatever you do, Priest, don't make it easy for me.'

Priest heard the sound of a keyboard tapping at the other end of the line.

'OK,' mumbled Giles. 'What about this? Born fifteenth of May, nineteen twenty-five. Deceased, second of June nineteen eighty-seven.'

'Could be. Who's listed as the next of kin? Is it Albert Ruck?'

A few more taps and Giles read out a name.

Priest faltered. *Jesus.*

'Thanks, Giles,' he murmured.

'Are you going to tell me what this is about?' demanded Giles.

Priest hung up.

❧

Priest stepped out of the bathroom wearing a pair of dark chinos and nothing else. The shower had been a short but welcome distraction from the darkness that seemed to be attaching itself to him. He'd tried to wash it off but it was sticking and he still felt dirty.

Jessica was now in the lounge, on his sofa next to the fish, the glow from the tank illuminating one side of her face. Her auburn hair was pulled back, showing more of her soft features, her high cheek bones and elegant neck. She had kicked off her shoes and hunched herself up against the arm of the sofa. He lingered in the doorway, wondering if he should have put a shirt on, but Jessica barely looked up. He remembered how her skin had felt as smooth as pure silk.

'Did you recognise anyone from the database?' he asked.

She shook her head.

On the coffee table his phone lit up. Two new voicemails. He picked it up and dialled. He heard an unfamiliar voice: 'Mr Priest. I'm a friend of Georgie's. She's in trouble. Phone me back. Please.'

Shit. He pressed the recall button. *Come on, pick up.* Jessica raised her head.

Eventually, the phone connected. 'Hello?'

'This is Charlie Priest.'

'Thank God! I didn't know who else to call.'

'Who are you?' Priest demanded.

'My name is Li . . . I'm a friend – a flatmate – of Georgie's.'

'She's mentioned you.'

'I didn't know who else to call.'

Li gave an account of her phone call with Georgie. As he listened, Priest felt the darkness claim a little more of his soul.

'She was in Cambridge?' he asked.

'Yes. I don't know why.'

'I think I do.'

What had he expected? That she would go home and play role-playing games with her nerdy friends? Forget all about the case? Fuck, he had been naive.

'Are you sure the phone cut out because of a struggle?' Priest asked Li. 'Why do you think that?'

'Because I heard some sort of scuffle . . . And there's something else,' Li said carefully. 'Somebody . . . somebody sent Georgie something. In the post.'

Priest swallowed hard. *No!* 'What kind of something?'

Jessica sat up.

'Like an insect. A dead bug,' said Li, her voice shaking.

'A mayfly.'

'Think so. Maybe. Does that mean anything to you?'

'Li, I want you to phone me the minute you hear from her, OK?'

'Sure, but –'

Priest cut the call, sinking down into the sofa. Jessica put her hand on his arm.

'What's happened?' she asked, panic rising in her voice.

'I think they have Georgie.'

'Who? Who has her?'

'I think it is the same people that have Hayley.' He sat still, trying to take it in.

Jessica swallowed. 'Charlie, I . . . I didn't mean for any of this to happen.'

'What?'

'I mean you were supposed to be looking into my brother's death. I had no idea how deep this thing went.'

'No, I mean, you called me Charlie. You usually call me Priest.'

She leant against him and he placed his arm around her shoulder. She nuzzled her head into his chest and he began to feel his heart rate increase. Her smell was familiar to him now; he wondered whether her scent might be enough by itself to bring light to his darkened soul. Gently, he kissed the top of her head. He was caught between worlds again in a black void. He was afraid; a feeling he hadn't known for a very long time. He was afraid that he now had something to lose.

'If I could stop time,' he told her.

She leant across him to pick up his phone. 'You have another message,' she whispered, passing it to him.

He dialled the voicemail again, standing up and crossing to the other side of the room so she couldn't hear what was said. He listened to Georgie's voice, excitable and fresh, ignorant of the danger she was in.

'Hi, Charlie. Please don't be mad but I went to Cambridge to look for Hayley. I know I shouldn't have but I just can't stand back while all this *stuff* happens around us. So, you know, I hopped on a train. Guess I shouldn't have. Like I said, don't be mad. I mean, I know you will be but let's try and keep it to just Attila the Hun mad and not Vlad the Impaler mad, OK? Sorry, I've just realised how inappropriate that is. Anyhow, I did get something helpful, I think. One of Hayley's neighbours said she saw a car outside Hayley's house recently and, although she couldn't identify it, she described a symbol stuck in the windshield, which was the Ellinder Pharmaceuticals brand logo. I guess it was a car park pass or something. And Hayley's room is a mess. It's clear something bad has happened in there. There are fingernail scratches on the dresser, and the table has been pulled off the wall. We need to find her. So, in conclusion, don't be mad, we need to find Hayley, there's something fishy about the Ellinder company. Bye.'

An Ellinder Pharmaceuticals car park pass. It was starting to fit together.

Jessica was staring at him, eyes wide.

'Who was it?' she asked.

'Georgie. Before they took her, I guess.'

'What did she say?' she said anxiously.

Priest checked the lionfish. *When was the last time they were fed?* He reached for a little tub of pellets and sprinkled some in. The fish flicked through the water to the surface and ate greedily.

'Nothing. She was just checking in.'

46

Georgie felt the van slow down and heard the unmistakable noise of tyres on gravel. She sat up, glancing at her watch. She had been in the van for the best part of an hour, the last half of which she had spent in a state of semi-consciousness, curled up in the corner, occasionally jolted awake as the vehicle lurched through traffic. It was so cold that she had lost the feeling in her hands.

There was a crunch as the handbrake was pulled on, then the sound of both cab doors opening. Two people got out of the van. She braced herself. Tried to measure the risk of bolting through the door when it was opened. Where was she? Could she outrun them? They could have guns. She wouldn't make it more than ten yards before they shot her down.

Georgie concentrated instead on controlling her breathing. She was light-headed, her brain swimming in oxygen and adrenaline.

The door opened. The view outside was blocked by two large men. Their heads were covered with hoods, similar to the conical headwear of the Ku Klux Klan, save that the peak of the hood was less exaggerated and the eye sockets were elongated slits set at an angle, rather than round holes.

They stood motionless, staring at Georgie. A cold, raw fear flushed through her, a sensation she had never experienced before.

'Wh-who are you?' The words tumbled out of her mouth.

One of the men beckoned for Georgie to get out of the van. She hesitated, feeling as if her legs would not work even if she wanted them to. After a few moments, the one who had motioned for her to come out dropped his hand and put a foot inside the van, arching himself through the doorway.

'OK,' Georgie croaked, holding up her hand. 'OK, I'll come out.'

The temperature outside wasn't much lower than it was inside the back of the Transit, but the icy wind that gusted across the courtyard felt like knives cutting into her skin. As she was led over the gravel she saw they had parked in the shadow of an enormous baroque mansion.

As they headed towards the house, Georgie noticed a row of cars lined up against the side of one of the wings. Porsches, Jaguars, Range Rovers, all gleaming. A handsome fleet.

They reached a side door. 'What is this place?' she said. The only reply was a sharp prod in the back to push her on into a dark hallway.

Inside, a worn red carpet spread down the middle of a stone floor. There was a flight of spiral stairs to the left and various closed doors to the right. The air was heavy but the warmth was a small relief. There was a musty smell she could not quite place – maybe just the smell of age, or rot.

Georgie was led to a room off the hallway – a study, its walls lined with old leather books and containing a green sofa and two writing desks. She was shoved in to the middle of the room where she stood alone and silent, her heart racing but her head held high. She would not give anybody the satisfaction of sensing her fear if she could help it.

After a moment she turned. Her guides had taken up sentry positions either side of the doorway, their arms crossed in perfect symmetry. Georgie stared, baffled.

'Where are we?' she demanded. 'What is this place?'

They did not move. They might has well have turned to stone.

Georgie felt her resolution starting to melt. 'Why won't you talk?'

'Because they are paid not to.'

She whirled around, shocked, the voice ringing in her ears. A man was lying, legs spread out, across a chaise longue in the corner of the room, a book in his hand.

'Who are you?' she said, trembling.

The speaker placed the book on a nearby table, careful not to lose the page, before slowly getting up and stretching. He wore no hood, his face clearly visible. He struck Georgie as someone who might be ill. He was no older than Charlie, but his face was gaunt and skeletal. His hair looked wet, dark streaks swept haphazardly across his head.

Georgie was short of breath. She quickly scanned the room but the only way out was past the two guards standing on either side of the door. She wondered whether she could make a break for it, but her arms and legs felt like lead. She doubted she would even make it to the door, let alone get through it.

'I have a name,' said the ill-looking man. 'But it is of no consequence.'

'My name is Georgie Someday,' she said with venom. *You will not see me afraid!*

'I know. Thank you for joining us, Miss Someday.'

She swallowed but her mouth was dry and the action made her want to gag. 'I didn't get much choice in the matter.'

'No,' he agreed, smiling at the floor beneath her feet. 'I doubt you did. And I apologise for the necessity of sedating you, if only for a short while, and for the unpleasantness of your transportation. And, indeed, generally for the inconvenience that has been caused.'

'Inconvenience?'

'Well –' Still smiling, he held his arms up defensively. 'We all know how frightened you must be, but I see no reason to compound it with inflammatory language. So, may we just call it *an inconvenience*?'

'Where is Hayley?'

'Here. Safe. You will see her shortly. I have found her to be, however, a little uncommunicative.'

He strode across the room until he was only a few feet away from her. He was not tall, or well built, but he was bigger than Georgie. She had an urge to shrink back but something made her hold her ground, despite the fact that the grip she had on her nerves was hanging by a thread. She stared at him, unblinking.

'What is this?' she asked.

'History, Miss Someday. A rebirth of something very old. You are honoured to be a part of it.'

'Why me?'

He shrugged. 'A hunch. Nothing more.'

'What hunch?'

'That you're one of those people who have spent their whole lives trying to fit in when in fact they stand out like a sore thumb . . . And because I feel it will increase our chances of being joined here by a mutual friend of ours.'

She fixed him with a look – the best version of hatred that she was capable of. A look she had only managed once before in her life. Then she understood.

'*Charlie*! You're using me as bait?'

Her captor smiled, although his mouth fell at the corners so it was an ugly smile. She could smell him – drink and cigarettes. He reached for her, cupped her face in his hand. Her heart jumped. She wavered. The urge to run was irresistible.

'Can you scream, Georgie?' he whispered softly. 'Can you scream? I hope so. Because people have paid me a lot of money to hear you scream tonight.'

47

'This is it,' said Jessica. 'Ruck's nursing home.'

The Volvo pulled up outside a red-brick building surrounded by dead trees and clumps of nettles. A sad waiting room before the final curtain call.

'How long has Albert Ruck been here?' asked Jessica.

Priest shrugged. 'No idea. But he's a hundred and three years old.'

They parked on the grass outside the main entrance. Priest had looked it up online. The Priory was a private nursing home where the residents could enjoy their time in the embrace of the Lord. Before, presumably, they were allowed to enjoy their time in His backyard.

'Sad place to spend your inheritance on,' Jessica said.

'Depends where your inheritance comes from,' Priest replied. 'The nurse I spoke to was very helpful. Bertie is lucid most of the time, prone only to the occasional bout of screaming madness.' *Much like my brother . . . we'll get along famously.*

The inside was as drab as the outside. It smelt of disinfectant.

The young nurse smiled as they approached the desk. 'Can I help you?'

'Are you Lina? I think I may have spoken to you an hour or so ago.'

'Yes! How nice of you to drop by. You're here to see Bertie, right?'

Priest returned her smile. 'Yes. We are. May we?'

'Of course!'

Lina ushered them down a beige corridor past a number of open doors. From inside, a few of the residents looked up from their tea and newspapers; most were asleep.

As they walked, Jessica whispered in his ear, 'Just how much of your investigatory work is achieved through flirting, Priest?'

'About half. Maybe more.'

'And what lie did you spin to get us in here?'

They reached a door at the end of the corridor. It was closed, but the sign read *A RUCK*.

'I didn't lie at all. I told her I was a priest.'

'This is it,' Lina announced, knocking gently and showing them through. 'Bertie, you have some visitors.'

A frail, emaciated creature lay on the bed. He was awake. Two glassy eyes were trained on Priest, although how much Bertie Ruck could see through the cloudy lenses was questionable.

Jessica hung back as Priest approached the bed.

Priest didn't speak until he heard the door click behind him and the sound of Lina's heels making their way back down the corridor to the reception.

'Mr Ruck?'

There was no response. Were it not for the methodical rising and falling of the old man's wheezy chest, he might have been dead.

'Mr Ruck. My name is Priest. This is Jessica Ellinder. We're private investigators. I wondered whether you would talk to us for a moment?'

The old man blinked once. 'I've nothing to say to you.' His voice was surprisingly clear.

'You know why we're here?' Priest asked.

Ruck coughed out a laugh. 'Of course. You want to know about the Cage. Everyone does. How we treated the prisoners, how we won the war. You're all the same.'

Priest cast Jessica a glance and raised an eyebrow.

'Actually we're here to talk about Eva Miller.'

Ruck held Priest's gaze for a moment, unblinking, and then turned his head away in disgust.

'Leave an old man in peace, Mr whatever your name is. I'm tired.'

'So am I, Mr Ruck. But I want to talk about the Mayfly.'

Silence.

'I will be brief. If you want, I'll ask the questions in a way that allows you to only answer yes or no.'

'Nothing you say, Mr Priest, will persuade me to talk about anything with you. Save your breath.'

Priest thought back to Eva's will. The only piece of information it had offered on Ruck was his rank. 'Please, Colonel. It's a matter of life and death.'

Ruck creased up his forehead and jostled himself higher up the bed. 'What did you say?' he wheezed.

'I said it's a matter of life and death.'

'No. Before that.'

Priest carried on uncertainly. 'I said, "please, Colonel".'

'How do you know my rank? Nobody knows my rank. I never used it.'

'You're Colonel Albert Ruck. Sir.'

'I am. And who did you say you were?'

'My name is Charlie Priest.'

'Mmm. I see. And you want to talk about . . .'

Priest took a small envelope from his jacket pocket and handed it to Ruck. The old man took it with quivering hands, slipped open the top and tipped the contents on to the bed in front of him.

'This was sent to you?' he asked gravely.

'To a friend of mine. Do you know what it is?'

'Of course I do. *Rhithrogena germanica*, of the genus *Epeorus*. More commonly known as the March brown mayfly.'

Colonel Bertie Ruck had hauled himself upright and was looking far more animated than a man of a hundred and three. He reached over to a bedside drawer, fished around inside and took out an envelope. He shook it open.

'They sent me this a few days ago,' he explained. 'It's an invitation, you see. Sick bastards.'

'Perhaps you ought to start from the beginning,' Priest suggested.

Ruck shook his head. 'Let's see what you're made of first, Mr Priest.' He paused, as if to gather further strength. 'Tell me, what drove the Nazis to what they termed the Final Solution?'

'The Nazis believed that they were the descendants of the Aryans, the master race. They sought to remove impurities from the gene pool – this is the essence of eugenics. It wasn't just the Jews, of course, but anyone considered to be defective – the feeble-minded, the lame, the infirm. The Useless Eaters, they were called.'

Ruck inclined his head. 'Fine. So, you read occasionally, but it's an incomplete answer.'

'How so?'

'Because it provides a starting point for Himmler's warped ideology but it does not explain what was, to me, the biggest unanswered question of that bloody conflict. That is, why, at the point at which the Germans' struggle against the Allies became desperate, they used their valuable resources not on transporting men and materiel to the front line but on getting Jews into gas chambers. Trains were crammed with intended victims to the detriment of German troops. Why did the Nazis miss the opportunity to bolster their defences in favour of transporting the Jews to the death camps? It makes no sense, unless the answer is far more complicated than you suggest.'

'The Nazis were in chaos at the end of the war,' Priest offered.

'To an extent their command chain was dysfunctional, but they were not incompetent,' Ruck countered. 'That does not account for their actions.'

'So what does?'

'I thought I might have part of the answer to that question in nineteen forty-five when I met a Nazi doctor named Schneider but, on reflection, I'm not so sure.'

Schneider. *That name again.* Both Tiff Rowlinson and Sandra Barnsdale had mentioned it. 'Schneider experimented on Jews at Buchenwald using poison.'

'That's right. He developed a poison that was capable of bringing about unimaginable pain and suffering to a victim without actually killing them. He had what I suspect was a sexual reaction to the suffering the victims brought about on themselves. He told me that, at the extremity of their suffering, he had opened a conduit directly to God.'

'In the same way that the point of orgasm gives a channel to God during a sex rite?'

'Something like that.' Ruck snorted. 'Nonsense, I say, but something like that.'

'And Eva Miller?'

Ruck looked away, his eyes filled with regret. '*Eva*,' he breathed. 'What purpose would it serve?'

Priest pulled up a chair at the foot of Ruck's bed. He looked around. The room was devoid of any personal possessions except for a single framed photograph on the bedside table, turned away from the bed. Priest wondered whether that was out of choice.

'Atonement,' Priest suggested.

'*Atonement*,' Ruck scoffed. 'What would you know about that?'

Priest leant forwards. 'I know that this might be your last chance to achieve it, Colonel.'

'Do you really think me giving you the answers you want will give me atonement? That's very presumptuous of you, Mr Priest.'

'Colonel Ruck – I don't give a shit. Your peace means nothing to me. All I want to do is make sure that the people I care about don't get hurt and that the people responsible have their black hearts torn out.'

For the first time since they had entered the room Ruck smiled. 'Then that is a good enough reason for me, too.'

∞

When Ruck had finished, he asked for water. Jessica handed him a glass and he gulped it, splashing it down his front.

'So after your time in the military was over, you joined the police force?' said Priest.

'That's right. I joined the Met in nineteen forty-nine. There were lots of us after the war, not sure what to do with the skills we'd acquired, the things we'd seen. Police work was the only thing that made sense; only thing I was good at. I worked my way up to detective chief inspector, but all the while I was looking for her. Eva. I never found her, until one day in nineteen seventy-two I was called out to a murder scene in a hotel in Kensington. It wasn't my remit ordinarily, but the killer had left a note addressed to me personally. The body had been poisoned using the same strain of alkaloid described by Schneider in his interviews with me. Only two people knew about that – me and Eva Miller. She had also sent me an ink sketch of a mayfly, just to make the point clearer, as if it wasn't already.'

'Why a mayfly?' asked Priest.

'It was the code name of the operation I was in charge of after the war ended. Britain's dirty secret. We were given the task of trying to salvage any intelligible data from the Holocaust experiments. We were trying to see if the Nazi doctors had achieved anything of worth. We called it Operation Mayfly.'

Priest clicked his tongue. 'And so you think Eva established some sort of group? A group that is still in operation today?'

'I believe,' said Ruck, 'that Eva found a rich reservoir of perverse individuals who wanted to buy in to what she was doing.'

'People are paying to watch the poisonings.'

'Yes.'

'But Eva's now dead and yet the group is still operating,' Priest pointed out.

Ruck nodded. He was beginning to tire. 'I suspect Eva Miller had an apprentice. Someone to whom she passed on her work.'

'Have you any idea who?'

'I would tell you if I did. I followed her as best I could over two decades. Attended every crime scene that seemed to have any possible connection with the Mayfly group. I set up task force after task force but we never got close. We could never find out who was involved. No one would talk.'

'I know,' said Priest. 'I have the names.'

Ruck stared at him. 'You have the names?'

Priest was about to reply when Jessica suddenly darted across the room and picked up the photograph from Ruck's bedside table. She looked at it for a second and then handed it to Priest without a word. It was faded, the edges worn white from over-exposure, but the face was striking. A woman with a half-smile. There was something familiar about her.

'Eva?' Priest asked gently. Ruck nodded. Jessica remained silent. 'Were you in love with her?'

Ruck looked away. 'I suppose I was. In a way.'

'Did you ever meet her again? I mean after that night in nineteen forty-six?'

'Yes. Just once.'

∽

14th November, 1978
A village near London

Ruck stirred. Something had disturbed his sleep.

This wasn't unusual in itself. He had slept lightly ever since the war, never daring to allow himself to drift off completely from the world. The tiniest noise would rouse him.

But this was different. Somebody was in his house.

He got up, careful not to make too much noise. There was a revolver in the drawer. If there was a trespasser downstairs, Ruck wanted to retain the element of surprise. Not many people would have anticipated that a man of his age would be so alert. He had the advantage.

He crept down the stairs. A streetlight outside penetrated the thin curtains, giving just enough illumination to allow him to make his way to the front room.

He cocked the gun. Held it upwards, ready to bring it down and around the door. Two shots, then back to cover again. Just the way he had been trained.

He peered around the door.

'Hello, Bertie.'

The gun dropped to the floor. For a moment, Ruck felt the bones in his legs melt away. He caught the side of the doorframe to stop himself from toppling over.

'Eva.'

'I'm sorry to intrude.'

She was an older version of the young girl who had sat timidly in the corner of the barn recording his interrogation of Kurt Schneider. But it was unmistakably her, even in the dim light.

She was sitting cross-legged, an unlit cigarette between her fingers. Her black-rimmed glasses suited her, emphasising her fine features. Her hair was an extraordinary shock of white.

'Do you have a light?'

Ruck walked across the room, keeping his eyes on the woman in his chair; he reached for a box of matches on the mantelpiece. Lit one and offered it to her. She leant across until her cigarette met the flame. She inhaled deeply.

'Thank you.'

'What are you doing here, Eva?'

She blew smoke around the room. 'I hear you've been looking for me.'

Ruck gritted his teeth. He felt nothing now for her but utter contempt. He should kill her. Shoot her in the head. How many lives would he save by doing so? He edged around back to the door and bent to pick up the gun.

'I've been looking for you to put an end to this.'

'Put an end to what?'

'Don't play games with me, woman.' Ruck pointed the gun at her. She didn't flinch but watched the end of the barrel curiously.

'Really, Bertie? Don't be silly. Put that thing away before you hurt yourself.'

'I'm close, Eva. Close enough to put you away. I know everything. I know about your little gatherings. I know about the men that pay you to see you poison innocent people. I know about the Mayfly, Eva.'

'Do you? Good for you. So shoot me and get it over with.'

'Don't tempt me!' Ruck took a step forward.

Eva smiled. She stood up and stepped closer to him so the gun was within her reach. He could smell her, even through the smoke. That same scent he remembered from thirty years ago. He could not hide the quiver in his hand.

'Bertie, if you were going to shoot me, you would have done it by now. So why don't we talk?'

'It's only a matter of time before I find out the names of the sick people you have recruited to your group, Eva.'

'And when you do, what then? Hmm? Will the angry mob grab their pitchforks and come rampaging through the countryside trying to find all the monsters and lynch them? Bertie, you are in danger of disappointing me. Have you lost all of your imagination?'

'Damn you, Eva!'

'That's more like it. A little more testosterone and you would interest me again, I think. Now listen, darling. This is important. I would urge you to cease your pursuit of my friends.'

Ruck laughed; the gun wavered dangerously. 'Now who's disappointing, Eva. You think I'll give up? Just like that?'

She took another drag on the cigarette. 'Well, yes.'

Perspiration was running down the back of his neck. His eyes were starting to blur. 'You're mad, Eva.'

'Not at all, Bertie. In fact, you know what they say. Don't get mad, get even.'

'What are you talking about?'

'I'm here to welcome you, Bertie. To the club. To our little group. A lifetime membership. Think about it.'

'Never.'

'Oh, it's not a choice thing, I'm afraid. It's quite necessary. You see, if someone ever found details of our membership, Bertie, do you know whose name is at the top of the list?'

'No . . .'

'Yes, I'm afraid so. It's really very simple, isn't it? No one is going to believe that a mere secretary is capable of orchestrating the most secretive society in London all by herself. But you? Now, that's very different. After all, with your experience in the Cage, torture is your profession, is it not?'

Ruck lowered the gun. Outside, he could hear birds waking and the glow of the sun was threatening to pierce the hilltops.

The dawn chorus was beginning.

∽

A silence hung in the little room at the Priory Nursing Home as Priest tried to take it all in.

After a while, Ruck spoke quietly. 'So now you see, Mr Priest, why I doubt the possibility of atonement.'

'You didn't create the monsters on that list, Colonel.'

'But I did nothing to stop them, either. And to avoid what? Being locked up as a lunatic, being administered drugs against my will by people wearing white coats and fake smiles?' He looked around and laughed. 'Hardly a fate I avoided, don't you think?'

Priest thought for a while. 'You said they invite you, still. To the gatherings. Even now?'

'The miserable bitch taunted me for years. A reminder, I suppose, of her hold on me. And her protégé continues the tradition.'

'You said you had an invitation recently?'

Ruck beckoned for Priest to come closer. He gave him the mayfly he had retrieved from his drawer. Priest understood: this was an invitation.

'So there is a gathering soon?' said Priest, his throat suddenly dry. *What if we're too late? What about Georgie and Hayley?*

'Open it and see.'

'What?'

Ruck took the insect with trembling fingers and held it up to the light. He cupped it in his hand and placed his thumbs on the underside, gently applying pressure to the creature's abdomen.

There was a squelching sound as Ruck prised the mayfly's body apart, like removing the shell from a prawn.

Lodged in the insect's body was a note. Ruck passed it to Priest, who unrolled it, then read it aloud. An address, a time and a date.

'My God,' said Jessica. 'That's tonight.'

❧

Bertie Ruck waited a few minutes. When he was sure they weren't coming back, he reached under his pillow and fumbled for his mobile phone. It had half fallen behind the bedhead but he managed to pull it out despite the arthritic pains in his hands.

He stared at the keypad, waiting for his eyes to focus. He had to wait for everything now. Wait before he stood up, wait before he pissed, wait before the tablets worked. How pathetic; how effete he was now.

Eventually, the screen lit up and he found the number just as they had shown him.

'It's Ruck. They've just left.'

The voice at the other end hissed in his ear. He had learnt to hate it, the androgynous voice that wouldn't let him live, or die for that matter.

'No. I did nothing. *They* came to *me*. They must have found out who I was somehow. Anyway, it is done.'

Ruck listened, but he no longer cared.

'Yes,' he said. 'They will be your guests, just as you wanted. Now, I have paid my debt. Leave me alone.'

48

Priest stared at himself in the mirror. There were lines under his eyes he hadn't seen before and a scar under his chin, although he couldn't remember cutting himself. He examined his hands. When he pressed the skin between his fingers, he felt the sensation of pain. But it wasn't sharp enough, no matter how hard he pinched. His nose had bled again over the sink, though he had barely noticed. Such things did not matter in the parody of the real world in which he lived.

His phone pinged. Georgie's friend, Li. *Any news? What are you doing?*

What *was* he doing? Labouring over his cufflinks, buttoning his dress shirt, putting on his dinner jacket? He had no choice. He was going to a party. In the bedroom, he picked up the Glock and studied it. The gun was heavier than he recalled, the edges were worn, the metal had lost its shine. A small, numb part of his brain registered alarm – the barrel was pointing at his face, his hand on the trigger. He had seen that image before. A long time ago. After they had handed down the special verdict to William. After his marriage to Dee was over, his career was in tatters, his parents were dead, he'd been drinking and his sister hated him. For a long time, all he had heard when he'd closed his eyes at night were the screams of the people his brother had murdered.

Priest thought about all of the people he had let down.

Not again.

He had offered Ruck the chance to atone. Was there anybody willing to offer him a similar chance?

He threw the gun on to the bed.

On the way out, he made sure the fish had extra food. If he didn't come back, it might take Sarah a few days to remember to feed them.

Jessica was waiting for him by her Range Rover, watching him as he made his way across the underground car park. She too had been home to wash and change. Her hair was immaculate. He took her hand and kissed it, eyes on her face. She met his gaze.

'You think we can just waltz up to this house and negotiate our way in uninvited?' she said.

'But we're not uninvited. Quite the contrary.'

'We're going as Colonel Ruck? And guest?' She sounded sceptical. 'Ruck is one hundred and three.'

'They won't have a clue who he is; he's never been. All we need to do is get in. We'll work the rest out when we get there.'

'But how can you be sure that Georgie and Hayley are at this gathering?'

'I can't be sure – but the Bagman told me that Hayley was at their *special house*. The address on the note is a mansion in the middle of nowhere. If that's where they have Hayley, that's also where they will have taken Georgie.'

'Fine. I'll drive.'

Priest glanced at the Volvo. 'Why?'

'I doubt this is the sort of affair where the clientele drive cars like yours.'

Priest stepped aside and clicked his keys. She turned at the sound of the alarm. Not the Volvo, but something else tucked away in the corner of the car park.

'You have an Aston Martin Rapide S?' she said. 'Five hundred and fifty brake horsepower and nought to sixty in under four point nine seconds.'

Priest nodded, impressed, although he had no idea whether she was correct.

'Why would you drive an old Volvo when you own one of the most luxurious saloons ever made?'

Priest shrugged. 'You can get more stuff in the Volvo.'

∞

The house was not visible from the road but there was a faint glow of illumination from behind a line of trees. Everything else was completely swallowed by the darkness.

Priest slowed the Aston to a crawl. The headlights glinted off a set of giant wrought-iron gates tipped with gold leaves. As they approached, three large figures emerged from the shadows.

'Did you bring the flash drive?' Jessica asked.

Priest patted the inside of his jacket pocket. 'It's the only thing we have to bargain with.'

He stopped just short, making the approaching figure bridge the final few metres while he waited. He wound down the window and a large, shaven head leant into the car, followed by the overpowering smell of tobacco.

'Can I help you?' said the skinhead.

'Ruck,' replied Priest.

'Of course, Mr Ruck. Welcome. If you would be kind enough to let me have your keys, I will take care of your vehicle. My friends will escort you to the house.'

Jessica glanced nervously at Priest. A valet service limited the opportunities for a quick getaway.

'Sir?' The skinhead sensed their hesitation. 'Your car will be in safe hands.'

Priest nodded to Jessica and she got out. Priest followed, surrendering the keys to the welcoming committee. He took a long look at the Aston, wondering if he would ever see it again.

'This way, sir, madam.'

The skinhead tossed the keys to one of his colleagues and led them through the gates to a waiting golf buggy. They climbed aboard and were driven down a winding drive through the trees.

There wasn't much to see. The occasional lamp cast a dull light over the oaks lining the driveway but there was little else to give them any clues as to what was lurking behind the greenery. They passed a large gatehouse and finally arrived at a set of stables that ran the length of a gravelled courtyard the size of a football pitch. Wherever they were going, it was big.

The buggy slowed and turned through a further set of gates before sliding to a halt in another gravelled courtyard. As they got out, Priest gave Jessica's hand a squeeze. She smiled at him weakly. He tried to focus on her face, but to his horror, it began to slip away from him. As he scrabbled to hold on to reality, he saw himself alight from the golf buggy and walk towards the entrance to an enormous baroque mansion. They were finally here – at the House of Mayfly.

The warm air of the house brought a welcome reprieve from the chill outside, but it was short-lived. A sense of dread had crept over Priest. His hands and fingers no longer felt like they belonged to him. He was slipping away, powerless to stop the descent. *Jesus, not now.*

'Mr and Mrs Ruck.' Priest heard the skinhead announce them as if from a long, long way away.

A gangly man in a pristine black suit came forward and offered his hand, first to Priest then to Jessica. Priest took it, but didn't feel the grip. *Here and now*, he told himself over and over again. *Here and now.*

'Welcome, Mr Ruck. And Mrs Ruck. Welcome to the House of Mayfly. May I take your coats?'

Dazed, Priest handed over his coat. He stumbled back a few paces but felt a firm hand on his shoulder, steadying him. He turned. In an instant, he had wrestled his consciousness back. *Here and now.*

'Sir, may I ask you for your invitation?'

Jessica had removed her coat and handed it to the butler. Beneath, she wore a blue gown that flowed like a meandering river to the floor. The material clung elegantly to her hips and waist. Her white neck was adorned with a simple gold chain, from which hung a single pearl. There was nothing fancy or extravagant, from the matching pearl earrings to the elegant cut of the dress; her understated beauty was simply breath-taking.

'Sir?'

The butler was looking at him expectantly. To Priest's relief he saw him through his own eyes, palm outstretched. Jessica took his arm.

From the inside pocket of his jacket, Priest pulled out an envelope and handed it to the butler, who inspected the contents, smiled robotically and then passed it to the skinhead, who placed it in a pile with other similar envelopes on a table behind them.

'Thank you,' the butler said. 'May I ask if you will be using the spa after the lecture tonight?'

'There's a spa?' Jessica asked.

'Of course. Towels can of course be provided, Mrs Ruck, so please do not fret if you are unprepared.'

'Thank you,' murmured Jessica.

'Now, a change to the order of play this evening,' continued the butler. 'Dinner will follow the lecture this time around.'

'Because?' Priest asked.

The butler smiled. 'We prefer our guests to go to the lecture with empty stomachs.'

Jessica squeezed Priest's arm. *The lecture*. If Georgie and Hayley were here, they had to be found without delay. *One or both of them might be playing a central part.*

'A drink first?' the butler enquired.

'Of course.'

'Very good. Myers will see you to the bar.'

Another man in a black suit stepped forward and indicated that they should follow. They set off, but the butler called them back before they reached the door on the opposite side of the room.

'Mr Ruck! Aren't you forgetting something?'

Priest stopped and turned, wondering if the game was up.

The butler was holding out two white hoods.

∽

His head having been stuffed inside an ill-fitting hood, Priest's anxiety level had notched up considerably. Not only was it extremely hot, it also stripped him of his peripheral vision – the material around the eye sockets was raised slightly, creating blinkers. *Still, at least I'm back in the present, inhabiting my own body.*

Myers led them through a labyrinth of hallways cluttered with ornaments and trinkets. Stuffed animals lined the walls alongside life-size oil paintings of arrogant-looking earls and ugly Victorian children dressed as dolls – all of them wearing ruffles. The house gave the impression of grandeur but it had ended up looking more like a film set.

They turned another corner. In the distance the sound of activity bled through the walls. Priest imagined people clinking glasses, talking excitedly, milling around drinking, as if they were waiting for a recital. Meanwhile, there was every chance that two girls were held captive, alone and terrified. He clenched his fists tightly. He felt sick.

Ahead of them was a grand staircase. As they climbed it, the noise grew louder. At the top, a set of mahogany double doors were thrown open and they were shown through to a large reception room occupied by perhaps fifty people – mostly men, squeezed into suits. A small group of more casually dressed academic-looking types in leather-patched jackets and designer jeans were huddled in a corner. There were a few women, but none as striking as Jessica. She had already drawn attention as she entered the room; they couldn't see her face, but beady eyes had latched on to her body.

'Let me announce you, sir,' their guide whispered to Priest.

'That will not be necessary.' Priest took Jessica by the arm and plunged into the crowd.

No going back now.

'A drink?' Priest said.

'Do we have to?' Jessica replied.

Priest felt the flap at the bottom of the hood. It had been designed to allow the wearer to eat or drink.

'Everyone else has glasses in their hands. It might look odd if we don't.'

Jessica nodded. There was a bar to the right, extending the width of the room. Four bartenders and beer on tap. Rows of spirits were racked up behind and little dishes filled with peanuts were on the side. As they approached the bar it became clear that the room, although sizeable, was actually a mezzanine balcony overlooking another much larger room beneath: in effect they were standing in the lower circle of a theatre. They leant over the brass railing and looked down. Below them was a raised dais on which stood a table. The backdrop was covered with a heavy white curtain.

'Is that where . . .?' Jessica's question tailed off.

'Yes. That's where the *lecture* is going to take place.'

'There's something about this place,' said Jessica. 'Something odd; I mean odder than all these masked people, odder than the whole set-up. It's almost *familiar* to me . . .' She tailed off again. 'What do we do now?'

'Not sure. But we have to find a way to search the rest of the house. The girls have to be here. We need to find them, and quickly.'

'Yes, please?' The bartender beamed at them. He was sporting a Victorian handlebar moustache and looked like a film extra. He even had a rag hanging from his back pocket.

'Madam?'

'Blue margarita.'

'Excellent choice! And for sir?'

Priest hesitated. *What the hell is a blue margarita?* 'Tonic water,' he said.

The bartender went about his work, whistling a tune and without any apparent concern for the hideous acts that had been planned for the stage below. Priest surveyed the room. Only one door in and out, which led to the stairs they had just climbed. Thereafter lay an infinite number of possibilities: this was a cavernous, sprawling mansion. Wandering around aimlessly in the hope of finding Georgie and Hayley was a poor plan.

'Charlie,' Jessica said.

'What?'

He followed her gaze. On the far side of the room, their guide, Myers, was talking intently to two other men, also in black suits but wearing gold cummerbunds. They were looking across. Myers pointed to Priest and Jessica and his two companions began to weave through the crowd towards them.

Priest took a sip from his drink and turned away, not wanting to demonstrate any alarm.

'Charlie? What do we do?'

'Drink,' he said to Jessica. 'Relax. I'll talk.'

At least the tonic water soothed his dry throat. Jessica slipped her hand around his arm. He gave her hand a squeeze. Her palm was hot; he sensed her confidence starting to wane.

'Mr Ruck?'

'Yes?'

The two men took up positions either side of Priest. He tensed, adrenaline surging through him. He was ready to fight hand to hand if he needed to. They hadn't come this far to fail now, not when the stakes were this high. Georgie hadn't signed up for this: she was in danger because of him. He had got her into this and he would get her out. And these men sure as hell weren't going to stop him.

'Your seat is ready, sir,' said the first man.

'My *seat*?' Priest tried not to show surprise.

'You have been designated a premium seat, Mr Ruck. Would you like to come down with us? You may watch the lecture from the balcony, Mrs Ruck.'

The first man stretched out his arm, gesturing towards the door. Priest shot Jessica a look. She raised her hand, letting him know it was all right.

He was about to follow his guide when she stopped him, placed a hand on his shoulder, leant in and kissed him on the cheek through the hood.

49

Priest was led out of the balcony room, back down the stairs and through a set of double doors into the theatre itself. Where one might have expected to see rows of seats bolted to the floor, there was only a large, empty space, save for a bank of cubicles set up near the front but off-centre. Four of them in all, staggered slightly so that, once you were sitting down, you couldn't see any of the other observers. There was a desk in front of each chair. Writing paper and pens had been provided, a phone and a small reading lamp.

'This is your seat, Mr Ruck,' said the first man, pointing to the third cubicle along from the left. 'May I get you another drink?'

'No, thank you.'

'Very good, sir.'

'Tell me, when does the lecture start?'

'In approximately forty-five minutes. In the meantime, please make yourself comfortable. If you need anything at all, please use the phone provided. It goes straight through to your personal attendant.'

'Thank you.' *Forty-five minutes to find Georgie and Hayley.*

The second escort pulled the chair back and Priest sat down. The two men bowed and withdrew.

As he had come in, Priest had noticed that one of the other cubicles was occupied. *Another premium seat holder.* A hooded head much larger than his appeared around the corner of his cubicle.

'Wow, this is unbelievable!' The accent was Deep-South American. 'Twenty-eight grand for this seat and it's not even real fucking leather!'

⁓

Jessica watched as Priest was escorted through the crowd. The doors shut after him and she suddenly felt completely alone. It was as though someone had thrown a bucket of ice-cold water over her face.

'Another blue margarita?'

The barman with the Victorian handlebar moustache was beaming broadly again.

'Yes,' she said. She pushed her glass across towards him. It was empty but she had no recollection of drinking it. Standing by the bar, she was conscious of the heads that were turning, one by one, to look at her, of people – hooded men, mostly – talking, laughing. She clenched her fist tight, tried to break the skin with her fingernails, but her hands felt numb.

The barman placed another drink in front of her but she didn't take it. Out of the corner of her eye, she saw trouble. A hooded man, leaning arrogantly against the bar, his body turned towards her, his gut barely contained inside his suit.

'Interesting choice of drink,' he remarked.

Jessica recognised his voice. *Shit!*

'What is it, now?'

She turned slowly. *Shit! Shit! Shit!*

'It's a blue margarita,' she said through gritted teeth.

'Lovely. A lovely drink for a lovely girl,' said Detective Inspector McEwen.

I must keep calm. It's possible he doesn't recognise me. Why should he? We barely met twice, but still . . . I'd know his voice anywhere, even if his fat face is squashed into a white hood.

'Goldie, I'll take one of those and another for the lady,' McEwen shouted across at the barman.

'I'm fine. Thank you.'

'You must. I have not seen you at one of these lectures before. Are you a newcomer?'

Jessica picked up her drink and took a sip – slowly, so as not to reveal her shaking hands. 'I was here last time.'

'No, no. I would have remembered you. Undoubtedly.'

She felt sick. He had moved to within an arm's reach. Close enough for her to smell his garlic-laced breath and stale sweat. She took a deep breath and tried to conquer her shock. He must not see how terrified she was.

'I hear we have a very interesting programme tonight.'

'Aye,' agreed McEwen. 'Intriguing, I'm sure.'

Jessica fought the urge to gag. 'Are you a doctor?'

'Oh, no, lass. I have more subtle interests in tonight's demonstration. You could say I'm staff, really.'

Jessica put the glass down on the bar. 'Staff?'

'Aye. Like Goldie here.' He nodded at the barman wiping a pint glass. The man grinned in return. 'We get paid in kind, if you know what I mean.'

Staff. Unlikely you would be a paying customer on a detective's salary. That also explains why you aren't on the Mayfly database.

I bet none of the staff *are. And paid-in-kind just means they get to watch the show for free.*

Jessica's stomach knotted.

'It's been nice talking to you,' she said. 'But I have to use the bathroom. Please excuse me.'

She made to leave but McEwen grabbed her arm. His hands were hot and sticky. He pulled her back so his stomach brushed against her dress. He stank of alcohol.

'Wait a minute, lass. Don't I know you?'

'No.' Jessica knew she had replied too quickly. She could see McEwen's small eyes through his hood looking at her, down her top, across her breasts, to her hips.

'Are you sure we've never met?' he slurred.

'Never.'

He let her go. 'Come back, when you're done.'

She nodded curtly, turned and walked away through the crowd.

50

Priest inspected the phone in his cubicle. It looked as if it should have been hung on a hotel bathroom wall. There was no keypad, just a single button adorned with a familiar symbol.

'Cute. A little mayfly,' he mumbled.

'What's that, partner?' The American craned his head round the divider again.

Priest pressed the button. After a few rings a woman answered.

'Yes, Mr Ruck? How can I help you?'

'How long is it until the lecture begins?'

'Just over forty minutes. Can I get you anything?'

'I'd like to use the facilities before the lecture starts, please.'

'Of course, Mr Ruck. An attendant will be with you very shortly.'

The attendant arrived in two minutes. Thirty-eight remaining. He was stocky, around Priest's height but lighter. Not the sort of person that Priest would ordinarily pick a fight with, but options were limited and time was short.

'This way, sir.'

The attendant motioned for Priest to follow him. He sounded Scandinavian, Danish maybe. Priest followed, wishing his guide would walk faster. *Come on, you slow fuck – time's ticking!*

It took them less than three minutes to get to the bathroom. Thirty-five remaining. The attendant pushed the door open and followed Priest in. There were no urinals, just a row of five or so cubicles.

'Is this the gents?' Priest asked. There had been no sign on the door.

'This is the premium customers' toilets, sir,' replied the attendant.

'So not many women pay for premium seats, then?'

'To my knowledge, none.'

Priest ran his fist as hard as he could into the attendant's stomach. Not a fatal or even incapacitating blow but enough to discourage any fight back. The shock of having the wind forcibly ripped from his lungs prevented the attendant from crying out or retaliating and he sank down in a heap against the door.

Knocking a man unconscious is a delicate business. Too much force might kill; not enough risks attracting attention.

Priest bent down. 'Now listen. My preference would not be to hurt you, but I will if you prejudice my chances of walking out of here without attracting attention. How do you feel about that?'

'Wh-who the fuck are you?' the attendant groaned.

'I'm here for the women.'

'What? Are you mad?'

'Where are they?'

Through coughs and splutters, the attendant actually wheezed out a laugh. 'You're crazy.' He managed to draw back some of the lost air into his lungs and putting out a hand to steady himself, started getting to his feet.

Priest grabbed the man's hand and twisted his wrist. He collapsed back down again, wincing with pain.

'Where are the women you are holding for tonight's performance?' he demanded, more forcibly this time.

'This whole place is crawling with guards – you can't possibly think you can just walk out of here!'

Priest twisted harder and the attendant writhed in response. But Priest had leverage over him, and an extra couple of stone in weight. He placed his knee on the attendant's chest and pushed down abruptly.

'*Shit!*'

'Look, I have dissociative disorder.'

'Wha—'

'So what? Means I bore easily and breaking your wrist then whatever other bone I can get hold of really isn't the big deal, for me, that it should be.'

Their eyes met. Priest saw panic – and realisation. He relaxed his grip, just a little. An invitation, nothing more.

'The wine cellar,' the attendant gasped. 'They are always kept in the wine cellar.'

Priest nodded, grabbed the man by the collar and dragged him across to a sink. He removed his belt and secured the attendant to the pipework. Priest tied the leather strap as tightly as he could – enough to stop the blood flowing to the captive's hands. In minutes, they would be numb and useless. When Priest had finished, the attendant laughed, although his face remained twisted with pain.

Priest forced off one of the attendant's shoes and a black sock.

'Do you think you have any chance of getting out of here alive?' the man spat.

Priest stuffed the sock into the attendant's mouth, tying a shoelace around his head to keep it in place. Then he grabbed him by the chin, forcing him to meet his gaze:

'The odds are even. But if you're lying about the wine cellar, I'll know where to find you.'

∽∾

Jessica walked out of the double doors past a small gathering of hooded figures talking in low murmurs. One of them looked over. Jessica ignored them and headed left along the corridor. She had no idea where she was going, but she didn't dare go back into the same room as McEwen. Good job the alcohol had clouded his judgement.

When she had got far enough away from the party and the sounds of people enjoying themselves had started to fade, she removed the hood. Her face was too hot and it was difficult to breath properly. Her hair was a mess. *People paid tens of thousands of pounds to be here?*

She rounded another corner, more certain now of where she was. An idea had started to take hold; a sense that this house wasn't as unfamiliar as she had originally supposed. At first, she had dismissed the feeling as déjà vu – this was the same corridor lined with old paintings and thick, velvety wallpaper that you would see in any number of grand houses open to the public.

But this feeling was more than that.

She stopped at a door. Looked at it carefully. *Behind this, there's a staircase leading down.* She was sure of it. She tried the handle, pushed open the door. In front of her, wooden stairs disappeared into a gloomy space below. Jessica swallowed. A sensation of uneasiness washed over her. She knew this house. She recognised the layout.

Slowly, she descended into the darkness.

She fumbled for a light switch. At the bottom of the staircase, another oil painting loomed over her. A mother holding a baby clad in ridiculous frills. Time had worn the paint away so that only the mother's face remained clearly visible. A pale, melancholy stain on a black canvas.

A memory from her childhood surfaced: that of a six-year-old girl who had played in the large room that lay beyond this one, through a set of double doors.

A door. An insect carved into the top panel.

Jessica froze. This was not déjà vu. She had been here before.

∞

Priest couldn't risk going back for Jessica. A premium seat holder who gave up such a prized place would attract the wrong sort of attention. She would have to look after herself now: there was twenty-two minutes left by his count.

He kept close to the walls, where the floorboards creaked less, moving as quickly as he dared down another hallway before he arrived at an iron spiral staircase. It only went upwards. He stepped back, infuriated.

He had to focus. Lift the fog. There was some detail he was missing, a blurred edge he needed to straighten. *What is it? Think!*

He tried to rearrange all the details he had collected, strip them apart and put back together again. The photograph of Miles Ellinder's ritualised death, Sandra Barnsdale's Mayfly list, Bertie Ruck's bitterness, Eva Miller's will.

His counter-terrorist contact Giles had said something almost offhandedly during their last conversation. What was it? *'The devil's in the detail, Priest.'*

He reached for his phone and brought up the post-mortem report Giles had sent him. Then the Mayfly list. He typed a name in Search. Then . . . *Yes, it matched. Of course!*

Priest knew what he needed to do. He looked right to a set of double doors. *A way through . . .*

Removing his hood, he tossed it in a plant pot and smoothed his ruffled hair. He turned through the doors, following the distant sound of clattering and the rumble of talk. Eventually, he came to another pair of doors. They swung open in front of him and he almost collided with a waiter who only just managed to prevent a tray of canapés crashing to the floor.

'Be careful!' the waiter cried.

'I'm so sorry,' said Priest, sliding past clumsily but whipping away the white cloth dangling from the waiter's trousers and stuffing it into his own back pocket.

In the kitchen, food was being prepared. The smell of fish was overpowering. Lemon sole, if he wasn't mistaken. *Where this whole sorry affair started.*

'Be careful not to get the oil too hot,' he commented to one of the chefs who was steering a frying pan around the hob. 'It burns easily.'

'Who are you?' the head chef shouted across the silver range. He was a tall man with frown lines as deep as trenches across his face.

'Mr Ruck has requested two bottles of the Château Mouton Rothschild,' Priest replied.

The chef clearly sensed something was amiss; this was a waiter he had never seen before. But Priest was gambling on the human instinct to avoid alarming conclusions when faced with uncertainty. It was a principle his father had taught him.

'We don't have two bottles of that,' the head chef said curtly.

'Then something similar?' Priest waited.

'Fine. Marco, you go.' The chef nodded to a waiter standing over by the door. The man had a military haircut, his shoulders were broad and his biceps bulged from beneath his black suit.

Twenty minutes, maybe less.

Marco led Priest down a series of staircases and hallways. He walked quickly but every step represented another few moments of lost time. Priest had kept track of how long he had left before the lecture began, almost to the second. He doubted it was going to be enough.

As they rounded a corner, Marco stopped so suddenly that Priest almost ran into the back of him.

'What?' Priest said, trying to disguise his panic.

'You don't work here.'

Priest's stomach lurched. He had managed to negotiate past the head chef, but not the bloody bottle washer.

'You don't work here,' Marco repeated.

Priest braced himself.

'Who are you?'

'I'm the guy that's going to break your neck if you don't do what I say.'

Marco nodded, as if he already knew. Priest felt uneasy – something wasn't right.

'You're here for the girls?'

Priest did a double-take. 'That's right.'

'Did someone tell you they're in the wine cellar?'

Priest hesitated. Marco looked totally unfazed. Priest said nothing.

'They're trained to say they're in the wine cellar. If, you know, someone breaks in undercover,' Marco said.

Priest thought about the attendant tied to the sink upstairs. It was conceivable he had lied but Priest had had nothing else to go on. *Wait –*

'Who *are* you?' asked Priest.

Marco looked at Priest for a moment and something passed between them. Then he turned back the way they had come.

'Hey –' Priest grabbed him by the arm.

'Down there,' Marco nodded to a door on the left. 'That leads to the great hall. Go across it to the other side. There's a set of steps leading to a cell. The girls are there. But you'll need to be quick. I'll tell the boss you got the wine and you're going to deliver it now.'

Priest turned to the door. It was marked – like a gang tag – with the outline of a black insect with long wings.

When he looked back, Marco had vanished.

51

The great hall of the House of Mayfly was circular, with six giant stone pillars supporting a domed ceiling. The only illumination was provided by the moonlight that filtered through thin windows cut into the base of the dome and a series of dim, artificial lights set around the edge of the room.

On the far side, the waiter had told him that there was a door leading to a cell where he would find Georgie and Hayley, but the room was occupied. Priest stopped short.

In the centre stood a round table and twelve seats. In one of the seats a figure sat with its back to Priest. The noise of the door opening resonated round the bare walls, but the figure in the centre did not stir.

On the far side of the room stood another figure, handgun trained on Priest. His face was hidden behind a white hood, but Priest recognised the masked man who had invaded his family home. He nodded at Priest and gestured with the gun to a high-backed chair in the corner. Priest sat down. For the first time in days, his head felt clear, a strange sense of peace had descended on him. *This is the end. The final solution.*

Another door close by, hidden by the gloom, opened. Nobody moved. Jessica took a few cautious steps forward. Her eyes darted around, taking everything in – the giant table, the masked man on the other side, Priest sitting in the corner, the sombre figure staring ahead.

'What is this?' Her voice shook but whether it was from fear or anger Priest couldn't be sure. Like him, she had removed her hood.

The sight of her panicked face looking at him expectantly was too much to bear. Priest looked away. He knew what was to come, what she was going to see unfold. The betrayal would be unforgivable.

The figure at the table rose slowly, chair legs scraping across the marble floor. The noise was amplified tenfold in the cavernous room.

Jessica stopped dead.

'Jessica,' the figure said.

For a moment, nobody moved.

Lucia Ellinder turned and faced her daughter. At the Dower House, Priest had met a fragile, ghostlike woman, whose meekness was as pathetic as it was pitiful. This, in contrast, was a woman at the height of her powers.

'What – what are you doing here?' Jessica stammered in shock.

Lucia Ellinder smiled. 'In a sense, I have always been here.'

'But . . . Daddy . . .'

'Is very ill, dear. Very ill. But we soldier on, don't we?'

'I don't understand.'

'Of course you do, Jessica. You *do* understand.'

Jessica looked at Priest. Her face had changed from one of confusion to defiance. Again, he struggled to hold her gaze.

'I'm sorry, Jessica,' he said. 'She's the one. The Mayfly.'

'You seem unsurprised, Mr Priest.' Lucia Ellinder turned towards him. She was almost the same height as Priest and presented a commanding figure, in a plain black gown with a high neck line and white frills around the wrists. Her stare made the hairs on the back of his neck rise.

'I knew it was you,' Priest said simply.

'Of course you did.'

'You're . . .?' Jessica spoke so quietly it didn't sound like her voice.

'Oh, come on, Jessica!' Lucia shouted. It was a tone Priest suspected Jessica hadn't heard often. She stepped back a few paces in surprise.

'But of course!' Lucia's tone was bitter. 'How could it be me? Your pathetic mother? For whom you have not an ounce of respect!'

Jessica stepped back in shock. 'Mummy, I –'

'Shut up! I do not resent you for it, Jessica. Why should you have known? Your father was such a great man, and I was but a small part of his long shadow. Or so he thought.'

'But – he loves you . . .'

'Oh, how feeble! Do you really think, child, that marriages amongst the privileged are founded on such ridiculous notions? Your father no more loved me than he loved his cars.' She waved her hand in dismissal. 'Now –' She turned to Priest. 'I'm very interested in hearing the conclusions to your investigations. My family did, after all, pledge to pay for your services. Perhaps we should see if we have value for money?'

'You did,' Priest agreed. 'But of course I was retained to find out what happened to Miles. And you knew all along, didn't you?'

Jessica opened her mouth but no words came out.

'Well, come on then, Mr Priest,' Lucia Ellinder taunted. 'Jessica deserves the truth, don't you think?'

Priest took a moment to consider this. Making him tell the story was all part of the show; it had been meticulously planned. At the back of the room, the hooded observer shifted his weight from foot to foot. He had not moved from his position since Priest had entered the room. He had a painful sense of foreboding: this was the moment before judgement was passed.

He tried clearing his throat but something was stuck there. The air in the room was stagnant, oppressive. A smell familiar to him from his early police work: death and decay.

He regained his composure.

'There was once a woman called Eva Miller,' he said slowly. 'She was a typist, a stenographer of sorts, during the war, assigned to an intelligence officer in the murky aftermath of VE Day. She was assigned to Operation Mayfly, the British government's dirty secret. In the days that followed the war, Europe looked about its ravaged lands for answers. It wanted to know why. The Holocaust was the greatest single act of ethnic cleansing ever to have taken place and yet nobody understood what lay behind the Nazi obsession with death on such a massive and focused scale.

'Eva Miller was one of those unfortunate people who was exposed to that dark world at a very young age. It corrupted her. Wove its way under her skin. She learnt the thrill of fear and the value of that thrill. She was the one who started the chain of events that eventually led to this evil. She was the first Mayfly.

'Over time, Eva built up a network. A unique club, the members of which may have had differing motivations for their participation but who all shared a common interest – they wanted to see the work of the Nazi doctors continued. The Allies may have thought the human experimentation that took place in those concentration camps was consigned to history – a tear in the fabric of normality – but it was something far more significant to those twisted minds. Something of value. And they came in significant numbers waving their cash at Eva to witness it.

'But a secret network rarely remains secret for ever. The Attorney General Sir Philip Wren established a task force to investigate the activities of the Mayfly. You threatened his family to pressurise him into calling the investigation off and that was working, until Sandra Barnsdale sent him the list of Mayfly names. You found out about that; not hard, if you have people in the right places. So you gave Wren an ultimatum: hand over the names, or you would take his daughter. How am I doing so far?'

'Extraordinary,' Lucia said. 'Perhaps not a complete waste of money after all.'

'The problem was that by then Wren had already sent the flash drive to me. That's what Miles discovered. So Wren had nothing left to bargain with except the name of the person who he sent the data to. Me. He gave you that, but you took Hayley anyway.'

'Wren had been a thorn in our side for a long time. He needed to be taught a lesson.'

'But then you still had to recover the data.'

'It was very upsetting to learn that our records had been compromised.'

'So you sent Miles to reclaim it from me.'

'What?' Jessica broke in. '*You* sent Miles?'

'Of course she did,' said Priest, getting up from the chair.

'Indeed,' Lucia confirmed. 'After Miles failed initially, we tried to get the data back from you via Hayley – given her connection to you – but she turned out to be quite useless.'

'Charlie . . ' Jessica choked on her words. There were tears in her eyes and her voice, fragile, barely audible in the great hall, seemed to have lost all its grit. 'Charlie, what are you saying?' Her eyes were fixed on her mother.

Priest ignored her. He had to get to the end of this. Time was short. 'And how does Eva fit into all of this?' he asked.

Lucia Ellinder smiled again. 'You tell me.'

'I'm sorry, Jessica,' Priest said gently.

'What?' she stammered. 'Tell me!'

'Eva Miller is your grandmother.'

Jessica didn't move.

'Eva Miller and Bertie Ruck had a child, Jessica,' Priest said. 'Ruck didn't want to expose Eva, not because his name was on the list, but because he knew their daughter had taken over her mother's role. You saw the picture on Ruck's bedside table and you recognised the family resemblance, didn't you? Lucia is the daughter of Eva and Bertie.' Priest looked at Jessica. He was worried. The clarity that had descended upon him when he'd first entered the great hall was beginning to dissipate. The dark veil had returned. *Not now, please God, not now. Not with only ten minutes left . . .*

Jessica broke the silence. 'You brought me here.' She addressed her mother. 'To this house. When I was a child, didn't you?'

'Yes,' said Lucia, her eyes lighting up. '*Yes*, Jessica. You remember!'

'I remember this house and this hall. You said it was our legacy. Our family's gift to the world.'

'I brought you here to show you. You played, over there by the table.'

'You lied,' Jessica cried. 'This is no *gift*. It's poison. *You're* poison!'

'You cannot escape your destiny, Jessica.'

'You're sick, Mother. You need help . . .' Jessica tailed off as if something had occurred to her. 'You said Miles failed. Did *you* kill him?'

Lucia lowered her hands slowly, carefully, and sat back down at the table, turning her back on them both.

'She didn't kill Miles, Jessica,' said Priest. *Come on.* He fought to keep himself in the present, pinched the end of his nose hard. *Come on! Here and now.* The pain grounded him, but for how long?

Nine minutes.

Jessica shot her head around and he felt her fierce eyes bore into him again.

'Then who in God's name did?' she whispered.

'No one.' Priest let the words bounce off the stone like a ricocheting bullet.

'I don't understand. What do you mean, *no one*?'

'Miles is still alive.' Priest nodded in the direction of the hooded figure. 'He's standing over there.'

The figure had stood stock still throughout the proceedings, arms folded, chest rising and falling with slow, rhythmic breaths. Now, he moved, slowly at first, peeling away the hood that covered his face and letting it fall to the floor beside him.

Jessica gasped, staggered backwards, and grasped at a pillar for support.

'Hello, Miles,' said Priest.

Miles Ellinder smiled broadly, a row of teeth spreading across his face. He looked better groomed than he had the night he'd threatened Priest with the drill. His dark hair was clean, swept back; his eyes were pinpricks, barely visible from this distance. There was something reptilian about them, Priest thought: dead eyes. He thought back to the Bagman. He hadn't made the connection quickly enough.

'You're alive,' Jessica whispered in horror. 'Then who . . .?'

'Who was impaled in the Ellinder warehouse?' asked Priest. 'A migrant, a vagabond? Just someone picked up off the street?'

Lucia shrugged. 'His name is hardly important now.'

'I doubt you even know it,' Priest said. 'There is no shortage of undocumented migrants you could prey on. Although I still don't understand why you had to impale him. It seems sensationalist, even for you.'

'There are limits to your understanding, then,' Lucia sneered.

'But how?' Jessica demanded. 'How did everyone think that was Miles?'

'Because his mother identified the body. I saw that on the interim autopsy report but it didn't register as significant at the time.'

Lucia stood up and pushed the chair aside. 'Of course I identified his body! What else could a faithful wife do for her sick and grieving husband? And besides, it was hardly a secret that Miles was mine and not Kenneth's.'

'No one questioned a mother's identification of her own son,' said Priest. 'And of course you have McEwen. He's part of the network, isn't he? And the pathologist who supposedly carried out the post-mortem. Also belongs to you.'

Lucia raised an eyebrow. 'McEwen? The pathologist? You've surpassed my expectations, Mr Priest. I doubted you would manage to identify all of my foot soldiers.'

The devil's in the detail, Priest. 'Easy when the name that signed off Miles's post-mortem report also appears on the Mayfly list,' Priest replied.

'But . . .' Jessica stammered. 'Why?'

'Miles had to fake his death and I suspect he shares your mother's love of theatre. So began the greatest wild goose chase of them all.'

Lucia nodded and clapped her hands. In the distance, Priest could hear the muffled hum of the crowd; they were waiting for the performance, restless and eager. In six minutes time, they would be satisfied.

'But why?' said Jessica again. 'Why did Miles have to fake his death?'

'I think there were two reasons,' said Priest, fixing his stare on Lucia. 'Firstly, Philip Wren was starting to get very close to the Ellinder family; that was a major concern. So, Miles had to be killed off in a spectacular way to cast your family as the victims and not the perpetrators. Am I right?'

Lucia nodded. 'Wren was becoming a nuisance but killing him would only have made matters more difficult – no doubt someone would have taken his place. We needed to confuse the investigation and allow Miles the freedom to operate from the shadows.'

'You ended up having to finish Wren off anyway once you found out he had got hold of the Mayfly list.'

'I don't understand . . .' Jessica looked at Priest, as if pleading with him to make sense of it all.

Be careful what you wish for, Jessica.

Priest continued to address Lucia Ellinder. 'The second advantage of faking Miles's death was that it gave you the chance to get to me. You needed to retrieve the data but also establish what I knew. Miles failed to recover the data first time around so you killed the stand-in and planted my business card on him.

You then persuaded your husband to instruct me to investigate Miles's death. Jessica was encouraged to shadow me. That way I could be drawn in to the Mayfly web and McEwen would have every excuse to recover the data – like his failed attempt at exercising a warrant to search my offices.'

'Bravo, Mr Priest.' Lucia Ellinder clapped again.

'But why involve me?' Jessica asked.

'To initiate you. To let you discover for yourself the glorious horror of what awaits you. Your mother has already said it, Jessica: this is your destiny, your house. This institution is bequeathed to you. As Eva passed her work on to her daughter, so in turn will your mother hand it on to you. You're her apprentice. You are the next Mayfly.'

Jessica shook her head. 'This is madness,' she whispered.

Lucia Ellinder extended her hand to her daughter. 'Have you not seen the wonder of what we have achieved, Jessica? The work of Kurt Schneider continued.'

'You're torturing people. For entertainment.'

'We are *living*, Jessica. Through fear, we are redefining our relationship with God. Achieving the ultimate. The power and control we command in this house, Jessica. Imagine, establishing a direct conduit to Him – the Creator.'

'People are *paying you*. To see you torture people.'

'And that money has allowed us to retain the lifestyle that you have enjoyed, Jessica. Do not forget that. Your father's businesses could not have sustained us. But this isn't about money. It's about the Mayfly. It's about *evolution*.'

Jessica buried her head in her hands. 'I don't understand.'

'No doubt *you* do, Mr Priest,' Lucia Ellinder tilted her head at Priest.

'It would be easy to dismiss this as a lunatic death cult,' said Priest slowly. 'But that would be too simple an explanation. You said it is about evolution, which is ironic, given that it is actually about God.'

Lucia's smile broadened. 'Go on.'

'You believe you can be closer to God – or perhaps even see Him – through the unimaginable suffering of another human being. It's like a sex rite, but whereas the conduit to God purportedly opens at the point of orgasm, here the channel is opened through pain and fear.'

'I've never heard of anything so insane,' Jessica whispered.

'The idea of sacrificing human life to appease a god has been around since the earliest civilisations,' Priest pointed out. 'This is – in a way – the evolution of that idea. That's what Kurt Schneider was trying to do.'

'This isn't happening . . .'

'Wake up! This is your inheritance, child!' Suddenly enraged, Lucia began to advance across the room towards Jessica.

Priest calculated. He needed more time but his chances were ebbing away. Miles was twenty yards away, maybe less, brandishing a gun. He'd only have to be a moderately skilled shot to take Priest out.

In the distance, a bell chimed. Nobody moved. Then, gently at first, rain started to patter on the opaque windows lining the circular room. *This is it. Time's up.*

'Enough of this,' Lucia declared. 'Come with me, Jessica.'

Miles brought the gun up, and gestured for them to follow him through one of the doors at the far end of the room. Priest thought of Georgie, and what might lie in wait for her. As Lucia disappeared through the door ahead of them, Priest glanced at

Jessica. Her cheeks were red and she looked exhausted, but she was not beaten. Far from it.

'Miles,' she said urgently. 'What on earth are you doing?'

'What I was born to do, sister.'

'You weren't born into this darkness, Miles. Open your eyes, for God's sake!'

'God, sister? I thought you were a non-believer?'

'I am. You can't tell me you believe any of this shit, you moron.'

He chuckled. 'Well, why don't we step forward and meet Him and see if you're right?'

52

Miles led them through another door off the great hall, down a dimly lit corridor and up the grand staircase to the balcony room overlooking the theatre. When they reached the final set of double doors, Miles paused. From inside they could hear the noise of the guests clearly. The performance hadn't started yet. Maybe Georgie and Hayley were still alive, but Priest's head was spinning. He had no plan.

'Last chance, Miles,' Jessica warned.

Miles was amused. 'You always were a tight-cunted bitch, Jessica. I don't care whether or not you join Mother and me, but it's in your blood.' He pulled her roughly towards him. 'Admit it,' he whispered. 'You *want* to see the bitch hurt.'

Priest felt Jessica shaking with fear beside him.

Miles marched them into the balcony room. In front of them a crowd of hooded people were craning to see over the edge of the balcony, jostling for position and applauding. The noise was deafening. If Hell existed, Priest thought, then this was how walking through its gates would feel.

Miles led them round to the back of the crowd, which had increased twofold since Priest had last been in this room. Televisions had been set up around the sides of the room, showing the stage below. Every screen displayed Lucia Ellinder, bowing in front of her public.

'Friends!' Her words were barely audible above the noise of the crowd. 'Welcome. Welcome!'

Priest turned to his right. Miles jammed the gun into his ribcage. To his left, Jessica was transfixed by the television screen. He felt her hand slip into his. He squeezed. She squeezed back. She turned away from the screen. Her eyes were cloudy with tears. In front of him, Lucia was still talking, but he could sense the words slipping away from him. The drone of the crowd seemed numbed, as if the noise had been trapped behind closed doors.

Not now, please God, not now . . . He was slipping away, into his own private dreamland.

Priest watched as the scene played out in front of him. He saw himself standing at the edge of a gathering of faceless ghosts, all swaying to the discordant whine of an invisible orchestra. Moving metrically as one, they seemed hypnotised by an energy source on the far side of the auditorium. He saw his hand clasped around something warm and comforting and knew he might never find it again if he let it go.

Suddenly both sides of the crowd began to implode, cascading inwards. Some of the ghosts began falling, toppling over like wooden soldiers, trampled by others. The intensity of the noise increased. There was screaming – the din of panic and distress. As he watched, the mob began to disintegrate, broken up by men and women in uniforms with heavy guns strapped over their shoulders, screaming.

'Armed police! Get down! Get down!'

Priest stepped back. Numb as he was, the noise was unbearable. He wanted to sink down, curl up, shut everything out, but someone had him by the lapels and was forcing him up against the wall.

'Charlie!'

He shook himself. *Here and now.*

'*Charlie!*'

'Jessica?' He blinked his way back to reality.

'Charlie! Miles. He went that way!'

She was pointing to a small door wallpapered to match the surrounding walls. Priest was just in time to see Miles Ellinder disappearing through it.

Priest pushed aside two hooded spectators trying to flee and sent them sprawling back into the crowd. He tore open the door.

He ran blind down a tunnel barely wide enough to allow free movement. Slivers of light breached cracks in the walls. The house was old enough to be riddled with passageways separating the servants from their masters. Conduits between two worlds.

He pressed on through the gloom, driven by the dark energy that had been building within him over the last week. Ahead of him, he could hear Miles stumbling through the dark, his progress laboured. The gap between them was closing.

At the next corner, Priest found himself at the bottom of a flight of stairs, ascending into darkness. Above him, he heard boots on the steps and heavy breathing.

Just as Priest was about to follow Miles up the steps, two shots ricocheted back down the stairwell. The bullets splintered holes in the wooden treads, missing him by several feet. Priest paused, calculating his next move.

From above him, a woman screamed.

Disregarding the risk, Priest took the stairs three at a time.

'Georgie!' he called out.

'Charlie!'

Her voice was distant and muffled. At the top of the stairs, Priest hurled himself through another door but rather than stumbling into another servants' passage, he was met by the howl of the wind and driving rain. The shock of the cold and the wet gale slapping into his face arrested him and for a moment he lost his bearings. He began to pick his way across a moss-covered roof.

'Charlie!'

The alarm in Georgie's voice was as unsettling as the change in atmosphere had been. He glanced ahead. Through the rain, he could see he was on a vast section of flat roof at the back of the house surrounded by four or five towers and bordered by turrets overlooking the grounds and lined with stone grotesques. On the far side, he could just make out Miles, standing facing him on the roof edge, his arm across Georgie's chest, the gun jammed to her head.

'Georgie!' Priest had to make himself heard above the sound of the pounding rain. He crept forwards, closing the gap between them to ten feet or so. 'Miles – give her to me!'

'Fuck you, Priest!'

Miles took a step backwards. Another two steps and he would go over the edge, taking Georgie with him.

'Georgie!' Priest yelled. 'Look at me. Look at me!'

Her head was twisted to the side but, with great effort, she managed to turn to look at Priest. She was white with fear, but otherwise seemed unhurt.

'Georgie, it's going to be OK,' he assured her.

She nodded uncertainly.

'You're a good liar, Priest,' said Miles. 'Useful for a lawyer.'

'It's over, Miles. There's nothing to be gained from carrying on. They'll get you one way or the other. Might as well give yourself a chance to plea bargain.'

Miles laughed. 'As if *that's* an attractive proposition.'

'You're not in a good position to argue, Miles.'

'I'm the one with the gun to your bitch's head, Priest! Give me the flash drive.'

'What? You think there's a way out for you, still?'

'It doesn't matter what I think, just give me the damn flash drive!'

Miles was deadly serious. Out of the corner of his eye, Priest saw a figure take up position on the other side of the tower. He checked the angle – it was out of Miles's eye line.

'You've lost, Miles,' Priest shouted. 'The ceremony is over. Your mother is in custody. The data's of no use now.'

'I'll do it, Priest!' Miles shouted. 'Putting a bullet through her head is child's play compared with what I've achieved!'

'And did you find God while you were doing that, Miles? Or just get off on it?'

'Priest!' Miles warned.

Priest fixed his gaze on Georgie. She looked back, pleading with her eyes. *I will not let you down. You will not become another ghost.* Slowly, he reached into his inside pocket and produced the flash drive.

Miles's face lit up. 'Throw it to me,' he instructed.

Priest gave Georgie one final look. Then he tossed the flash drive in the air towards Miles. It fell a couple of feet short. Enraged, Miles pulled Georgie closer and leant forward and around her to retrieve it. In that moment, a single shot from the other side of the tower ripped through the darkness and into Miles's arm. He yelled out and tumbled to the ground, releasing his grip on Georgie, who immediately ran forward.

Priest was quick off the mark but Miles had reared up and returned fire in the direction of his attacker. The bullet slammed harmlessly into the tower.

Priest hurled himself at Miles and they both fell to the ground, sending the gun spinning away out of reach. Priest's leg dangled dangerously over the edge of the roof as, off balance, he found himself thrown sideways.

From behind the tower, the waiter, Marco, surged across the roof towards Miles but lost his footing on the wet moss. He recovered, but it was enough to bring him to one knee only a few feet away from Miles, who catapulted forwards and punched him in the face.

The waiter fell backwards, blood pouring from his nose, his gun clattering across the roof. He scrambled back towards the tower but slipped again. Behind him, Miles picked up the gun.

Priest watched as Marco whirled around but only to look down the barrel of his own gun. Priest searched the rooftop desperately. To his right, only a metre or so away, he saw Miles's gun lying in a puddle.

'Goodbye, whoever the fuck you are,' Priest heard Miles say.

Priest dived for Miles's gun. *I'm too late . . .*

The gunshot cut through the night sky like thunder.

Marco was on the ground. For a moment, Priest thought he hadn't fired in time. But as he watched, Miles Ellinder began to stagger, clutching his side.

And then he fell over the side of the roof.

Priest made his way to the edge and peered down into the courtyard below. He removed the magazine from the handgun and pocketed it before turning to Georgie.

'Are you OK?'

'I've had a rough day.' She attempted a watery smile.

'I'll bet.'

'Thanks for coming all this way and saving me, Charlie.'

Priest took her into his arms. 'I'm a really thoughtful employer,' he whispered into her hair.

'Nice shot,' Marco observed, getting to his feet.

'I take it you don't work here for the tips.'

'NDEU,' said Marco. 'National Domestic Extremist Unit.'

'How long have you been undercover?'

'About a year now.'

'Guess I almost blew it for you.'

'Pretty close, but you made up for it with that shot. So, can you tell me who you are?'

Priest sniffed and tightened his arm around Georgie. The rain had let up a little but he was drenched and incredibly thirsty. Georgie hadn't let go of him.

He shrugged. 'I'm just a lawyer.'

53

By the time they had made their way back down and into the front courtyard, the Met had things under control. The drive-way was packed with police cars. A kaleidoscope of blue lights danced off the stone walls as handcuffed spectators were led into the back of riot vans. A few people had managed to slip through the net but the dogs would soon catch them. One man had been found upstairs having turned a gun on himself.

In the end, the demise of the House of Mayfly was a pitiful sight.

Priest and Jessica huddled around an ambulance waiting for Georgie to be checked over. None of the three of them had spoken since they had come down from the rooftop. Priest felt anaesthetised, drained of all feeling.

Two paramedics wheeled a stretcher past them. Priest caught Jessica's arm. 'Just a minute,' he said, gesturing for the paramedics to slow. He followed the stretcher party to a second ambulance.

'Is she OK?' he asked.

'She's weak,' said one of the paramedics as he helped lift Hayley Wren into the back of the ambulance. 'Her body's taken a hell of a lot of stress. That's all I can say.'

'Listen,' said Priest urgently. 'She's been poisoned with a modified version of strychnine. You need to contact Detective

Chief Inspector Rowlinson of South Wales CID. He has details of similar cases – the information he has will help you treat her.'

'Thanks, that's appreciated. Are you police?'

'Not anymore.'

Inside the ambulance, Hayley opened one eye and looked at Priest. She didn't appear to recognise him at first, but just as the doors were closing, she lifted her hand and smiled. A small piece of him felt restored. Atonement was perhaps not as elusive as he had thought.

The feeling was short-lived.

'Oh, shit,' he muttered.

'What?' said Jessica.

'It's my ex-wife.'

Assistant Commissioner Dee Auckland strode purposefully across the gravel, her face warped into a look of raw hatred. She was flanked by two other officers. Priest vaguely recognised them as the policemen who had accompanied McEwen to Philip Wren's house. She had aged since he had last seen her – there were crow's feet around her eyes he didn't recognise. Priest sensed Jessica tensing up.

'Hello, darling,' he said.

'Shut up, Charlie. Just what do you think you're playing at?'

Priest took his time. His short marriage to Dee Auckland had ended principally because he'd failed to think through what he said to her first.

'I think I have just uncovered the biggest public scandal of the twenty-first century,' he said.

Auckland opened her mouth and took a deep breath. Priest braced himself, but she was interrupted.

'That's the one! That's him! Arrest that fucker!' McEwen was wading across the courtyard, his face red and blotchy. He had lost his bow tie somewhere along the way and his shirt was hanging open, revealing a bulging, sporadically haired chest. He was pointing frantically at Priest.

The two CID officers with Auckland looked at her for guidance.

'DI McEwen,' said Auckland drily. 'Remind me. How is it that we came to find you here?'

'I've been working undercover, ma'am. Ratting out these perverted bastards, under the instructions of your predecessor.'

'I see. Probably an arrangement I would have known about if it were true, don't you think? And the grounds for arresting Charles Priest are what, exactly?'

'Perverting the course of justice, ma'am. Priest was in on it from the start.'

'Indeed. Well –' Auckland turned to the two CID officers. 'You'd better arrest him, hadn't you.'

'Dee –' Priest protested, but she put up her hand. Priest glanced at Jessica.

'Provided,' Dee said calmly, 'that DI McEwen can explain why it is that the *real* undercover officer can't verify *his* cover.'

From behind the ambulance, Marco appeared. He had removed the waiter's uniform he'd worn earlier and was now wearing civvies and SCO19-issued body armour. He stood behind McEwen, arms folded, blocking his way.

'M-ma'am?' McEwen stuttered.

'We already had an undercover officer working at the House of Mayfly, Inspector. This is Graham Sanderson. NDEU.'

'Well – I wasn't aware –'

'Aware that your sordid little enterprise was being monitored from the inside? No, I don't suppose you were.'

McEwen stiffened. Priest saw his beady little eyes dart from side to side, like a trapped animal calculating his chances of escape.

'And him?' Auckland nodded at Priest, her eyes on Sanderson.

'Ellinder had taken one of the women to the roof. I freed the other but without this man, the outcome wouldn't have been so positive. I found him on the roof, about to be shot by Ellinder, which is when I opened fire.'

'Very well.' Auckland turned to McEwen. 'Get this one out of my sight then, please, Sanderson.'

Sanderson nodded at Priest, who returned the acknowledgement with a wry smile. Then the undercover officer took McEwen's arms behind his back and slapped on the cuffs. The Scot objected but there was no fight left in him.

As Sanderson led McEwen away, Priest and Jessica turned back to Auckland. Priest wished he had turned quicker – he could have sworn that Dee was smiling to herself.

'And now,' she said thoughtfully. 'I'll need statements from you. Tomorrow will do. I trust you can manage that, Priest?'

'I'll give it a go.'

'Yes. You will. And now get out of here before I change my mind.'

Priest wasn't a man who looked a gift horse in the mouth. He took Jessica's hand and walked away to where the Aston had been parked.

'And you –' Auckland called out.

Priest stopped and they turned back.

'Miss Ellinder.' Auckland nodded at Jessica's hand locked in Priest's. 'For fuck's sake, don't be so bloody stupid.'

Inside the car, Priest ran his hands over the wheel. The blue lights flashed rhythmically across the mirror. He turned to look at Jessica. She was staring straight ahead.

'What will you tell your father?' he asked.

She sighed heavily. 'I'll tell him the truth.'

'That'll be hard to hear.'

'It might even kill him.'

'And Scarlett?'

Jessica didn't respond. Just shook her head.

Priest studied the scene in the rear-view mirror. Four uniformed officers were dragging a woman kicking and screaming down the stone steps. She was thrashing her arms and legs; her dress was torn. It was taking all of their strength to keep her from escaping their grip. Eventually, they managed to bundle Lucia Ellinder into the back of one of the riot vans, all four officers climbing in after her. Even after they had slammed the door shut, her cries drifted across the misty air.

'Infidels! God hates you! God will swallow your souls, cut out your tongues, mutilate your bodies . . .'

Priest dipped the mirror. Jessica hadn't looked, but he knew she had heard.

'At least they got her,' she whispered.

'You couldn't have known, Jessica.'

'I *should* have known.'

Priest nodded. He felt the same thing about William.

The rear driver's side door of the Aston opened and someone climbed in. Priest and Jessica spun around.

'Georgie?'

'Hi.'

'You really should stay with the ambulance crew,' Priest pointed out.

'They gave me tablets. I feel fine.'

'Georgie . . .'

'Charlie, I don't want to be labelled a victim. Can we please just get out of here?'

Priest looked at Jessica. She was smiling. He sighed. *Bloody stubborn employees*. He fired up the Aston's engine and pulled away, up the drive, and out on to the main road.

'Charlie, do I get paid overtime for this?'

'We'll talk about it later.'

He pressed the accelerator and the House of Mayfly disappeared in the haze behind them.

54

On Priest's insistence, Georgie checked herself in at the local hospital. Fortunately, her injuries were minor and she needed little treatment other than bandages and sleep.

Priest had offered to stay with her but she had lied and said someone was on their way to pick her up. She suspected he would have more important things to do than sit in a busy A & E department on a Saturday night. Instead, she had walked home in the early hours of the morning, despite the young doctor suggesting she ought to stay. Georgie hadn't told him how she had got the injuries.

After several hours of disturbed sleep, she got up, showered, dressed and registered with a local agent to look for a flat closer to the office. When she emerged from her room, she found Li sitting outside in the corridor.

'I didn't want to disturb you. So I waited here,' Li said.

'Thanks.'

Georgie sat down next to her.

'Georgie, what the hell happened to you?'

Georgie thought about it. *What* has *happened to me?* There was so much of it she didn't understand but she had the rest of her life to find out. And tomorrow she was due back at work.

'Do you want to get a house with me closer to the centre?' Georgie asked.

Li waited a moment. Then she smiled and nodded. 'Sure.'

They sat in silence for a while. Then they heard someone coming up the stairs.

'Li, where have you – Oh. It's you.'

Martin stopped short when he saw Georgie and started to walk back the other way. There was a time when Georgie would have flushed with embarrassment. But not now. She got up.

'Actually, Martin,' Georgie said. 'Wait. Please.'

He hesitated and she could tell he was debating ignoring her, but he didn't. He stopped, and turned to look at her. 'Yeah?' he said.

Georgie stepped forward a few paces, swung her fist back, and planted it into his face. Martin's chin cracked. He fell heavily and wheezed out a cry of pain and surprise. Li scrambled to her feet.

'You are a rapist,' Georgie said. 'But you have *no* hold over me.'

55

Priest closed his eyes and listened to the sound of Sarah's voice at the other end of the phone. He had no idea what the last fifteen minutes of conversation had been about. Normally, he found listening to Sarah babble on about the glass ceiling – however justified – fairly tedious. Today though, the sheer normality of it was glorious. It reminded him that he was still alive.

'I mean, have you any idea just what percentage of directors of the top FTSE 100 companies are female?' she was saying.

'I have no idea.'

'I have no idea either, but I bet it's like, less than five.'

'Sarah,' he said. 'You've got bigger balls than most men.'

She replied but he didn't hear it. The doorbell had just rung.

'Listen, Sarah, I have to go. Love to Tilly, OK?'

He opened the door and Jessica walked in, as usual without saying a word and without really looking at him. Considering what they had been through in the last twenty-four hours, she looked incredible, although, judging from her grim expression, it was going to be a short meeting.

'Can I get you a drink?' he asked.

'I'm not staying.'

She was wrapped in a long, off-white designer trench coat. Like everything about her, from the way her hair fell over one eye to the bag elegantly hung over her shoulder, she made it look understated.

'You look –' he stroked his chin, searching for the right word. 'Flawless.'

If she was pleased with the compliment, she didn't show it. Except for maybe the smallest quiver of her lip.

'So there was a task force after all,' she said. 'They had been watching my mother for months, ever since they'd identified her as . . . whatever she was.'

Priest nodded. 'You couldn't have known, Jessica.'

'Then why do I feel such heavy guilt?'

He didn't have an answer to that.

'The Mayfly has operated successfully for decades,' Priest said gently. 'First through your grandmother and then your mother. Its reach went as far as the highest echelons of government. There are arrests happening simultaneously across the country. Almost every police force in the UK is involved to some degree. Politicians, bankers, lawyers, coppers. Even a fucking geography teacher.'

'And that man, the waiter, he was part of Philip Wren's task force?'

'A specialist, covert group. One that had its origins, I believe, with our friend, Colonel Ruck. Just as the House of Mayfly has had its successive commanders, so has the task force. After Ruck retired, they gave the job to an MI5 spy and eventually they selected Wren to head it up because he had a military background but wasn't directly involved in the police.'

Jessica was staring at the floor, gently shaking her head, as if she was still trying to process everything that had happened. Priest wanted to take her into his arms and tell her that everything would be fine. But that would be a lie. He doubted she would ever be fine again.

'How did your father take it?' he asked.

'He's not spoken since. Just stayed in his office. Scarlett's staying for a while longer to look after him, but I can tell all she wants to do is get back to the States and forget the whole thing ever happened.'

'I can sympathise. You know, she's the one who showed me your father's insect collection?'

'They're just specimens,' Jessica murmured. 'My father was interested in entomology. I took a look around recently. There aren't actually any mayflies in the collection.'

'I see. We all just – assumed.'

Jessica nodded. 'One thing,' she said, looking up. 'How did you know Miles wasn't dead?'

'I didn't know for sure.' Priest sighed. 'But on the interim autopsy report that Giles sent me, there were a few important details that didn't click with me until later. One was the fact that Miles's body was identified by your mother and the second was that the toxicology report was clean.'

'Whereas you knew Miles was a user.'

Priest nodded. 'The pathologist was on the Mayfly list, too. I gave Dee the details. He wasn't found at the house but they picked him up at Dover. He must have heard about what happened and fled.'

'And the impaling? Why did they impale that poor man?'

Priest looked away. 'When the police raided Miles's house, they found a shrine to Vlad the Impaler. Books, posters, comics, blogs, figurines, artwork, a pendant bearing his image.' He turned back to Jessica. 'You couldn't have known,' he said.

'You never went there. Miles was obsessed with one of the most evil tyrants in history. He chose to fake his own death to celebrate him.'

Jessica shuddered and walked over to the fish tank. The lionfish were weaving in and out of their little plastic bridges. She put her hand against the glass.

'There were three,' she said softly. 'Now only two.'

'One of them died. I think I overfed them.'

She turned to him. 'I'm sorry, Charlie Priest.'

He looked at her. 'You're sorry because you can't stay or because one of my fish died?'

'Because I can't stay. I'll buy you a new fish.'

The words got stuck in Priest's throat. 'You're here to say goodbye, then.'

She nodded slowly.

'It has to be this way.'

She took his hand. Held it for a moment. Her touch was warm, full of life and promise. He wished the moment would never pass. Then she let it go and turned to walk out.

'I'm sorry, Charlie.'

'No. Wait.' Priest held up his hand. 'You're going to say you can never see me again,' he said. 'But you're wrong. It doesn't have to be that way. The guilt you're feeling is crushing you, isn't it?'

'Charlie, those people . . .'

'We all need a blue sky, Jessica. I feel guilt too.'

'What did you say?'

'I said I feel guilt, too.'

'No, the first bit.'

Priest swallowed. It had just slipped out. 'I said we all need a blue sky. It's something my mother used to say.'

It was her turn to falter.

'Don't you see, Jessica? We're the same.'

She bit her lip. Her face was flushed and there were tears in her eyes. As they stood in silence, the mid-morning sun pushed through the clouds and flooded the apartment with glorious colour.

Priest studied the Risk board carefully but it wasn't obvious where he could move. The majority of the board was awash with red, save for a small stronghold in Eastern Europe controlled by his blue army.

William rapped his knuckles on the table.

'How long is it going to take you, brother, to realise that the statistical probability of you winning this game is next to nothing?'

'Give me a moment.'

Priest moved a unit west and rolled the dice.

'I do enjoy our games of Risk,' William said.

'I used to prefer it when we played Guess Who.'

'That is natural because you are a rotten chess player – but a fine brother.'

William totted up the dice and laughed gleefully as he removed the advancing unit from play.

'How have you been, Wills?'

'Worried about you, as it happens.'

'Really?'

'Yes. That surprises you? That I am capable of such benevolent and altruistic thoughts? After what I've done?'

Priest pointed to the board. 'It's your move.'

'Really? You don't want to move these troops here?' William gestured to a unit on the far eastern corner of the board.

'It's your turn,' Priest insisted.

William shrugged. 'Suit yourself.' He began checking his cards and moving reinforcements to areas already heavily populated with red infantry. 'So, was the matter taking up your time satisfactorily resolved?'

'It was resolved, if that's what you mean.'

'I hear on the news that a neo-Nazi ring has been exposed in our backwater country. Did you have something to do with that?'

'Can I ask you something?'

'Of course. No secrets between kin.'

'When you murdered those people – you didn't meet God at any point along the way, did you?'

William was about to throw the dice but he stopped and looked up. Priest stared into his brother's eyes. For the first time as far as he could remember, he saw a small flash of humanity.

'Only once.'

'What did you do?'

William sat perfectly still for a moment before throwing the dice across the board.

'I turned myself in. My work was complete.'

∽

Outside Fen Marsh, the rain had let up. Priest walked across the car park, head down, his hands thrust deep into his mac. Okoro was standing by the car, arms folded.

'How was he?' he asked as Priest approached.

'Not too bad. I beat him at Risk. He's losing his touch.'

'It's a game of chance, Priest.'

'Isn't everything?'

'Hmm.' Okoro opened the door to the passenger seat and motioned for him to get in.

'Can't I drive?'

'*My* car? No, Priest. You can't drive my car. You can barely walk. You're exhausted. When was the last time you slept?'

Reluctantly, Priest climbed in the passenger side. Okoro sat behind the wheel. Everything smelt of new leather.

'If you think about it,' Okoro said, 'McEwen told us about the Mayfly right from the start. Why did he mention it? He didn't need to.'

'Arrogance, stupidity. I think McEwen just liked knowing more than we did.'

Okoro looked over, his finger hovering over the start button. 'So, what next, Priest?' he asked.

Priest reached inside his coat pocket and picked out a hip flask. He unscrewed the top and let the last swig of warm malt whisky slide down his neck.

'Drop me off at home, Okoro. I've got a date with a former client to get ready for.'

AUTHOR'S NOTE

Thank you to the three most influential people in my life – Oliver, Grace and Archie. Without your inspiration and encouragement, this book would never have been written. I accept of course that, Archie, you had no idea I was writing it, but you helped invaluably in your own way. I only ask that you all remember me when you are famous.

Thank you also to Pat Hazel – your support and attention to detail were second to none. Dad would have been proud of us both.

To Richard and Denise, thank you for your encouragement, generosity and support. You accepted a dishevelled moppet with a dream of becoming a writer into your family all those years ago and, for that, the moppet is eternally grateful.

I am indebted to Nicki Richards and the good people at Totally Entwined, whose skill and inexhaustible patience taught me how to write.

It has been a privilege to work with the team at Bonnier Zaffre, whose tenacity and passion run through the spine of this book, and I wish to pay particular tribute to the hard work of my editors, Katherine Armstrong and Kate Parkin.

Finally, to my wife, Jo, I owe you the biggest thanks of all. Mainly for continuing to put up with me.

The Holocaust remains one of the darkest periods of modern history: a genocide so unfathomable, it has been referred to as a tear in the fabric of time. I read widely when researching *The Mayfly* but I was particularly influenced by *Doctors from Hell* written by Vivien Spitz, a harrowing eyewitness account of the Nuremberg doctors' trials.

A conversation with author
James Hazel

Your background is in the law. How did you get into writing? Have you always written?

I've always been fascinated by stories and how the idea of telling a story has pervaded human evolution since we developed language. It is one of the few things that every civilisation, every culture, every race and creed have in common: we all tell each other stories.

What's also fascinating is that, throughout history, billions of people from different backgrounds and cultures have basically told the same stories, in their own ways, sometimes with astonishing similarities. Every religion has a story of creation, for example.

I've always enjoyed creative writing (most lawyers will tell you that this represents a good percentage of their trade anyway!) but I only started writing serious in my mid-twenties, at a point when I felt ready to do so. And what started out as a therapeutic outlet turned into a hobby, which turned into an obsession, which turned into a life-goal – and this eventually became *The Mayfly*.

How do you write? Are you a plotter or a starter (i.e. you just get on with it)?

I would love to pretend that I plan everything meticulously, every twist and every revelation, mapping out each novel in storyboard form before even thinking of typing the words 'Chapter One'.

I can't say that, however, because that's not the case. So I guess that makes me a starter. Hit the keys with determination and vigour, and see what happens, with only the vaguest of notions of where everyone will end up.

Having said I'd love to say I'm a plotter, I heard that Stephen King wrote *Misery* in a similarly unplanned way, a lot of the first few chapters on a hotel napkin; so perhaps there's something to be said for starters.

Charlie Priest is a whip smart, wise-cracking protagonist that readers will really enjoy getting to know. Where did the idea for him to have dissociation disorder come from?

I guess the idea developed from the desire I had for Charlie to have an unusual vulnerability to something; I wanted him to have his own personal kryptonite. In the absence of something like that, I thought his heroism might become predictable. In that sense, Charlie had to be flawed. At the same time, I was looking for a way for Charlie to have a connection with William that would partly explain their relationship and feed Charlie's biggest fear: that he might be just as capable of killing as William was. It's a useful teaser to have them share a psychological condition.

Charlie and William as brothers obviously have the same background, yet one became a lawyer and the other a killer. What do you think about some geneticists' belief that people can be born with an evil gene – that they are predestined to be violent because of their DNA? With many cases, particularly in America, exploring this option as a defence, where do you think that leaves the UK legal system – not to mention crime fiction?!

Apparently, there is evidence that a variation of a particular gene that produces low levels of an enzyme called mono-amine oxidase (MAOA) can, in certain circumstances, increase the prospect of a person developing antisocial tendencies in later life. Thus, I suppose we are not a million miles away from discovering an 'evil gene'.

There are examples of genetic evidence persuading juries in the American legal system to downgrade murder to manslaughter.

It seems to me to be a chilling ideology that the accountability a man has for his actions might be diminished, or even extinguished, because of his biology. I cannot accept that our genes mean we are predestined to do anything; to do so would mean I have to accept that the concept of free will is an illusion.

However, that is not to say that there is no debate to be had. Making the subject taboo would impede further research, from which a lot of good may come.

The English legal system will eventually have to address the point of the evil gene. I don't profess to be a moral philosopher on any scale but, it seems to me, that if we don't condemn William for his crimes because of his genetic makeup, we can't then call Charlie a hero either because his benevolence is also undoubtedly the product, at least in part, of genetics.

Which authors inspire you?

I'm a huge Jo Nesbø fan and one of the people who felt they had found a soulmate in Harry Hole. It's a real disappointment to end each book and remember he's only a fictional character.

I grew up reading James Herbert, Iain Banks, Stephen King and Terry Pratchett and anything fantastic and gothic. H. P. Lovecraft occupies a particularly dear place in my writer's heart, if for nothing else than his extraordinary vocabulary and pioneering monsters. How extraordinary that we are still reinventing his ideas a hundred years after they were first spawned.

There are too many crime fiction writers to mention that I am both admiring and envious of in equal measures: James Patterson, Martina Cole, Chelsea Cain, Karin Slaughter, Lee Child, Sarah Hilary, Chris Carter, to name but a few.

What next for Charlie and the team?

The second Priest novel will pick up six months or so after the end of *The Mayfly* and chronicle a new case for Priest & Co. Expect more adventure, more devious plans, more Georgie brilliance, more socially awkward moments and a rival for Jessica!

If you enjoyed The *Mayfly* why not join the James Hazel Readers Club by emailing me at james.hazel@myreadersclub.co.uk?

Turn over for a message from James Hazel . . .

Dear Reader

The Mayfly took me two years of writing late at night, usually after the kids were in bed and the lights were out. Writing was, and still is, my obsessive passion, but I never actually considered what might happen if I was published. It all seemed too much of a pipe-dream.

So, thank you. Because now my book is finished. Not when I wrote the last few words, or my editors straightened out the last few kinks. When you finished reading it – that's when the book was properly complete.

After all, a book without a reader is just . . . well, paper with symbols on it.

Charlie Priest and his motley crew have lived inside my head for years before I was able to properly unleash them on the world. I hope you enjoyed their emancipation. There's lots more to come and you'll soon get to hear about a new Priest & Co adventure with even more cutting one-liners, socially awkward moments, and raw heroism from Charlie. And, yes, more Georgie brilliance.

If you want to be the first to hear about it, then you could join the James Hazel Readers Club. You can do so by visiting www.bit.ly/JamesHazel to sign up. It only takes a moment to register and, to say thanks, I'll send you a free short story. There'll be regular updates about forthcoming titles and some exclusive VIP content, including details of a competition to become a character in a new Priest novel! (don't worry: you get to be a good guy).

It's also a really great way to get in touch. I'd love to hear from you and get to know what you liked and what you didn't like. Writing is a pretty solitary pursuit so it's nice to know I'm not totally on my own here.

Your data will never be passed to a third party and I'll only be in touch now and again. You can unsubscribe at any time. I hope you stay with me though, because we've started this adventure together, you and me, and it's going to be a great ride!

I'd also love it if you were able to spend a few moments leaving a review on Amazon or Goodreads, or anywhere else that supports reviews. All authors appreciate fair and constructive reviews but first time writers like me live or die by them, so anything you can do would be fantastic. If you liked Priest, spread the word, people value a good book recommendation.

Once again, thank you for reading.

With best wishes,

James Hazel

Want to read
NEW BOOKS
before anyone else?

Like getting
FREE BOOKS?

Enjoy sharing your
OPINIONS?

Discover

READERS
FIRST

Read. Love. Share.

Get your first free book just by signing up at
readersfirst.co.uk

For Terms and Conditions see readersfirst.co.uk/pages/terms-of-service